THE GIRL
AND THE
GRAVEDIGGER

ALSO BY OLIVER PÖTZSCH

The Ludwig Conspiracy

The Castle of Kings

The Gravedigger Series

The Gravedigger's Almanac

The Faust Series

The Master's Apprentice

The Devil's Pawn

***The Hangman's Daughter* Series**

The Hangman's Daughter

The Dark Monk

The Beggar King

The Poisoned Pilgrim

The Werewolf of Bamberg

The Play of Death

The Council of Twelve

The Black Musketeers Series

Book of the Night

Sword of Power

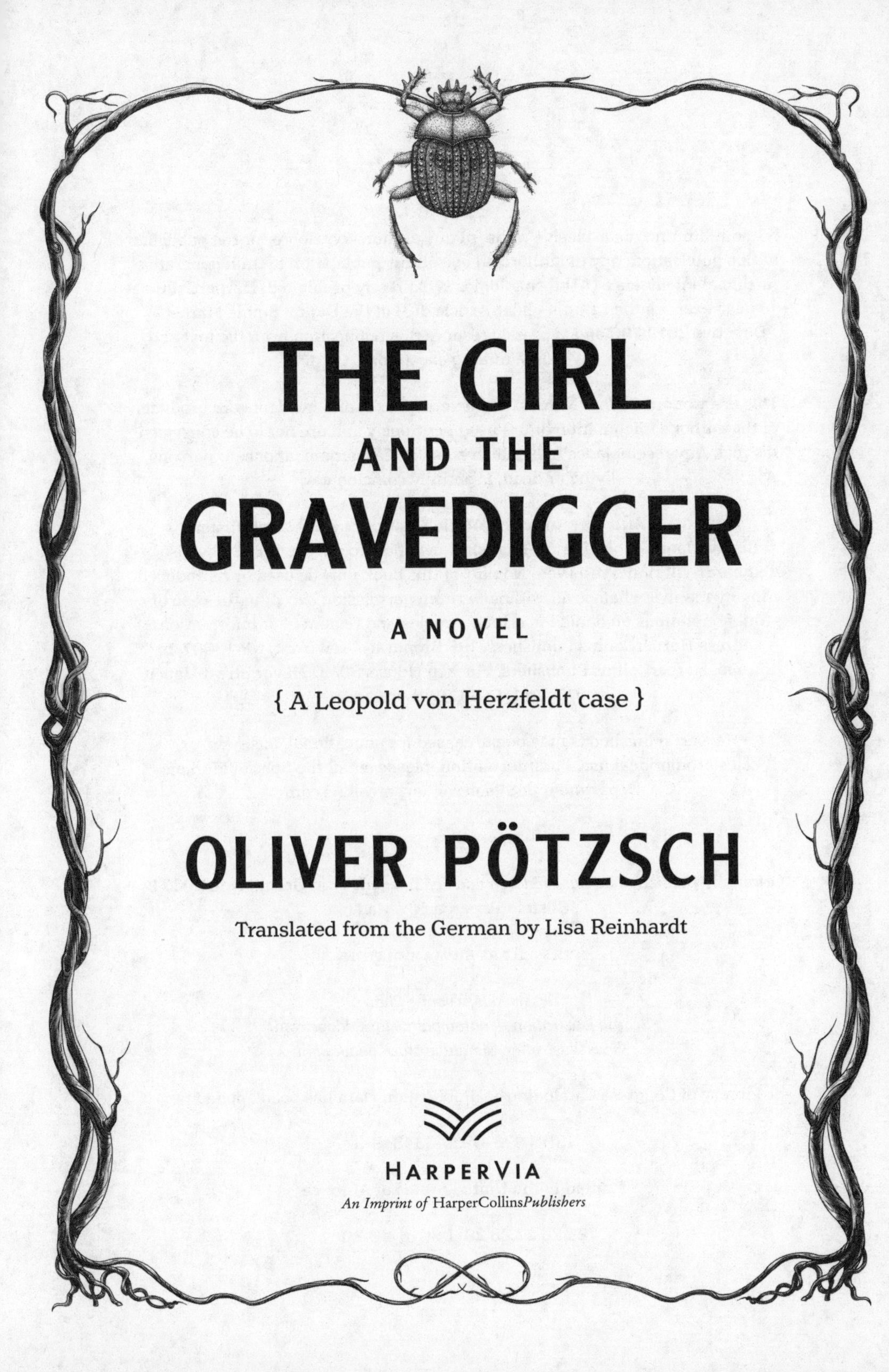

THE GIRL AND THE GRAVEDIGGER

A NOVEL

{ A Leopold von Herzfeldt case }

OLIVER PÖTZSCH

Translated from the German by Lisa Reinhardt

HARPERVIA
An Imprint of HarperCollins*Publishers*

HarperCollins books may be purchased for educational, business, or sales promotional use. For information, please email the Special Markets Department at SPsales@harpercollins.com.

harpercollins.com

Originally published as *Das Mädchen und der Totengräber* in Germany in 2022 by Ullstein Paperback Verlag.

FIRST HARPERVIA EDITION

Designed by Yvonne Chan
Scarab illustration © natalypaint/stock.adobe.com
Vines illustration © natalia/stock.adobe.com

Library of Congress Cataloging-in-Publication Data has been applied for.

ISBN 978-0-06-334849-3

Printed in the United States of America

25 26 27 28 29 LBC 5 4 3 2 1

For Katrin, my sun, once again! Because you always believed in me (and Augustin) . . . Growing old alongside you is like a daily fountain of youth.

And for a little Belgian detective whose fictional cases I read frequently while writing this book. The grand finale *with the final resolution is dedicated to you, Monsieur Hercule Poirot!*

"At first I could see nothing, the hot air escaping from the chamber causing my candle flame to flicker, but presently, as my eyes grew accustomed to the light, details of the room within emerged slowly from the mist, strange animals, statues, and gold—everywhere the glint of gold."

Howard Carter on the discovery of Tutankhamen's tomb

CONTENTS

DRAMATIS PERSONAE

Vienna Police Headquarters

Leopold von Herzfeldt, inspector

Erich Loibl, inspector

Paul Leinkirchner, chief inspector

Moritz Stukart, superintendent and director

Julia Wolf, crime-scene photographer

Vienna Central Cemetery

Augustin Rothmayer, gravedigger

Anna, an orphan

The cemetery director

Vienna Archaeological Society

Professor Alfons Strössner, Egyptologist

Charlotte Rapoldy, Egyptologist and Strössner's daughter

Dr. Clemens Rapoldy, Charlotte's husband and Strössner's son-in-law

Professor Walter Kerfeld, Egyptologist

Dr. Alexander Dedekind, curator of the Egypto-Oriental Collection

Dr. Friedrich Carl Knauer, director of the Vienna zoological garden

Carl Rebers, zookeeper and Knauer's assistant

Professor Eduard Ritter von Hofmann, director of the forensic institute

Archduke Rainer Ferdinand of Austria, nephew of the kaiser

Other Persons

Adelheid Rinsinger, Leo's landlady

Big Elli, owner of the Blue Dragoon brothel

Bruno, security at the Blue Dragoon

Margarethe, a friend of Julia's

Saidrovuni, Matabele chief

Eugen Lenz, zookeeper

Yurek, leader of the kanalstrotters

Father Gregor Mayr, Egyptologist

Dr. Adolf Landinger, Egyptologist

From *Death Rites Around the World* by Augustin Rothmayer, written in Vienna, 1894

The ancient Egyptian craft of mummification is doubtlessly one of the most sophisticated funerary rituals in the world, a technique that was refined over millennia.

The Greek chronicler Herodotus reported that the Egyptians inserted a long, curved metal rod through the nose in order to mince the brain before stirring it and removing it with the aid of the hook. Next, embalming oil was poured up the nasal passage to dissolve any last remnants of brain. The embalmer then used a sharp-edged obsidian tool to open the torso and remove the entrails from the abdominal cavity, which was then rinsed with palm wine and ground herbs. The hollow body was then filled with bundles of linen, pouches of sodium bicarbonate, and sawdust, stitched back up, and immersed in soda lye for 70 days. At last the dehydrated corpse was wrapped with countless bandages and placed as a mummy inside a sarcophagus.

During funerals of pharaohs in ancient Egypt of the first and second dynasties, numerous servants and royal officials were also mummified and placed inside the grave alongside their ruler. Since those servants and officials were still alive, they were killed in ritualistic manners, preferably with a stone adze or by snakebite or poison. In some cases, the poison may have failed to kill the victim, paralyzing them instead. Presumably, more than a few poor souls thus experienced their own embalming while alive and breathing. The horror they must have endured during their slow deaths go beyond even my imagination, and I am a gravedigger.

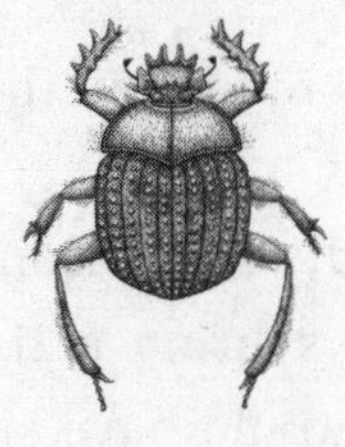

PROLOGUE

Egypt, among the ruins of ancient Thebes,
in the late spring of 1892

Professor Alfons Strössner—venerated Viennese scholar and world-renowned Egyptologist—tripped on a dried camel pie and tumbled face first into the sand.

He uttered a curse at Ra, the blazing god of the sun, his tongue sticking to the roof of his mouth like a scrap of leather. Countless tiny grains of sand trickled from his hair, itching his nose, ears, and eyes. He felt for his flask and greedily drank up the last remaining drops before sitting up, the soft ground beneath him burning like fire. How could he be so stupid and lose his way—as if he were some kind of snobbish British lord! Dunes of sand stretched endlessly into the distance around him like waves in a sea of brown and yellow, broken occasionally by rugged rocks and mountains. Somewhere behind one of those mountains lay the necropolis of Deir al-Bahari, which he'd left just a few hours ago. Only, where exactly? It couldn't be more than a few miles, but the paths wound through the mountains like a labyrinth.

Strössner had left the dig site because he needed some quiet. For weeks now he'd been sharing a tiny tent with his Austrian colleagues—colleagues he would have struggled to tolerate in one of the spacious lecture halls at the University of Vienna, let alone in close quarters, enclosed by no more than thin canvas walls and the wide Egyptian desert. Fat Father Gregor Mayr's snoring and smacking, Adolf Landinger's never-ending complaints about the weather, the bilious comments from his old enemy, Walter Kerfeld . . . He just couldn't bear it any longer.

That said, their work here represented one of the greatest finds in decades, any Egyptologist's dream! The discovery of Deir al-Bahari was already a sensation. New mummies were being unearthed all the time, along with jewelry, amulets, and precious figurines. Each country had sent its most learned experts to Egypt, and so farno agreements had been made as to who would take home which treasures—thus bringing honor and glory to their nation. The various teams of archaeologists behaved as jealously as maidens on the hunt for the most suitable husband.

Strössner straightened up, removing his linen-covered safari helmet, and desperately tried to regain his bearings. His stubborn camel—loathsome creature that it was—had thrown him off an hour ago before trotting away. He'd turned back on foot and seemed to have taken a wrong turn somewhere among the rocks. The way back couldn't be particularly long, but this terrain was treacherous, studded with crevices and soft, hip-deep sand, which, once stepped into, wouldn't let a man go. If he didn't keep his wits about him he could end up a mummy himself. Here, in the hot desert sands, he would desiccate faster than a rotten apple.

Thirst was already beginning to dull his senses. Should he cry for help? But who, aside from a handful of mangy jackals, would answer his cries? Why hadn't he at least brought more water? His mouth and throat were parched, and he struggled to concentrate.

Furious, Strössner hurled his flask against a nearby rock face. The tin vessel clanged hollowly, an echo sounding from between the rocks. Then came a clacking as if a marble had rolled down some steps.

The professor paused, listening.

Rolled down steps?

Intrigued, he rose and approached the rock face. Right where he'd thrown the flask was a hole about the size of a hand. The bottle must have tumbled inside. Strössner kneeled and began to clear away the sand with growing excitement. Soon he made out a shaft leading downwards at an angle, steep stone steps disappearing in the twilight. He guessed that the big sandstorm that had descended a few days ago might have exposed the shaft; before then, the entrance might have remained hidden for millennia.

Strössner's heart thumped wildly in his chest and his right hand started to shake—was it the illness that had been plaguing him for some time now or excitement about the unexpected discovery? Swiftly, he strode back to his field pack, which he'd abandoned in the sand. Aside from a small trowel, it held a kerosene lamp. The professor struck a match, then another . . . at last, the third one lit the wick.

The burning lamp in his hand, he climbed down into the shaft. After only a few steps, the world above all but faded out. He stepped down through the sand which covered the steps in ever thicker layers. Soon he needed his spade to make any progress at all. Thirst and exhaustion were forgotten, and he worked like a man possessed. In the dark of the tunnel, his spade struck something solid. Strössner burrowed in the sand and retrieved a mummified head, followed soon thereafter by a dried hand. He dropped both with disappointment. No, this was no carefully embalmed mummy—no priest, no pharaoh—only the pathetic earthly remains of some unknown stranger.

The corpse of a grave robber, perhaps?

But no, the professor had yet to reach the burial chamber and any so-called false doors—meaning that the would-be plunderer probably hadn't entered the inner parts of the tomb either. He glanced about nervously for potential traps. He knew of clever mechanisms the ancient Egyptians employed to protect their tombs, of deadly apparatuses and poisons that were little studied. But he found nothing, and so he carried on working furiously, shoveling aside the deep sand until he struck a brick wall etched with hieroglyphs. As far as he could tell, it seemed intact.

A smile spread across Strössner's sunburnt face.

There we go . . .

In the dancing light of the lamp the professor recognized the symbol of Osiris, the god of the underworld, as well as the symbol of Thoth, the god of wisdom and magic. There also were several hieroglyphs he couldn't make out. But what he did know was this: the tomb in front of him had not yet been plundered. Maybe it even was the tomb of a yet unknown pharaoh. He would enter the history books with this find!

Strössner only hesitated briefly, then grabbed the spade and smashed it against the wall with both hands. Clouds of dust billowed around him, and grains of sand flowed down the walls in wide swaths. The sand reached his hips. Nervously, he looked upward, where sunlight streamed in through a tiny rectangle that seemed very far away indeed. If much more sand flowed in, he would be buried alive down here. Maybe other explorers would find his desiccated corpse a hundred years or more from now, next to the one he had stumbled across earlier. He shuddered.

Don't give up now!

Again he thrust the spade against the wall, and at last a hole roughly the size of a head burst open. Chunks of clay clattered into the darkness beyond. A musty, slightly sweet smell drifted out from it, carrying notes of dried frankincense. It was a scent the professor knew all too well. His hand trembled as he felt the wall around the hole before shining his kerosene lamp inside, its flickering glow moving across a wall of natural rock beyond.

Good God . . .

The chamber behind the wall was only hip high, and its walls were painted with images. It clearly was a burial chamber. A single sarcophagus stood in the center.

Strössner's hand now shook so violently that he almost dropped the lamp. He could scarcely believe his luck.

The tomb, it's wholly untouched. . . . And those strange symbols on the sarcophagus, the signs of Thoth . . . and a single painted eye . . .

One symbol stood out in particular to Strössner. It was the image of a hand, pointing straight at him with the fingers spread apart.

Like a warning.

Engrossed by the miracle before him, the professor hadn't noticed that sand had continued to trickle down the shaft—grain by grain, inch by inch, as if filling the bottom half of an hourglass.

The trickles turned into streams, then torrents; then, all of a sudden, the entire shaft collapsed like a wave breaking over the top of him.

Strössner gasped with surprise, flailing his arms about. From the corner of his eye he saw the hole to the burial chamber vanish, then his lamp, then the spade . . . Eventually, he was unable to move, the sand reaching up to his throat. A hoarse cry tried to escape him but it came out as a croak. A terrible thought shot through him.

The hand . . . it really was a warning . . . a curse! A trap!

A small black dung beetle crawled directly past his nose. Another beetle tickled his ear; Strössner thought he could practically hear the scratching from the insect's legs.

"PROFESSOR, IS THAT YOU DOWN THERE?"

At first, dazed and confused, Strössner thought he was hearing his own voice. But then he realized that the voice was coming from an opening farther up, where a thin ray of light shone down from above. It was the cutting voice of his archnemesis, Walter Kerfeld. Never in his life had Alfons Strössner thought he would be this glad to hear it.

He gasped, coughed, and spluttered sand. "I'm . . . trapped . . . !" he managed to shout.

"Good heavens, Professor Strössner! We've been looking everywhere for you! Blessed be Our Lady, my prayers have been answered." This was clearly Father Gregor Mayr.

The professor peered up into the speck of light above. He was able to make out the gray, sunken face of Adolf Landinger beside those of Kerfeld and Father Mayr. His colleagues had formed a search party and found him just in the nick of time.

"A rope!" Strössner shouted up at them. "Hurry!"

In an almost superhuman effort, he managed to pull his arms from the sand. When the rope at last appeared in front of his dirt-encrusted eyes, he grasped it and tied it around his chest, and his rescuers began to pull him up. When he reached the surface, he spat out more sand, dry heaving and shaking. The three men stared at him as if he had just escaped from the underworld.

One of them handed him a flask. He gladly accepted it and drank greedily. Then he looked at each of his colleagues in turn. Wiping the last few grains of sand from his eyes, he spoke in a low, husky voice.

"Gentlemen, what I'm about to tell you remains between us. I have discovered a miracle! And I don't intend to share it with the

Brits, the French, or—God forbid—the Prussians. Let alone with a bunch of camel herders. This discovery is a sensation, and it belongs to Austria! Can I count on your word of honor as men of our country?"

All three nodded silently, and the pact was sealed. Walter Kerfeld alone shot him a distrustful look but said nothing.

Then Strössner told the others of the tomb in hushed tones.

None of them could have known then that the spectacular find would prove to be the downfall of them all.

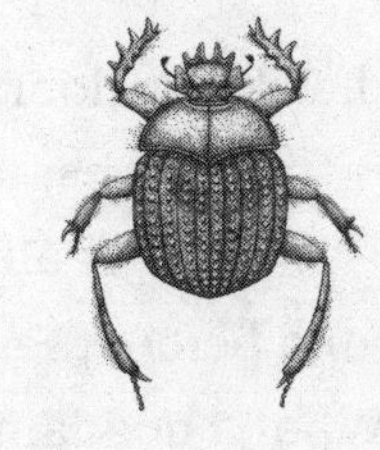

CHAPTER 1

Two years later in Vienna, mid-May 1894, evening in the twelfth district

"Three, two, one—now!"

The combination of magnesium, potassium chloride, and antimony sulfide detonated with a loud bang. There was hissing and smoke, and for a brief moment, the gloomy storage shed was lit up by an abnormally bright glow—almost perfectly circular, like a bell of light. It still seemed like a miracle to Julia every time, even though she knew that the miracle was nothing more than a chemical reaction. Simple modern technology, just like the photographic camera in her hands, an awfully expensive Goldmann with a wide-angle lens and a stand. At almost the same moment that she gave the command, the nervous constable beside her lit the powder and she squeezed the trigger. The camera shutter opened, allowing the light to touch the silver bromide–covered plate behind it and thereby capturing the scene: the cobwebbed windows; the paint cans knocked over on the hard dirt floor; the countless shards of glass and broken bottles on the shelves; the blood, rendered black on the photographic plate . . . Most of all, though, it captured the young man lying on the ground before them, his arms outstretched, his eyes wide with terror. "What a goddamned mess," grumbled inspector Erich Loibl. "Worse than the slaughterhouse over in Sankt Marx. At least it smells better here."

The shed they were in belonged to a dye shop, and the air smelled faintly of the caustic bleaching agent leaking from the toppled tins.

Julia said nothing as she unscrewed the camera from the stand, willing her hands to keep steady. She knew the half dozen men in the room were watching her. During one of her first assignments, a domestic crime in the tenth district, she'd vomited. The murderer had bludgeoned his wife to death with a hammer, and the murder weapon was still lodged in the victim's skull. Instantly there'd been the murmurs that women were unfit for police work—too sensitive, too squeamish—when in fact two long-serving constables had also spewed. But she was always scrutinized more closely.

"You all done there?" asked Loibl, standing right behind her. His watery gaze shifted lazily across the scene. She could smell alcohol on his breath. When the call came in the inspector was probably in some tavern or other, in the middle of drinking his way into the end of his shift. Loibl looked as if he longed to return there as quickly as possible.

"I'd like to take a few close-ups," Julia said. She swapped out the lens and crouched down to adjust the distance on the back of the camera, aware that several of the men were staring at her behind. She then turned to the constable handling the flash apparatus. She'd built it herself—rubber bellows with a hose leading to a burning candle, and a small pocket mirror as a reflector.

"Ready?" she asked.

The constable nodded sullenly before squeezing the bellows once more. Again there was hissing and smoke as a cloud of the powdered mixture reached the candle's flame. For a few brief moments, blinding white light engulfed the corpse.

The victim seemed no older than seventeen or eighteen, dressed in a threadbare, hole-ridden shirt that was sodden and red with blood. Beneath it, they could see signs of at least a dozen knife wounds. The lad had been stuck like a pig. Julia's gaze wandered down to his naked groin, which was matted in blood. Despite the mess, it was clear that the boy was missing some important parts. There was a gaping hole where the testicles ought to have been, and the penis had been cut off, too; only some sinews where it used to be.

A wave of nausea washed over her. She turned to the side and set down the camera. She could practically feel the police constables' eyes on her, as hungry and alert as predators. She'd planned to go out with Leo, and in the rush, there had been no time to change out of her lime-green, figure-hugging evening dress, which was only poorly covered by her thin coat. It was the Saturday before Lent, but it seemed like they'd have to postpone.

"Everything all right, Fräulein Wolf?" Loibl's voice sounded almost empathetic—but only almost. "Are you finished with the camera now?"

"Don't worry, I'll tell you when I'm done. Flash, please."

There would be three more bangs with hissing and smoke before Julia was satisfied. "I think we've got everything." She nodded, as she packed the Goldmann into its wooden box, her lips tight. "Who in God's name does such a thing?" she murmured, almost to herself. "And why?"

"If you were a fellow you'd understand. A man without a willy or balls, well—that's no longer a man." Loibl pushed his bowler hat back on his head. With obvious revulsion he gestured at the body bathed in the flickering light of the kerosene lanterns. "Handsome kid. I have no doubt that he was a street hustler. My guess is he poached on someone else's turf, maybe repeatedly. Someone higher up the food chain made sure the boy'd never do it again. They pick him up in the street, drag him in here, there's a brief struggle, and it's good night, pretty boy. A warning to others not to get any ideas." He motioned at the shards and toppled containers. "The prostitution business is a merciless one. Over in the Prater, you can buy a lad for pennies—some of them not yet fourteen years old. Perhaps this lad here wanted to strike out on his own and his pimp took exception. Chances are, we'll never find out for certain."

"So, you're saying this is a warning to other hustlers?" asked Julia. "Hmm . . ."

She studied the dead body once more. His face was indeed handsome, somewhat feminine. Now she noticed that he was wearing a hint of rouge on his cheeks, and his mouth bore traces of smudged lipstick—a recent trend popularized by the French actress and diva Sarah Bernhardt. The boy looked like a broken doll that had been tossed in the trash.

"It's a rather effective warning, if you ask me," said Loibl. "I've seen something similar before, over in Leopoldstadt, close to Prater Park. A while ago now. Question is, did they chop off his sacred bits *before* they killed him or after? Granted, it's not a pretty sight, but no worse than two fellows getting it on like a pair of dogs. Wouldn't you agree, fräulein?" he asked with a wink in Julia's direction.

"Like you said, you'd know more about that sort of thing, being a man and all," she replied, packing up her photographic plates.

Behind the ramshackle shed the Wien Canal flowed past, flushing away the toxic chemicals from the neighboring dye shop. Some days, the water ran bloodred. This area—Meidling, the twelfth district—wasn't without dangers. It was a workers' quarter, marked by crumbling workshops, factories, tanneries, and glum tenement blocks, where people lived by the dozen in cramped rooms. One of the neighbors had heard some noise and checked on the shed; just half an hour later, the constables and inspector Loibl from the Vienna Security Bureau had arrived, with Julia following shortly. The telephone call reached her during supper with Sisi, all dressed up and ready to go out. She'd kissed her daughter before leaving her with Big Elli and rushing off with her camera and stand.

Had she known what awaited her here, she'd have decided against supper.

"When will the images be ready?" asked Loibl, looking bored as he chewed a toothpick. He was one of the few police agents at Vienna headquarters who wasn't constantly smoking. Loibl was lanky as a beanstalk with a bushy walrus mustache, in contrast to his direct superior, chief inspector Paul Leinkirchner, a beefy bloodhound of a detective. Julia had been relieved to find Loibl at the crime scene, not Leinkirchner. Leinkirchner would have spotted even the slightest tremor of her hands and shown her up in front of everybody. By comparison, Erich Loibl was practically a lamb.

"I'll bring the photographs over on Monday if that's all right?" said Julia.

"That should be fine." Loibl nodded. "The case is quite clear." He shifted the toothpick from one corner of his mouth to the other. "To be honest, I don't see why everything's gotta be photographed now, anyhow. We're already drowning in files! I'm gonna send out a few men; one of the poofters is bound to talk. Those faggots are worse gossips than a bunch of Vienna housewives over afternoon coffee." He gave a dry chuckle and almost choked on his toothpick.

Julia said nothing as she folded together the camera stand and stowed it in its canvas bag. She knew better than to argue with the inspector and possibly jeopardize her position. She needed the money, at least for her daughter. The medicines were expensive.

She smoothed down her dress and straightened her hat before

picking up the stand and case. She cast one last glance at the disfigured corpse before addressing Loibl. "If that's all . . . ?"

The inspector had already turned to a constable in a green surcoat, issuing instructions. He glanced briefly in her direction. "Yes, that'll be all, Fräulein Wolf. We're still waiting for the investigative judge. The real work begins now, and that's men's business."

Julia was already walking out the door when Loibl called after her, ogling her evening dress: "By the way, maybe give your nose a powderin' before your rendezvous—you look a little green around the gills. Enjoy your evening!"

Several of the men laughed, and Julia said nothing as she walked out of the shed.

Outside, darkness had fallen; it was probably close to eight in the evening. The air was warm, and even here in Meidling—a district reeking of bleaching agents and lye, close to the Vienna sewage ponds—a hint of summer lay in the air.

A summer that boy will never experience, thought Julia.

Loibl's words from earlier sprang to her mind.

Question is, did they chop off his sacred bits before they killed him or after . . . ?

She shuddered despite the warm breeze. Maybe it wasn't too late to go out with Leo. It would help dispel the gloom.

A horsecar tram jingled closer. Julia waited at the nearby stop and climbed on board among the many sweaty, visibly exhausted passengers. She clung to a rope handle, closed her eyes, and tried to focus her thoughts on her daughter. Sisi was probably fast asleep by now, dreaming lovely dreams.

Julia had a hunch that her own dreams wouldn't be quite so lovely this night.

LEO RUBBED HIS EYES TIREDLY, STRAINING TO DECIPHER HIS handwritten notes through the thick cigar smoke. The two gas lights hanging from the wood-paneled ceiling cast only a faint glow through the smoky room.

"Blood, my dear colleagues, usually doesn't look anything like the authors of cheap crime novels would have us believe," he said, trying to sound more awake than he felt. "It is a very special juice, to quote good old Goethe. As you probably know from your own experience, blood can take on any color, depending on the degree of desiccation. From rusty red to brown to greenish yellow . . ."

He cleared his throat and lifted his gaze. The two gas lights below the wood-paneled ceiling struggled to dispel the tobacco haze. Looking at the two dozen police agents in front of him, Leo suddenly felt unsure if these men had in fact seen blood before. Most were quite young, fresh police agents who had only completed their law studies the previous year. The lot of them looked as though they came from money and knew more about horse racing, women, and expensive cigars than about murder most foul—typical spoiled sons of academics, Leo thought to himself. *Just like me. Except for the bit about murder . . .*

"Murder weapons are often carefully cleaned, but blood sticks in invisible places," Leo carried on. He held up one of the objects that he had fetched from the evidence room beforehand. "A butcher from the sixteenth district used this pocketknife to stab a colleague to death during an argument. He cleaned the knife thoroughly. But when our experts examined it, they found particles of blood under the wooden grip. Consequently, the man confessed. Also, blood splatters on walls are a useful way of determining whether the blood is arterial or venous, and how the body was positioned, as well as—"

Someone chuckled and Leo broke off. In the last row of seats, a young man was passing a small piece of paper to another.

"Would you be so kind as to share what you find so amusing?" asked Leo.

The young man, a wheat-haired young lad with a freshly healed cut on his cheek quickly hid the paper under his desk. "Beg your pardon . . . ," he mumbled. "It's nothing . . ."

"Lovely. If it's nothing, then I'm sure you've got time to come up here and assist me with this evidence." Leo beckoned and the young man made his way to the front, accompanied by gleeful cackling from his peers. Leo realized that he sounded just like his senile law professors back in Graz. Had it really come to this already?

He drew a deep breath. He'd had a gut feeling right from the start that this presentation was a bad idea. But superintendent Moritz Stukart, the new director of the Vienna Security Bureau, had personally asked Leo. A little over six months ago, Leo's former mentor, Graz investigative judge Hans Gross, had come to Vienna to hold a series of talks at Vienna police headquarters. Gross's recently published *Handbook for Investigative Judges* was a milestone of modern criminalistics, but apparently, Vienna wasn't ready for it. Gross's monotonous, yes, outright boring presentation style hadn't helped. Superintendent Stukart had expected a fierier turn from Leo.

But this here isn't even a dim glow, thought Leo.

While the blond youth with the scar made his way to the front at a leisurely pace, Leo's gaze wandered across the room. Stukart had assigned him a fourth floor meeting room; which housed larger meetings during the day. The space was hopelessly crowded with two dozen participants: up to four men shared small, wobbly desks. Visibility was terrible due to the cigar smoke, and Leo could barely breathe. He counted six overflowing ashtrays. On top of everything else, it was past eight o'clock on a Saturday night. He, too, struggled to suppress a yawn. Like himself, his younger colleagues had had a long day and they were ready to drink and dance with their sweethearts. They didn't want to listen to the uppity speech of some fop from Graz—especially if said fop talked like a German.

"Take this axe," said Leo once the young man arrived at last at his desk. Leo handed him the axe. "At first glance, it appears clean. Do you see any stains?"

The lad turned the axe this way and that, and eventually pointed to a tiny speck on the cutting edge. "There," he declared, sounding bored.

"What if it's rust?" asked Leo.

"Hmm . . ." The blond boy moved his head from side to side. "Well, then I don't know. . . ."

"Then, my dear colleague, you ought to know from your studies that we're now able to detect blood thanks to the Van Deenschen test, even if the sample is old and dried up. The test makes use of the fact that the blood colorant hemoglobin—"

The door opened. To Leo's surprise, it was chief inspector Paul Leinkirchner, his superior. Leinkirchner squeezed his bulk onto one of the last remaining seats and gave Leo a nod. "Carry on, Herr von Herzfeldt," he said in his deep voice. "I'm all ears."

"Um, the fact that hemoglobin possesses the . . . the quality of binding oxygen," stammered Leo, thrown by the sudden appearance of Leinkirchner. "Experiments with West Indian guaiacum plants have shown that extracts from this plant turn blue when they come in contact with blood, and—"

"With what kind of blood?" Leinkirchner leaned back lazily and played with the silver watch chain on his waistcoat.

Leo paused, confused. "Beg your pardon?"

"Well, what kind of blood, I wonder. That there's a butcher's hatchet." Leinkirchner pointed at the axe in the young man's hands. "How can you tell that it isn't the blood of a calf or a lamb? Or do you class those as murder now, too? But don't mind me, dear colleague—I didn't mean to interrupt your presentation. Please, carry on."

Several of the young men chuckled, and Leo bit his lip. Leinkirchner was absolutely right. While they might be able to differentiate blood from other substances such as rust, mold, or saliva mixed with chewing tobacco these days, there was no way of determining which creature the blood originated from. It could be human blood, or it could be that of another mammal, or even that of a bird.

"The difference lies in the size of the blood cells," tried Leo lamely. He straightened his notes. "If the blood is fresh, one might be able to find indicators of whether it's human. Under a microscope—"

"But it's not fresh. You said so yourself, earlier. It's old and dried up. I believe that's what I heard just outside the door." Leinkirchner lit a cigar, taking contented drags. Leo was increasingly under the impression that Leinkirchner had come with the sole intent of sabotaging his presentation. In addition, he seemed to have eavesdropped.

That would be so like him. . . .

"I am certain that we're close to cracking blood analysis," said Leo curtly. "Before long we'll be able to differentiate between animal and human blood with absolute certainty. And who knows—maybe one day there'll be a way to tell the blood of one person from that of another."

"Well, one thing is for certain—*your* blood doesn't flow in the veins of the likes of us," replied Leinkirchner.

Leo flinched. "What are you trying to say, chief inspector?"

"You may draw your own conclusions, Herr *von Herzfeldt*. Being the clever criminalist that you are."

A frosty silence settled over the room. Leo noticed several men stifling a grin, including the blond one with the scar who still stood at the desk holding the hatchet, focusing hard on the tips of his shoes. The meaning of Leinkirchner's words was obvious. Leo knew it, and so did all the young men in the room.

He opened his mouth to make a retort when Leinkirchner flipped open his pocket watch.

"Past eight. I think you better continue your talk another day, Herzfeldt. I actually came here to fetch you."

"Fetch me? What for?" Leo's voice trembled.

"Superintendent Stukart wants to see us both," said Leinkirchner.

"At this hour?" asked Leo, surprised.

"Vienna never sleeps. Murder doesn't take time off." Paul Leinkirchner rose and headed toward the door. "Oh, and leave the axe, Herzfeldt. We wouldn't want any accidents."

As Leo stepped past his grinning colleagues to follow the chief inspector outside, his eye caught on one of the desks in the back row. The scrap of paper the young blond man had passed around earlier sat on the tabletop. It almost looked as if he'd left it there on purpose.

Drawn on the paper was a hastily sketched portrait of Leo—with an enormous hooked nose.

OUT IN THE CORRIDOR, NEITHER MAN SPOKE. LEINKIRCHNER walked a few steps ahead, which allowed Leo to observe him from behind. He was a burly man in his midforties, bald with broad shoulders. An experienced policeman, he had fought his way up from humble beginnings all the way to chief inspector at the famous Vienna Security Bureau.

He walked with a slight limp, adding to his sullen appearance. Leinkirchner had disliked Leo from day one. Leo felt this was at least partly because Leo was his polar opposite: young, dapper, well dressed—a dandy from Graz who—worst of all—spoke with a High German accent. By comparison, Paul Leinkirchner, with his loose-fitting coat and the poorly healed scar on his cheek, bore closer resemblance to a gangster. All the more surprising, then, that Leinkirchner had moved Leo to his department six months prior. There were days when the two of them, both experts in their field, worked side by side. But sooner or later there was always an unpleasant scene such as what had just happened.

They arrived at the end of the long corridor. Stukart's office was the last on the right-hand side. An enamel sign on the door read: "Moritz Stukart, Superintendent, Security Bureau."

Stukart ranked directly beneath the president of the bureau—and therefore, to more than a few colleagues, higher than the dear Lord and Savior. As the new director of the security bureau, for a few months now he'd been in charge of murder and serious crime—and there was plenty of both in Vienna.

Leinkirchner's knock was answered with a brisk "come in!"

When they entered, Leo noticed yet again how much the superintendent had made this room his own in such a short space of time. Stukart's office was the epitome of accuracy and orderliness: a large, tidy desk; several immaculately polished filing cabinets; clunky, uncomfortable set of corner furniture with no cushions. It smelled of . . . nothing. No cigar smoke, no scent of wurst buns or coffee. The office was as sterile as an operating room.

Stukart was sitting at his desk studying files, a dozen pencils lined up in front of him like a perfect row of tiny soldiers. He looked up and pushed the files aside.

"Herzfeldt, good of you to make time. How was your presentation?"

"Enriching," said Leo with a sidelong glance at Leinkirchner. "For both."

Stukart nodded, contented. He was a supporter of the new methods, and he expected Leo to introduce them to the Vienna police. It was a laborious task, as Leo had just had the pleasure of experiencing yet again.

"You ought to hold such talks more often now," said Stukart. "We must convince our young colleagues of the advantages of modern criminalistics. Paris and Scotland Yard are miles ahead of us in that respect." He tapped one of the pencils on the table, sounding like a telegraph operator. "Have you heard? Our colleagues in London have their very own chemical laboratory now, and they have a telephone in every single tiny office. By comparison, we still wallow in the dirt like pigs!"

As usual, Moritz Stukart was dressed in a tailored waistcoat and a tight choker collar, his fine hair combed and perfectly parted with brilliantine. It was hard to believe he was the same man who had single-handedly brought down several of Vienna's most notorious criminals in his younger days.

"Please, sit, gentlemen," he said, waving impatiently toward the furniture in the corner.

Leo felt increasingly certain that he wouldn't get away from work until late. And he had a date with Julia, damn it. Things weren't going so great between them anyway, and now he had to go and stand her up!

"I have a somewhat delicate assignment for the two of you," began Stukart once they were all seated. "A body has been found in the Museum of Art History."

"In the Museum of Art History?" Leinkirchner frowned. "A robbery gone wrong?"

Leo followed Leinkirchner's train of thought. The Museum of Art History was one of the most magnificent buildings along the newly built Ring. Alongside its sister organization, the Museum of Natural History, it had only been completed a few years earlier and was a veritable crowd magnet. The museum housed one of the world's most significant art collections, on par with the Louvre in Paris or the Hermitage in Saint Petersburg. Had a painting been stolen, or perhaps precious jewelry from the Kunstkammer, and one of the museum wardens slain by the intruders?

"No, not a robbery." Stukart twirled his mustache, shiny with brilliantine. "It's a little more . . . well, complicated. That's why I asked you both here. This matter must be treated with the utmost discretion. It mustn't leak to the press under any circumstance. It would cause a scandal!" He gave a cough and leaned forward. "Does the name Alfons Strössner mean anything to either of you?"

Leinkirchner said nothing while Leo racked his brain. He felt as though he'd read the man's name in the paper some time ago. Something about a lecture at the University of Vienna, an expedition to Egypt . . .

"Isn't Strössner an Egyptologist?" he asked.

"Not just any Egyptologist, but one of Austria's finest." Stukart nodded. "A world-class academic! He led a group of Viennese archaeologists to Egypt two years ago, and now works as an advisor in the Museum of Art History—or rather, worked."

"So, the professor is the murder victim?" asked Leinkirchner.

"It's not entirely clear yet whether he was murdered, let alone when or how." Stukart sighed. "But yes, he is dead. They found him this evening, shortly after the museum closed. Inside a sarcophagus. That alone would be strange enough. But that's not all."

"What are you suggesting, sir?" asked Leo, wrinkling his forehead. "Could it have been suicide? Is that it?"

"I doubt it. Unless Professor Strössner removed his own intestines and bathed in lye before wrapping himself up in bandages." Moritz Stukart leaned back in his wobbly wooden chair, and there was a creaking sound as if a long locked door had opened.

It was dark when Julia finally arrived home in Neulerchenfeld, in the sixteenth district. The moon was a pale sickle high above the rooftops, shining down on the usual suspects in Vienna's biggest amusement patch. Whores with painted faces stood leaning against gas streetlights waiting for clients, their garishly dressed pimps watching over them from the doorways of taverns, smoking. So-called flower girls walked the sidewalk, proffering bouquets and swaying their hips; everyone knew they were just another kind of prostitute, albeit much younger ones and without a bill of health. Two inebriated figures emerged from a wine bar and approached a flower girl, a haggard young blond thing in a tattered shift. They agreed on a price and vanished into a backyard.

Julia turned away with disgust. Men were sometimes no better than beasts. She thought back to how years ago she, too, used to bare all to get by. She'd sworn to herself that her daughter would be better off than herself one day. Julia was willing to do whatever it took, even if that meant photographing horribly mutilated murder victims.

With the busy evening traffic, it had taken more than half an hour to get here by the horsecar tram. Not too long ago, Neulerchenfeld had once been a separate village outside Vienna, but a few years ago it was incorporated as a part of the city. People came to the neighborhood to amuse themselves in its many taverns and bars—or to procure a *Blosengerl* or a *Bordsteinschwalbe*, a "pavement swallow," as the people of Vienna affectionately called their prostitutes. Julia walked toward an aging, multistory building from the Biedermeier era. It had rusty balcony railings and blackened wooden figurines. The windows were covered with heavy red drapes. She pulled on the doorbell, and a hatch at eye level opened.

Behind it a rough-hewn man with a fearsome visage and flattened boxer's nose grinned at her. "Our Julia. Been taking some lovely photos, have you? You sure you don't wanna take my picture sometime? I'm a handsome fellow, aren't I?"

"I'm afraid your face would shatter the glass plate, Bruno," Julia replied with a tired smile. "Sisi sleeping?"

"Like an angel. I sang her a lullaby." Bruno opened the door. He was a giant at six foot five, his forehead as angular as if it had been hewn from rock. Julia pictured this monster of a man humming softly to her daughter. Bruno was one of the few men in her life. Bruno and Leo. And the fearsome colossus was probably gentler with Sisi than Leo. Sisi would happily spend hours bouncing on Bruno's knee.

Julia nodded at Bruno warmly before heading down the corridor, her steps muffled by heavy rugs. As always, the air was rife with strong perfume and musk, and from behind the doors, moans, squeals, sighs, and laughter could be heard—the usual nighttime noises. Well-worn steps, also covered in carpet, led upstairs. Julia stopped outside a door on the second floor and opened up quietly. A smile spread across her face.

Inside, in a wide four-poster bed among plush bedding and down pillows, beneath a painting showing a copulating faun, her three-year-old daughter lay blissfully asleep. She lay curled up like a kitten, sucking her thumb. Julia stepped over and gently covered Sisi with a blanket, taking care not to wake her. Julia moved quietly even though there was no need: Sisi had been deaf and mute since birth. They had tried everything—water cures, draft candles, other obscure and expensive remedies. Therapies and medicines gobbled up Julia's meager wages more quickly than she could earn them. Sisi was the result of a rape, conceived on the filthy kitchen table of a former employer. Regardless, Julia loved her child more than anything.

More than I could ever love a man, she thought, engrossed by the angelic face of her daughter. *Even with the way Leo is wooing me . . .*

"You're late, girl. I was starting to worry."

Julia turned. Big Elli stood in the doorway, her arms folded. The brothel keeper tried to glower at Julia but failed. Swaths of red taffeta billowed down her voluminous body, which always reminded Julia of one of Wagner's Valkyries. Her fine-featured, doll-like face suggested she must have been a stunning beauty in her younger days.

"What was it this time?" asked Elli. "Someone put on a permanent necktie or jump off a bridge? Tram run 'em over?"

Julia sighed. "You don't want to know, Elli."

"I'm not gonna stand by and watch this for much longer." Elli gave her a sharp look and raised a chubby forefinger. "You're growing skinnier by the day, and I can hear you screaming at night. It's no job for a woman! Dead bodies, day in, day out."

"Spreading your legs for all these dim-witted mutts, that's a job though, is it?" It came out harsher than she intended. "Just now, two men disappeared around the corner with a girl out there. She couldn't have been fourteen!"

"That's against the law. Bruno will go see to those bastards."

"Then there'll just be more." Julia shook her head. The brawling of drunken men outside could be heard. "It never ends."

Julia had been living at the Blue Dragoon bordello for more than three years now, since she'd turned up on Elli's doorstep, pregnant. Elli would have liked to employ Julia as a prestige whore, but Julia refused. Nonetheless, the brothel keeper and other girls cared lovingly for Sisi when Julia was at work—to Sisi, they all were like aunties.

Very scantily clad aunties, thought Julia.

"Have you heard from Leo?" she asked Elli. "We were planning to go out tonight."

Big Elli shook her head, and Julia said nothing, disappointed.

"Listen." Elli lowered herself onto the foot of the bed, causing it to creak. She patted the covers with her soft fingers, signaling Julia to sit down beside her. "Menfolk all believe they're gods. But in reality, they're pathetic little creatures. We can do whatever we please with them—that's how thick they are! You only need to bat your eyelashes and before you know it, they'll throw themselves off a bridge for you or shower you with money."

Julia smiled sadly. "But that's not the kind of man I want."

"I know very well what you want. And you know how I feel about that. It's a crock of shit!" Big Elli never tried to hide the fact that she thought very little of Julia's relationship with Leo. The two of them had been a couple for six months, and took care to ensure no one at police headquarters found out.

Elli continued in a stern voice, "Leo is a spoiled brat. I know plenty of his ilk. Don't go getting serious with someone like him—it'll only end in tears. You're not one of them—you belong here, in Neulerchenfeld! And voilà, he's let you down yet again. How much longer are you planning to put up with that, girl?"

Julia rose from the bed. "I've got to go to work, Elli."

"You'll think back on my words. At the latest when he sends you packing! I promise you'll—" There was a ringing somewhere downstairs, and Elli rolled her eyes. "That goddamn telephone. I never should have agreed to having one of those things. It's worse than any punter . . ." Elli left, dragging her feet.

Julia kissed her sleeping daughter's cheek softly and stroked her lovingly.

She looks so beautiful, she thought. *Beautiful and fragile.*

Then she picked up her camera suitcase and left the room. She hadn't been planning to develop the images until the next day, which was Whitsunday. But now that Leo hadn't shown, she might as well do it straightaway. Then at least it would be done and over with.

She took the stairs to the top floor, past the many rooms in which Elli's female employees noisily earned their nightly bread. Their workdays were only just beginning. Listening to the cries of delight, the fake moans, the men's puffing and grunting, Julia experienced a moment of gratitude for Sisi's deafness.

On the fifth floor, a ladder led to the attic, where Elli stored old chests of undergarments, moth-eaten silk cushions, and retired leather boots and masks. Hanging from the old, rotting rafters were crops and other implements menfolk liked to be tortured with or enjoyed torturing women with. Julia dragged the suitcase up the ladder and entered her realm. Up here, she'd set up a laboratory for developing her photographs. She lit a small gas lamp with a red shade and set to work.

There was only one small, dusty window full of cobwebs, and she covered it with a heavy curtain, making sure that no outside light could get in. The room was now bathed completely in red from her lamp. She poured the developer and fixer solutions into two separate tin basins, and clean water into the third. She then removed the magazine holding the glass plates from the camera. Leo had taught her everything in great detail, and she'd been a good student. As she dipped the plates into the first basin, her thoughts drifted back to Leo. Big Elli's words popped into her mind.

You're not one of them—you belong here, to Neulerchenfeld. . . .

Leo had gifted her the camera and bought the laboratory equipment. It had been he, too, who had even secured her the crime scene photographer position—previously at the police headquarters she'd worked as a switchboard operator. Leo was always generous not least because he could afford to be. His mother sent money from Graz on a regular basis. He wore expensive suits and took Julia out to good restaurants. Twice he'd taken her to the opera on the Ring; on both occasions, she'd borrowed an elegant dress from the brothel. Throughout her childhood in the Inn region, meals were oat gruel during the day, boiled potatoes at night, and, if they were lucky, a starved chicken in broth with beets on the occasional Sunday. The only opera her parents knew was The Magic Flute, and only because it was performed with puppets and a barrel organ in the village square.

Leo, by contrast, knew Italian Mozart librettos; he knew which wine went with which meat and which cutaway went with which tie.

You're not one of them. . . .

Julia sighed. Perhaps Elli was right, and she and Leo were ill matched.

Were they even a couple? They slept together and went out every now and then, danced, laughed. But they hadn't yet developed a deep sense of trust or ability to rely on each other. And now he'd stood her up yet again.

Absorbed by her thoughts, she realized she almost forgot to take the images out of the developer—she nearly botched the entire job! She would have struggled to explain herself at the police station come Monday morning. . . .

Julia swiftly removed the plates from the first bath and dipped them first in the fixer solution and then in clean water. She'd done this so many times now, but it never ceased to amaze her how the images suddenly appeared on the plates, like sunken treasures emerging from the sea. She'd loved this work from the moment she first watched Leo do it. Julia dreamed that one day she'd photograph living people, not just dead ones. Elli was right—she often slept poorly following the nights spent in the attic. The corpses—cut up, stabbed, shredded, run over, shot—followed her into her dreams. The boy whose testicles and penis had been cut off would visit her this night, Julia felt certain.

She placed the plates on the wooden rack to dry and lit another lamp. She studied the photographs, thinking. There was the wide-angle image that also showed half of inspector Erich Loibl, the chaos in the shed. The close-ups of the horrific injuries, the blood, showing in black in the pictures; the youth's painted face, the eyes, wide with fear . . . Something bothered her. Something was different than it ought to be. Only, what?

Julia lit a cigarette, even though she knew how risky that was, up here in the attic, with a highly flammable liquid nearby. Smoke rose and spread among the rafters and roof tiles. Again she studied each image.

What is it?

Eventually, she gave up. She would lie down beside Sisi and try to fall asleep, with or without Leo. Sometimes, problems solved themselves during sleep.

She put the cigarette out in an old can, packed the plates into the case, and climbed down the ladder.

But once she lay in bed with her eyes closed, Julia saw the made-up boy who had been murdered so horribly.

He appeared to shout something at her desperately, but she couldn't understand what he was saying.

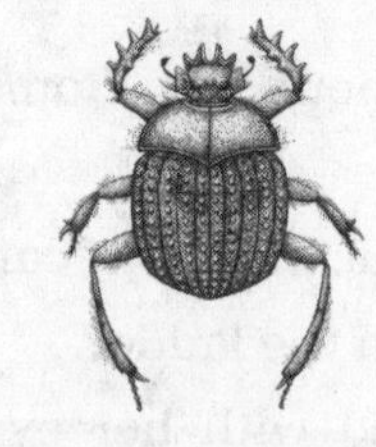

CHAPTER 2

From *Death Rites Around the World,* by Augustin Rothmayer, written in Vienna, 1894

> Mummies can result from natural occurrences: preservation from hot desert sands, or cold glacier ice; from cool, dry drafts of caves or cellars, or by sour waters of moors. Once removed from their original surroundings, they soon begin to rot and smell. That is not the case with man-made mummies. Even thousands of years later, they can appear young and fresh. The mummies of Memphis are black, dry, and extremely brittle, while those of Thebes are yellow, supple, and moderately shiny. Unfortunately, Egyptian mummies are still frequently used as fuel by today's citizens. Who knows how many pharaohs have gone up in smoke!

It was but a short ten-minute walk from the police headquarters at Schottenring to the Museum of Art History, past city hall and Volksgarten park. Fiacre carriages rattled past, and the streets were busy with night owls on their way to the opera or the fine restaurants along the Ring on this Saturday night.

Paul Leinkirchner appeared not in the mood for conversation, which suited Leo just fine. He hung back, letting Leinkirchner limp sullenly ahead, and thought about what superintendent Stukart had told them. It wasn't a lot, and it struck Leo as strange—yes, eerie, even. The fact that Stukart was sending the experienced chief inspector together with the young champion of modern criminalistics showed how important this matter was—and how delicate.

The phone call had only come in from the museum about an hour ago. That was why Stukart didn't know many details. But at least he had gathered some information about the deceased, who was relatively well known in Vienna.

Professor Alfons Strössner had been well into his sixties and was indeed a world-renowned expert on Egyptology. His curriculum vitae demonstrated a picture-perfect academic career: degrees from the Universities of Vienna, Paris, and Cairo; various publications in esteemed journals; committee member of the exclusive Vienna Archaeological Society; as well as adviser at the Vienna Museum of Art History, one of the largest museums of its kind worldwide. Just the year before, Strössner had returned from a lengthy expedition to Egypt, bearing treasures from antiquity—statuettes and sarcophagi—which were on loan to the museum at no cost by the country of Egypt. The professor had lived in a large house in Hietzing together with his daughter Charlotte, also a trained Egyptologist. Apparently there was also a son-in-law—Charlotte's husband—by the name of Dr. Clemens Rapoldy. All three of them were welcome guests at receptions, generous patrons of science and sparkling jewels of Viennese society.

The two inspectors meanwhile reached the sprawling Maria Theresien Square, where two magnificent Renaissance-style buildings housed the Museums of Natural History and Art History. Helden Square and Wiener Hofburg were located not far away on the other side of the Ring. Leo hadn't yet found an opportunity to visit the museums—not least because dusty paintings, weapons, stuffed zebras, and butterfly collections didn't carry the same appeal as Viennese nightlife. The Museum of Art History lay on the left; the huge statue of Archduchess Maria Theresa in the center of the square seemed to point its hand at it. The square was still busy at this hour with small groups standing here and there, the men dressed in tailcoats and top hats, the ladies in evening gowns and elegant hats, ready for a social Saturday night.

Leinkirchner still wasn't speaking. The incident from earlier hung between them. Leinkirchner had intended to provoke Leo—worse, he had yet again bullied him for his Jewish roots. On his father's side, Leo came from a Jewish family of bankers, and the chief inspector continued to drop sneering remarks. And he wasn't the only one. At police headquarters, yes, in the whole of Vienna, anti-Semitism was practically bon ton.

In Vienna, the Jews get blamed for everything, thought Leo. *For the weather as well as the ongoing construction and pigeon infestation.*

The tall windows of the Museum of Art History were dark; a handful of gas lights burned at the entrance. As the two inspectors approached, they were met by a middle-aged man wearing a tidy three-piece suit and a pince-nez, which he held on to nervously as he walked. The ash-gray color of his suit matched that of his face.

"Are you the gentlemen from the police?" he asked in a low voice.

"We are indeed," replied Leinkirchner. "And you are . . . ?"

"Alexander Dedekind, curator of the Egypto-Oriental Collection." He looked about anxiously. "Please, follow me. We're trying to create as little fuss as possible."

"Might help if you stop sneaking around like a thief in the night," Leinkirchner suggested.

"I apologize, but it's all . . . I'm still in shock . . ." Dedekind shuddered. "Well, you'll see for yourselves in just a moment."

They followed the man inside and Leo stopped short. There wasn't much light, but even so, the first impression was imposing. The ceiling was high above the floor and came together in a stucco dome with a circular hole in its center, like a divine eye. Several wide flights of stairs led up in different directions, and farther back, Leo made out a large marble statue. The ground was covered in mosaic, and the numerous columns and arches made Leo think of a temple.

A temple of art and science . . .

"Can't we get more light in here?" Leo asked their guide. His voice echoed eerily in the vast building. "I can barely see."

"The architects, Semper and Hasenauer, decided against artificial light," explained Dr. Dedekind. He reached for a kerosene lamp on the ground. "That way, the paintings are shown in a better light during the daytime. That's why we have different opening hours depending on the time of year."

"And we can barely see where we're putting our feet," grumbled Leinkirchner. "Where are the night watchmen?"

"I sent them all home bar two. Like I said—we want to cause as little fuss as possible." Dedekind gestured to the right, where a staircase led to an entrance flanked by two black pharaoh statues. "Officially, there is a burst pipe in the Egypto-Oriental Collection. I barred the doors from the inside to avoid anything . . . uh, leaking."

"Leaking?" asked Leo. "How do you mean?"

"Well, no gossip. Nor . . ." Dedekind hesitated. "Nor anything else. Follow me. We'll go a different way."

Without further explanation, Dr. Dedekind led the two inspectors up another set of steps and down a corridor. The only light came from the kerosene lamp. From the darkness in front of them emerged Greek statues like giants that seemed about to attack, followed by stone coffins, then stone torsos and a figurine of a woman with four heads. Leo strained to see as much as possible. Each hall they passed through was like an entire museum in its own right.

"Bloody hell, how big is this place?" swore Leinkirchner. Apparently, he hadn't been to the museum yet either.

"The museum houses over eighty rooms," replied Dedekind as they continued past statues and glass display cabinets. "This is the Antiquity Collection. There also is the Numismatic Collection, the Imperial Armory, the paintings, the library, the Egypto-Oriental Collection, of course. . . . We even have our own in-house restoration department. If you visited all our halls, you'd be walking two miles—half the Ring!"

"Couldn't imagine a nicer stroll," muttered Leinkirchner.

Eventually they arrived at a large hall that, in the dim light of night, felt like the inside of a pyramid. The walls were lined with wooden sarcophagi standing upright and stone covered in Egyptian designs, protected behind glass. Columns carried a high ceiling adorned with blue ornaments and bird motifs. Glass cabinets held gilded masks, statuettes of deities, and jewelry, among them several obsidian scarabs.

"This . . . this is really impressive," Leo said, tilting back his head to admire the paintings.

"Isn't it?" Dedekind beamed like a child on Christmas Day. "I think the hall is a huge success. The columns are originals from Alexandria. It really gives our visitors an idea of what a powerful empire ancient Egypt was. Three thousand years of history! Habsburg has a lot of catching up to do."

Chief inspector Leinkirchner meanwhile had walked up to one of the sarcophagi. The lid had been removed, displaying the body inside. It was wrapped in brownish bandages, dead eyes staring at them from a dried up, black face. Leinkirchner turned to Dedekind with a grin.

"The professor?" He pointed at the mummy. "His suit has seen better days, I've gotta say."

"This is the mummy of Pa-di-set of the twenty-second dynasty," explained Dedekind, a little peeved. "It was an age that peaked around 800 BC. We're very proud to be able to display this sarcophagus."

"800 BC?" Leinkirchner whistled appreciatively. He began to light a cigar, but Dedekind gave him a stern look. "In that case, the old feller doesn't look too shabby at all."

"The preserving techniques of the ancient Egyptians are unmatched, to this day. You'll see for yourselves shortly. If you'd care to follow me."

Dedekind led them to a smaller side wing where, Leo noted to his surprise, mummified dogs and cats were displayed. He even spotted a large bird, some kind of crane.

"Is that what I think it is?" Leinkirchner gestured at a huge and long mummy of an animal.

"Yes, this is a Nile crocodile," replied Dedekind. "To the Egyptians, crocodiles were holy. There even was a crocodile god."

"I wonder if we could get this done with our dachshund when it dies?" asked Leinkirchner. "My wife would love it."

Alexander Dedekind said nothing and opened a heavy door concealed inside an alcove. A sign read that only staff had access.

"Please, follow me," said Dedekind. "And mind the stairs. They can be slippery."

They climbed down a narrow set of steps that ended outside a solid steel door. When Dedekind opened it, Leo felt a dry, chilly breeze carrying an unpleasant, musty smell, almost as if he were entering a giant sarcophagus. He was looking at a long, low-ceilinged room. At least there was more light here. Several gas lamps hung from the ceiling, illuminating a scene that Leo struggled to make sense of at first.

In the center of the room stood a large workstation with a stone top, and on it rested an open sarcophagus. There were alcoves on the left and right with three levels each, somewhat like berths on a ship. The alcoves could be closed with sliding doors, but many of them stood open. Inside the berths, Leo saw colorfully painted sarcophagi and mummies, all stacked up tidily. Stored on shelves and inside glass cabinets were statuettes, heads made of clay, and shards; a few more sarcophagi stood leaning against a wall. Leo suddenly realized just how cold it was down here.

"The rest of our collections," explained Dr. Dedekind. "We have too many artifacts to display all of them upstairs. These rooms here are for . . . er, research alone." He glanced about nervously, as if he was looking for something.

"Are all of these pharaohs?" asked Leo.

"The belief that pharaohs alone were mummified is a common misconception," said a familiar voice. It sounded like it was coming from one of the alcoves. "Practically everyone was mummified in Egypt. Kings and priests, of course, but also tradesmen, even farmers and day laborers. Though the bodies of the poor were mostly just buried in the sand where they dehydrated into leathery bundles. It is fair to assume that the soil is laced with mummies. A strange thought, don't you think, Herr von Herzfeldt? Like a giant cemetery."

A man with glasses and a well-kept beard stepped out from the darkness of one of the alcoves. He wore a waistcoat and neatly buttoned white shirt with the sleeves rolled up. He blinked tiredly at Leo and took off his glasses to clean them.

"Professor Hofmann!" exclaimed Leo with surprise. "What are you doing here?"

"I was asked to perform an initial examination in these special circumstances," explained the professor. "I was happy to oblige, for my own particular reasons."

Leo knew Professor Eduard Ritter von Hofmann from his first

few days with the Vienna police. Hofmann was the director of the forensic institute and one of the greatest experts in his field. His intelligence and vast knowledge were undisputed, as were his meticulous methods and his vanity. Leo thought it seemed unusual for Hofmann to go to the trouble of conducting an examination in situ—and in the museum's repository.

Eduard Hofmann waved them closer. "Take a look at this. You've never seen anything like it."

When they stepped up to the open sarcophagus, Leo gave a start. Inside was the corpse of a man around sixty, his pale cheeks hollow and his lips black, wrapped in new, white bandages. Some had been removed so that his face and neck were visible. His mouth was stretched in a grin, and the little hair he had was parted neatly. The most bizarre feature of his face were his eyes, shimmering green and severely cross-eyed. In the poor light, it took Leo a few moments to realize that the eyes were in fact two emeralds set in gold. The pupils, irises, lids, lashes . . . everything was reproduced with great precision. The gemstones had been pushed firmly into the sockets.

"This is Professor Alfons Strössner?" asked Leinkirchner.

Hofmann nodded. "Good old Alfons. He almost looks as if he's merely sleeping, don't you think?"

Leo looked from the mummy to Hofmann, surprised. "You knew the man?"

"Indeed I did. Though I wouldn't say I knew him very well. We were both members of the Vienna Archaeological Society, along with Dr. Dedekind. It truly is a strange case."

"Are you absolutely certain this is the professor?" asked Leinkirchner. "I realize you can see his face, but still. . . . I mean, those awful button eyes alone. What's that about?"

"The eyes decay very quickly, and so it's imperative to remove them as soon as possible, right after the brain," explained Hofmann with a shrug. "It's an ancient technique. Most often, glass marbles were used in place of the eyes in ancient Egypt, or also onions." He looked at Dr. Dedekind. "Emeralds are rather unusual, wouldn't you say? And expensive. Am I right, Alex?"

The doctor nodded distractedly, and Eduard Hofmann carried on: "Believe me, this is Professor Alfons Strössner. I'm sure. We've raised the occasional glass together. And we have this." Hofmann produced a pocket watch on a silver chain, dangling it in front of Leo's face. "It's Alfons's watch. I recognize it—plus, his name is engraved on it."

"The watch was with the body?" asked Leo. "You discovered it?"

"Uh, not I, the cleaning lady."

"The cleaning lady?" growled chief inspector Leinkirchner. "Are you joking?"

Behind them, Dr. Dedekind cleared his throat. "Perhaps I ought to explain how the body was found. Well . . . at six o'clock this evening, just before closing time, I heard someone screaming down in the museum repository. I went there immediately and the cleaning lady came running toward me. She was beside herself, as if she'd seen a ghost."

"Don't tell me the mummy staggered toward her with outstretched arms," jeered Leinkirchner.

"No, no. Why would it?" Dedekind appeared confused for a moment, then he continued. "The woman gets paid to clean and dust, once a week—she knows what to expect. The sliding doors with the mummies are always locked. Well, normally." He paused again. "I must have forgotten to lock one of them. That nosy, thieving woman looked inside and messed with the bandages."

"She did *what*?" asked Leo, astounded.

"It's not uncommon for precious items to be found among the bandages of mummies—amulets, gold scarabs, and the like," explained Professor Hofmann. "They are meant to protect the mummy in the realm of the dead. At times there can be dozens of precious items. As an employee of the museum, the woman was familiar with this custom."

"So, these mummies are bundles full of surprises." Leinkirchner gave a dry laugh. "I wasn't aware you're such an expert on the subject, professor."

"Like I said, I'm a member of the archaeological society. And of course, I'm a pathologist . . ." Hofmann seemed nervous for some reason not yet known to them.

Leo nodded at the collection's curator. "Go on, doctor."

"As I was saying," Dr. Dedekind said slowly, "the cleaning woman fiddled with the bandages and found the pocket watch. When she uncovered the face of the mummy, she recognized the watch's owner. She knew the professor from when he used to come here." He gave a shrug. "You can imagine how she felt. The mummy was at the far back of the room—it might have been years before we examined it. These rooms are like one enormous morgue."

"And where is the poor woman now?" asked Leo, unable to tear his gaze away from the mummified doll-like face with its cross-eyed emerald eyes.

"We brought her to my office," said Dedekind. "I thought you might wish to question her."

"Indeed." Leinkirchner nodded. "I hope your office doesn't look like this repository. If you ask me, the woman has been punished enough. Who has access to this room?"

"Only me and the cleaning woman. The sliding doors to the sarcophagus shelves are locked separately, and I'm the only one with a key." Dedekind paused to think for a moment. "Well, and Professor Strössner. He used to come here regularly."

"Do you have any ideas how Professor Strössner's body might have gotten in here?" asked Leo.

"That's the strange thing." Dr Dedekind gave a sigh. "We believed the professor was still on an expedition in Egypt. Just last year he and the other leading Egyptologists of Austria returned from a longer expedition. It was a difficult task, getting all the mummies and artifacts here undamaged. Customs alone, and then the journey across the sea. Not to mention the temperatures—"

"Spare us the details," said Leinkirchner, glancing at his watch impatiently.

"Well, all right, uh . . . where was I?" Dedekind wiped beads of sweat off his forehead. He looked quite stressed. He seemed to grow more nervous by the minute. Leo felt increasingly certain that the two scholars were keeping something from them.

"When Professor Strössner returned to Vienna last year," continued Dedekind, "he spent most of his time down here in the repository—most days of the week, even Sundays. He studied and documented all these artifacts. And then he said that he needed to go back to Egypt. All of a sudden. He needed to check something very important. He was gone from one day to the next!"

"When was that?" demanded Leo.

"About three months ago, in February."

"Three months, hmm . . ." Leo turned to Professor Hofmann. "And how long does it take to look like our body here?" He motioned at the sarcophagus.

"If you followed the old rituals, you'd have to steep the body in soda lye for about seventy days," said Hofmann, polishing his glasses yet again. "A little less, perhaps, but not much. Otherwise it will smell."

Again Leo noticed how musty it was down here, smelling of rot, of old tombs and moldering bones.

Of mummy, I suppose, he thought.

"A little over two months, then." Leinkirchner nodded. "That might work. So, the professor suddenly vanishes and reappears a while later at the museum, well preserved. Did he tell you personally of his plans to travel to Egypt?"

"Yes, he even telephoned. Though the call was brief and a little . . . odd. Something was wrong with the connection." Dedekind frowned. "We received two or three letters from Cairo. Nothing significant—the weather, the food. It did strike me as a little strange because he normally wrote to us about his finds."

"And you don't know what it was the professor wanted to check in Egypt?" asked Leo.

"No, I don't. I'm sorry." Dedekind shook his head. "His daughter, Charlotte, might be able to tell us more. I was going to visit her and her husband, Clemens, tonight to relay the news of her father's death personally. I know them well, and so I thought—"

"You can go ahead and forget about that," interrupted Leinkirchner, "the thinking and especially the visiting. Both are jobs for the police, not you. That aside, we'll also require those letters and any other personal files the professor kept here at the museum."

"Whatever you say." Dedekind gave another shrug. "If that's all. . . ." He looked about nervously again, almost as if he expected one of the sliding doors to open by itself. "I'd be grateful if we could finish up down here soon."

"Don't tell me you're afraid of your own mummies!" said Leinkirchner with a laugh. "You'd be in the wrong profession. That would be like an inspector of blood crimes who's scared of murder victims."

"At least your dead stay dead, Herr Inspector," replied Dedekind softly. "I can no longer say the same with absolute certainty about ours. Not after what's happened here."

A WHILE LATER, LEO AND LEINKIRCHNER WERE BACK UNDER the large dome of the entrance hall. Professor Hofmann and Dr. Dedekind had gone over to the archive to retrieve the documents Leinkirchner had requested.

"What a strange story," said Leo, staring pensively into the darkness. "I can't make heads nor tails of it. And why is the doctor so nervous? Professor Hofmann too seems to be hiding something. Strange . . ."

"We'll get to the bottom of it, but not tonight." The chief inspector put on his hat and nodded at Leo. "I think that's all for now. You can handle the rest by yourself."

Leo gave his colleague an astonished look. "But we've yet to question the cleaning lady. She's still waiting in Dedekind's office!"

"Have her taken to the detention cells at Theobald Lane. We can question her in peace on Monday. That's better anyway—the longer she spends alone in a cell, the less she can blab about what happened here. The last thing we need now is a scandal! Professor Hofmann can arrange the transfer of the body to the forensic institute. Other than that—not a word, to anyone! Not even to our colleagues." Leinkirchner lowered his voice. "Listen, Herzfeldt, I have tickets for the Deutsches Volkstheater for tonight. Something by Nestroy. I'm already late and my wife is going to kill me."

Leo sighed, not bothering to mention that he too had a date tonight. "Do I have a choice?"

"I'm afraid not. Order from your superior." Leinkirchner bared his teeth in a grin, but then his face darkened. "I promised my wife I'd also spend tomorrow with her. Twentieth wedding anniversary, and she wished for a Sunday with no work. The first in a long time. Plus it's Whitsunday. So tomorrow we're headed to opening day at the new zoological garden in Prater park. There's some sort of ethnic show with Hottentots, or something along those lines. And I've yet to buy flowers . . ." He groaned and ran the back of his hand across his forehead as if he were heading to the scaffold.

Leo tried to stifle a grin. Leinkirchner with a wife in the park was a strange image. Hadn't he even mentioned a dachshund earlier? In his mind's eye Leo pictured Herr and Frau Leinkirchner strolling past the monkey cage with their doggie, stopping to buy some roasted almonds. He realized that even though they'd been working together for almost six months, he knew nothing about Leinkirchner's personal life. Was the chief inspector happily married? Did he have children? There were no photographs in his office, not even one of his wife.

"Give my best to your wife," said Leo. "And say hello to the camels at the zoo. I hear they're just as bullheaded and grumpy as the people of Vienna."

"Save your mockery, Herzfeldt!" Leinkirchner moved his face closer to Leo's and raised a finger. "And to make sure you don't get bored over Whitsunday, I have another task for you: tomorrow you're to take a ride out to the Rapoldys and deliver the sad news to the daughter."

Leo was about to reply when Professor Hofmann and Dr. Dedekind reappeared in the hall. The doctor was carrying a heavy bundle of papers, which he passed to Leo.

"This is everything personal of Professor Strössner's I was able to find at short notice. The letters are all there. If there's anything else you need, let me know. The inventory alone from the Deir al-Bahari archaeological site fills ten folders."

"Too kind," replied Leo with a tired smile. "This will be my summer reading."

With that, Dedekind and Leinkirchner took their leave. Professor Hofmann went with Leo to use the telephone in Dedekind's office. Hofmann ordered the hearse to transport Strössner's body to the forensic institute, and then Leo called the prisoner transport for the cleaning lady—the so-called Grüner Heinrich, or Green Henry.

They then went back to the entrance hall and waited under the tall dome for the hearse and the Green Henry. The pair of black pharaohs stared darkly at Leo from the top of the stairs.

"A strange story, isn't it?" said Leo after a while.

"Beg your pardon?" The professor gave a start; it seemed he'd been wholly absorbed by his thoughts. "Oh, yes, indeed."

"It must be awful for you, having to examine the body of someone you knew."

"I . . . I didn't know him all that well. We met a few times, had a few glasses of wine, that's all."

Leo thought. "Do you have any idea what Dr. Dedekind meant when he spoke of dead that don't stay dead?" He frowned. "It almost sounded as if he were mightily afraid of something."

"I think I know what he's afraid of," said Hofmann quietly.

"Really?" Leo gave the professor a look of surprise. "What is it?"

"What do you know about curses, Herzfeldt?" Hofmann lowered his voice even more. "And I'm not talking about the kind of choice curses Leinkirchner employs so skillfully, but dark, evil curses. Curses that have the power to kill, to spread disease, that conjure up storms, and, yes, that may be able to bring back the dead. Bring them back as . . . avengers. . . ."

Several of the gas lamps by the entrance flickered and the professor gave a start. He laughed, but it wasn't a cheerful laugh. "What am I saying? I sound like an old washerwoman, not a scientist. What a load of nonsense!"

"Are you suggesting that—" began Leo, but just then a long black carriage drove up outside the museum.

"Ah, the institute's hearse. Punctual as death himself." The professor checked his pocket watch before stepping outside and beckoning at the driver. "We'll have Strössner taken away in the sarcophagus. We'll tell the men that I'm assisting with the study of some dried-up old mummy. That way there'll be no fuss." He took a few steps toward the carriage before turning to Leo once more. "If you want to find out more about curses, perhaps you should ask your gravedigger."

"*My* gravedigger?" Leo raised his eyebrows. "Are you talking about Augustin Rothmayer from Central Cemetery?"

"He's well read, as you know. I thought you two were friends."

"Friends? I wouldn't go that far." Leo gave a wry smile. "Is it even possible to be friends with a gravedigger?"

"In any case," Hofmann said, shrugging, "as far as I know, Herr Rothmayer is working on his next book. He borrowed some technical literature from me."

"Oh God, so he's writing another book. Is it going to be just as macabre as the last?" Leo sighed. A few months earlier, Augustin Rothmayer had published *The Gravedigger's Almanac*, proudly supported by Hofmann, who declared it an instant classic.

"The new book is called *Death Rites Around the World*." Hofmann nodded enthusiastically. "I came up with the title. A fascinating project, don't you think? Our friend knows a lot about Egyptian curses. And now if you'll excuse me." The professor turned to the two broad-shouldered hearse drivers dressed in black and tipped his hat. "Good evening, gentlemen. Let's not make our friend wait for too long."

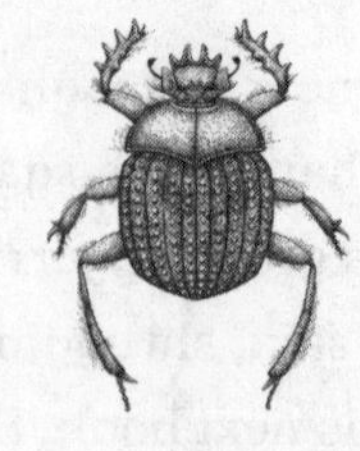

CHAPTER 3

The following morning, Leo woke to the smell of coffee and Frau Rinsinger's bright voice seeping into his room from the hallway, warbling a May song as she noisily dusted and shifted things around.

Leo gave a hearty yawn and turned to the nightstand to check his pocket watch. Eight in the morning, and it was Whitsunday. . . . He'd have to broach the subject of noise levels with Frau Rinsinger. After all, he was paying good money for his measly hundred square feet and hallway bathroom—a solid twenty-five kronen per week, which included cleaning and regular meals and nosy questions.

Adelheid Rinsinger, his landlady, highly valued peace and quiet at night, but apparently she didn't apply the same concept to mornings. Leo had moved into the tiny room on the third floor immediately upon his arrival in Vienna; he was the only tenant. The apartment was on Lange Lane in the district of Josefstadt, not too far from the police headquarters. It was large, cluttered with Biedermeier furniture and faded landscapes.

Leo's bed creaked as he rose—the signal for Frau Rinsinger to knock.

"Good morning, Herr von Herzfeldt!" she said in a singsong. "Coffee will be ready in five minutes, as well as fresh pastries. The early bird catches the worm!"

"And hopefully chokes on it," muttered Leo. Cursing under his breath, he scratched his unshaved chin. It probably wasn't for the worst, getting up early today. He had plenty to do. There was the trip to the Rapoldys that Leinkirchner had dumped on him, and he needed to talk to Julia as soon as possible. He would take her out to a nice coffeehouse and explain everything. Would she still be mad at him for last night? He'd had to cancel quite a few times lately, but it never was his fault. In the last six months, Vienna had experienced numerous spectacular crimes, and consequently, the Vienna Security Bureau and its police agents had been working overtime almost every single week. There'd been violent robberies, attacks by anarchists, child prostitution, and plenty of knife fights. The city was a pressure cooker that might explode at any moment.

And now there's a mummy to add to the mix. . . .

As Frau Rinsinger continued to trill her merry tune, wiping and dusting, Leo thought of last night's terrible events. The mummy with its emerald eyes had haunted his dreams. The case was just too bizarre: a mummified professor of Egyptology inside a sarcophagus at the Museum of Art History! When he arrived home last night, Leo had skimmed through Strössner's personal documents from Dr. Dedekind, including the strange letters Strössner sent from Egypt. Most of it meant nothing to him: there were lists of findings, plenty of numbers, a few sketches from digs . . . At first glance, there appeared to be no mummy among the treasures brought back to Austria.

When Leo finally heard Frau Rinsinger enter a different room to dust, he darted down the hall into the bathroom to freshen up and shave. Back in his room, he stood in front of the tall wardrobe, wondering what to wear. He ought to look smart for his visit at the Rapoldys'. After dithering a few moments he decided on the Harris Tweed three-piece with a light chesterfield coat and his homburg hat. He smoothed down the waistcoat's lapel and studied himself in the small, chipped mirror on the inside of the wardrobe door. He saw a handsome and well-dressed man in his early thirties, with blond hair and clean-shaven cheeks—a dandy, as the English would say. Leo had mastered their language, as well as French, Latin, and a few phrases of Italian.

With the Viennese dialect alone he still struggled.

Leo took after his mother, who was from Hannover and had retained her High German accent. She loved her second-born son above all else. If his father knew that she was sending Leo money each month to supplement his sparse police salary he'd probably have a stroke.

He wouldn't forgive me, even on his deathbed, thought Leo. For the past six months, neither had contacted the other by telephone or by letter—ever since Leo's sudden departure from Graz. Bitter silence reigned between them.

When Leo walked into the living room, Frau Rinsinger had set a plate for him and placed the *Neue Freie Presse* beside it. He lit one of his beloved Yenidze cigarettes and skimmed the headlines of the Pentecostal edition: the kaiser was paying a visit to the Bavarian prince-regent Luitpold; Archduke Albrecht was spending time in Sarajevo; farther back there was a brief notice about water damage at the Museum of Art History—no mention of any mummies, which was good. Leinkirchner's idea to have the cleaning woman taken into custody probably hadn't been a bad one; that way, at least, they would gain a couple of days.

"Well, you had plenty of sleep?" Frau Rinsinger entered the room with a steaming pot of coffee and filled his cup.

"Is it even possible to have plenty of sleep at half past eight on a Sunday morning?" retorted Leo sullenly. "At least your singing drowned out the furniture moving and cleaning." He took a sip of Frau Rinsinger's strong coffee. There was cream in an ornate little porcelain jug and sugar in a horrendous green glass bowl. All rooms, but worst of all this room, were chockablock with trinkets, porcelain tea sets, vases, sickly sweet shepherdesses, and, most plentiful of all, kitschy angel figurines of which his landlady owned so many, the heavens were bound to be empty.

"It was Mozart," replied Frau Rinsinger, seemingly a little offended. "I wanted to give this beautiful holiday morning its due welcome." She eyed his suit. "Are you going into work today, Herr von Herzfeldt? On Whitsunday?"

"Yes, I have a few work-related errands. Crime knows no holidays, Frau Rinsinger." Leo smeared butter and honey on the warm croissant. Then he slid an envelope toward her. "Would you be able to send a messenger to Neulerchenfeld with this? You'd be doing me a huge favor."

"To Neulerchenfeld, huh?" His landlady picked up the letter and scanned the address, winking at him. "An invitation to a cozy Sunday stroll, perhaps, for Fräulein Wolf?"

Leo bit into his croissant and said nothing. Frau Rinsinger's nosiness was almost as vast as her love for porcelain angels and dusting. Three times now she'd asked him when he would finally get engaged.

"Do feel free to bring the fräulein here again sometime," his landlady continued amiably. But then her expression turned serious and she raised a finger. "Only until eight at night, of course. Overnight stays by lady friends are—"

"Prohibited by police orders, I know." Leo grinned, wiping crumbs from the corners of his mouth. "I should know—I work for the police, after all."

Frau Rinsinger had met Julia a handful of times, and thankfully she took a liking to the young woman. It had probably helped that Leo told his landlady Julia too was working for the police. Anything to do with police work Frau Rinsinger thought awfully exciting. Thank goodness the woman didn't know that Julia's home address housed a brothel.

"By the way, you left these in here last night. Very messily, too, if I might add." She handed Leo the bundle of papers from the museum with one of the letters lying on top. "Don't tell me you're traveling to Egypt for work, are you, Herr von Herzfeldt? A death on the Nile—how exceptionally interesting!"

Leo almost choked on his dry pastry. How could he have left these important papers lying in the living room? "Not as far as I'm aware," he mumbled. "If I ever do have to travel there, I'll take you with me, Frau Rinsinger—who else would make my coffee and fill me in on the latest gossip?"

He rose, picking up his coat and hat as he said goodbye. Before leaving the apartment he stowed the papers under his bed. Hopefully Frau Rinsinger wasn't going to clean there, too.

A SHORT WHILE LATER, LEO WAS STANDING IN LANGE LANE, waving down a fiacre. In the letter he'd given his landlady he begged Julia's forgiveness and asked her to meet him at a coffeehouse on Prater Road at lunchtime. He hoped very much that she'd come and accept his apology. Afterward he would drive out to visit the Rapoldys.

A fiacre stopped and Leo climbed aboard. He'd spontaneously decided to visit Central Cemetery before heading to the coffeehouse. He hadn't forgotten Professor Hofmann's comment from yesterday.

If you want to find out more about curses, why don't you ask your gravedigger . . . ?

Leo sighed. Why did his and Augustin Rothmayer's paths have to keep crossing in these uncanny ways? It was almost like a curse, too.

The fiacre rattled along the streets of the suburbs, through poorer quarters that began past the so-called Gürtel, or belt. Leo saw the huge slaughterhouse and the central livestock market drift past. The stink wafting all the way over to him reminded him of the smells of death at the various crime scenes he'd had to examine in the last few months—but it also reminded him of Augustin Rothmayer. Leo had met Rothmayer while working on his first major case in Vienna. Since then he had visited him whenever he had questions about a particular cause of death or the stages of decomposition. Rothmayer was an expert, blessed with an astounding intelligence. He wasn't easy to be around, and yet Leo had learned to appreciate the quixotic old codger. He thought about Professor Hofmann's words from last night.

I thought you two were friends. . . .

Well, if it was friendship, it was a strange one.

Half an hour later, the fiacre reached Simmering Road, which led out to Central Cemetery. Several horsecar trams plodded along the tracks, filled with the typical Sunday visitors dressed in mourning. The cemetery had been operating for twenty years now. More than half a million dead lay buried here, and their number was only growing. Up to a hundred coffins were unloaded from the funeral parlors' black carriages here in a single day. Especially during the summer, when bodies soon began to smell, the neighboring residents' complaints also grew. For a while, therefore, the city had considered building a corpse tube mail system for transportation of bodies—but the idea had soon been abandoned due to a lack of funding.

They came to a halt on the square outside the main entrance, near the horsecar tram's final stop. The carriages belonging to various funeral parlors stood lined up outside the three large entrances, and close by, some barracks served as provisional waiting halls.

Leo handed the sour-faced driver a few coins and entered the cemetery through one of the gates in the tall wall. Today, on Whitsunday, the cemetery was busy. Men in top hats and black suits and women in black dresses strolled about, looking like a gathering of sad ravens and penguins. There were families, too, the children seemingly unaffected by the burden of death who ran laughing past the rows of tombstones, playing catch or hide and seek until one of the parents would reluctantly call them to order. Leo smiled. It was nice to see that life prevailed everywhere, even at a cemetery.

Rothmayer's cemetery housing—his only housing—was situated by the east wall at the very far end of the cemetery, close to the suicide graves. His house wasn't hard to find if Leo paid attention, so long as he didn't take any wrong turns. But to his surprise, he ran into an obstruction. A makeshift fence had been erected across the path and a sign had been attached to it, hastily scribbled words reading: "*Closed because of earthworks. Danger!*"

Dismayed, Leo searched for a detour, which proved difficult. All the other paths in view led in a different direction. He decided on the one that seemed most likely to lead him to the gravedigger's house, but to Leo's annoyance, this path soon turned west. With a sigh Leo left the narrow path and headed across the fields of graves, walking over freshly dug grave mounds and stepping over low bushes. Burs tugged on his trousers and his shoes sank into mud. Already he cursed his idea of visiting Rothmayer. How was he supposed to meet Julia at Prater Road in this state? Let alone his visit to the posh Rapoldys!

Orienting himself by the sun, after awhile, Leo arrived back on the path he thought led to Rothmayer's hut. And indeed, not long thereafter he saw the cemetery wall and, not too far along, a pretty little house with flower boxes in bloom. Old roses surrounded the cottage like a miniature version of Sleeping Beauty's hedge.

Leo passed by a large compost heap of decaying flowers, a crate with misshapen candle stumps, and a stack of old coffins. Just then, Leo's foot struck a length of timber that was sticking out from under the stack of coffins, well concealed under leaves. The rotting coffins swayed, tilted, slid, and finally crashed to the ground noisily. Leo only just managed to save himself by leaping into the compost pile.

The hut's front door flung open, and out came a tall, haggard man wielding a spade like a bayonet.

"Jesus, Mary and Joseph, get outta here you bleedin' mutts, or else—"

He broke off when he realized who was kneeling in the compost next to the pile of coffins. "Herr von Herzfeldt, what a pleasure!" Augustin Rothmayer's mouth formed the smile that always reminded Leo of a wolf. "What a surprise! What are you up to? Looking for a coffin for yourself? I can sell you the lot for a bargain price. Unbeatable deal! A nail or two and they'll come up like new."

"By the devil! This is seriously dangerous!" Leo waved at the toppled stack. "One could be forgiven for thinking you'd stacked these coffins crookedly on . . ." He faltered when he noticed Rothmayer's expression of feigned innocence. "Hold on—you stacked them crookedly *on purpose*? Was this meant to be a trap?"

Augustin Rothmayer gave a shrug. "Well, you should have stopped at the sign about the earthworks. What did it say? 'Please feed'? No. It said 'Danger.'" He nodded grimly. "There you have it."

"This is hardly earthworks, Herr Rothmayer. Do you want to know what I think? I think you put up the sign so that no one comes to bother you, and if someone does make it past the sign, they get buried by coffins!"

"I beg you, that's far too dramatic! It was more of a . . ." Rothmayer thought for a moment. "An alarm system."

"And what on earth would you need an alarm system for?"

"Well, why d'you think? Can't you guess, Herr Inspector? You're usually so clever." The gravedigger gave a sarcastic chuckle before gesturing for Leo to follow him into the house.

Leo patted the dirt off his knees as best as he could and entered the cottage. There were only two rooms: the living quarters and a bedroom. A cast-iron stove stood next to the kitchen table, and there was a large bookshelf and a well-worn standing desk. Curled up in an armchair, a large tomcat lay snoozing in the sunshine falling in through the clean windows. A fiddle hung on the wall next to a dirt-encrusted coat and floppy hat.

"It's because of Anna," said Rothmayer, not bothering to offer Leo a seat. "Twice already the woman from the welfare has been. They want to take Anna away from me. If that blasted woman turns up again, at least I'll have some warning. Gives Anna time to disappear."

"And where is she now?" asked Leo. Anna was an orphan girl who had been living with Rothmayer since he helped Leo with his first case. She worked alongside the gravedigger as his apprentice, but Leo had long thought that this arrangement couldn't last forever.

"In the greenhouse, binding flowers. She likes the work, inspector. And she likes living here with me! And those fools want to stick her in an orphanage. Not on my watch, I'm telling you, not while Augustin Rothmayer's here."

Leo gave a wry smile. "I remember a time when you couldn't wait to get rid of Anna."

"Can't a man can change his mind?" retorted Rothmayer gruffly.

Leo was certain that Anna reminded the gravedigger of his own deceased daughter. He'd worried from the beginning that the welfare office would pay Rothmayer a visit sooner or later. And if Leo was being honest, this wasn't an ideal situation: a young girl living inside a shack on a cemetery together with a batty unmarried old gravedigger. Anna ought to be going to school. Not to mention the depressing surroundings . . .

"How is Fräulein Wolf?" asked Rothmayer abruptly.

Leo looked up. "What makes you think of Fräulein Wolf now? She's well, thanks for asking. I'll probably see her today."

"Then please pass on my regards."

Leo looked out the window. The sun had climbed higher above the cemetery wall. "Herr Rothmayer, I'm not here to talk about Fräulein Wolf or about Anna. I have a serious matter to discuss. I've been told that you're working on a new book. Something about . . . uh, death rites?"

"Ah, so that's what it is." Rothmayer grinned. "It was Professor Hofmann told you, wasn't it?"

"It was indeed." Leo nodded. "There's been an incident and I was hoping you might be able to help me." In slow words he told the gravedigger of the strange discovery at the Museum of Art History the previous night.

When he had finished, Rothmayer tilted his head to one side. His eyes sparkled with interest. "Hm, so Professor Hofmann spoke of a curse, did he?"

"I must ask you to treat this matter with the utmost discretion! But yes, those were his words. And, like I said, Dr. Dedekind, the curator of the Egytpo-Oriental Collection, seemed to be terribly afraid of something. Afraid of a curse? Is that what Professor Hofmann meant?"

Rothmayer scratched his nose, then walked over to his bookshelf, drew out a heavy one with a stained cover, and began to leaf through it. Leo's eyes turned to the desk, where he could see several loose pages covered in neat and very small handwriting. Words had been crossed out and replaced, and the margins were crammed with notes. He read the first sentence on the page lying on top: *"An especially interesting death rite is the Buddhist sky burial, practiced in parts of Tibet, Mongolia, and India."*

Leo cleared his throat. "Is this your new book?"

"Hmm?" Rothmayer looked up from his book, a look of concentration on his face. He'd clamped a pince-nez on his nose, giving him the mien of a blind mole-rat. "Yes, but it's quite unripe still. There'll be a chapter on curses, too. Hmm . . . Oh, here it is!" He brandished the book in triumph. "The Egyptian Book of the Dead by Edouard Naville—an instant classic! The professor kindly lent it to me."

"And what does it say?" asked Leo.

"Well, I think this might be what the professor meant." Rothmayer placed the open book on the kitchen table and skimmed. "Naville writes that the entrances to Egyptian tombs, and even walls and sarcophagi, occasionally bear hieroglyphs suggesting a curse—a curse that strikes whoever disturbs the rest of the dead person." Rothmayer blinked behind his pince-nez. "Which mummy was Alfons Strössner examining before his death?"

"Uh, I don't know yet," replied Leo, wondering if he should have spent more time perusing Strössner's notes. "But I'm sure I can find out. So how does a curse work?"

Rothmayer licked his finger, cemetery soil under his nails, and leafed through the pages. "Oh, there's a whole range of possibilities. There are curses for the afterlife and curses for this side of the grave. Those for this side are especially nasty. They promise diarrhea, paralysis, vile diseases, the falling sickness, and sudden deaths from lightning, tidal waves, falling boulders—the kinds of things that suggest divine punishment. And then there are the perfectly ordinary curse formulas. Here, for example." Blinking a few times, he read from the book: "You shall be ravaged by an ass."

"Not a nice thought, indeed," Leo said. "But it's all a load of nonsense, isn't it?"

"Have you heard of the tunnel sickness?" asked Rothmayer abruptly.

"The what?" Leo shook his head. "I'm afraid I haven't. Why?"

"Well, about twenty years ago during the construction of the Swiss Gotthard Tunnel, a series of mysterious afflictions: fatigue, dizziness, fainting, anemia. Many miners died, including the supervisor, who collapsed during a routine check. Some believed it was a curse, because the mountain was being damaged so gravely—until an Italian doctor figured out what was actually behind it all." Augustin Rothmayer gave a wide grin. "Shit."

"Beg your pardon?"

"In the narrow tunnel, the workers were literally working in their own feces, ankle deep at times. Tiny worms that lived in the feces and bored into the men's skin were responsible for the disease. No curse. Just shit." The gravedigger returned the tome to the shelf. "Do you get what I'm trying to say, Herr Inspector? Maybe there's something entirely different behind the curses of the Egyptians, something we don't yet understand. Maybe pyramids, too, have some kind of . . . alarm system. A bit like mine out there. And we just don't understand it yet. And your Professor Strössner triggered something like that."

"A mummified professor? Come on! How's that supposed to work?"

"Hmm, you're right. That's hogwash. Still, it would be interesting to know what Professor Strössner was working on at the end." Rothmayer set aside his pince-nez and looked sternly at Leo. "Did he get a decent embalming at least? Brain out through nose with a hook, clean cut in the side, innards stored in separate jugs? Or did they merely squirt acid up his derrière? Cause then the guts dissolve while still in the body, and the whole sludge—"

"Christ, stop, please!" Leo began to feel sick. "I didn't check that closely. I'm sure Professor Hofmann from the forensic institute will be able to tell us those details soon. As well as the manner of Strössner's death. We don't even know yet whether he was murdered or what went on. We know nothing, really!"

"Well, it would be interesting to find out what exactly Strössner's mummy looks like now." Augustin Rothmayer nodded pensively. "Because one thing's for certain: if your dead body was embalmed according to Egyptian tradition, it must have been done by an expert." One of his bushy eyebrows went up. "You get what I mean?"

"An Egyptologist," said Leo, slapping his forehead. "Of course. Damn it, you're right! That rather limits the pool of suspects."

He cursed himself inwardly for not thinking of this sooner. It was a real clue, or at least a lead that was worth following up. Perhaps his visit at the Rapoldys' that afternoon would shed some more light on the matter.

"Please thank Fräulein Wolf again for the stockings and new shoes for the lassie," said Augustin Rothmayer suddenly. "Can't believe Anna's grown again already. Perhaps the fräulein might help find some undergarments for her next visit?"

"Undergarments? Next visit?" Leo started from his musings. "Fräulein Wolf visits you and Anna regularly?"

"Well, every now and then. More often than you, in any case. The last time was about two weeks ago. Anna gets very excited each time the young lady comes. She has no mother, and Fräulein Wolf is always so kind. Undergarments, yes? Please try to remember, Herr Inspector."

"I'll pass it on." Leo bit his lip. Julia hadn't told him she came here on a regular basis. Why hadn't she? He placed his hat on his head and turned to leave. "Thank you, Herr Rothmayer."

"Do you know when Strössner's mummy will be autopsied?" asked Augustin. There was a conspicuous twinkle in his eye.

"Are you planning to . . . ?" asked Leo.

The gravedigger waved dismissively. "Purely for research reasons, for the new book. No trouble, inspector. I'll call Professor Hofmann myself." He grinned, baring his surprisingly white teeth. "It's not such a terrible invention after all, this telephone apparatus. The cemetery director has one. I might almost grow used to it. Take care, inspector!"

Leo stepped outside, his eye pausing on the toppled coffins. He thought of their former inhabitants, long since decayed and forgotten, and a shudder ran down his spine. Then he kept walking. He had a feeling he would be seeing more of Augustin Rothmayer in the near future.

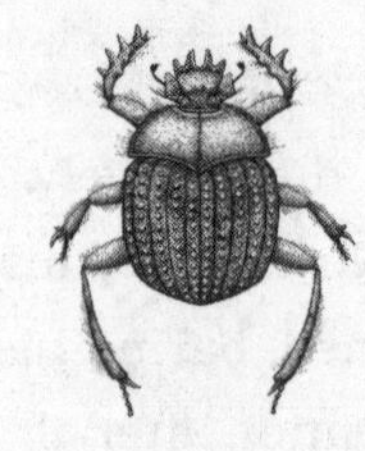

CHAPTER 4

From *Death Rites Around the World* by Augustin Rothmayer, written in Vienna, 1894

> An especially interesting death rite is the Buddhist sky burial, practiced in parts of Tibet, Mongolia, and India. Since the ground is often too hard to dig graves and there is little wood for incineration, bodies are cut up and fed to the vultures. The quicker a body is eaten up, the more exemplary was the life of its former owner. In some places the bodies are placed atop high towers for this purpose. Subsequently, one can occasionally find scraps of human flesh accidentally dropped by the vultures on house roofs or in gardens near such towers.

Julia sipped on her May wine and turned her face towards the sun. It was her second glass, and it was delicious. She was sitting outside under an umbrella, liveried waiters scurrying between the tables, fulfilling their customers' every wish. She had to admit that this coffeehouse was an excellent choice. Still, it bugged her that Leo had chosen to meet on Prater Road, the ostentatious boulevard of the second district. Why not a humble tavern somewhere near the Danube Canal? He was probably trying to make up for failing to show last night.

What Leo didn't know was that she, too, had worked late on Saturday night. Never mind—let him roast for a while longer. He'd written her quite the charming letter; he was good with words, was Herr von Herzfeldt, that's for sure: *In the quiet hope of spending a lovely Whitsunday with you, your Leo with love . . .*

She smiled despite herself. Leo was so different from her, so different from most people she knew. How he spoke alone! And his attire, too, as if he were stepping straight out of a Scottish country manor. Not that Julia had been to any Scottish country manors—but that's how she imagined the lord of one. Like Leo.

That's what made it so beautiful, and so tricky at the same time. . . .

Sometimes she wondered at the twist of fate that had brought the two of them together. Leo had come to her like an angel from far above. Back in Graz he'd already made it to the position of investigative judge; his father owned a bank, and the family had celebrated a promising, advantageous match—an engagement that Leo dissolved nonetheless, with dramatic consequences. And then fate had carried him to Vienna.

Maybe we aren't so different after all, thought Julia. *Both of us washed up in Vienna . . .*

Her eye drifted over the many holiday revelers strolling down Prater Road, wealthy families perhaps on their way to nearby Prater park. The boys were smartly dressed, the girls with ribbons in their hair. Julia thought of Sisi, who was at this moment back in Neulerchenfeld playing with her so-called aunties. She'd almost brought

Sisi along, but Elli had promised to serve her cake on a tiny porcelain set as if they were at the royal court, with Bruno pretending to be her fairytale prince. Her little daughter was happy, no doubt about it.

Julia looked up at the clock on the front of the department store across the street. A quarter past twelve! If Leo didn't turn up soon she'd pay and leave. She didn't need this, even with a likely hefty bill.

Just then, a fiacre pulled up right beside the restaurant and Leo disembarked. He looked exhausted. His tweed trousers had dirty knees and mud was stuck to his shoes. Julia smirked. His arrival bore something comical, something fragile she found touching.

My Scottish lord. Apparently, he's been out hunting. . . .

"Apologies for being late," said Leo, slumping into the chair opposite her. He pulled a monogrammed white kerchief from his chest pocket and dabbed his sweaty forehead. "I've just been to Central Cemetery."

She raised an eyebrow. "Central Cemetery? What were you doing there?"

"It's a long story—I'll tell you shortly." Leo beckoned a waiter and ordered a small beer and roast beef sandwich with mustard and cucumber. Once the waiter had left, he said, "Augustin Rothmayer sends his regards. He asks if you could please bring undergarments for Anna next time." He donned a petulant expression. "Why didn't you tell me you were visiting them?"

She shrugged. "It didn't seem important. I wasn't under the impression you'd want to join me."

It was true—she had taken Sisi for a few walks at Central Cemetery. Over the last few months, she'd grown fond of Augustin Rothmayer and Anna. And Leo didn't seem too comfortable around children. He lacked patience and the ability to make a fool of himself every now and then.

"What made you visit Herr Rothmayer?" she asked again.

The sandwich and beer arrived, and Leo took a few hungry bites of the white bread before starting to talk. "It's a strange story. Probably the strangest I've come across. And it's also the reason I stood you up last night. It wasn't my fault, Julia, please believe me."

"Never mind." Julia brushed Leo's apology aside impatiently. "Go on, spill."

The story Leo told her between mouthfuls truly was unbelievable: a mummified professor in the storage rooms of the Museum of Art History! And then there was the mention of a curse . . . Listening intently, Julia didn't notice her wine turning warm.

"Later I'm going to visit the Rapoldys in Hietzing. Perhaps they know something," Leo said, finishing his report. He wiped his mouth with his handkerchief. "It's all rather mysterious."

"First you'll have to tell Frau Rapoldy that her father is a mummy," observed Julia dryly. "That's not going to be easy. Someone from the family will have to identify the body at the forensic institute. I'd hate to imagine seeing my father like that . . ." She shuddered despite the fair weather.

Neither spoke for a while.

"Do you believe in things like curses?" she asked eventually.

"Balderdash!" Leo gave a snort. "I stick with facts and motives. If Rothmayer's suspicion is true and the body was embalmed with all the trimmings, then the perpetrator must be an expert—an Egyptologist or someone with similar training. There can't be many of those in Vienna. And it would be interesting to know what the professor was working on when he died. It might give us a clue to his murder."

"If it was a murder," pointed out Julia. "The autopsy results aren't in yet."

"I beg you, Julia. He'd hardly mummified himself."

Julia thought. "What about the letters Professor Strössner wrote from Cairo? It doesn't add up. If his body really did spend seventy days in lye, he'd hardly have written home."

"The letters all date to the time immediately following his supposed departure," explained Leo. "They were all stamped in Cairo. I compared them to his notes and it does look like his hand. But no one knows what happened next."

"So, that would mean Professor Strössner decides to travel to Cairo for unknown reasons, writes a few letters, and then someone murders him there and sends him posthaste back to Vienna packaged as a mummy? You can't seriously believe that."

"No, that doesn't sound particularly plausible." Leo sipped on his beer. "Hmm . . . then maybe the letters are forged after all and Strössner never went to Cairo. He was here in Vienna the entire time."

"But didn't he call the museum personally and tell them he was leaving?"

"Christ, Julia, I don't know! This case is as foggy as the banks of the Danube in November. All I know for sure is this: there is no curse. This isn't a dime novel, this is reality!"

"Reality can be more frightening than any dime novel," said Julia. Lowering her voice, she went on: "Last night, I was called in to take some crime-scene photographs for Loibl. People can be such monsters . . ." She told Leo about the dead boy in the twelfth district. "Inspector Loibl suspects some kind of revenge act among pimps," she said in the end. "He thinks the boy might have poached in the wrong patch and his murder is meant to warn off other hustlers. But do you know what I find strange?"

"What is it?" asked Leo. He'd pushed the rest of his roast beef sandwich aside; apparently he'd lost his appetite.

"If Loibl is right, then why were the boy's pants gone? And his . . . his . . . too." Julia shook herself as the image formed in her mind's eye. "Well, I couldn't find anything anywhere in the pictures. Why would bastards like that clean up after the murder? You'd leave it lying there, wouldn't you, especially if it was meant as a warning?"

"Hmm, you're right." Leo thought. "Maybe the murder took place elsewhere and they only used the shed to dump him?"

"With all the blood there? I don't think so." Julia frowned. "And there's something else. I studied the photos until late last night. Something . . . something's not right. But I just can't put my finger on it!"

Leo sighed. "Sounds like the security bureau has not one but two new cases. A castrated body and a mummy . . . We already have enough murders to solve. Vienna is one giant madhouse! Leinkirchner is leaving most of the work in the mummy case to me. He's enjoying a day off with his sausage dog and his dear wife, visiting the new zoological gardens in the park, and—" He stopped short, and his face suddenly brightened. "Come with me to visit the Rapoldys! What do you say? We could go for a walk in Schönnbrunn park afterward, maybe visit the menagerie—I hear the lions have cubs. A proper spring outing." He winked at her.

Julia raised her hands defensively. "I'm no police agent, Leo. There are no women in this profession, as you know. If chief inspector Leinkirchner finds out—"

"How would he? I'll simply tell the Rapoldys that you're my assistant, something like a . . . a secretary that accompanies me."

"Uh-huh, secretary. You'd love that, wouldn't you."

Leo gave her a pleading look. "You'd be doing me a huge favor, Julia. It's not easy telling someone that a loved one has passed away. Even more so in this macabre case, as I'm sure you can imagine. Besides, two pairs of ears hear more than one." He lit a cigarette. "If Leinkirchner chooses to leave me to deal with this on my own, he has to accept some new methods. I've always thought women have better instincts during interrogations. Especially when questioning other women."

"I don't know . . . ," said Julia, although she knew that Leo had her. The case intrigued her. As a little girl she'd been fascinated by sunken treasures and archaeology. The stories of Heinrich Schliemann and his spectacular discovery of Troy had made it all the way to her native Inn region. Her father once gave her a picture book about Troy, as well as ancient Egypt and its pyramids. As a child she read the book over and over with fascination.

"Sisi is in good hands with her aunties," insisted Leo. "She'll hardly notice you're gone what with all the cake and fun. Please, Julia!"

"Is this what you consider a successful spring Sunday outing?" she said, trying one last time to resist. "Delivering news of a relative's passing?"

"Come on, Julia. Leinkirchner won't find out." He looked at her with puppy eyes.

She sighed. "All right. On one condition."

"Which is?"

"We're taking the good old tram. This restaurant here is enough for one day; I don't like pretending I'm posher than I am. Speaking of posh." She gave him a look of mock admonishment as she handed him a napkin. "Clean your shoes and pants. Or else they'll never let us in at Hietzing. Not even as police agents."

THE TRAM MOVED AT WALKING PACE, GIVING LEO AMPLE OPportunity to study the elegant villas of Hietzing—the front lawns, verandas, gables, and turrets; the marble statues beneath decorative willow trees . . . They'd been traveling for a good half hour and it felt as though they were in the countryside. Open meadows bordered cafes with garden seating. Hietzing was once a tiny village, but since it neighbored the imperial palace of Schönbrunn it was becoming more and more popular with wealthy burghers. Whoever in Vienna society could afford to own a villa here—and evidently, the Rapoldys could.

They had already passed the magnificent palace and were now looking out at a large construction site in Wiental, the ground ripped open in a long strip. Workers were installing heavy steel tracks. Plans for the new city tram to run all the way out here had been in the making for years, and it now looked close to completion.

About time, thought Leo. In London they'd had an electric tram for years now, and it ran *underground.* And Leo guessed it was much faster than the slow Vienna tram, let alone the horsecar tram.

Now they rattled past Casino Dommayer, where old Strauss had given celebrated concerts. The women strolling past wore large summer hats with flowers pinned to them; the men wore top hats. Here and there particularly brave folk were riding two-wheeled Rover bicycles to a Sunday picnic. Julia gazed out the window, pointing at this or that pretty chateau, as if they were alone on the Orient Express. Leo could smell her subtle lily-of-the-valley perfume. He loved it so much—as much as he loved her sharp mind, her interest in technology, as well as her graceful movements when she danced, when she undressed, or when she merely leaned up against him as she did now.

He didn't really know why he'd asked Julia along. But this case was so strange, he was simply glad to have someone by his side. And he looked forward to strolling through Schönbrunn park together. At the same time, he was aware that he was disregarding countless police regulations. Julia was a photographer, not a detective. Technically, he shouldn't have even told her about the case.

Nor a gravedigger from Central Cemetery . . .

Leo sighed. If Leinkirchner found out, he'd rip his head off. Well, tough luck—that's what he got for leaving Leo on his own on Whitsunday while strolling in the park with his wife and dog.

They hopped off at the corner of Wenz Lane. This area had been an amusement park until just a few years ago, when the stock market collapsed in 1873 and it was forced to close. Mansions scattered across the rural landscape like huge exotic flowers, far from the noise and traffic.

The Rapoldy residence wasn't far from the tram stop. At the end of the long driveway stood a two-story villa surrounded by a beautiful fenced-in garden, both overwhelming and ridiculous at once. There was a stone pyramid as tall as a man, and a sarcophagus planted with daffodils and ivy. Several statues among the trees looked like Egyptian deities. Two granite pillars in the fence were flanked by sphinx, and a sign on the gate between the pillars displayed the name of the house: "*Villa Thebes.*"

"Welcome to Egypt," murmured Leo. He pulled the bell rope next to the garden gate. There was a low, soft gong somewhere inside the house, like a greeting from a distant world.

After a while the door opened and an older woman in a white apron and bonnet looked outside.

"Yes?" she asked indignantly from the doorstep. The garden gate remained shut.

Leo produced his badge, embroidered in gray and black with the Habsburg double eagle, and held it between the iron bars. "Inspector Herzfeldt and Fräulein Julia Wolf, my assistant. We're from the Vienna security bureau and we—"

"It's all right, Mathilda," said a melancholy-sounding female voice from inside the house. "I'll handle it."

"As you wish, madam." The maid vanished.

The woman who appeared did not look like any woman Leo had ever met. Bathed in sunlight, she stepped into the garden. She was perhaps in her midthirties, wearing a wide, flowing, deep blue dress adorned with mysterious patterns that seemed to shimmer in the light. Leo squinted. The dress was entirely unfitted, not at the waist or the chest; it hung like a . . . well, like a sack. Leo had heard of such dresses, and that "enlightened" women from the upper classes were increasingly wearing them. He thought that they weren't particularly flattering, but nevertheless, or perhaps because of this, the woman radiated majesty. She held her chin high as she strode down the steps, her black hair cut at chin length and, above the brow, in a straight line. Her nose was narrow and a touch too big for her face. Leo couldn't help but think of Queen Cleopatra. And then he noticed something else.

The woman was barefoot.

"Yes?" she said when she reached the gate. Her voice was smoky and almost as deep as that of a man.

"Are you Charlotte Rapoldy?" asked Leo.

She nodded. "I guess you're here because of my father. Good old Alexander came this morning and shared the news with us. It's . . ." Charlotte Rapoldy paused, shaking her head. Her eyes were slightly reddened. "Well, the world is an eternal puzzle, is it not?"

"Dr. Dedekind came here?" asked Leo, astonished.

"Yes, kind of him, wasn't it?" She smiled sadly. "Alex wanted to tell us before we heard from elsewhere—or from the police."

Leo was speechless. He wasn't sure whether because of Frau Rapoldy's strange appearance or Dr. Dedekind's blatant disregard of police orders. "Well, in any case . . . ," he stammered eventually, "can we come in?"

"Of course, how silly of me." She opened the gate. "I'm sure there's plenty to discuss. Follow me. We'll go to the library. I'll ask my husband to join us, if that suits you."

They followed her inside. The entrance hall was decorated with tall clay vases bearing Egyptian motifs. Leo couldn't say whether they were originals or reproductions, but either way, they looked expensive, just like the silk wallpaper and the Impressionist paintings on the wall. The Rapoldys seemed to be swimming in money.

Toward the back, the hall ended in a bright conservatory with wicker furniture. Charlotte Rapoldy opened a door on the left and asked them to enter. “Why don’t you make yourselves comfortable in the library and I’ll be right with you. Would you like tea or coffee?”

“Uh, no thanks, don’t trouble yourself on our account.”

“Clemens, are you coming?” She disappeared up the hallway, her flowing dress rustling softly. Leo and Julia looked around the library.

“Heavens,” whispered Julia. “Is this a temple?”

Leo nodded. “A temple of books.”

“And madam is the priestess,” said Julia. Leo thought he heard sarcasm in her voice.

His gaze traveled up the many shelves that stretched across the two stories. They were mostly filled with books, but there were also some technical implements, presumably for research. Leo recognized a petroleum torch, a modern phonograph, and what looked like a large camera. A freestanding staircase wound up to the second-floor gallery, and farther up still, a glass dome formed the roof, allowing in bright sunlight.

This room, too, was decorated with Egyptian vases and deities. Jackal heads made of basalt served as bookends; the walls were wallpapered in blue with Egyptian symbols. Leo carefully lifted one of the jackal heads and studied it.

“Anubis, god of death rites and embalming,” a male voice sounded from the second floor. “He accompanies the dead on their final voyage through the underworld, and weighs the heart. If the heart is too light, the soul is fed to Ammit, the great devouress.”

Leo looked up and spotted a man in middle age. He was dressed in a light-colored summer suit with a wide-brimmed hat, as if he had just been in the garden. He was lanky and tanned and wore his beard in a goatee, reminding Leo of a French painter. The man removed his hat and gestured at the symbols on the wallpaper.

“Those are excerpts from the ancient Egyptian Book of the Dead. The parallels to the Bible are astonishing. My father-in-law was always highly interested in the Egyptian origins of Christianity." The man descended the stairs slowly and somewhat cumbersomely. Leo saw only then that he leaned on a cane.

Charlotte Rapoldy entered through the downstairs door with a tray holding a jug of water and some crystal glasses. Her hands shook and the glasses chinked softly. She gave a strained smile.

"I sent our housekeeper home," she said. "It's Whitsunday, after all. But the dear woman won't go. She worries about me." She set down the tray. "Please, sit. You've already met my husband, Clemens. He's a doctor and can probably handle such gruesome news better than I can." She pressed her lips together, and Leo thought her pallor made her appear even more dignified. "We still can't believe it . . . and the nature of his death . . . it's like a terrible ghost story. I'm just so glad I have Clemens by my side. We haven't been married long."

Together they sat down on a suite upholstered with zebra skin. Clemens Rapoldy leaned on his cane even while he sat, placing his other hand soothingly on Charlotte's knee. After a couple of moments, he addressed Leo. "Dear Alexander told us there was no mistake, but I'm sure you'll understand if we'd like to see for ourselves that . . . that it's true."

"Of course." Leo nodded. "You can see the body as soon as the forensic institute gives their permission. However I must point out that Dr. Dedekind had no right to speak with you before us."

Charlotte Rapoldy sighed. "Alex is a family friend. He wished to break the news gently. But how is anyone to break news like this gently? It's . . ." She groped for words. "Absurd! Horrifying and absurd. Like a nightmare!"

"And yet it happened," said Leo. "Let's summarize what we know." He leaned forward, noticing at the same time that the ivory knob of Clemens Rapoldy's walking stick was a carved jackal head, just like the bookends. The Rapoldys were a strange couple. He continued, "Professor Strössner wasn't just any archaeologist—"

"My father was a world-renowned scientist, an eminent authority in the field of archaeology. His specialty was the so-called New Kingdom of Egypt, which existed more than three thousand years ago." There was something mesmerizing about Charlotte Rapoldy's smoky voice. From the corner of his eye Leo noticed she still wasn't wearing any shoes. "That is why the court of Vienna entrusted him to lead the archaeological investigation at Deir al-Bahari." She looked at Leo and Julia in turns. "Are you familiar with the findings at Deir al-Bahari?"

"Uh, I'm afraid not," said Leo. "Please educate us."

"Well, I'll have to backtrack a little." There was a soft splashing sound as Charlotte filled their glasses with water. "About twenty years ago, antiques of dubious origins started to appear on Egyptian markets. The trail led to a local family by the name of Abd el-Rassul, who had discovered a rock grave of enormous proportions in a remote valley. Such rock tombs are known as caches, and this one contained sarcophagi from various tombs that had been moved there long ago for protection from tomb raiders. The three brothers plundered the cache but were eventually arrested and interrogated." Her eyes gleamed excitedly as she continued:

"The discovery was indescribable! Several pharaohs from the twentieth and twenty-first dynasties, among them immortal names such as Amenophis, Thutmose, and Ramses, as well as jewelry, canopic jars, figurines . . . And that wasn't all. Ten years later another cache was discovered in the same valley. This one contained the mummies of over a hundred and fifty priests. Over a hundred and fifty! The find was so enormous that the Egyptian government decided to distribute part of it to the most important museums in the world by drawing names out of a hat."

"And some of it went to the Museum of Art History in Vienna," concluded Julia, who had listened in silence until then.

Clemens Rapoldy nodded before giving a cough. "Sarcophagi,

ushabti statuettes, canopic jars and chests—a treasure straight from Aladdin's cave. My father-in-law was in charge of the Austrian group tasked with examining the findings assigned to them and then safely transporting them to Vienna. He spent over a year there."

"Who were the other archaeologists?" asked Leo.

"The other archaeologists?" Clemens Rapoldy seemed to hesitate briefly. "Well, Adolf Landinger from Innsbruck and Father Gregor Mayr from Graz. And of course Walter Kerfeld from Vienna. Why do you ask?"

"Would it be possible to get their addresses?" Leo produced a pencil. "Even telephone numbers, perhaps, if those universities own telephones? We'd like to speak with the gentlemen." He didn't mention that all three men might be suspects—as leading Egyptologists, most likely, all three of them knew how to embalm a person.

Clemens Rapoldy swallowed uncomfortably, and his wife said nothing. "I'm afraid that . . . well, that won't be possible in two out of the three cases," he said at last. "Unfortunately, Dr. Adolf Landinger and Father Gregor are both deceased."

"They *what*?" Leo almost dropped his pencil.

"Yes, unfortunately Dr. Landinger died of a fever while still in Egypt, quite unfortunately in the last few days of the expedition. Apparently it stemmed from a poorly healed wound from during the dig," said Clemens Rapoldy. "And Father Gregor Mayr had a weak heart. He passed just a few weeks ago; his faculty informed us not long ago."

"And what about . . ."—Leo checked his notes—"Professor Walter Kerfeld from Vienna? Were he and your father-in-law in regular contact?"

"Not very regular," replied Clemens Rapoldy. "There was no love lost between the two of them. Professor Kerfeld was the deputy leader of the expedition, and I believe he would have liked to be in charge. Later, in Vienna, he resented the museum for asking my father-in-law to document the find instead of him. They had one or two professional disagreements."

"Well, Professor Kerfeld at least is still alive," observed Leo. "Unlike the other two gentlemen."

"I know what you're thinking," said Charlotte Rapoldy. "Three out of four researchers from an Egyptian expedition dead: it sounds like a curse."

"Your words, not mine," said Leo.

"But all three men were elderly. Fever, a weak heart—there's nothing untoward about that."

"There is about a mummified professor, though," interjected Julia.

Charlotte Rapoldy looked affronted, and Leo shot Julia a warning glance.

"Forgive us, Frau Rapoldy," he said. "That was a little rude of my assistant. We only wish to find out what happened."

"So do we, for heaven's sake!" Charlotte Rapoldy ran a hand through her hair. "How . . . how can all this be possible? We thought my father was still in Egypt, and now this . . . We were concerned, of course. The letters stopped coming, and—" She began to sob. Leo noticed not for the first time that she was beautiful in a special way, as if she belonged to a long forgotten world.

"Why don't we start at the beginning," suggested Leo gently. "Did you accompany your father on his first expedition? You're an Egyptologist yourself."

"We visited the group at the site last year," said Clemens Rapoldy, coming to his tearful wife's aid. "It . . . it was our honeymoon. A cruise on the Nile, that's what Charlotte always wished for. We'd met a few months prior in Cairo—a whirlwind romance. Wasn't it, Charlotte?"

Charlotte Rapoldy nodded and blew her nose while her husband went on: "My father-in-law wasn't the youngest and he wasn't well. He suffered from diabetes melater, a pancreatic disease not uncommon in the elderly. Symptoms are thirst, fatigue, exhaustion, and increased urination—well, that's probably of more interest to those with a medical background." He gave an impatient wave. "In any case, during the expedition it was helpful for someone to check on him from time to time. That became my task, as a sort of personal physician. All went well, aside from poor Dr. Landinger's injury, of course. We all returned home last September. Since then, my father-in-law spent almost all his time at the museum. Charlotte assisted him from time to time." He smiled weakly and stroked his wife's hand. "You know, she's the first woman researcher in this field. In Austria at least."

"Congratulations," said Julia. "Your father must have been very proud."

"He was." Charlotte smiled too, now, even if it was just a small smile. "My mother died when I was a child and I was very close to my father. And even now we lived under the same roof. Last year we spent so much time down in the museum repository, and it felt almost like . . . like the old days. One find especially fascinated my father . . ." She broke off and shot her husband a worried look.

"Is there something we should know?" asked Leo.

She only spoke once her husband gave a nod. "I ask you to keep what I'm about to tell you to yourself. The find I speak of came to Vienna in, well, not entirely legal ways. It is a mummy that my father had shipped, uh, privately."

"Your father *stole* a mummy?" asked Julia, stunned.

Clemens Rapoldy raised both hands. "That's not quite right. My father-in-law found the tomb himself by chance, when he got lost in the desert. It was his find! He almost died in the process. Old tombs can be treacherous, you know. Ceilings collapse, sand comes pouring in . . ."

"So, he had the mummy brought to Vienna secretly?" asked Leo.

Charlotte Rapoldy nodded. "With the consent of the other researchers. At the time of the discovery, Clemens and myself hadn't arrived yet. We only found out later. The mummy lay in a tomb of its own, far away from the others, as he wasn't a priest of Amun. This one served a much older and darker deity." She lowered her voice. "He was a priest of Thoth."

"The god of magic," added Clemens Rapoldy. "The priest's name was Ta-bek-en-chon. We believe that it was because of this mummy that Alfons traveled back to Egypt. It wouldn't give him any rest. He probably hoped to learn more about it over there. That was in February this year."

"And he didn't say goodbye?" asked Leo skeptically. "That sounds more than strange."

"It is, isn't it?" Charlotte Rapoldy's hand trembled when she reached for her water glass. "Clemens and I were away for the weekend, a conference in Munich. When we got home, there was only a letter. Father wrote that he was taking the next train to Genoa and from there a ship to Cairo. He would explain everything upon his return."

"May I see the letter?"

"Of course." Clemens Rapoldy rose and, with the help of his walking stick, walked over to a small desk. He opened a drawer and retrieved a bundle of letters.

"We received a few more letters," he said when he handed the bundle to Leo. "But then, at the end of March, all contact ceased. It's not that unusual—in the desert, it's not hard to lose contact with civilization. The Egyptian postal service is a catastrophe. But after a while we began to worry. And now this . . ."

Leo compared the Rapoldys' letters to those he had received from the museum. They contained the same warm words, a few scientific comments he didn't understand, but nothing that raised any concerns, at least not at first glance. All bar the first bore a postage stamp from Cairo. The writing was identical.

"And you're certain this is your father's hand?" asked Leo, looking at Charlotte.

She nodded. "A hundred percent. There's no doubt in my mind."

"Then please explain to me how your father can write letters in Egypt when he's now lying at the Museum of Art History in Vienna as a mummy? It's impossible. Dr. Alexander Dedekind assured us that mummification takes more than two months."

"I don't know, Herr Inspector! All I know is that this is more than mysterious. It is frightening." Charlotte Rapoldy, still trembling, leaned against her husband. "Believe me, if I wasn't a scientist, I would believe in a curse, too. Please help us solve this terrible riddle! It's the only way my father—all of us—can find peace."

A SHORT WHILE LATER, LEO AND JULIA WERE BACK OUTSIDE the villa. It was afternoon now; the sun had lowered, and the first shadows enveloped the statues in the garden. A shiver rippled down Julia and she buttoned up her thin summer coat.

"So?" asked Leo. "What's your impression of it all?"

"A fairly nebulous one." She tried to ignore the pair of sphinxes who seemed to stare at her as they passed through the gate. "At this point, we don't even know how exactly the professor died. And then those letters . . . But Charlotte Rapoldy truly did seem to have been very close with her father. It was obvious."

Julia thought of her relationship with her own father, a smith, tinkerer, and inventor from the Inn region. He was her great role model. She couldn't imagine how she would have reacted had something similar happened to her father. Charlotte Rapoldy was holding up well, considering. The marriage, though, had seemed a little strange—like the whole family, Charlotte especially. Julia hadn't failed to notice the furtive looks Leo had given the mistress of the house. She had felt a quiet stab of jealousy, but immediately called herself a fool.

"At least we have our first suspect," said Leo, interrupting her musings. "Professor Kerfeld. He is the last survivor of the expedition and he argued with Strössner. Perhaps about the priest mummy with the unpronounceable name? Plus, Kerfeld would know how to embalm someone, being an Egyptologist. I'm definitely going to pay him a visit."

"And you think this Kerfeld might also have murdered the other two members of the expedition?" asked Julia, dubious. "Why would he? And besides, their causes of death sounded natural. Fever and heart failure."

"We can check. I can make an inquiry at Graz at least—I have contacts there. There has to be a death certificate for Father Mayr. And then we'll see." Leo frowned. "The Rapoldys are seriously wealthy. Where did all the money come from? I wonder if this mummy wasn't the only thing Charlotte's father misappropriated during his expeditions."

"Or maybe they're just rich," replied Julia. "Old money, you know." She could easily imagine Leo as a wealthy passenger on a Nile cruise. Inside the mansion, she'd felt that the other three were conversing at eye level while she'd been but a spectator.

"Well, in any case, the Rapoldys are definitely snobs. The way they dress! And all that Egyptian junk." Leo smirked. "Thank you for coming with me. Shall we go to the park at Schönbrunn?"

"I don't know, Leo. The whole thing has kind of put me off. Maybe let's leave it for today. Sisi is probably waiting for me—"

"But you said yourself she was in good hands. What's one more hour?"

"You can't understand, Leo. You're not a woman."

"Clearly." Leo held up his palms and gave a conciliatory smile. "Then let's at least take a fiacre back so we don't have to end our

Whitsunday breathing in the collective sweat of all the holiday-makers."

A short while later, seated in a cab taking them back to the city, they snuggled close together. But they didn't speak, and Julia's hands were cold. It was as if this mysterious curse had clasped hold of their hearts, too.

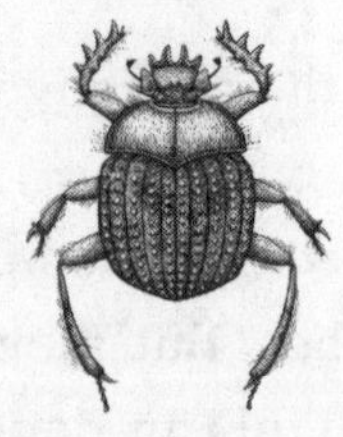

CHAPTER 5

On Whitmonday, Leo arrived at work early. He had much to do. The events from the previous day kept playing in his mind. Once again he had read through Professor Strössner's notes late into the night, but found nothing he deemed relevant to the case. The priest's mummy that Strössner had shipped illegally was mentioned nowhere. At least he spotted the name of Strössner's colleague a few times, Walter Kerfeld, who was listed as the second-in-command of the Egypt expedition. It appeared that both men were members of the Vienna Archaeological Society. Didn't Professor Hofmann say that that's where he met Strössner? The society seemed to boast an illustrious circle of members.

Leo entered the police headquarters, nodded at the porter, and went up to the third floor. The building on Schottenring was a former hotel from the world's fair of 1873. The walls were paper thin, the stairs creaked, and the maze-like hallways and corridors smelled of cold cigar smoke, floor polish, and cabbage. Leo still didn't know how many rooms were under the roof of the castle-like building; he still discovered new rooms from time to time. Because of the holiday, police headquarters were quiet today, which suited him.

Carrying his briefcase, he strolled down the corridor, greeting the few colleagues he saw until he reached the last door on the left. Inspector Erich Loibl, with whom he shared the office, looked up from a steaming cup of coffee. An open file lay on his desk, together with several photographs. Leo could tell right away that they were images of a murder victim. No sleeping man would lie like that . . .

"Morning," said Loibl into his walrus moustache. Leo thought he could smell a faint whiff of alcohol. Had Loibl tipped a shot of schnapps into his coffee this early in the day? It was no secret that his colleague enjoyed a drink or two, but so far, his drinking had never been an issue; although recently, Leo had been under the impression the drinking had become heavier.

"Are those pictures from the murder in the twelfth district?" asked Leo, coming closer to Loibl's desk.

Erich Loibl winked at him. "Aha! Fräulein Wolf already told you?"

"I just bumped into her outside headquarters," lied Leo. "We had a quick chat."

"I see, a quick chat . . ."

Leo didn't respond to Loibl's suggestive tone. Like Loibl's drinking, Leo's relationship with Julia was something no one really spoke of. Relationships among colleagues were strictly forbidden. Besides, nothing had even happened last night. Following their visit to the Rapoldys, Julia had gone home to Sisi. Leo had received nothing but a few hasty kisses.

"Stukart asked for the pictures," said Loibl after a few moments. "Your little lamb just dropped them off. A goddamned outrage it is, this. But we'll catch those filthy dogs. Our men are already checking out every known criminal in the twelfth district." He pushed the photographs toward Leo so he could see for himself.

Leo bent over the desk and breathed deeply. Julia hadn't exaggerated. He could understand why she struggled to sleep after developing such awful images. At first glance he didn't know which was worse: the horrific mutilation of the genitalia or the smudged lipstick around the boy's mouth, making his face, rigid in death, look like a terrible mockery of a Kasperl puppet from the Wurstelprater.

"And you reckon it's meant to be a warning to other hustlers?" asked Leo skeptically.

"Our investigations should bring some clarity soon, but yes, that's what I think. I beg you, Herzfeldt!" Loibl leaned back and sipped on his coffee, milky brown froth clinging to his beard. "Cutting off a man's holiest of holies? The message couldn't be any clearer: leave your knob in your pants or else you'll fare the same way. Someone marked his territory."

"Do we know who the boy was yet?"

"Like I said, inquiries are underway. You're welcome to help me work through the results."

Leo pointed at one of the pictures. "I don't see any pants. Did your constables find any? Nor do I see what you just called a knob—where is it?"

Loibl shrugged. "They probably cut him up somewhere else and dumped him there."

"What about all that blood?" Leo pointed at the images again, the blood black against the floor. "How do you explain that?"

"Christ, now you sound like Wolf! That's what she was on about too, earlier, just as if she were an inspector. We have to watch out for those women, make sure they don't take over one day. Hmm . . ." Thinking, Loibl slid the images back and forth on his desk. His confidence was beginning to crack. "Let's wait and hear what Professor Hofmann from the forensic institute says. Then we'll see. Until then—"

He broke off when the door flew open noisily. Paul Leinkirchner marched in, clearly in a foul mood. Leo thought he looked even more sour than usual, and that was saying something. Leinkirchner's cigar glowed in his face like a third eye.

"A wonderful morning, chief inspector," said Leo with a smile. "How was the zoo yesterday? Did you feed the monkeys with your lovely wife?"

"Save your cleverness, Herzfeldt," replied Leinkirchner without taking his cigar out of his mouth. He looked at Loibl. "Well, Erich? Any news from the twelfth?"

The two inspectors had known each other for many years. Leinkirchner often treated Loibl as if he were his errand boy, and Loibl let him. Erich Loibl wasn't a bad police agent, but he only ever did what he was told, task after task. And when he'd had too much to drink, occasionally a task was dropped.

"We're on it, Paul," he replied. "I'm still waiting for the report from the local constabulary."

"Those scoundrels are getting cheekier all the time. Beatings, blackmail, and now this! Sooner or later we'll have to crack down hard on them." Leinkirchner sighed. "Well, at least it's a pretty straightforward case. Hopefully soon it'll be cleared up." He turned to Leo. "You—come to my office. You and me have something to discuss."

Ignoring Loibl's curious gaze, Leo followed Leinkirchner to his office, on the opposite side of the corridor. It was larger and more comfortable than his and Loibl's, and even had its own telephone. And it stank even worse of cigar smoke than other rooms in this building, if that was even possible.

"Well, what did you learn from the Rapoldys?" asked Leinkirchner, getting straight to the point.

Leo reported on his visit without mentioning that Julia had accompanied him. Nor did he mention his trip to Central Cemetery. But he did speak of his suspicion that the suspect had to be an expert on mummification. Leinkirchner listened carefully, chewing on his now cold cigar.

"Hmm, it's all still rather mysterious," he muttered eventually. He scratched the scar on his cheek, as he often did when he was thinking. "But at least we have our first suspect with Professor Kerfeld, provided your theory holds true. An argument among scholars that got out of hand. It's a motive. What sort of a man is this Kerfeld? Probably another one of those arrogant academics."

"According to the museum's records, Professor Walter Kerfeld is just as recognized an Egyptologist as Strössner was," explained Leo. "The two of them had known each other for years. I was planning to find out more about Walter Kerfeld today and then pay him a visit."

"And you believe this Egyptologist also killed the other members of the expedition?" Leinkirchner brushed a few crumbs of tobacco from his beard. "It's quite the leap, if you ask me."

Leo gave a shrug. "I'll admit it's a lot of unformed ideas. But maybe we'll find something else. It could be about money. Professor Alfons Strössner was quite wealthy. Maybe the money came from earlier undocumented finds, like the priest's mummy."

"That Ta-bek-something. Hmm, damn, you might be onto something." Leinkirchner nodded thoughtfully. "Perhaps it wasn't such a bad idea of Stukart's to involve you in the case, Herzfeldt." The chief inspector grinned suddenly. "Your people know all about Egypt and curses."

"My people?" Leo sat up straighter in his seat. "How do you mean?"

"Well, the Egyptians enslaved you Jews, didn't they? And then didn't God help you get out of Egypt with ten curses? Water to blood, frogs raining from the sky . . . stuff like that."

It was clear that Leinkirchner was baiting Leo.

But Leo didn't bite. "In any case, the villa in Hietzing is a palace," he said calmly. "It's bursting with money. And if there's one thing I know about crime, it's this one truth—"

"Follow the money—it will often lead to the culprit." Leinkirchner scratched his bald head and thought. "All right, go dig," he said after a while. "With regard to those two dead researchers, too. And keep me informed! I'll handle the cleaning lady at the detention. I'll make sure she stays locked up a little longer before she can spill the whole affair. If she hasn't already blabbed to one of the guards."

Leo drew out a cigarette and Leinkirchner lit it for him. It was strange. Moments ago he had teased Leo for his Jewish roots, and now he once again appeared to respect him, value him, even. Then where did the man's hatred of all things Jewish come from? Leo couldn't understand why Leinkirchner had brought him in to work in his division in the first place. He thought about how sometimes, working together could be invigorating, and Leinkirchner had even saved his life once. Maybe it had been for a simple reason.

A good policeman knows another good policeman when he sees him . . .

The chief inspector was still chewing pensively on his cigar. "This case is very important to the police president," he said. "The Rapoldys aren't just rich; they're influential. Their connections include Archduke Rainer Ferdinand of Austria, a relative and close confidant of the kaiser, who is apparently also crazy about all things Egypt. If we're unlucky, the court will stick its beak in. That's the last thing we need! So, not a word to anyone. Not even Loibl." Leinkirchner drummed his fingers on the table. "When can we expect a report from Professor Hofmann?"

"Tomorrow at the latest, I'd think. The Rapoldys are yet to visit the body, to identify him."

"Perhaps Frau Rapoldy will identifiy the mummy as Ramses-something-or-other, and then her father will arrive on the next ship from Cairo. Wouldn't that be something." Leinkirchner grinned. "Alas, I don't see it happening."

"Nor do I, chief inspector."

The telephone rang. Leo still struggled to grow accustomed to its metallic sound.

Leinkirchner reached for the apparatus, which looked like a kind of black lampshade, with one piece to speak into and another to hold to one's ear. "Yes, what is it?" He listened for a while before barking, "And why do you come to me with this?" More listening. "Hmm, I see. Very well, I'll send someone."

When he hung up, he gave Leo a thoughtful look.

"The world's a small place sometimes, isn't it, Herzfeldt?"

"Sir?"

Leinkirchner scratched his bald head again. "As you know, my wife and I visited the new zoological garden at the Prater yesterday. We saw the lion enclosure, too. They have a good-sized specimen there, the size of a calf. What can I say?" He sucked on his cold cigar. "Last night, the beast crunched up one of the keepers."

"And it was no accident," guessed Leo. "Or else they wouldn't have called up the security bureau."

"Clever deduction, colleague. Is that part of your modern criminalistics?" Leinkirchner pressed the cigar stump into an overflowing ashtray and picked up the earpiece. "I'll send our pretty photographer straightaway, together with one of our detectives. And don't you think for a minute that it could be you, Herzfeldt. Zoos are overrated, anyway."

Strange news from China tells us that people there bury their dead in hanging coffins. The coffins sit upright in a rock wall and . . .

Augustin Rothmayer chewed on his quill pen and stretched his back with a groan. The early morning May sun streamed through the window of his small hut, which did nothing to improve his mood. Why did people get all excited about sunny May? Although, there actually seemed to be less dying in May. As if those on death's doorstep wished to experience one last summer.

He wrote standing up at his beloved desk, as sitting had been causing him pain for a while now. He estimated that over his lifetime so far he had dug well over a thousand graves, some in frost-hardened ground, others in baking heat or pouring rain—no wonder his back had stopped cooperating at some point.

This morning had been especially bad. The day before, in the late afternoon on Whitsunday, they had brought him three unexpected burials, after he'd just filled in the shaft grave in sector 23. Damn, he was getting old!

He brought the pencil down to the paper again.

They stand upright in a rock wall and . . .

Behind him, someone hummed melodiously, a chair scraped across the floor, and the cat hissed.

"Jumpin' catfish, can't I have a moment's peace and quiet!" Augustin turned, glowering. "How am I supposed to work in concentration, huh?"

"Beg your pardon, Herr Rothmayer." Anna pouted. She was sitting at the table with coffee, bread rolls, and honey, wiping the crumbs from her lips. The sleeves of her dress, which were much too short, were smudged with honey. She had grown a good deal in the last six months. "Lucie got his tail pinched and—"

"I don't want to hear it! No excuses, no hissing, and no bleedin' singing. What was that, anyhow, that you were humming so tunelessly?"

"The song you played me at bedtime last night, Herr Rothmayer. The Schubert one with the trout. I like it."

"I see, the *Trout Quintet*," grumbled Augustin, though he sounded somewhat pacified. Anna still called him Herr Rothmayer as if he were some distant uncle she'd only just met. And as far as the cemetery administration and the welfare office were concerned, that's just what he was—until the day someone asked too many questions.

And Augustin would do anything to prevent that.

"Will you play me something?" asked Anna. She was about twelve years old—no one knew for certain. But if there was something she wanted from Augustin, she could whine like a six-year-old. "It's so quiet here. As quiet as . . . as . . ."

"As the grave, is that what you were going to say?" Augustin gave her a stern look and lifted a finger. "My dear girl, you live at a cemetery. If you'd prefer to play with marbles and other little children, go to Simmering."

"But I like being here with you, Herr Rothmayer. I only want a little music. Please!" Anna gave him one of those looks that Augustin struggled to resist. He might be grumbly and rude, bark at her and grouse, but deep down he liked her—more than that, he loved her. Even if he'd never say so.

Like my own daughter . . .

It had been years since he told anyone this.

Would he ever tell Anna that he used to have a daughter, with the same name?

With a sigh, he set down his pencil. He wasn't really concentrating anyway. He hadn't really been able to since yesterday, when that dandy Prussian of an inspector had visited and told him about the mummy. A truly interesting case. Augustin couldn't stop thinking about it. The story would go well with his new book. The year before, Augustin had compiled *The Gravedigger's Almanac*, which he hoped would someday become a classic, a guide to others in his profession. No one knew as much about grave digging as he did, even Professor Hofmann said so. It had been Hofmann who had published the book, and even written a personal dedication at the front! Normally, writing brought Augustin peace and focus, but not today.

"Fine," he grumbled. "One tune, but only one! Then you go outside to play, all right? And remember that we must clear the old bones from the shaft graves in sector 22 by lunchtime. I'll need your help with those. And later we'll sow chrysanthemums in the glasshouse."

Anna nodded eagerly. Her mother was buried in sector 22, and the girl sometimes went to the grave and spoke with her. One time Augustin secretly listened. She'd told her mother that she lived with a strange man who liked to gripe even if he didn't mean it. And she'd said that she was happy. Augustin had quietly trudged off and wiped a few tears from his eyes.

"I'll play you some Schubert. But don't you sing along off-key again." He rose and walked over to the sacred corner where his violin hung. Its timber was dull with age and it bore a few scratches, but its sound was still excellent. Augustin tuned the instrument before drawing the bow across the strings, producing a mournful, melancholy melody. Anna closed her eyes and smiled blissfully. She loved music more than anything. It was like a language to her. When she first moved in with Augustin, she didn't speak, not a single word. Music had helped her find a new way into the world. She and Augustin used music to communicate.

When he had finished, her eyes were full of longing.

"What's it called?"

"Oh, it's called "The *Linden Tree*." It's about memories that no one can take away from you. They stay forever in your heart. An old linden tree, a beautiful fountain, or a loved one."

She nodded earnestly. “I like that.” Suddenly she stood up from her chair, sending the cat leaping off her lap with an indignant meow. “Can I try?”

“Are you barking mad, lassie?” He returned the violin to its hook. “It’s not a toy. It was gifted to me. It used to belong to a famous man, a long time ago.”

“Who was he?” asked Anna.

“Don’t be nosy. One song was our agreement, and that’s that!” He pointed at the door. “Out with you. I have an idea. You go look for Schubert’s grave. If you find it, I’ll play you something else by him. Maybe the song about wandering. But I don’t want to see you back here for at least an hour.”

Anna snatched another bun with honey before running outside.

“Hey, put a coat on, girl!” Augustin called after her. “You’ll catch your death.”

But she no longer heard him or chose not to.

Cursing under his breath, Augustin returned to his desk. Maybe he’d manage to write the chapter on hanging coffins in the next hour. He kept getting stuck on the same sentence!

His eye snagged on Naville’s book on Egyptology. He hesitated. Something had been nagging at him since the day before, something the inspector mentioned in passing. Augustin hastily leafed through the pages until he found what he was looking for.

Look at that . . .

He was right.

A grin spread across his face. This very morning he would walk over to the administration building and telephone Professor Hofmann at the forensic institute. This mummy case really was highly interesting, not least for reasons that no one had paid any attention to thus far.

Augustin picked out a few fresh pages, dipped his quill pen into his inkwell, and started to write with concentration. The Chinese death rites would have to wait until tomorrow.

Egyptian funeral ceremonies deserved a chapter of their own.

When Julia climbed out of the fiacre together with inspector Loibl, she immediately spotted the entrance to the new zoological garden. The zoo was situated at the Prater's edge, in the same location where years ago the old zoological garden had been, an area known as am Schüttel. A long queue had formed outside the pay booth. Vienna's newest attraction had opened its doors only yesterday, on Whitsunday, and it seemed today would be another busy day.

"Me, I've never really understood why everyone gets excited about staring at animals," grumbled Loibl as they crossed Laufberger Lane to get to the entrance. "Those beasts sleep all day anyway. Every now and then a monkey will have a scratch, or a lion yawns—that's it. And the stink!"

It was true, a pungent smell blew over to them from the animal enclosures. Julia didn't point out that Loibl also stank, of smoke and sweat from the previous night's schnapps. She felt a moment of pity herself—that she had to visit yet another crime scene so soon after the murder in the twelfth district.

Chief inspector Leinkirchner had telephoned the Blue Dragoon about an hour ago—luckily, no one at the police station knew that a brothel lay at the other end of the phone line. Leinkirchner had sent her to the new zoological garden with Loibl, who had been unwilling to take the case.

"I've no idea what we're supposed to do here," he grumbled as they lined up outside the entrance, an archway flanked by two turrets with stone lions. "A mauled keeper . . . some idiot must have left the gate open, and a lion is no pussycat. And now they even want pictures of the crime scene. *Crime scene* . . . That term alone!" He rolled his eyes. "What crime scene?"

"Chief inspector Leinkirchner said there were clues that someone was involved, that it was done on purpose," said Julia, lugging her heavy case. At least Loibl was carrying the tripod for her. "And besides, the zoo only opened yesterday with a big hoo-ha and a whole number of important guests. They can't afford a faux pas."

"Even the police president came, and our dear colleague Leinkirchner, I know." Loibl nodded. "And now we have to jump through the hoops. As if we have nothing better to do!"

Julia was grateful for every commission, even if it meant leaving Sisi at home for half the day. But she had to agree—Leinkirchner's assignment seemed an overreaction. Besides, she'd seen enough blood in the last few days.

Loibl pushed past the queue impatiently and showed his badge at the booth.

"The fuzz gets in for free?" complained an older man behind them. "And skipping the line! I'm a veteran from Königgrätz, you hear me, and I still pay my ten kronen!"

Ignoring the man, Loibl entered the zoo with Julia.

"I see how it is—the missus don't pay either," the old man continued to heckle behind them. "What's in the case? Chocolates for the zoo director? If the kaiser knew, I tell you!"

Apparently they were expected. A man in his fifties trotted toward them, clad in a stained overcoat and tall, muddy boots. Underneath his overcoat, Julia could see a waistcoat with silver buttons, a tightly buttoned shirt, and a tie. His long black hair was combed back and his mustache neatly trimmed. The man looked like an upper-class merchant dressed up as a peasant.

"The, uh . . . gentlemen from the police?" He darted a confused look in Julia's direction.

"Fräulein is here to take photographs—it's what we have to do these days." Loibl flashed his badge again. "And you are?"

"Friedrich Carl Knauer, director of the zoological garden." The man in the coat lowered his voice and glanced at the visitors around them nervously. "Please follow me. We don't want to cause a stir."

Dr. Knauer led the way past several enclosures and aviaries. Julia noticed how beautifully the new zoo had been designed. There were playgrounds and small parks where peacocks strutted, as well as a medieval-looking bear cage and even a fake ruined castle for visitors to walk through. They passed giraffes, zebras, and camels, and cages with babbling parrots and screeching monkeys. Farther back, Julia could see the roof of a pavilion from whence came the sound of a trumpeting elephant. She decided she would bring Sisi here sometime soon. This was much nicer than the grimy stalls at the Wurstelprater next door.

"It's lovely here," she said to Friedrich Knauer as they walked.

The director nodded distractedly. "You should see the arena where we show our ethnic displays. You'll truly believe you're in Africa. And now this!" He sighed. "If the public finds out about this accident, we might as well shut shop again. So soon after we opened!"

"So you believe it was an accident?" asked Julia.

"Leave that to us police agents to determine, Fräulein Wolf," said Loibl next to her. "You're here to take the photos." He turned to Knauer. "Who's the dead man?"

"A young assistant keeper, Stefan Moser, not yet twenty. We've informed his family." Knauer dabbed his forehead with a handkerchief. "Terribly tragic, truly."

Meanwhile, they had reached a wide gravel path that was cordoned off with a ribbon. A warden was standing guard. A sign dangling on the ribbon read that the lion enclosure was under renovation.

Loibl gave a dry laugh. "Renovation? One day after opening? Who's supposed to believe that?"

"All the more important that we can reopen this part as soon as possible." Knauer nodded at the warden and slipped under the ribbon.

Together they entered a large pavilion that imitated an Indian pagoda. Inside, a semicircular arena was surrounded by stone seats, and in the center stood an enclosure about twelve feet high and just as wide. The back wall of the cage was designed as a rock wall, and logs and boulders lay on the ground.

Julia could see the pool of blood between the rocks immediately.

"Where is the body?" asked Loibl.

"The hearse came an hour ago and took it," replied Knauer. "We wished to spare the men the sight. And—"

"You wished to spare the men the sight? Why the hell are we here, then?" Loibl kicked the metal bars hard, causing a loud clatter. "To mop up the blood? Didn't anyone tell you that you mustn't touch a possible crime scene?"

"I'm sorry, I . . . uh, didn't know. But what was there to see? I mean, the poor boy was . . ." Knauer hesitated. "Well, there wasn't much left of him. If you know what I mean."

Loibl said nothing, casting his eye across the enclosure. "Now, what makes you think it may not have been an accident?" he asked eventually.

"It's not me who thinks so, but one of my chief keepers, Eugen Lenz. He's one of our most experienced men and responsible for the predators, including Nathan."

"Nathan?" Loibl frowned.

"The lion. Well, Herr Lenz, he . . . he has a suspicion."

"A suspicion, I see. Then Herr Lenz better get here pronto to tell us about his suspicion before we waste much more of our time."

"He was meant to be here . . . Herr Lenz!" Director Knauer held his hands to his mouth like a funnel, his voice echoing through the pagoda. "Herr Lenz! Are you there?"

There was a creaking and squeaking, and a concealed vertical sliding door lifted at the rear of the enclosure. Out stepped a short, emaciated-looking man carrying a mop and bucket, eyeballing them suspiciously. His thinning black hair was combed to the side. His mustache reminded Julia of a hairy caterpillar.

"Herr Lenz, the police are here," said Knauer. "Please tell them what it is you noticed. I would like to point out that I still believe it was an accident. But Herr Lenz insists."

The keeper walked with a hunched back, dragging his feet, and unlocked a gate on the side of the enclosure. "Come in, then," he said sullenly. "But don't walk all through the blood. I've yet to clean up. Poor Nathan!"

"Poor Nathan?" Julia stepped into the enclosure with her case, trying not to picture what had happened here last night. The pool of blood, which had begun to dry, glimmered in the light of the morning sun that slanted in through the greenish windows in the roof. "Don't you mean the poor lad that was killed by the lion?"

"Yes, him too, of course." Eugen Lenz slumped over to the blood. "Stefan was a good lad. It was his first time working as an animal keeper. He was a handsome, friendly sort of fellow, reliable. Now they're both gone. Stefan and Nathan. What a waste!"

Dr. Knauer cleared his throat. "We were forced to shoot Nathan. You understand, following an incident like this . . . We took him straight to animal carcass processing."

"Wonderful," said Loibl gruffly. "Victim and murderer are dead and both corpses gone. Again, I ask what we're supposed to investigate here."

"What makes you think it was murder?" Julia asked the keeper.

"Well, Stefan was highly reliable! And he wasn't stupid. He'd never have left the gate open—in fact, you can't leave it open. Come here, I'll show you."

Eugen Lenz walked to the sliding door in the rock wall, which, upon closer inspection, turned out to be made of gypsum. Julia noticed a pulley system that moved the door up and down. On the other side, a small room reeked disgustingly of rotting meat. A cloud of flies buzzed around some large bones that had been chewed clean—presumably a cow or sheep. At the back of the room, another small door led outside.

"This is the feeding room," Lenz explained. He pointed at a chain next to the sliding door. "It's locked during visiting hours. The keeper enters it through the small door at the back, tosses half a mutton inside, goes back out, locks up, and opens the sliding door to the enclosure from outside." The keeper pointed at the heavy padlock installed on the outside of the enclosure which prevented the chain of the pulley system from being able to move. "Nathan goes into the feeding room, the sliding door shuts, and the keeper can clean out front. It's a very safe system."

"Only this time, the sliding door was open," guessed Julia.

"Listen, there's no way anyone could be this stupid. We shut the door every single time! The only way I can imagine this happening is if someone opened the sliding door from the outside while the keeper was inside the enclosure out front."

"So, you're suggesting, the boy locks the lion in at the back, cleans the front enclosure, and then someone opens the sliding door from the outside. Hmm . . ." Loibl thought for a moment. "Don't you need a key to pull the chain? The lock looks pretty solid."

"Well." Lenz seemed embarrassed. "We sometimes leave the key in the lock. I mean, who would expect a dirty bastard to come along and open the gate? It was after the zoo was closed—no visitors were left in here."

"And where is the key now?" asked Loibl.

"Uh, we haven't been able to find it," confessed director Knauer. "It's strange. It wasn't in the lock."

"And you believe you know who messed with the door?" asked Julia, looking again at Eugen Lenz.

"Of course." The warden nodded with conviction. "I believe it was the African chieftain."

"Beg your pardon?" Loibl raised an eyebrow. "Are you drunk or something?"

Dr. Knauer took a step forward. "Uh, I believe Herr Lenz is referring to chief Saidrovuni. We currently host an ethnic show here at the zoo. Africa expert Dr. Meyer was kind enough to lend us representatives from a Matabele tribe. Natives of East Africa. Saidrovuni is their leader."

"And why would this Saidro-what's-his-name want to kill a young keeper?" asked Loibl. He scratched his head. The whole affair was turning out to be more complicated than expected.

"I don't think he meant to." Keeper Lenz lowered his voice conspiratorially. "I don't think he wanted to nail Stefan but me! That black feller and me, we had beef."

"The two of them had a bad argument a few days ago," explained director Knauer. "I was called in. Herr Lenz said a few ugly things."

"He's a heathen and he acts as if he's the emperor!" exclaimed Lenz indignantly. "He demanded better conditions for his people when they're already being treated much better than they deserve. Please! They aren't even proper humans—"

"Herr Lenz, mind yourself!" snapped Dr. Knauer. "Of course they're humans. Wild ones, perhaps, but nonetheless God's children, like you and me."

"Either way," growled Lenz. "That feral one stirred trouble, and so I told him just what I thought of him, nothing terrible. But the feller blew his lid straightaway, yelling and screaming at me in his tongue . . . Sounded just like a curse, I swear, like a curse!"

"And you believe this chief mixed up Stefan with you?" asked Loibl skeptically. "How so? A young lad and you . . ."

"Listen, man, I'm not that old! Besides, we always feed the lions after sundown. It was dark. And who else could have done it? There was no one else left in the zoo apart from the Africans. It wasn't a monkey!"

Julia frowned. "They live here?"

"They do." Knauer nodded. "In their huts in the show arena, just like back in their homeland."

Like animals, thought Julia.

"Well, then we better pay this chief Saidro-thingy a visit," said Loibl. He turned to Julia. "I guess you won't be taking any photographs here, am I right?" He grunted. "What of? An empty enclosure?"

Julia said nothing. In a way she was glad the body had been removed. Two mangled young men in three days was too much.

"You can take pictures of those savages and sell them to the papers. They like things like that. Impressions of exotic lands." Loibl ran his fingers over his walrus mustache and strode ahead. "Well, let's go catch ourselves some Hottentots."

JULIA AND LOIBL LEFT THE LION ENCLOSURE TOGETHER WITH keeper Lenz and director Knauer. After following a narrow path, they arrived at an aviary as tall as a house. Nets enclosed large areas that were filled with the chirping, cooing, whistling, and trilling of exotic birds. Julia spotted red and blue parrots, tiny hummingbirds, and mangy-looking vultures that sat hunched on branches or picked at unrecognizable cadavers. There was an intense tang of rot and damp—how Julia imagined the jungle. Only the marching music drifting over from a brass band in Prater park didn't fit the scene.

Director Knauer led them past the crowd of visitors, through a tunnel of nets that opened onto a wide square strewn with dirt and sawdust. Tiny monkeys climbed along nets stretched very high up, and birds screeched as they chased through the greenery. Like the lion's arena, this area too was surrounded by seating, except there was enough space here to hold several hundred spectators.

"Our ethnic show arena," said Friedrich Knauer, visibly proud. "The heart of Vienna's new zoological garden. There's no other construction like it in Europe!" He motioned at the middle of the arena, where around a dozen sad little huts had been erected, roughly cast with clay and covered with reeds. A group of dark-skinned children dressed in loincloths were playing with a small shaggy dog. A fire smoldered in the square's center, with a few women with green headscarves seated around it, stirring something in wooden bowls. Some of the women were singing a foreign tune.

"A traditional village of the Matabele," declared the zoo director. "We built a detailed replica."

When the children spotted the visitors, they ran to their mothers, screaming. The women scrambled to their feet and vanished into the huts with their children.

"Why do they run from us?" asked Loibl. "Do they have something to hide?"

"It's their day off. The opening yesterday was incredibly busy. It was one performance after the other." Knauer shook his head. "Vienna is crazy about our Matabele. They perform song and dance, and the men display their skills in combat. In the fight against the English, the Matabele proved worthy adversaries, even if they lost the war against us civilized nations in the end. They're nimble and strong, and they can perform amazing tricks."

"You speak as though they are animals," murmured Julia quietly. She thought it disgusting how they were being put on display here. Director Knauer seemed to catch something of her dismay.

"These people are here of their own free will," he explained. "There are fixed rest times, contracts . . . Africa expert Dr. Meyer put this troupe together for us. After Vienna, they will go to Berlin, then Hamburg, and then back home by ship." Nodding to himself, Knauer gazed at the display with a dreamy look. "There's so much we can learn from these wild people. They radiate an almost paradisial innocence, don't you think? This is how it must have been in the Garden of Eden."

"But there the lions slept next to the lamb. These days the lions eat their keepers," said Loibl. "Where's this chief?"

Keeper Lenz gave a jeering laugh. "I bet he's lazing around somewhere, making his wives work for him. Those heathens are allowed to keep more than—"

"That's quite enough, all right?" snapped the director, cutting Lenz off. "It's hardly surprising if Herr Saidrovuni dislikes you! You just focus on looking after our predators, Lenz, that's what you're good at. Leave the Matabele be!"

Lenz, clearly taken aback by the director's angry outburst, said nothing.

Knauer turned to Loibl and Julia. "We are going to pay the chief a friendly visit. Friendly!" He glared at Lenz sharply. "No more rude comments, yes? Follow me, please."

Together they walked up to the huts. The doorways were hung with hides behind which they could hear murmurs, singing, and the crying of young children. Friedrich Knauer approached the biggest hut and stopped outside it.

"Herr Saidrovuni," he said loudly. "It's me, Friedrich Carl Knauer, the director. May we speak with you a moment?"

"Do these people speak our language?" asked Loibl quietly.

"Well, I suppose a parrot can learn all sorts," whispered Lenz, too softly for Knauer to hear.

After a few moments a tall, slender man emerged from the doorway. He wore a loincloth. Green bird feathers were braided into his shoulder-length hair. It took Julia a moment to realize that the headpiece was a wig, probably made from horsehair. Julia had expected an old man, a gray man, but chief Saidrovuni was very young, not quite thirty. He was tall and muscular, towering over the director by at least a head. He glanced at Eugen Lenz and an angry furrow formed on his forehead. Julia noticed his fists clench. Then his expression cleared and he looked at Knauer.

"Herr Director, how may I help?" Saidrovuni spoke with a foreign accent, but his German was good. Julia wondered how long it would take her to learn the tongue of the Matabele.

"Well, uh, you may have heard. There's been an accident."

Saidrovuni nodded. "The young keeper, yes. We heard. Very sad."

"Huh, sad!" snarled Eugen Lenz, hiding behind the director. "The lion was supposed to eat *me*. Admit that it was you who pulled up the door!"

The chief didn't respond, merely looked at the director.

"I'm from the police, do you understand me?" said Loibl then. "There is a suggestion that you wanted to take revenge on keeper Lenz. You argued, is that correct?"

"That man said bad things about us. He refused to give us our food."

"What a load of bollocks!" protested Lenz. "Müller has been off sick for a while, and so it was my turn to bring them their lunch that day. Pork sausages in a bread roll with mustard and cabbage. There's no better food on this earth!"

Julia gave Lenz an incredulous look. "You brought them sausages? Why not a pint of beer to go with it?"

"I was in a hurry, so I sent for something from the Wurstelprater. It's cheap and there's always lots of it. Those lads eat like hippos." Lenz gave a shrug. "But the food wasn't good enough for Herr Chief here."

"A misunderstanding," said director Knauer. "Normally the Matabele receive potatoes, vegetables, grain porridge, beef, things like that. But Müller has been ill for a while now, and Herr Lenz helped out. I'm sure it won't happen again."

"He said bad things," repeated Saidrovuni stoically. "We cannot forgive."

"Huh, there you have it!" cried Lenz. "First he cursed me, and then he tried to get the lion to eat me!"

"Jesus Christ, won't you all shut up for a moment!" Loibl was visibly struggling with the situation. He took a step forward. "First of all we'll search this here hut."

"Hoping to find what?" asked Julia, a mocking note in her voice. "A handwritten confession?"

Loibl gave her a furious stare before turning to Saidrovuni. "Step aside!"

The chief didn't budge.

"Step aside, I said!" repeated Loibl.

When Saidrovuni still didn't move, Loibl barged past him. With an apologetic shrug, Julia followed him, and Knauer and Lenz did too.

The hut's interior surprised Julia. There was a fireplace in its center, and seated near it were two women. The younger of the two cradled an infant, and both of them stared fearfully at the intruders. The rest of the furnishings were rather European, with a stained mirror propped on a shelf in the corner, and a clothes rack, holding three pocket watches dangling from silver chains, among other things. Further, there were two large travel trunks bearing labels from various train and shipping companies. It was as if the space was trapped between two worlds.

"What's in there?" demanded inspector Loibl, gesturing at one of the trunks.

When Saidrovuni said nothing, Loibl started rummaging through the chest. He pulled out items of clothing, many of which also looked European: linen pants, skirts, a few wide shirts. When he couldn't find anything suspicious, Loibl opened the other chest. He paused, astonished.

"What do we have here?" He lifted out a blue visored cap of the kind the zookeepers wore. A few thin black hairs hung off it.

"My cap!" exclaimed Lenz. "I don't believe it—I've been looking for that for days. The bastard's got my cap!"

"More interesting is what lay under the cap." Loibl's fingers played with a key ring. The inspector shot a questioning look at Knauer. "Is this the key to the lion enclosure?"

Director Friedrich Carl Knauer's mouth gaped. "It . . . it is!" he managed eventually. "Good God, it is." He turned to Saidrovuni. "Do you have an explanation for this?"

Still Saidrovuni said nothing, his muscular arms crossed on his chest. The women inside the hut started to wail; the baby cried.

"Well, it looks like we have our culprit." Loibl turned to Julia. "Fräulein Wolf, let's call the Green Henry and lock this fellow up. Should be a quick trial. The case is solved."

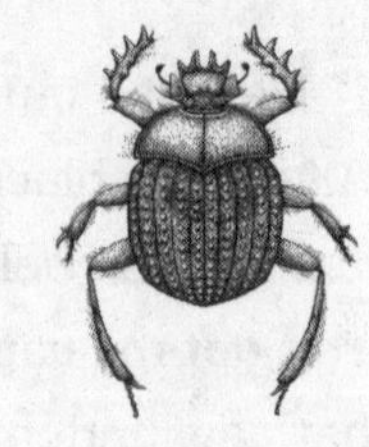

CHAPTER 6

From *Death Rites Around the World,* by Augustin Rothmayer, written in Vienna, 1894

> One of the most bizarre funeral rituals we know of comes from the East Indies. The Toraja mountain people embalm their dead but fetch them out from their coffins every three years. The corpses get washed, combed, dressed in new clothes, and are permitted to spend ten days partaking in the everyday life of the living. There is competition among the families as to whose corpse looks the freshest. This way, folk get to meet their great-great-grandfather or their great-grandmother, almost as if they were sitting at the table together. Only once the bodies begin to fall apart are they left in their coffins.

Walking through the large door of Vienna University, Leo felt as though he'd time traveled into his past. Students walked toward him, laughing, their hands full of stacks of books, some of them reading even as they walked. It was busy even though it was Whitmonday. The "Alma Mater Rudolfina," one of Europe's oldest universities, was exclusively for young men. Women were not permitted at Vienna University. In this regard, France, England, and even Switzerland were ahead of Austria!

During the morning, Leo had tried to gather some information about Professor Walter Kerfeld. There was nothing in the police files, but Kerfeld did have a telephone number in the ninth district; however, there was no answer. Leo suspected he was at work at the university even though it was a holiday. And so Leo had walked over from headquarters. But once he arrived, everything became a little difficult. The porter explained to him that much of the faculty were housed elsewhere. Egyptologists were part of the classics department, which in turn belonged to philosophy. Once he'd asked his way there, Leo was told that Professor Kerfeld currently worked in the university library, which was back in the main building. Running from place to place and back again, Leo cursed under his breath. How small and cozy Graz University had been!

When at last he arrived at the large university library on the second floor, his feet ached. He entered the hall, a temple of knowledge that reminded him of the Rapoldys' library, only on a much larger scale. The space was two stories high with columns, a milky glass ceiling, and pompous stucco. Students sat hunched over their books at the many tables under low-hanging gas lamps. Leo sought out one of the librarians shuffling along the shelves of books, balancing a stack of books in his arms. He wore sleeve protectors and his face was an unhealthy shade of gray.

"Excuse me, I'm looking for—" began Leo. The librarian shot him an angry look and Leo realized he was speaking too loudly.

"I'm looking for Professor Walter Kerfeld," Leo whispered.

"The Egyptologist?" The librarian studied him sternly, presumably struggling to categorize Leo. He seemed too old to be a student and too young to be a teacher. "Try room III A, where the classical works are kept."

"And where's that?"

His hands still clutching the books, the librarian nodded his head in the right direction. Leo thanked him quietly and walked over to the smaller adjoining hall, which was much emptier than the main room. Only a handful of students occupied the tables, and an ancient grandfather clock ticked in one of the corners. A gaunt older man stood at one of the bookshelves with his back to Leo, his hair long and gray, tousled like a lion's mane. Leo walked up to him and cleared his throat.

"Herr Professor Walter Kerfeld?" he asked, trying his luck.

"Who wants to know?" The man didn't even turn. "If you have a question about the oral exam, come see me during my office hours," he continued in a melodious Viennese accent.

"Inspector Leopold Herzfeld from the Vienna Security Bureau," said Leo, introducing himself. "I have a few questions."

"If I am in fact Professor Kerfeld." The man still had his back to him. He pulled a book from the shelf and opened it. "The question hasn't yet been answered, the proof not provided. *Quod erat demonstrandum.*"

"Well, are you or aren't you?" asked Leo with slight annoyance. The man was infuriating.

"Of course I am! What kind of a question is that?" The man returned the book to the shelf and turned around. He wore a pince-nez, and had bushy eyebrows and an absurdly large mustache. With his stained jacket and stiff upright collar, he looked a little like Friedrich Nietzsche, that mad German philosopher who was fashionable in scholarly circles at the moment.

"What do you want from me?" asked Professor Kerfeld. "Not a final grade, I presume. You look too old for that."

"I would like to talk to you about your dear colleague Professor Alfons Strössner."

"Strössner?" The bushy eyebrows went up, and Leo watched closely, looking for any emotion in Kerfeld's face. Had he glimpsed a nervous twitch behind the eyeglasses? "What business of mine is Strössner?"

"What I want to talk about is better discussed in private," said Leo. "Is there anywhere we can go?"

Kerfeld didn't respond at first, and Leo half thought the professor would simply turn around and march off. But then he nodded. "Let's go to the map room. We'll be undisturbed there. Come."

Leo followed Kerfled through a smaller side door into another room, musty with hundreds of rolled up maps piled on its shelves. More maps lay open on a table in the center. Leo noticed that they were old maps of Egypt, with a blue ribbon clearly recognizable as the Nile. He also spotted the ancient cities of Memphis and Thebes. Kerfeld pushed the maps aside and they sat down opposite each other.

"What about Alfons Strössner?" asked Walter Kerfeld. "I thought he was still in Egypt. That's what I heard, at least."

"Your colleague is dead. I thought you might like to know."

Leo studied Kerfeld's expression, but the professor stared at him blankly. "What happened?" he asked after a few moments.

"It's . . . well, bizarre. Please keep the following details to yourself for the time being." Leo told the man what had happened, and still there was no emotion showing in Kerfeld's face, as if it were perfectly normal that his colleague and competitor should suddenly turn up as an embalmed mummy at the Museum of Art History. "We have no leads yet. We're not even sure how exactly Strössner died. When was the last time you saw your colleague?"

Professor Kerfeld twirled his enormous mustache. "You think I have something to do with it?"

"We have to follow up on everything. So, when was the last time you saw him?"

Kerfeld thought. "Must have been about three months ago. Yes, in February. At the palace of His Excellency the Archduke Rainer. Shortly before he up and left back to Egypt."

"Archduke Rainer?" This gave Leo pause. Chief inspector Leinkirchner had also mentioned a connection between the Strössner family and the archduke. "You were invited at the home of a member of the imperial family?"

"Not just me and Strössner—the entire committee of the Vienna Archaeological Society. His Excellency has an avid interest in Egyptology. Several years ago, the archduke made it possible for us to purchase a large number of papyrus scrolls from the city of Faiyum. It is likely to be the most significant papyrus collection in the world."

"So, you were invited at the archduke's," said Leo, trying to get back on topic.

"Yes, the whole committee. That is, Strössner, myself, the Rapoldys, Dr. Alexander Dedekind from the Museum of Art History—"

"I hear that Professor Hofmann from the forensic institute is also a member of this illustrious circle?" said Leo, interrupting the man.

Kerfeld gave a thin smile. "You're well informed, inspector. We are indeed a rather distinguished group."

And a rather secretive one, too, thought Leo. He wondered who else might be a member of this exclusive society. "So, Strössner left for Egypt soon after this reception," he continued. "Did he mention his intended departure at this last gathering?"

"No! I was as surprised as everyone else when he left so suddenly. Not a word. Nor about what he intended to do there."

"Was Strössner acting strange at all during this last meeting?"

"Why should he have?" Kerfeld shook his head. His long hair rustled, and Leo noticed the man's old suit jacket was covered in dandruff. "Alfons was just as self-righteous and full of himself as ever. Perhaps even a little worse than usual. After all, the archduke personally bestowed upon him the curation of the Egyptian donation."

"Something you coveted," observed Leo.

"Who wouldn't? The findings of Deir al-Bahari are the greatest archaeological gift this country has ever received. Cataloging it and conceptualizing an exhibition from it is an honor for any scholar. And the archduke yet again picked the loudest of us." Kerfeld's lips pressed into a thin line. "Yet again."

"I hear you would also have liked to been in charge of the expedition," Leo went on, probing.

Professor Kerfeld hesitated, then waved his hand dismissively. "Listen, Herr Inspector, there's no point beating around the bush. Alfons Strössner and myself couldn't stand each other. He's from a wealthy family with connections all the way up. I, on the other hand, am from the village of Klagenfurt, the son of a teacher. But when it comes to qualifications, I don't need to hide my light under a bushel. On the contrary!"

"I presume you've heard of Father Gregor Mayr's passing in Graz." Leo leaned forward over the maps, studying Kerfeld closely. "What happened in Egypt?"

"Well, I'm sure the Rapoldys already told you."

"I want to hear it from you, professor," replied Leo.

Kerfeld took his time with his reply. "We shouldn't have done it," he said at last. "I still despise myself for partaking as well. It was a crime."

"You mean the theft of the mummy," clarified Leo.

Kerfeld nodded. "Following the find of the second cache, the Egyptians made it very clear that while they were happy to give various treasures to the museums of the world, the mummies were out of bounds. But Strössner was of the opinion that Ta-bek-en-chon was his mummy." Kerfeld laughed. "His! As if a dead person could be owned like a house or a bond. Fine, he found it, in some remote valley where he got lost. But that didn't give him the right. That mummy was in a solo tomb far away from the other tombs. Alfons was besotted with it! He kept examining it, even when we were back in Vienna. And then, at the archduke's reception . . ." He trailed off.

"What is it?" asked Leo.

"Nothing." Kerfeld shook his head. "My guess is that Alfons returned to Egypt because of Ta-bek-en-chon. Whatever happened there or why he turned up at the museum as a mummy—I can't tell you anything about that."

"Professor Alfons Strössner isn't the only one of your party who died unexpectedly."

"You're insinuating that it's a strange coincidence that three out of four members of our expedition are no longer alive." Kerfeld paused. He seemed to consider something. "Dr. Adolf Landinger died of a fever in Egypt. Such things happen in hot climates, and Landinger was no longer young. And Father Gregor Mayr—"

"Suffered a heart attack, I know," said Leo, cutting him off. "We're already looking into it. Still, I'd like to know more about what exactly happened in Egypt two years ago. Did you argue? Maybe because you disagreed with the theft of the mummy? Or was there something else?"

"Researchers bicker worse than quarrelsome wives." Kerfeld's eyes came to rest on the map on the table, as if he were traveling back to Egypt in his mind's eye.

Both men were silent for a while.

"Have you ever wondered where all the money came from, that of the posh Strössners and Rapoldys?" asked Walter Kerfeld eventually. "It is assumed that back in Deir al-Bahari, a number of finds went missing, not just the one mummy. And earlier, too, it was not uncommon for precious items to be slipped to dealers of stolen goods. Gold masks, jewels, scarabs . . . Many such items land in the villas of wealthy Europeans."

"Are you suggesting Alfons Strössner grew rich from the treasures of pharaohs?"

Professor Walter Kerfeld smiled an evil smile, and for a moment he looked like an emaciated mummy himself. "That's what you said, inspector. All I'm saying is, if there really were a curse, then it found just the right victim with Alfons Strössner."

"Aren't you afraid the curse might strike you, too?" asked Leo. "You're the last surviving member of the group."

"To be honest, I fear something entirely different. And now excuse me, Herr Inspector. My students are waiting." With that, Walter Kerfeld rose and left Leo alone in the dank room. Amid all the maps, Leo felt a little as if he were in a tomb.

SEVERAL HOURS AND TWO GLASSES OF ABSINTHE LATER, FOR the first time that day Leo was able to forget about work. It was past nine in the evening, and he was enveloped by the warm tones of a slightly out-of-tune piano. With relish he smoked one of his beloved Yenidzes, feeling the tension slowly fall away from him. Tired, he stretched out his legs and leaned back in his chair, watching Julia, who stood leaning against the piano, perform a French chanson. It was a mystery to him how she could sing perfectly in French, Italian, and Spanish without being able to speak the languages whatsoever. He, on the other hand, was also fluent in English and French, but singing? He couldn't even do that in German.

They were at a cavernous cellar bar not far from the Blue Dragoon. Big Elli owned both establishments, the brothel and the bar, the latter being a typical dance and entertainment nightclub. At the end of the night, the ladies would take their punters over to the brothel, and Elli reaped the rewards twice over. Several times a week

Julia sang here until late. It didn't pay much, but singing and dancing were her great passions. Leo knew they were her original reason for coming to Vienna: she'd dreamed of a career as a singer.

And now she takes pictures of murder victims, thought Leo.

Well, it could have been worse. Most girls who washed up in Vienna with big dreams ended up working as maidservants for a pittance or earned their living as prostitutes. Or they ended up as the pitiful creatures Julia photographed.

Un fiacre allait, trottinant . . . Derrière les stores baissés, on entendait des baisers . . .

Julia's smoky voice still aroused Leo every time. He cast jealous looks at the other men in the bar, who stared with lustful eyes at the singer in the tight blue dress and the fur stole. This was precisely why Leo didn't like Julia singing here. He avoided coming on the nights when she sang. Tonight was meant to be her night off, but some of the regulars had begged her to sing a song regardless, and she'd agreed. Leo felt that she hadn't tried very hard to say no. Maybe the performance was distracting her from the events of the last few days. Julia had been telling him about the zoo incident when the customers demanded a song.

The music ended, the guests applauded, and Julia returned to his table. She motioned at his empty glass. "Looks like you needed it today."

"Maybe I need it to enjoy my evening here," Leo retorted.

"What do you mean?"

He was about to make a nasty reply but stopped himself, waving a hand. "It's been a long day," he groaned instead.

He felt as if he'd worked a double shift. Following his conversation with Professor Kerfeld at the university library, he'd returned to police headquarters, where Leinkirchner had assailed him with questions. It seemed to Leo that the chief inspector would have liked to arrest Kerfeld straightaway as the main suspect. But what did they actually have against him? Nothing more than a weak motive. They didn't even have a time at which the crime was committed, nothing to compare an alibi with. But Leinkirchner was eager for results.

Leo had made no progress in Graz, either. Because Father Gregor Mayr's official cause of death was a heart attack, the case hadn't been investigated by the police. Leo had telephoned every Graz hospital into the evening, trying to get ahold of the doctor who issued the death certificate, but he hadn't made it past the receptionists. As if a mummy in Vienna weren't enough, he'd had to contend with Graz hospital bureaucracy!

"Professor Kerfeld is an odd fellow. I struggled to read him," said Leo, telling Julia about this afternoon's trip to the university. "He didn't try to hide his dislike for Strössner and the Rapoldys." He sipped on his absinthe, tasting aniseed and herbs. "And then his suggestion that Strössner might be responsible for the theft of countless antique treasures—though I do have to admit that there's a ton of money in Villa Thebes. I don't want to know where all those sculptures in the garden alone come from. Does Charlotte Rapoldy get them from some antiques markets?"

"You seem to be quite taken with Charlotte Rapoldy," observed Julia dryly.

He frowned. "What makes you think that?"

"A woman can tell. The two of you seemed to get on swimmingly." She gave a wan smile. "Let's leave it." They sat in silence, drinking and smoking.

"What sort of priest's mummy was it that fascinated Strössner so much again?" asked Julia eventually. "Maybe you should look into that some more."

"The Ta-bek-en-chon that the Rapoldys mentioned. What a weird name! Remember, Clemens Rapoldy said he was a priest of some Egyptian god of magic. There was nothing about him in

Strössner's papers." Leo gave a bark of laughter. "If I didn't know better, I might think Ta-bek-en-chon was responsible for the three deaths. As revenge for tearing him from his grave and shipping him to cold Vienna."

"And now he haunts the city." Julia grinned. "You're seeing ghosts."

Leo turned serious. "Kerfeld mentioned at the end that he was afraid of something. I wonder what it is?"

"Let's leave the mummies to rest in peace for a while." She stood up. "Before you order your third glass of absinthe and can't walk in a straight line, I'd like you to dance with me."

Leo raised his hands defensively. "Julia, please! I've had a long day . . ."

"Don't be like that. Or else I'll ask one of those handsome boys from the next table." Julia nodded her head in the direction of a corner table where three young students whispered and quite obviously blushed.

"Julia Wolf, every undergraduate's wet dream," sighed Leo. "Very well, before you run off with a first-year medicine student."

"If he's a better dancer . . ." She winked at him. Then she turned to the old pianist. "Alfredo, please play us the tango. You know, the one from Paris."

The pianist began to play a sad, slightly abrupt melody, a wistful greeting from a distant, warmer world. Leo knew this style of dance was also called tango. Alfredo had brought this style from Argentina, where it was controversial on account of being considered indecent. Julia loved the tango! She'd taught him the steps. They pressed their bodies as closely together as if they were one. Julia's legs wrapped around his and she threw back her head. It was like an amorous wrestling, a kind of foreplay that went on forever.

The melody carried them both away. Leo barely noticed the other dancers—for him, there was only him and Julia. When they danced the tango, they were closer than ever, and all those things that stood between them were forgotten, at least for a few minutes.

The melody ebbed like a wave on the shore, and the piano player started a slow waltz. They spun in circles, the spell broken, but they were still close. Julia suddenly struck Leo as very earnest and sad, and a little distracted.

"What is it?" he asked.

"This young chief, Saidrovuni, at the zoo today," she said. "For some reason I can't believe that he really murdered that boy."

"But he didn't want to kill the young keeper, but the old one," said Leo as they continued to sway to the music. "And that one is, by the sound of it, a real asshole. All the evidence is against your chief. He had motive and they found the keys to the lion enclosure in his hut."

"But what about the cap that Lenz supposedly lost? And then the body was taken away and the lion shot, as if they were trying to destroy evidence! It all seems too convenient to me. You should have seen Saidrovuni, Leo! His direct, honest eyes . . ."

"Oho, the noble heathen!" Leo smiled. "Don't you think you're being a little too romantic?"

"Loibl had him taken straight to the prison," said Julia, ignoring Leo's jest. "The women and children cried . . ." She suddenly tore herself free, dropped heavily onto a chair, and helped herself to one of Leo's cigarettes. She stared into thin air with empty eyes, still flushed from dancing.

Leo sat down with her and lit her cigarette.

She drew hard and exhaled the smoke. "They keep them like animals," she said after a few moments. "Like animals! The director, that Knauer man, calls it an ethnic show. But it basically is no different than people gaping at zebras or elephants. Like . . . like an animal show. It's revolting!"

"You're right," Leo conceded. He signaled the waiter and ordered two more glasses of absinthe. Pensively, he placed the sugar cubes on the absinthe spoon and poured water over them. A milky green fog spread in the glass.

"At least those cases are solid, tangible," he continued, picking up his glass and gazing into the fog. "A stabbed hustler, bloody revenge at the zoo . . . Me, on the other hand . . ."

Leo trailed off when he noticed Julia wasn't really listening. She was staring at a couple who had been dancing next to them earlier. The young woman had flipped open a small pocket mirror and was using one of those modern lipsticks to trace her lips.

Leo rolled his eyes. "Don't tell me you're going to buy into this new fashion. One day all women will be made up like theater divas and—"

"The lipstick," murmured Julia. "Now I know what it was in the picture."

Leo wasn't following. "What do you mean?"

"The dead boy in the twelfth district. He was wearing lipstick!"

"You already said. So what? The queers like it, apparently. It's the latest fashion from Paris."

"The line wasn't drawn neatly, it was fat and messy. The boy would never have done it like that himself."

Leo shrugged and picked up his glass once more. "It simply got smudged in the process."

"It wasn't smudged, Leo! Someone painted lipstick on his face afterward, and this someone didn't try particularly hard. I'm guessing they didn't have much time."

"But why would anyone do that? Why . . ." His voice trailed off and he lowered his glass. Then he answered his own question. "Because someone wanted it to *look* like a prostitution murder. The lad wasn't a hustler at all. And he was probably murdered for something unrelated. Damn, you might be right."

The piano player started another tango tune. This time it was Leo who rose and held out his hand to Julia.

"Let's dance," he said. "Before all these spooky cases ruin our night."

As they danced, Julia pressed herself close to him with her eyes closed. He could sense that in her thoughts, though, she was still with the poor dead boy with the lipstick.

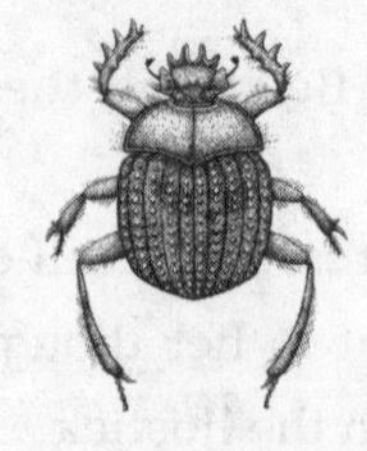

CHAPTER 7

When Leo arrived at the office the next morning, still feeling sleepy, Erich Loibl was sitting at his desk with a glass of brandy. Briefly it looked like he was going to hide the liquor, but then he raised his glass triumphantly at Leo instead.

"Cheers," said Leo. "Do we have something to celebrate?"

"I'd say so." Loibl grinned. "No murder case has been solved this quickly in a long time."

"The murdered boy from the twelfth?"

"No, not that one, unfortunately." Loibl's grin vanished and he lowered his glass. "Well, at least we know the boy's name now. He was a certain Jakob Markowitz, presumably an occasional hustler from Ottakring. He liked to hang out at the usual dives. He was just seventeen. His sister reported him missing and identified him from the crime-scene photographs."

"From Ottakring? That's the sixteenth district. What was his body doing in Meidling? The twelfth? That's a fair way."

"Maybe he was visiting a friend, or one of those underground speakeasies for the gays? I said from the start that the boy must have been poaching in the wrong patch." Loibl lifted his glass once more. "No, I'm talking about the shredded keeper at the zoo. Classic case of revenge. The murderer is a Hottentot! One of those heathens from the ethnic show."

"Oh, that case." Leo sat exhaustedly in his chair. "I heard about that."

"And I can guess who from," replied Loibl with a wink. "Out late last night? It shows." He drained his brandy in one gulp and returned the empty glass to his drawer.

The smell of the booze made Leo feel sick. His head was heavy from last night's absinthe. But at least he and Julia had spent a lovely night together, filled with gentle caresses and passionate moments. They'd danced until late and then gone back to hers. The events from the last few days, which weighed so heavily on them while they were at the nightclub, had vanished for a brief time. Sisi had been blissfully asleep. Nights like these happened much too rarely for them, not least because Big Elli didn't like Leo staying the night. He decided he would take Julia out more often, and maybe not to shabby establishments like the cellar bar. There were plenty of lovely taverns and small theaters in Vienna, more than in many other European cities. He would study the programs in the papers this very day.

In spite of or maybe because of the successful night, Leo felt exhausted. He'd come straight from Neulerchenfeld this morning, hadn't even changed his shirt, let alone shaved. He hadn't even had time for a coffee.

Erich Loibl raised a fatherly finger.

"I don't care what you get up to at night or who with, Herzfeldt. And Fräulein Wolf is a pretty little thing. But do be careful that Leinkirchner doesn't find out, or worse, the dear Lord himself, superintendent Stukart! You know his Excellency cannot abide liaisons within our house. They bring nothing but trouble." Loibl burped softly into his hand. "And I must say I do agree. Women have no business at police headquarters. It's like on a ship; they bring nothing but ill luck. And our little lamb can be bloody obstinate, as lovey as her jugs are . . ."

"How dare you!" started Leo. He was rising from his chair when Paul Leinkirchner walked into the office. Thankfully, he didn't look like he'd overheard their conversation.

"There you are, Herzfeldt," grumbled Leinkirchner. "Late enough. I came looking for you earlier." He looked Leo up and down. "What's the matter with your clothes? You don't usually look this rumpled." The chief inspector sniffed the air. "And the smell. Is that alcohol on your breath?"

Leo said nothing, and Leinkirchner turned to Loibl, who suddenly looked very busy. "Any news from the twelfth, Erich?"

"Well, I had to finish the report from the zoo. I can't do magic. And I reckon I was really rather quick with the keeper—"

"Yes, yes, I know, good work, Erich," Leinkirchner cut in. "But that was yesterday. Today we're back on the hustler murder. Our victim, Markowitz, came from Ottakring. It should be possible to find out what he was doing in Meidling, who he knew there. We need to close this one. I need every man on deck!"

"I might have something concerning that murder," said Leo. "It's about the pictures Fräulein Wolf took." He walked over to Loibl's desk, where the photographs lay in a careless pile. Some of the photos now bore fresh brandy stains and glass rings. Leo soon found the picture Julia had been speaking of.

"Look at the lipstick." He held the photograph up to Leinkirchner, pointing at the dead boy's face. "Not a neat line—a child could do a better job. It looks as if the lipstick was applied later, after his death, and in a rush. It's possible the boy was made to look like a hustler to divert our attention from the real motive?"

"Afterward?" Leinkirchner gave a grunt. "How can you judge that, Herzfeldt? Are you wearing lipstick and women's dresses these days?"

Leo hesitated. Leinkirchner was right. As a man, he was in no position to make these calls. "Fräulein Wolf told me," he said eventually. "I met her briefly last night. She felt quite certain about this. And it's still strange that his penis and testicles were nowhere to be found."

"Wolf again," growled Loibl from his seat. "She was causing me trouble yesterday, too. I think Wolf has been shooting off her mouth too much lately. She's sticking her nose in where it don't belong. I don't stick my nose in other people's business—or at least not until now." He shot Leo a look of warning.

"Fräulein Wolf is a photographer here and nothing else," said Leinkirchner. "I agree with Erich. She needs to keep out of police investigations. If it were up to me, we'd do without all the photographic nonsense. Our archives are already bursting at the seams. What did God give us two eyes for? But that's not why I came." He handed the picture back to Leo. "I want you to go over to the forensic institute, Herzfeldt. Professor Hofmann called earlier. He's finished examining the dead hustler. And someone else, too," he added under his breath, so that Loibl wouldn't hear. He gave Leo an intent look.

"Understood." Leo nodded. "I'll be on my way."

"If you come past a tap, hold your head under," suggested Leinkirchner, his voice loud again. "You look like you've been swallowed and spat back up. And don't vomit onto the corpse."

"Thanks for the advice," muttered Leo.

Behind them, Loibl gave a cough. "Shouldn't I go with him, Paul? I mean, it's my case, and—"

"He can handle it. I want you to find out what our victim was doing in Meidling. I'll expect a report by tonight." Leinkirchner wrinkled his nose with disgust. "And for heaven's sake, open the window! It stinks like a distillery in here."

WHEN LEO, A SHORT WHILE LATER, TURNED ONTO LAZARETT Lane, he felt much better. He'd bought a pastry at one of the many stalls and a bitter coffee to go with it, which the grim-faced proprietor had poured from a steaming tin pot. He had also combed his hair and fixed his collar as best as he could.

As he slurped the hot coffee, Leo reminded himself that Leinkirchner wasn't sending him to the institute so much because of the hustler boy, but because of Strössner's mummy. Word of the eerie incident mustn't get out, hence Leinkirchner's secretive behavior at the office. Presumably, Hofmann had called up superintendent Stukart directly to let him know that Strössner's autopsy was completed. Did Erich Lobl notice that Leinkirchner hadn't sent him along on purpose? Leo grinned. Most likely, Loibl was glad he could stay at the office with his brandy while someone else did the dirty work.

At the entrance to the institute, Leo spotted a familiar couple—the Rapoldys. Luckily they hadn't seen him yet. He spontaneously decided to cross the street to watch them for a bit. He guessed they had just visited Professor Hofmann to identify the body. From the corner of his eye, Leo watched the couple pick their way through the many pedestrians, carriages, and handcarts. Unlike at the villa, Charlotte Rapoldy wore shoes today, and a more typical costume instead of a shapeless dress.

Leo recalled how Julia had claimed he liked Charlotte the night before. He couldn't deny that he found the tall, elegant woman fascinating. She really did remind him of Cleopatra; even her expressive nose fit the picture. Now, it was obvious that she was crying. Her husband, dressed again in a light-colored, slightly crumpled summer suit, handed her a handkerchief. She wiped the tears from her pale face, and he draped an arm around her shoulder, consoling her. He, too, looked strained, leaning heavily on his walking stick.

Leo suddenly felt ratty in his role as the secret voyeur. What had he expected? They had just seen a dead relative under nightmarish conditions. Of course they were upset. Had he hoped to catch Charlotte Rapoldy as cold and unfeeling? Perhaps even as a murderess, with her husband as an accomplice? What Leo saw instead before him were two broken people.

He waited until the Rapoldys boarded a fiacre, and then crossed the street and entered the forensic institute. As always, the inside of the building smelled of different chemicals. Noisy medicine students in white laboratory coats poured out of a nearby lecture theater. In the last few months, Leo had visited almost weekly. There were always murders in Vienna, one of the biggest and most dangerous cities in Europe, and many of the victims landed on Professor Hofmann's table.

Leo walked down the familiar narrow corridor until he reached a closed door. He thought he could already smell the odor of corpses. He drew a deep breath and knocked.

"Come in, come in, if you're not an impoverished student," sang out Professor Hofmann's familiar voice.

Leo was about to use the door handle when the door opened as if by magic. Leo sighed when he saw who awaited him on the other side. On some level he'd half expected it. "Herr Rothmayer. We meet again."

As so often, the gravedigger wore his black coat, its hem crusted with dirt. At least he wasn't wearing his floppy hat, and it seemed he had shaved and washed for his visit at the institute—although Leo wasn't entirely sure whether the stench of dead bodies in the autopsy room didn't in part emanate from Rothmayer.

Augustin Rothmayer grinned widely, not abashed in the

slightest. "Herr Professor was kind enough to invite me over. Too kind—"

"After you pestered him with your questions over the telephone, no doubt," said Leo sarcastically.

"As usual, Herr Rothmayer not only has good questions but also good answers," said Professor Hofmann, who was standing at one of the three autopsy tables. He wore a white, blood-stained coat over his old-fashioned black suit. His shirt and coat sleeves were rolled up. "I told you it would pay to speak with him, inspector. Wasn't I right?"

"I'm grateful for any clues, no matter where from—even if they're from the cemetery." Leo stepped closer, his feet wading through fresh sawdust. The long room was bathed in the warm morning light streaming in through the talcum-coated windowpanes. Leo pointed at the table, where a body lay under a sheet. "Is that our mummy?"

"No, Alfons is next door. The Rapoldys have just been by to identify the body. I wanted to offer them some privacy."

"Then what's the gravedigger doing here?" asked Leo grumpily.

"Herr Rothmayer used the time to peruse my private library. You know, he's in the process of writing his new book." Hofmann turned to Augustin Rothmayer. "Did you find something useful for your research?"

"If at all possible, Herr Professor, I'd like to borrow *The New Dictionary of Technical Clinical Terms*. There's a section on burns that—"

"If the gentlemen would be so kind as to save their undoubtedly highly important conversation for later," interrupted Leo. "I still have murderers to catch today."

"Yes, forgive us, Herr Inspector. We're all busy. Speaking of murderers—" Hofmann drew aside the sheet. "This is the other body of interest to you. It came in on Saturday night, but I hadn't had a chance to examine it until now. You know how busy things are at the moment. All those gas suicides alone . . ." The professor sighed. "You're familiar with the hustler murder from the twelfth district, yes?"

"I am." Leo looked down at the body, recognizable from Julia's photographs. The boy's chest had been cut open and sewn back up, like a goose stuffed with apples. The terrible wound in the groin area was still quite obvious, as well as multiple knife wounds. The lipstick, however, had been washed off.

"It looks worse than it is," said the professor, as if they were talking about a broken watch. "At least the lad wouldn't have felt much."

"But all those stab wounds," objected Leo. "And then his. . . . uh, most sacred—"

"His most sacred, as you call them, were cut off postmortem. Penis and scrotum. A clean cut, almost as if it had been done by a doctor. I couldn't have done a neater job. Most of those stab wounds, on the other hand, are amateurish, and they did not lead to his death—they, too, were inflicted postmortem. What killed him was a single stab to the heart. Here." Hofmann pointed at a small cut right under the ribcage. "It looks as if this was the first cut, on an angle upward. A long dagger, presumably. The victim would have died instantly."

"You're saying this first stab wasn't amateurish like the rest?" asked Leo, his interest piqued.

"That's what I said. This stab was executed with high accuracy. Cardiac tamponade cuts off blood supply, leading to immediate loss of consciousness. The ancient Romans used this technique for executions."

Leo frowned. "But then why the blood bath afterward? As a diversion? Hmm . . ." He thought of the messy lipstick. Evidently, the makeup had intentionally been applied postmortem, too, just like the knife wounds.

"Answering that is the police's task," said Hofmann with a shrug. "My work here is done." He covered the body with the sheet as if closing a curtain. "Now, if you'd care to follow me next door, inspector. The other case is far more interesting."

Accompanied by Augustin Rothmayer, they moved to a smaller adjoining room that contained one single autopsy table of polished steel. There was a barred window, a few dried old flowers in a vase on the sill. A plain wooden cross hung on the wall.

"Our, uh, funeral hall," explained Hofmann. "For when relatives come. It's meant to look a little less sterile, more . . . homely."

"I'd say you hit the mark." Leo glanced at the withered roses, a petal sailing to the floor. Then his gaze turned to the mummy on the table. By daylight, the body didn't look quite as frightening; it looked more like one of those little prune men that pastry shops made for children at Christmastime. The creepy stone eyes had been removed, as well as the bandages. The body was covered with a sheet up to its waist. There was a fresh seam running up the sternum, and a long incision on the side. After a while, Leo noticed something he hadn't until then: aside from the hair on the head, there wasn't a single hair on the body. The corpse was as smooth as paper.

"The embalming techniques of ancient Egypt are truly fascinating," said Professor Hofmann enthusiastically. He turned to Rothmayer. "Wouldn't you agree? The technique used here corresponds exactly to what Herodotus described around 500 BC! The body is dehaired, the brain removed through the left nostril. Through a five-inch cut in the side, the inner organs are removed. Only the heart is returned later."

"The heart is returned?" asked Leo, surprised.

"To the Egyptian, the heart is the soul," said Rothmayer from his spot in the background, hovering like a living shadow. "The dead person needs it at the entrance to the realm of the dead because it gets weighed there. If the heart is heavier than a feather, the journey comes to an abrupt end. Then the big devouress comes, with her crocodile head and lion's rump, and gobbles up the poor sinner hide and hair."

"The great devouress, I see . . . quite the graphic image of the afterlife," said Leo, unsurprised at the gravedigger's knowledge of Egyptian mythology. He'd known Augustin Rothmayer long enough. Death was his hobbyhorse, no matter the millennium.

"No more graphic than judgment day, after which sinners face the worst tortures and a hell with nine circles that comes with boiling oil and stabbing devils," observed Professor Hofmann. "You wouldn't believe how much of ancient Egyptian mythology is contained in our oh-so-enlightened Christendom! All the way to the Virgin Mary and baby Jesus in her lap."

"So, this is the handiwork of someone who really knows their business?" asked Leo.

"Absolutely." Hofmann nodded. "An embalmer three thousand years ago couldn't have done a better job. But if you're going to ask me about his cause of death or time of death, I'll have to pass. I found no broken skull, no bullet hole, or anything of the kind. And besides, the innards are gone, save the heart."

"Hmm, how annoying." Leo's eye traveled up the shriveled-up corpse again. "And what about the emerald eyes? Any information on those? Where have they gone?" He looked around. "I can't see them anywhere."

Suddenly, the silence in the room was thick enough to cut with a knife. "The eyes . . ." began Hofmann, nervously polishing his glasses. "Well, since you mention the eyes . . . it's the strangest thing . . ."

"Out with it! What is it?"

"I probably should have told you on Saturday at the museum. I . . . I wasn't sure. Herr Rothmayer confirmed my suspicions."

Leo took an impatient step closer. "Herr Professor, I'm imploring you! Please get to the point."

"The eye of Horus," piped up Augustin Rothmayer. "Horus was a powerful Egyptian god. Kinda like Zeus for the Greeks. So, this Horus had beef with another god, Seth. Seth then ripped out one of his eyes and—"

"Herr Rothmayer, if I want to hear a story, I'll read a book or go to the theater," said Leo. "What in God's name are you trying to say?"

The gravedigger and the professor exchanged furtive glances. Then Rothmayer went on: "Well, it's like this. Those two emerald eyes are very valuable jewels, inspector. They're often found with mummies, sort of like a protective amulet. Like . . . like . . ." He searched for a comparison. "Like a rosary or a cross. But when you told me about it, I thought right away that something was off. There only ever is *one* eye of Horus, never two. It's always the left one."

Professor Hofmann nodded in confirmation. "I checked the textbooks. There has never been a single case where two eyes were found with a mummy."

"Never two," murmured Leo. He remembered that the eyes had looked slightly cross-eyed when he saw them for the first time at the museum that night.

Because they had been two left eyes . . .

"Yes, and then I remembered that the professor told me about one of those eyes a while ago," went on Rothmayer, shooting another intent glance at Hofmann. "Isn't that right, professor?"

Professor Hofmann cleared his throat. Then he walked over to the vase, lifted out the dried roses and tipped the vessel upside down. There was a tinkling as both emerald eyes rolled onto the windowsill. In the sunlight, they shone almost unnaturally bright.

"I hid these here temporarily," said Hofmann sheepishly. "They really are highly valuable. And, well, I've seen at least one of them before."

"When was that?" asked Leo.

"At the archduke's reception I told you about. About three months ago. There was an incident that I'd really rather not talk about . . ." The professor clearly agonized over his words. Then he seemed to reach a decision. "His Excellency had purchased a mummy in Egypt through contacts, uh, presumably not entirely legally. That night, when he hosted the Vienna Archeological Society, we withdrew into a side room that contained the mummy. We were given permission to undress the mummy together and examine it for . . . for precious items."

"You're telling me the archduke gave you permission to *plunder* a mummy?" asked Leo, stunned. "Just like the cleaning lady at the museum did with Strössner's mummy?"

"Plunder, no!" Hofmann raised a hand in indignation. "We put all the items back. It was a sort of game. A silly game that's played in England, too. Wealthy noblemen buy a mummy and host a party where the mummy is unwrapped. One often discovers surprises."

"And what kind of surprise did you discover at the archduke's palace?"

"Well, first of all I soon realized that it was a female mummy. Probably a high-ranking princess—a rarity." Hofmann gave a shrug. "There were a few pretty items, like small amulets, scarabs, scraps of papyrus bearing protective spells. Nothing outstanding. Then it was Alfons Strössner's turn. Under the bandages, he found the eye of Horus. I'm quite certain it was one of these two. The jewel is unique. But that wasn't the strange part . . ."

"But?"

Hofmann swallowed. "Well, it seemed as though Strössner knew the eye. He was obviously agitated and left the reception quite swiftly. Later it turned out that he'd taken the emerald, much to His Excellency's dismay. But the archduke had bestowed the curation of the collection onto Strössner after all, and so we assumed that Strössner intended to examine the eye and would return it later."

"And shortly thereafter he vanishes without a trace," murmured Leo. He gave Hofmann a stern look. "You should have told me about this sooner, Herr Professor."

"I wasn't certain. And dear Alexander begged me not to say anything."

"Dr. Alexander Dedekind, curator of the Egypto-Oriental Collection? He begged you not to mention the incident?" Leo thought about how Dedekind had visited the Rapoldys despite Leinkirchner's order not to. What was going on?

He picked up the two jewels from the sill and turned to leave.

"What are you planning to do?" asked Hofmann.

"I'm going to pay your dear friend Alexander another visit at the museum. Maybe he remembers things better in the daytime than he does at night. The emeralds are herewith confiscated."

"But, you can't just . . ." began Hofmann, trailing off as he saw Leo's look of determination.

With a grim expression on his face, Leo slipped the pair of emerald eyes into the pocket of his waistcoat and strode into the large morgue, past the murdered boy under the sheet and toward the exit.

He was itching to ask some questions.

He was so angry that he didn't notice until he was outside that Augustin Rothmayer was following him. Leo turned without stopping. "What do you want?"

"Listen, inspector, be careful with those eyes. They didn't bring much joy to their last owner."

Leo stopped abruptly. "What do you mean?"

Rothmayer awkwardly knitted his long, calloused fingers together. "I don't believe in curses, Herr Inspector. But I do believe that the professor's death is connected to the eyes of Horus."

"I agree, and that's why I'm going now to interrogate Dr. Dedekind again."

Rothmayer shuffled his feet, giving him the appearance of a clumsy raven. "Would it be terribly impudent of me to ask to accompany you, inspector?"

"You want to come along?"

"It's research for the book, you see. You're going to be discussing curses, and there are very few books on the subject."

"You just said yourself you don't believe in curses," jeered Leo.

"I don't. Nor do I believe in the great devouress with her crocodile head and lion's rump, or that each person's heart is weighed at the gateway to the realm of the dead. But these are all death rites, and that's what I'm writing about. Please, Herr Inspector. You'd be doing me a great favor!"

Leo was about to say no when he remembered that Augustin Rothmayer had only just helped him out, too. Plus, he didn't look as unwashed and disheveled as usual today—he almost looked like a normal person, though perhaps not like someone who would visit a museum. Well, nothing wrong with startling Dr. Dedekind a little. He deserved it.

"Fine," said Leo. "But stick to the background. I'm asking the questions."

Rothmayer nodded gratefully and together they walked toward the Ring, and from there, south toward the museums.

"Did you pass on my regards to Fräulein Wolf?" said the gravedigger, attempting the art of conversation. When Leo nodded, he continued: "And will she remember to bring undergarments for Anna?"

"She will remember the undergarments, yes. Now let's consider why Dr. Dedekind didn't tell me about the two emerald eyes. After all, he must have noticed them just like Professor Hofmann had. He was also at the archduke's reception."

"I have a hunch, inspector. Well, we'll find out in a moment." Augustin Rothmayer clapped his hands together merrily. "I've never been to the Museum of Art History before."

They wouldn't have let you in in your gravedigger's garb, anyway, Leo was about to say. But then he bit back the comment. He liked the old codger, after all. And he had been of great help to him, once again. And still Leo struggled to get used to Rothmayer's eccentric ways, especially here on the busy and ostentatious Ring. He felt as though he were going for a stroll with Death himself.

Augustin Rothmayer moved confidently among all the elegantly dressed people with their top hats, tailcoats, silver-pommeled walking sticks, skirts, and hats with flowers. Leo caught one or two furtive glances cast in their direction. What did people see in the unlikely pair? Despite himself, he smiled.

A dandy and his death . . .

At last they arrived at Maria Theresien Square with its two museums. Leo hurried toward the second of the two buildings and showed his badge at the entrance.

"I'm here to see Dr. Dedekind," he said curtly. "The curator of the Egypto-Oriental Collection."

The porter gave a shrug. "The doctor could be anywhere in the museum. Best you come back in the afternoon. He'll be back at his office then."

"I can't wait that long." Leo walked past the ticket booth into the museum.

"Hey, what about him?" called the porter, pointing at Rothmayer, who was studying the museum map on the wall.

"He's, uh, my colleague. Now if you'll excuse us. We're in a hurry."

Leo dragged Rothmayer into the large entrance hall, where they turned right. The museum was well attended. The entrance to the

Egypto-Oriental Collection was open, and visitors walking toward them cast irritated glances at the haggard figure in his long coat and heavy boots.

"If Dedekind isn't in his office, he's bound to be somewhere in here, or else he's in the mummy repository," explained Leo as they hurried across halls, past upright sarcophagi and stone artifacts. More than once, Rothmayer stopped to admire an exhibit, and Leo had to pull him away.

"Did you see that black mummified hand?" asked Rothmayer. "Highly interesting! The stage of decomposition—"

"You're welcome to come back another time to complete your research on death rites," said Leo, cutting him off. "For now, I have a few questions for the living."

He didn't have to search for long. Dr. Dedekind stood next to a glass display case containing figurines and clay jugs. He appeared to be giving a speech to a group of well-dressed older gentlemen.

". . . makes this canopic jar one of the oldest ever to be found," Dr. Dedekind was saying. "We assume it dates from the Old Kingdom, suggesting—"

"Dr. Dedekind," said Leo quietly. "We need to talk."

Dedekind gave a start and turned. "You can see for yourself that I'm in the middle of a presentation!" he hissed.

"Oh, I'm more than happy to hold a presentation. On the subject of the eye of Horus, or rather on the *two* eyes of Horus . . ."

The curator paled instantly. With a smile, he addressed his audience. "Uh, please excuse me, sirs. I must go clear up a very minor misunderstanding. We'll meet later in room III. Meanwhile, please enjoy our exhibits." To Leo, he whispered, "Follow me to my office. We can talk there."

Neither of them spoke on the way there. Dedekind turned with confusion when he realized that Rothmayer was following them.

"My assistant," explained Leo. "Don't worry, I will be asking the questions. He's only here in case . . . well, in case we get stuck. I asked the two constables to wait outside by the prison wagon in order to keep this discreet."

"Constables . . . prison wagon?" Dr. Dedekind grew even paler, and Leo was beginning to enjoy himself. Why not let the arrogant fop quiver in his boots a little?

Dedekind's office was bulging with books, tomes, and dusty artifacts of all shapes and sizes. It looked like an antique junk room. The doctor nervously swiped aside a few notepapers and offered them a seat.

"So . . . so you found out," he said once they were all seated.

"Which part?" Leo eyeballed the man opposite him severely. "That at least one of the eyes comes from a female mummy? A princess that you and the other esteemed gentlemen from the archaeological society plundered like common grave robbers? And inside the archduke's palace!"

Dedekind raised both hands. "Please, understand! We had His Excellency's explicit permission. He himself was present! And the mummy was later taken to the repository here."

"Still, you should have told me. Also, you went to see the Rapoldys even though we specifically told you not to! Why? To warn them about my visit?"

"God no! I . . . I . . . well, we've known each other for such a long time. Poor Charlotte . . . I just didn't want . . ."

"Some inspector to show up and stir things up," snapped Leo. He reached inside his pocket and placed the two emeralds onto the table. "Professor Hofmann told us Strössner was quite agitated after the evening at the archduke's. Professor Walter Kerfeld confirmed this."

"So you've spoken with him, too," murmured Dedekind. "Then you probably know about the death of the two other members of the expedition."

"We do. And I believe I know where the second eye came from." Leo moved the jewels across the table like pawns. "Before his sudden departure, Professor Alfons Strössner was working on a special mummy. You know the one I'm talking about? The same mummy the professor presumably returned to Egypt for. Am I right? The same mummy the Austrian research team illegally smuggled to Vienna."

"Ta-bek-en-chon . . ." Dedekind's voice was quiet, almost inaudible, as if he feared that even mentioning the name might bring misfortune. "A priest of Thoth . . ."

"God of wisdom, writing, and magic," Augustin Rothmayer said, speaking for the first time. He nodded sagely. "Later, the Greeks called him Hermes, and our wizards and witches danced and sang to a fellow names Hermes Trismegistus. They're all one and the same. Very old and very powerful. In the Egyptian realm of the dead, he was the clerk, kind of like a secretary."

Dedekind looked startled. "Your assistant is surprisingly knowledgeable."

"His specialty area is . . . uh, the underworld," said Leo. "But carry on, doctor. The second eye comes from Ta-bek-en-chon's mummy, am I right?"

Dedekind nodded. His eyes fixed on the two stones on the table as if he were hypnotized. "Alfons told me about it shortly before he vanished. Ta-bek-en-chon was his very personal find—he wouldn't let anyone else touch it." The doctor swallowed. "You see, it's highly unusual for two such stones to be identical. And such a precious pair! Only one copy was made of each individual eye. As the *one* left eye of Horus. So, Alfons and I came up with a theory."

"Which is?" asked Leo.

"It could have been something like wedding rings: a married couple these days exchanges identical rings. A symbol of their love, so to speak."

"You believe this priest, Ta-bek-en-chon, and the priestess, whose mummies now both reside in Vienna, used to be in love?" Leo frowned. "I thought those stones were protective amulets, not marriage symbols."

"They are. But they're also a symbol for eternity. For the eternity of love. Love that . . . that . . ." Dedekind struggled with his words. "That goes beyond death." He let out a deep sigh. "We should never have unwrapped the mummy the way we did at the archduke's palace! As if . . . as if we were undressing her. A disgusting defilement! He is never going to forgive us."

"He?" Leo raised an eyebrow. "You aren't talking about this dead priest?" He laughed out loud. "You actually believe this priest returned from the realm of the dead and took his revenge on Strössner because he defiled the mummy of his beloved? Come on! That's hogwash."

"I wish it were! Listen, inspector, I'm a rational scientist. But the fact is, things have happened that . . . that can't happen. Not in any rational way, at least." Dedekind shook his head. "Why does Alfons Strössner vanish, write letters from Egypt, and then turn up as a mummy here at the museum? Why is he the third member of the expedition to die? And why does the archduke bring this second mummy—of all mummies—to Vienna? Almost as if the princess followed her lover!"

"That's why I'm here, to answer all those questions, by leading a police investigation," said Leo. "Not relying on superstition and witchcraft." His tone came out only half as confident as he'd intended it to sound. "Maybe a good first step would be to closely examine those two mummies again."

"You see, inspector, that leads us to the next puzzle. Yet another event that defies reason." Dr. Dedekind leaned across the table, his voice not much more than a whisper. "Both mummies have vanished!"

Leo was taken aback. "What do you mean, vanished?"

"They're no longer here at the museum! Call me a liar, but it seems to me as though the pair of them are haunting the streets of Vienna, on a restless quest to come for all those who disturbed their peace!"

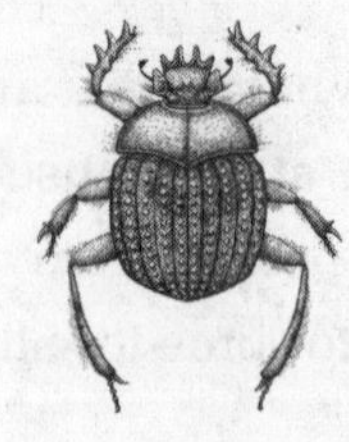

CHAPTER 8

From *Death Rites Around the World* by Augustin Rothmayer, written in Vienna, 1894

Mummia (also Mummia vera aegyptiaca, Mumiya, mummy powder): this powder made from ground-up mummies is sold in many pharmacies as a cure-all. Occasionally, the mummies arrive at the pharmacies in chunks, with bones and arteries still clearly discernable, and are freshly ground up in situ.

Mummia helps with coughing, soreness of throat, dizziness, palsy, heart complaints, trembling, weak kidneys, and headaches. There have been, however, cases of brazen fakes using more recent dried-up corpses. During the siege of Vienna by the Turks, imperial soldiers sometimes killed their prisoners, skinned them, dried them, and sold them as Egyptian mummies. Bog bodies, too, have occasionally been passed off as Egyptian. I am in no position to judge whether the efficacy differs and how.

Julia buttoned up the top button of her blouse, fixed her hair, and entered the foyer of the criminal courthouse. The four-story Renaissance-style building on Landesgericht Street filled her with awe every time—probably due partly to the fact that the executions by hanging took place in the prison courtyard. In contrast to the police jail at Theobald Lane, where brawling vagabonds or drunk beggars spent the night, this judicial complex was much more serious. The nation displayed all its power.

Her steps echoed as she walked inside past two uniformed guards. She was relieved to see a porter she knew behind the reception desk. Julia had met him several times before when dropping off photographs that were needed for a trial. Donning her loveliest smile, she cleared her throat. "Alois, isn't it?"

The man looked up from his files and returned the smile. "Oh, Fräulein Wolf, what a pleasure. Do you have some pictures for the judges? Has there been another shooting or knife fight over in the fifth?"

"Not this time, Alois," said Julia, raising her camera case. "I've come to take pictures. We have no identification for one of your prisoners."

The porter frowned. "Uh-huh, and why aren't you doing that over at Theobald Lane? That's where you normally take those."

"It's urgent. And besides . . ." Julia lowered her voice. "To be honest, I'd like to take a few more pictures than necessary. I don't get one of these heathens in front of my camera every day."

"Ah, now we're getting to the truth!" The man grinned. "That chief from the zoo, right? I heard about him. Ate one of the keepers—a proper cannibal!"

"Uh, that's right. Like I said, it's urgent . . ."

"Of course, Fräulein Wolf. Why didn't you say so right away? Looking lovely today, by the way! God bless!" He beckoned to one of the guards. "Please take Fräulein Wolf to the prison ward, Schorsch, would you?" With a wink, he turned back to Julia. "Perhaps she'll take a photo of the cannibal for us, too?"

"I'll see what I can do," said Julia.

She followed the chubby guard down several corridors, which branched off into flights of stairs or other corridors. It seemed like a never-ending maze. Uniform rust-red doors lined the walls. Julia thought she could just about hear the millstones of bureaucracy grind slowly in the walls of this palace of justice.

Earlier, she had gone to Theobald Lane to take a few identification photos, in the morning shortly after Leo had left. Their night together had been intimate and passionate, just like their dancing at the cellar bar. During such moments, she realized how much she loved Leo—never mind the endless list of faults Big Elli found with him. Maybe they were a better match than Elli thought.

After her visit to Theobald Lane, Julia rushed home for lunch with Sisi. The entire time, Saidrovuni's case nagged at her. She simply couldn't believe that the incident at the zoo was as clear-cut as inspector Loibl claimed. Sure, the keeper's cap and the keys to the lion enclosure had been found in Saidrovuni's possessions, and it seemed he was the culprit—but something told Julia that this wasn't the whole truth. Perhaps it was Saidrovuni's eyes, his upright bearing, even during his arrest. He'd climbed into the prisoner wagon with his head held high, not downcast like an exposed criminal. Julia decided she would pay Saidrovuni an unofficial visit. She only hoped that no one would ask questions about the photographs. If they did, she would just say she wanted to take a few exotic photos.

They finally reached the prison tract. The doors were painted red and reinforced with iron. Each door had small spy holes and a hatch for passing meals. The guard eventually stopped outside one of the doors and cast a probing glance through the hole. When Julia also took a look, she stepped back, startled.

"You chained him up like an animal!"

"Orders from the investigating judge," replied the guard monotonously. He was quite corpulent, pimply, and young. He certainly had the hang of police jargon. "The prisoner resisted when he was taken to his cell."

"And now you're afraid he'll fly away?" said Julia sarcastically. "Like a parrot?"

Instead of replying, the guard unlocked the door with his keys. "I'll wait outside," he said. "How long will you take for the photographs?"

Julia thought for a moment, then slapped her forehead. "Silly me! I left the camera stand down by the entrance. Would you be so kind as to fetch it for me?" She gave him a charming smile.

The pimple-faced guard hesitated, then nodded. "All right. The fellow's in chains, I don't suppose anything can happen. But be careful, yes? They're like animals."

He closed the cell door behind Julia and shuffled back down the corridor. Julia guessed he'd only be away for a few minutes; a quarter hour at most. Not a lot of time for an undisturbed conversation with the prisoner.

Chief Saidrovuni was sitting on a narrow metal cot firmly attached to the floor. The only other furnishings were a bucket to relieve himself, and a table and stool that were also fixed to the floor. Both his hands were chained to the bedframe, so that he couldn't lie down. Instead, he sat leaning against the cold, damp wall, directly underneath a small, barred window that allowed in the afternoon sun. At least someone had draped a blanket around his naked upper body. His face was expressionless. Julia wondered how long the chief had been sitting here like this. Since yesterday? Bruises on his face suggested he'd been beaten, too.

Who are really the animals here? she thought.

"Do you recognize me?" she asked, setting down her camera case. "I was at the zoo together with the inspector. I'm a photographer." She gestured at the case. "That means I take pictures with a small box in there that—"

"I know what a photographer is," said Saidrovuni. "I'm not as ignorant as you think."

"I'm sorry. That . . . that was silly of me." Julia pressed her lips together.

"I've been traveling with the Meyer ethnic show for three years. I've been to Paris and London. I've even been to the world's fair in Chicago. Have you been to America?"

"No, I haven't."

"They have boxes with pictures that move. Very interesting."

"Herr . . . Saidrovuni, we don't have much time. I came because I don't believe you killed the young keeper. I'd like to help you."

The chief looked at her directly for the first time. He seemed surprised. "Why do you want to help me?"

"Because I think it's wrong what they're doing to you. How they're treating you like . . . like an animal! We might be able to get you out of here. But to do so, you have to answer my questions honestly. Did you kill the keeper?"

"No. But I know who did."

"You . . . you know who did?" Julia held her breath for a moment. "Who?"

"It was the *Asanbosam*. An evil spirit."

Julia sighed. That wasn't the answer she'd hoped for. "An evil spirit. Oh, well . . ."

"You don't understand, miss. The *Asanbosam* isn't a made-up ghost who frightens little children. He really exists. He's a demon! Our people believe in him, and I've seen him. He has teeth made of iron. He used them to tear that poor boy apart. I saw it myself!"

"What did you see?" Julia sat down on the stool. She was close enough to touch him. She wasn't afraid of him—rather, she was afraid of what he might have seen at the zoo.

Saidrovuni swallowed. Then he began, "I went for a walk through the zoo that night. I sometimes do that when I can't sleep. The lights and all the noise of your big city, everything's so loud, so bright . . . When I came past the predators' enclosures, I heard a sound, a . . . ripping."

"A ripping?" asked Julia, leaning closer. "Do you mean . . . perhaps the squeak of the gate in the lion's cage?"

"No, a ripping. As if . . . as if someone was ripping a person to pieces. And then I saw him! The *Asanbosam* stood leaning over the boy, drinking his blood. He looked right at me. I . . . I ran away." Saidrovuni took a deep breath. "I was a coward."

"And the lion?"

"There was no lion. The lion was at the back, where they always take him to be fed."

"No lion . . . no squeaking gate . . ." Julia paused to think. They had assumed that the young keeper had locked the lion into the rear enclosure in order to clean the front one, and then someone opened the gate from the outside. But Saidrovuni told a different story: someone was with the keeper *before* the lion, when the animal was locked away—his murderer? "But then why was the key in your hut, if you had nothing to do with it?" she asked. "Was it in the gate? Did you take it?"

"There was no key, I swear! Maybe the *Asanbosam* gave me the key later because he wants to drink my blood. Once the men here kill me." He nodded grimly. "Because that's what they're going to do. Kill me. I want to die fighting, not on the gallows. My spirit will never rest, just like that of the *Asanbosam*."

"Can you describe this . . . this demon to me?" asked Julia.

"It was too far away." Saidrovuni shook his head. "But believe me, miss. It was the *Asanbosam*! Who else would do such a terrible thing? Only a demon could get into the enclosure without a key."

"And the keeper's cap?" asked Julia hastily. She knew they didn't have much time left.

Saidrovuni didn't answer right away. After a few moments, he said, "We stole it. But that was a few days earlier."

"Stole it? Why on earth would you steal it? It's worthless!"

"Because . . . because . . ." Saidrovuni faltered. "The old keeper isn't good to us. He said nasty things. The women wanted to weave a spell to punish him. They needed his cap."

Julia sighed. "That wasn't very wise, Herr Saidrovuni. How is anyone supposed to believe that you had nothing to do with this when you speak of spells and demons? If you—"

There were footsteps in the corridor. The guard was returning. A key turned in the lock and the door opened. The guard looked around the cell, then handed Julia the tripod, which she'd forgotten in the foyer on purpose.

"Did the savage touch you?" he asked. "Insult you? You look a little pale, fräulein. Is something wrong?"

"No, no, everything's fine. Thank you for fetching the tripod." Julia struggled to produce a smile and set up her apparatus. "Now let me quickly take my photographs before it gets too dark in here."

The pimple-faced keeper grinned. "Can't see the Moors at night, can you? Same with panthers in the jungle. All you see is their eyes."

Julia said nothing, focusing entirely on her work. She watched Saidrovuni from the corner of her eye. He was once more staring blankly ahead, sitting as if the dirt the world tried to throw at him beaded off like rainwater.

She was done in a quarter of an hour. Saidrovuni hadn't moved once the entire time, hadn't even blinked. It was as if she'd photographed a statue.

"What about my picture?" asked the fat guard, having waited impatiently by the door as she'd worked.

"The photographs need to be developed first," replied Julia. "That takes time."

"Of course." The guard seemed disappointed, but he was clearly trying not to let on that he knew nothing about technology. "Well then." He jangled his keys.

"Can't you at least give him a jacket?" asked Julia.

"They're always naked." The guard gave a shrug. "They don't mind, believe me. And besides, anyone could—"

"Do you want the picture or not?" snapped Julia. "Get him some clothes, and I will leave a picture for you with the porter. Promise. Deal?"

"Deal," grumbled the man.

"I'm going to check up on you, believe me."

With one last look at Saidrovuni, Julia left the cell. The door closed, and to Julia it sounded like the gate of the lion's cage clanging shut.

"It turned out exactly as I feared," complained Leinkirchner, lighting one of his fat cigars before sitting down. He had summoned Leo to his office as soon as Leo had arrived back at headquarters.

Leo too lit himself a cigarette—he badly needed it after this morning's events. He hadn't had a chance yet to process what Professor Hofmann and then Dr. Dedekind told him. He had asked Rothmayer to find out more about Egyptian curses and mummies—not that he seriously believed it would get them anywhere, but at least he'd shaken off the gravedigger that way. Rothmayer had seemed about to accompany him to the police station.

"The police president declared the mummy case a matter for the top level," Leinkirchner went on gruffly. "It appears Strössner's connections reached very high up. The Archaeological Society is quite the powerful circle, and Strössner sat on its committee. You'd be surprised at the names on their membership list—the people who're interested in archaeology! As if everyone with a title had turned tomb raider, all the way up to Archduke Rainer." He snorted. "We won't be able to keep a lid on this for much longer."

"What about the cleaning woman?" asked Leo.

"I went to Theobald Lane myself yesterday. The woman is charged with attempted theft. I'm guessing she'll see the judge as early as this week; things like this go fast. The remand prison is overflowing as it is."

"Well, it was to be expected," said Leo.

"Don't you get it, Herzfeldt? How dumb are you?" Leinkirchner's face turned red. "Once she's on trial, she'll testify! Then the story is out there. Journalists hang around the courthouse like vultures, just waiting for a story. Mummy professor at the museum. Ha, they would lap it up! We only have a few days left." He took a long drag on his cigar and appeared to calm a little. "So, what have you learned so far? Was Professor Hofmann able to determine Strössner's cause of death? Time of death?"

"Neither. Unfortunately, it's not as straightforward as that," replied Leo. "The case has taken an interesting turn—after the forensic institute, I went back to the museum. Dedekind didn't tell us the whole truth last Saturday."

He briefly told Leinkirchner about the archduke's reception, the mummy desecration, and the two emerald eyes. The chief inspector listened in silence, puffing like a locomotive.

"Dr. Dedekind thinks the two mummies are closely connected," said Leo in the end. "He's talking about a kind of romantic relationship, united eternally by the two emerald eyes of Horus."

"And both mummies are missing?" asked Leinkirchner.

Leo nodded. "They were down in the museum repository. The

priest's mummy's been there since the return of the expedition form Cairo, while the princess's mummy arrived three months ago, after the gentlemen from the Archaeological Society plundered it at the archduke's palace. However Dedekind never checked until today—both sarcophagi are empty."

"Empty. I see . . . And now the doctor seriously believes the two mummies are walking through Vienna, taking their revenge on everyone who took part in the desecration? That's utter nonsense!"

"Well, at the very least it's interesting that several people who've been connected with both mummies are now dead. Adolf Landinger and Father Gregor Mayr, both members of the expedition. And now Strössner, too . . . Dedekind must be fearing for his life."

"Because of two missing mummies? The man belongs in the nuthouse! I still believe Professor Kerfeld's our man. The fellow wanted revenge because he wasn't put in charge of the expedition. Bring him in, Herzfeldt! We'll put him under a little pressure here at the station. Kerfeld has motive, and the skills to undertake a mummification. And ask Graz again about that Father Gregor Mayr's death—maybe Kerfeld had something to do with it, somehow."

"I already have." Leo sighed. "The wheels of bureaucracy turn slowly, even in Graz. I'm still trying to find the doctor who issued the death certificate."

"Your family is from Graz, aren't they?" said Leinkirchner. "You Jews are connected. And you have money. Ask your father to use his contacts to speed things up. Money always makes things happen."

"If you need the Jew, he's well liked," murmured Leo.

"Beg your pardon?"

Leo squared his shoulders. "I think I'll pay the Rapoldy's another visit today, too," he replied. "They didn't tell me everything. They didn't mention the archduke's reception. Something's not right."

"Do that." Leinkirchner nodded. "But handle them with kid gloves. Apparently they're frequent guests of His Excellency the archduke's. And now the archduke even partook in this mummy spectacle! How embarrassing, the whole affair . . ." The chief inspector suddenly seemed to remember something. "What happened to the two emerald eyes?"

"I took the liberty of confiscating them. They're evidence, after all."

"Then you better take them down to the evidence room immediately before something happens to them. Those rocks must be worth a fortune. Oh, and Herzfeldt." Leinkirchner stabbed his cigar in Leo's direction. "Don't forget—not a word to no one! No even to Loibl or to Fräulein Wolf, if you happen to run into her again. This case remains in the smallest circle, you hear me? The very smallest circle!"

Leo nodded, saying nothing. He hated to imagine what would happen if Leinkirchner found out about his little excursion with Julia, or an investigating gravedigger.

If that gets out, Augustin Rothmayer may as well dig my grave, he thought. He tipped his hat and left Leinkirchner's office, feeling the chief inspector's eyes boring into his back.

The same evening, Julia set to work developing the pictures from the courthouse.

She didn't technically need to develop them. The photographs had been an excuse to speak with Saidrovuni. But she'd promised a picture each to the fat guard and the porter, and she worried that the chief would be treated even worse if the pictures failed to appear. If she was honest with herself, though, there was another reason: she was eager to see the photographs, too. She didn't often photograph living subjects, and Saidrovuni made an interesting one. And it meant that for once, she could develop the photos in the company of her three-year-old daughter—unlike the usual gruesome crime-scene images.

Sisi watched with interest as Julia dipped the plates into the three liquids, one after the other, and eventually balanced them on the wooden rack. Julia spoke loudly and clearly as she worked. She knew of course that Sisi couldn't hear her. But she also knew that deaf people sometimes read lips. Julia also knew a few words in sign language. Only yesterday she'd studied a book on the subject. But this language was these days considered an imbecile language, and they forbade it at the schools of Austria a few years ago.

Julia knew her daughter would never have it easy, least of all as an adult. She'd sworn to herself to be a good mother. But she didn't always succeed.

Not while she had to work hard for their daily bread as a solo mother here in Vienna.

"Mama can do magic. Watch," she said, placing a plate into the basin. "Hocus pocus . . . fidibus!" She lifted the previously dark plate from the liquid with an exaggerated gesture and held it for Sisi to see. As if by magic, Saidrovuni's face began to appear on it. The image showed the chief in profile, and it was clear and detailed: the tight curls of his hair, his dark eyes, gazing into the distance. The photo showed the uninjured side of his face.

Sisi's forehead crinkled. The photo plate didn't show colors, and yet Sisi seemed to notice that the man's skin looked different than her own. Julia realized that her daughter had never seen a dark-skinned person before.

"This is Herr Saidrovuni," she said clearly. "He comes from Africa. Everyone there has dark skin like his. But they're just the same as you and me."

Sisi's eyes turned to the developing images on the rack. Some of them showed the cuts in his face. Sisi pointed at them and gave her mother a questioning look.

"He . . . he fell," said Julia hesitantly. She couldn't bring herself to tell her daughter that Saidrovuni had been beaten.

By men with white skin . . . people like us . . .

Suddenly, the pictures seemed dirty to her. As if she'd stolen part of the chief's soul in taking his picture. She felt sick at the thought of the pimple-faced guard showing one of these photos off to his drinking buddies, that they made fun of Saidrovuni's alleged wildness, their greasy fingers poking at his face. Swiftly she moved the last few developed pictures to the drying rack.

"Time for bed," she told Sisi. "Let's go. If you're good, I'll sing you something."

Even if Sisi couldn't hear her, she seemed to feel it when Julia sang her to sleep—though maybe it was only the gentle rocking as she cradled her daughter in her lap.

She took Sisi by the hand and began to head downstairs when she heard heavy steps below. There was a knock, and Big Elli appeared in the doorway, breathing heavily.

"Don't think I'll do this regularly," gasped the landlady. "I'm not your maidservant, just so you know."

"What is it?" asked Julia nervously. Something out of the ordinary must have happened for Elli to tackle the steep stairs.

"The fuzz called," said Elli, wiping sweat off her forehead. "They say you're to come to the sixth quick as you can. To take photographs. The bloke on the telephone said to tell you it's another case like the last one."

"The last one . . ." Julia instinctively squeezed her daughter's hand so hard that Sisi gave a small squeal. "Good God . . ."

"You've gone all pale, child," said Elli, much gentler. "Is it another horrible murder, yes? I told you to give up that god-awful work!"

"I'm . . . I'm all right, Elli. Will you take care of Sisi? I won't be too late."

Elli nodded, and Julia planted a kiss on her daughter's cheek. "Aunt Elli will tuck you in, darling. Mama will be back soon."

Like the last time . . .

There'd been another murder.

And Julia knew what awaited her at the crime scene.

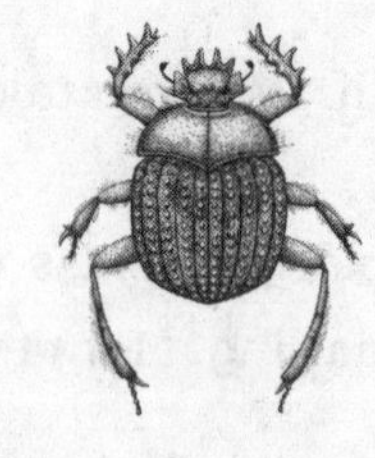

CHAPTER 9

It was after dark when Leo finally arrived back in Hietzing. The gas streetlights showed the driver the way, past cozy wine bars and posh restaurants that were busy even midweek. Laughter and the sound of a violin wafted out from ivy-covered verandas. But Leo wasn't headed there.

"To the New World, you say?" the driver asked, turning to his passenger. He probably assumed Leo was headed to somewhere like Casino Dommayer in his elegant getup. "The fields where the amusement park used to be?"

Leo nodded. "I'm visiting the Rapoldys. They have a private road—I'll point it out."

"As you wish, sir." The driver cracked his whip and the fiacre turned off Hietzinger Main Road onto Wenz Lane as a soft drizzle set in. The bars and restaurants gave way to scattered villas and fewer streetlights, which cast a milky glow. Lights burned behind large windows, and in some gardens, in colorful Chinese lanterns. But beyond the glow from the lights, complete blackness reigned.

Trees, bushes, and shrubs stood as stark silhouettes against the cloudy sky.

Leo had called ahead to the Rapoldys that afternoon, and Charlotte Rapoldy had invited him to come for dinner. After a moment's consideration, Leo had accepted. Maybe he'd achieve more in a relaxed setting rather than a sober interview. Also, chief inspector Leinkirchner had asked him to proceed tactfully.

Leo hadn't made any progress with regard to Professor Walter Kerfeld. Leinkirchner had pressed him to bring the professor in as a suspect, but Kerfeld wasn't at home nor at the university, even though he had a lecture scheduled . . . Leo bit his lip. Had the man run, or had something happened to him? Was there some truth to the curse after all?

There was no news in the case of Father Gregor from Graz, either. No one seemed to know the doctor listed on the death certificate. It almost seemed as if any traces of him had been covered. The whole affair was growing more mysterious by the day.

Pull yourself together! Leo shook himself. *You're beginning to sound as hysterical as Dedekind. You'll end up believing in curses. . . .*

The Rapoldys' villa appeared at the end of the driveway. The library's glass dome shone in the dark like a monstrous eye. At night, the Egyptian statues in the garden suddenly appeared menacing, as if they might start to walk at any moment. The two sphinxes by the gate glowered at Leo.

He handed the driver a few coins, climbed out of the fiacre, and pulled on the bell pull. This time, Charlotte Rapoldy opened the door personally. It was still raining.

"Herr Inspector. I hope you didn't get too wet."

"Not at all, madam, I took a covered fiacre." Leo walked up the steps and tipped his hat. "Thank you for the generous invitation. Truly, it was quite unnecessary. I only have a few questions."

"Which I'm sure we can answer over dinner. We set the table in the conservatory for the first time this year. To be honest, we were hoping for better weather and warmer temperatures. Not as hot as in Egypt, of course." She smiled. "Welcome to Villa Thebes, Herr von Herzfeldt."

Charlotte Rapoldy wore a plain black dress. Her hair was adorned with an expensive-looking tiara into which a green scarab had been set. Her face darkened when she noticed Leo's eye on it.

"I wear this tiara in memory of my father. It likely once belonged to a high-ranking Egyptian woman from the late Ptolemaic dynasty. Father always liked it on me." She stepped aside, gesturing invitingly. "Come in already, before you're completely soaked. It would be a shame—your lovely suit."

Together they walked past the vases in the corridor to the conservatory, where a table was set for three. The silver cutlery was polished to perfection; the plates were of the finest Meissner porcelain.

Charlotte was right—it was a little chilly. Three sides of the room were made entirely of glass, and large glass doors led out into the garden. Planters held roses and clematis climbing up small bamboo ladders. Leo was reminded of his parents' conservatory back home in Graz, in the posh quarter of Geidorf. Even the polite but superficial conversation was the same.

Clemens Rapoldy arrived moments later, leaning on his walking stick. He looked as though he'd had little sleep, his pale and unshaved face in contrast to his otherwise elegant appearance. Leo was grateful that he himself had stopped by his room after work to change. He wore black trousers with flat seams and his chesterfield coat over a waistcoat and a shirt with a folded collar—neither too fancy nor too casual.

Clemens Rapoldy indicated for Leo to sit. "Please forgive us, inspector, that we're receiving you this late. My wife and I had to organize my father-in-law's funeral. They've released his body." He swallowed hard. "We're . . . we're still in shock."

"My condolences," said Leo and sat. "I don't want to impose on your hospitality for long. Like I said, just a few questions."

The Rapoldys also sat down. As if there'd been a secret signal, a door opened and the maidservant, dressed in a white apron and mobcap, served them steaming bowls of soup. Leo could smell that it was crawfish soup. It was delicious.

After a few spoonfuls, he broke the silence.

"I hear you're occasionally invited at the archduke's," he began.

Charlotte Rapoldy nodded. "That's right. Archduke Rainer is a great friend of Egyptology. We owe him our gratitude, him and the imperial family."

"Then why didn't you mention that you were at his palace three months ago? Together with your father and the rest of the archaeological society's committee? And that something . . . well, unpleasant happened that evening. I might call it corpse defilement."

Clemens Rapoldy's spoon clinked loudly as he set it down. "Herr Inspector, how dare you! You cannot—"

His wife placed a hand on his arm. "He's right, Clemens. It was a mistake not to mention it. It was a mistake to let it happen in the first place!" She sighed. "The idea to unwrap the mummy came from His Excellency. That makes it difficult to say no."

"I know of the two emerald eyes and of Dr. Dedekind's fears," Leo carried on. "I'm guessing that was another reason he visited you on Whitsunday, even though we instructed him not to. He wanted to warn you." Leo shook his head. "Warn you of two mummies that used to be in love and that are now haunting our city as avengers. He says both mummies have mysteriously gone missing."

"We . . . we heard that, too," said Charlotte Rapoldy reluctantly.

"Tell me, inspector. What do you make of all this? Of the curse, I mean?"

"That's what I wanted to ask you. I would have liked to ask Professor Walter Kerfeld, too, but he seems to have vanished into thin air. No one at the university knows where he is."

"Professor Kerfeld likes to disappear for a few days at a time," said Clemens Rapoldy. "That doesn't necessarily mean anything. He's rather eccentric."

"That's the impression I got, too," replied Leo. "And that he harbors grudges." He watched the Rapoldys closely. "He accused your family of illegally selling antiquities in Egypt. Were you aware? He says the family's wealth was built on theft." Leo's eye brushed the precious tiara in Charlotte Rapoldy's hair again.

"Nonsense!" Clemens Rapoldy laughed hoarsely. "Kerfeld has been saying this for years. He's never been able to prove anything. And if it's our furnishings you mean, let me tell you that many of them are replicas. Still valuable, but not genuine. Like, for example, the sarcophagus in the garden. And for everything else, we have sales agreements. Including for my wife's tiara, which you're studying with such fascination." He leaned forward. "Is that why you came here tonight, inspector? To accuse us of theft? I wouldn't have thought you this naïve. It's blatantly obvious that Kerfeld merely tried to divert your attention from himself."

"I'm looking for answers to what has happened," said Leo. "That's all."

For a while they sat in silence, eating the now cold soup. Leo sipped on the exquisitely dry white wine, suspecting it was a Bourgogne Chardonnay rather than an Austrian one. The rain outside had intensified and a wind was blowing. Behind the glass doors, trees bent slightly in the breeze.

"When is the funeral?" asked Leo in a bid to break the awkward silence.

"Tomorrow evening at Central Cemetery," replied Charlotte Rapoldy, evidently grateful for the change of topic. "We decided to keep the details of his death to ourselves. It will be for close friends and family, after the cemetery gates shut. The society's committee alone is invited. No one knows what's happened apart from Dr. Dedekind and Professor Hofmann. The official version is that my father passed away a few weeks ago in Cairo from malaria and his body only just arrived home."

Leo nodded. "That sounds plausible."

At least until the true story comes out, he thought. *When will the papers find out?*

He took another sip of wine. "Tell me more about Professor Kerfeld. He told me he comes from humble beginnings, worked his way up on his own merit . . ."

"Yes, yes, the same old story," grumbled Clemens Rapoldy. "Don't let it fool you—Kerfeld always was unscrupulous when it came to his career. He copied the work of others and claimed it as his own; and even though nothing has been proven, he falsified old documents. And at the archduke's reception, he was the first to search the mummy for valuables—practically elbowed his way to the front. But he likes to point the finger at others and cast himself in the role of the innocent lamb."

"Do you think he's capable of the murder?" asked Leo. "Out of vengeance? Or perhaps if your father-in-law knew more about these falsified documents you just mentioned?"

Clemens Rapoldy said nothing.

His wife replied eventually, her voice brittle: "I no longer know what to believe, inspector. All I know is that strange things are happening that—"

Something clinked and rattled, and Leo looked around. The table was shaking slightly and one of the wine glasses had toppled, as well as the bottle, spilling the wine on the tablecloth. A gust of wind shook the glass doors.

"What on earth . . ." he began.

"There!" Charlotte Rapoldy pointed trembling fingers at the veranda doors. "My God . . . do you see it?"

And then Leo saw it.

Behind the bushes, right next to the ivy-covered sarcophagus, something moved. It was an upright figure, standing in front of the whitewashed wall, its arms outstretched toward the villa. It was taller than a man, at least seven feet. At first Leo thought it was naked, but then he noticed the gray bandages wrapped all around the figure, including its face. In the places where the eyes should be, there was a green shimmer.

Like two emeralds.

"That . . . that is impossible," whispered Clemens Rapoldy, his fingers cramped around the pommel of his walking stick. "Impossible . . ."

For a moment, Leo was rooted to the spot. Then he jumped to his feet.

"Stay here, no one leaves the room!" He ran to the veranda door and shook the handle. It was locked. "Damn it, where's the key?"

Charlotte was shaking all over now, and her husband seemed too stunned to reply. On instinct, Leo hurled himself at the door. Wood splintered, and one of the large panes burst. At last the door crashed open. Leo ran out into the garden.

"Herr Inspector!" Charlotte called after him. Her voice was barely audible over the rushing wind. "Don't do this! Stay here!"

But Leo had already raced past the Egyptian statues and small pyramid toward the wall. It was pouring now and the lawn was soft and muddy, the wind tearing at the trees like a deity gone mad. The giant mummy was still standing by the wall next to the sarcophagus, its hands stretched toward him. Leo thought he could hear howling. Or was it just the wind? One lonely gas lantern on the other side of the wall shed a little light. The mummy shimmered greenish and seemed to move toward him. Leo didn't have a pistol. Instead, he grabbed a branch and planted his feet.

"Stop where you are!" he shouted. "Police! This mummery ends now before—"

All of a sudden the figure vanished.

Leo started. One moment it was standing in front of the wall and the next it was gone. How was this possible? He dropped the branch and ran to the wall, running his hands over the white plaster. Nothing. No door, no secret hole. He kneeled down and examined the ground in the poor light.

He couldn't see any tracks.

That couldn't be right! If the mummy had been standing here, there ought to be tracks, prints on the wet—

There was a flash and then unbearable pain filled his head.

He tilted forward onto the wet lawn, and darkness washed over him.

WHEN LEO CAME TO, HE WAS LOOKING AT THE FACE OF CHARlotte Rapoldy. She was holding a wet cloth, apparently having wiped his forehead with it.

"What . . . happened?" he asked laboriously.

"Thanks heavens, you're waking up! I already tried ice and smelling salts, nothing would work. We were beginning to fear the worst . . ."

He tried to sit up and was instantly punished by a sharp pain in his forehead.

"Stay down, inspector," said Charlotte in a soothing voice. "Someone struck you down. You've a nasty bruise."

"The . . . the mummy," tried Leo. "What . . . happened to it?"

"Clemens searched the garden with our servants, but they found nothing. No mummy, no sign of an intruder. The storm has passed and that . . . that thing has gone. It's all very strange." Charlotte

Rapoldy sighed. "Maybe we imagined it? But it was too real for that. After all, all three of us saw it, didn't we?"

Leo saw now that she had been crying. She still wore the black dress but had removed the tiara with the green scarab. Her hair was a mess and her makeup smudged, making her somehow more human.

"Where am I?" asked Leo. He was lying on something soft, maybe leather. Someone had wrapped him in a wool blanket. A bandage felt tight on his head.

"You're in the library," replied Charlotte. "On the chaise longue, to be precise. We had you carried in here and bandaged your head. I think perhaps it isn't as bad as we'd feared. Mild concussion, probably. Still, we should be careful."

Leo tried to get up but was overcome by nausea. Charlotte gently pushed him back down. "I think it's best if you stay overnight. I can't allow you to leave in this state."

"But I must—" Leo protested weakly.

"Hush, I won't hear it." Charlotte smiled mildly. "Besides, you're not wearing any pants, inspector. You were drenched—we worried you might catch a fever."

Leo winced. "How mortifying . . ."

"Don't worry." She wiped the cloth across his forehead again. "You'll be pleased to know it was our servant who undressed you. Quite a pity, I thought."

Leo wasn't sure whether Charlotte had spoken the last sentence or whether his imagination had added it. His eyes were closed and he was drifting out of consciousness.

In his dreams, Charlotte as Cleopatra was kissing his lips passionately. But then the romantic vision changed.

A mummy as tall as a tower staggered toward Leo with outstretched arms. He ran and ran but couldn't get away.

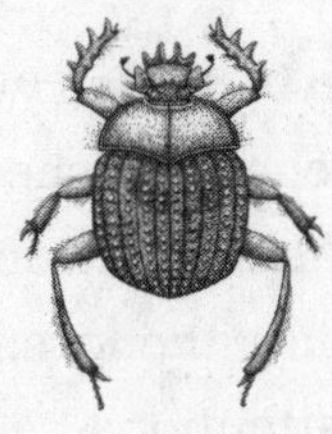

CHAPTER 10

From *Death Rites Around the World* by Augustin Rothmayer, written in Vienna, 1894

> In some regions of India, the death rite of burning widows alive still persists today. Each year, thousands of women are burned alongside their deceased husbands on the pyre—in most cases, not voluntarily. The women are pinned down with long bamboo sticks. Sometimes they're locked inside cages or huts that are also burned. Another method is the digging of a pit in which the fire is lit. A curtain blocks the view from the unhappy wife, until she either jumps into the flames or is pushed by her relatives.

Leo stayed in bed almost the entire following day.

He'd spent the night on the Rapoldys' chaise longue, drifting in and out of sleep. His head had ached despite the cold compresses Charlotte Rapoldy had applied. She'd shown herself very kind and caring toward him, checking in on him twice during the night. She'd placed her hand on his forehead to check his temperature. In the morning, Leo had reached the conclusion that he'd only imagined her suggestive words, just like the kiss. He had to admit, though, that he hadn't disliked her attentions.

The Rapoldys had sent him home in a carriage with their best wishes, and Leo had telephoned chief inspector Leinkirchner, who demanded a detailed report as soon as possible.

The problem was, a report about *what* . . . ?

For hours now Leo had been brooding over what happened the night before. That . . . *thing* that had been there. It had appeared like a larger-than-life mummy that had struck him down before vanishing without a trace.

All three of them had seen the figure in the garden. And still Leo couldn't accept that it was the mummy of an Egyptian priest taking his revenge on the Rapoldys for their defilement of his beloved. The thought alone was ridiculous!

And deeply unsettling at the same time . . .

There was a knock on the door, and before Leo could say "come in," his landlady entered, balancing a heavy tray holding a teapot, cup, bowl of sugar, and large steaming bowl of breakfast.

"I made you a thick bread soup, inspector," she said warmly, setting the tray down on the bedside table. "That'll give you strength. You must eat or you'll get a fever."

With a sigh Leo sat up in bed. This was the third time Frau Rinsinger had visited him at his sickbed. She fussed more than his own mother and was twice as exhausting. He was lucky she didn't spoon-feed him.

"Thank you, Frau Rinsinger. I'll have some soon."

She raised a stern finger. "Don't let it get cold or I'll get cross! Oh, and I went to the coffeehouse across the road to telephone the police station. They are informed."

"What would I do without you, Frau Rinsinger!"

Leo had told his landlady that he was struck down by an intruder during a nighttime assignment. Frau Rinsinger thought police work extremely exciting—a gruesome murder or wild shoot-out was a welcome diversion in the widow's otherwise quiet existence—so long as it didn't interfere with her nocturnal rest.

"Maybe I will get one of those telephone apparatuses," she said pensively. "Apparently that's what one does these days. Frau Schlesinger also has one, and she was only married to a councillor, whereas I—"

The doorbell rang and Frau Rinsinger broke off, irritated. "Who could that be? You need absolute rest, Herr Inspector!" Still cussing, she walked out to the hallway.

A short while later, Leo heard scraps of conversation through the thin walls.

". . . honestly don't know if you should visit him now, fräulein," Frau Rinsinger was saying. "He's very feeble. Any disturbance . . ."

"I don't think he'll consider a visit from *me* a disturbance, Frau Rinsinger," replied a bright voice. "And besides, I'm bringing news from the police station. You might say I'm here on official business."

Leo smiled. It was Julia. Followed by irked mutterings from his landlady, she walked into his room.

"But no more than half an hour!" protested Frau Rinsinger from the hall. "Or it's your fault if he catches his death. He must eat his soup, remind him! And he took off his bandage."

"Thank you for your kindness, Frau Rinsinger," said Leo without much energy. "If you'd please leave us now."

Julia shut the door and rolled her eyes. "Next time I'll bring a sword to help me past the dragon."

"Shh!" Leo placed a finger on his lips. "Lower your voice. There's a good chance the dragon's still right behind the door."

"Well, I didn't say it was an *evil* dragon . . ." Julia spoke right at the door. Then she became turned serious. She stepped up to his bed. Leo noticed that she looked tired and pale, as if she hadn't slept much. "How are you?" she asked sympathetically. "I found out at work earlier. Loibl told me. I went in to drop off some photos. Loibl didn't know any details, though. Something about a covert investigation. You should have called me!"

"It's . . . it's not that bad. A nasty blow, that's all. Though my head's still ringing like a bell." In halting words Leo told her about the eerie night at the Rapoldys'. Julia listened, stunned.

"A mummy." She shook her head. "How scary . . ."

"More like someone pretending to be a mummy. Even though I haven't the foggiest idea how they might have done it. There were no tracks and the thing was really big. If it was a person, we're looking for a giant. Someone with Bruno's stature." Leo straightened up. "As soon as I'm back in the office I need to try and get hold of Professor Kerfeld. It bothers me that he was neither at the university nor at home yesterday. What if something really has happened to him?"

"Like a visit from a giant mummy?" joked Julia. Then her eyes softened and she squeezed his hand. "Why didn't you call me after it happened? You could have come to me last night, I would have looked after you! If I were cynical I might say you enjoyed spending the night on the Rapoldys' chaise longue."

"Julia, don't be silly. I had a bad blow to the head. I wasn't going anywhere, not even to you. That aside, you know how much Elli dislikes me spending the night at yours. She's threatened to throw me out more than once." Leo changed the subject. "You said before you had news from work. Let me guess. It's got something to do with the photographs you brought in?"

"You're right." Her face darkened. "There was another murder. This time, in Mariahilf, the sixth district, and it was the same awful sight. Someone stabbed a young man to death and cut off his private parts. A nasty bloodbath. Loibl called and asked me to come."

"Do they know who the victim is?" asked Leo.

"Looks like it actually was a hustler this time. A few of them were at the crime scene and recognized him. A young lad, not yet eighteen!" She shuddered. "Sometimes I wonder how much longer I can do this work without becoming damaged myself. But do you know the worst part? You grow used to it. When I developed the pictures this time, it didn't affect me nearly as much as the first murder, the one in Meidling . . ." She trailed off.

"What is it?" asked Leo.

"I just remembered something. At the first crime scene, Loibl said he'd seen something like this before. I think he said it was in Leopoldstadt, near Prater park."

"Leopoldstadt?" Leo gestured in alarm, almost swiping the tray with the soup off the table. "Loibl never mentioned this to me or Leinkirchner, damn it! That would make it three cases. It can't be a coincidence."

"Loibl still insists it's a dispute among pimps," said Julia. "But I don't believe it. The first victim's lipstick was applied later on, and his pants were missing. In Mariahilf last night I couldn't see any pants, either . . ."

"Apparently, the victim in Meidling worked as a prostitute at least occasionally," said Leo. "A certain Jakob Markowitz from Ottakring. He worked other districts so that no one would recognize him, especially his family. That's what the investigation turned up. And you just said that the second victim was a young hustler, so Loibl is right insofar as the cases involve hustlers. But still, it's strange. The three victims were found in different districts. Meilding, Mariahilf, and apparently Leopoldstadt? Doesn't sound like an act of revenge by a band of procurers. Those fellows usually stick to their own turf. This god-awful headache . . ." He scrunched up his face in pain. "Loibl is an idiot! Just because he solved the murder at the zoo so quickly, he seems to think he can pull a few quiet days at the office, guzzling brandy all day long."

"I don't know if the murder at the zoo is really solved," said Julia in a thoughtful tone. "Yesterday afternoon, I visited chief Saidrovuni at the judicial complex. I just couldn't stop thinking about the case." She told Leo about her visit to Saidrovuni's cell and what he'd told her.

"A demon?" Leo snorted. "As if a mummy weren't enough! I'm sorry Julia, but that sounds like a lame excuse. They found the key in his possessions, and the warden's cap. And he stole the cap, admitted it himself. Don't be mad at me, but I think you're allowing yourself to be guided by misplaced empathy. And you put yourself at risk with your recklessness! If Leinkirchner finds out, you're out of your job faster than you can squeeze the release."

"You didn't speak with Saidrovuni. Something tells me that he isn't lying. Call it female intuition. I think the security bureau would do well to reopen the investigation."

"Julia, please understand that I can't be involved with every case! Leinkirchner made it very clear that the mummy case is top priority. The funeral's today and—" Leo hesitated. "What time is it?"

Julia checked the pocket watch lying on the nightstand beside the soup and teapot. "Quarter to five. Why?"

Leo frowned. "The funeral is this evening at Central Cemetery. It's private, only close friends. If we hurry, we can make it before the gates shut. I'm sure our friend Augustin Rothmayer can point us in the right direction."

"And why do you want to go there?" Julia raised an eyebrow at him. "Want to offer Charlotte Rapoldy your condolences? You had all night for that."

"Offering one's condolences isn't the silliest idea at a funeral," replied Leo curtly. "More importantly, though, the whole committee of the Archaeological Society is going to be there. I keep thinking that all these puzzles could somehow be answered by this club. And maybe we'll bump into our missing Professor Kerfeld. He's on the committee, after all." Leo struggled to his feet. "Could you pass me my suit, Julia? If we hurry, I might even have time to shave."

"There is a clothing store on Lange Lane, isn't there?" asked Julia.

"Yes, but why—"

"Tell you what. You shave and I'll go ahead and look for some undergarments for girls." She winked at Leo. "Or have you forgotten Herr Rothmayer's request?"

An hour later, Leo and Julia rushed down the narrow paths of Vienna Central Cemetery, heading for the gravedigger's house. Frau Rinsinger hadn't wanted to let Leo go. To mollify her, he'd had a few spoonfuls of the then cold, bland soup and mentioned an unavoidable work assignment. He'd had to promise her not to do anything strenuous, which wasn't difficult with his intense headache.

Late afternoon was turning to dusk—the birdsong gradually quieting, the shadows growing longer. They passed the occasional visitor, but they were all headed toward the exit. The porter had told them the gates were closing in half an hour, but Leo mumbled an excuse and rushed inside anyway with Julia. At least he looked the part in his black suit.

Leo knew the way to the gravedigger's hut, including its perils. When he reached the "danger—earthworks" sign, he continued straight ahead instead of turning off the path.

"Can't you read?" asked Julia. "We need to take another way."

"Sure, if you don't mind being crushed by rotting coffins or falling into a pit," replied Leo. "Rothmayer has practically barricaded himself in back there. He's afraid they'll take Anna away. Apparently, welfare has already visited several times."

"So that's how bad things are," murmured Julia. "I always suspected something like this would happen."

They continued on the main path, which soon brought them to the suicides field and then to the small cottage with its flower boxes. Leo went to knock but Julia yanked him back.

"Watch out!" she hissed.

At the last moment Leo spotted the board he'd been about to step on. A thin wire stretched from it to the roof. Leo stopped and coughed.

"Herr Rothmayer, are you there? It's me, inspector Herzfeldt. You have nothing to fear."

Something clattered inside. The door opened, and Rothmayer's grumpy face stared at Leo. The gravedigger blinked, his eyes flicking upward.

"If you're checking on your new alarm system, it's most likely functioning," said Leo. "At least if your visitor doesn't notice it first. What is it this time? A bucket full of coffin nails? A scythe swinging down?"

"Pah! Only horse dung," growled Rothmayer. "I'm not trying to kill anyone."

"Oh, how considerate of you. I'm glad to see you're learning. Your last so-called alarm system nearly knocked me out."

"No one but yourself to blame if you can't read. At least the suicides field is nice and handy." Rothmayer eyed him suspiciously. "Whatcha want, inspector? I'm finished for the day. Anna and me are playing dominoes and I'm losing. Meaning I'm already in a foul mood. I don't need no copper on top."

"Pardon the intrusion, Herr Rothmayer," Julia said from behind Leo. "We're looking for a funeral that's meant to take place this evening. And I brought something for Anna." She held up a bundle.

"Undergarments and a few other bits and pieces. You had asked for some?"

Apparently Rothmayer hadn't noticed Julia in the twilight. He smiled. "Ah, Fräulein Wolf! Why didn't you say so." He gestured invitingly. "Come in, come in. Anna will be pleased to see you. Perhaps you'll bring Sisi again sometime? How is she?"

"Later, Herr Rothmayer," piped up Leo. "First, we need your help. Apparently there's an exclusive funeral being held tonight after closing time. Professor Strössner—you already know his body from the forensic institute."

"The mummy? You needn't have hiked all the way out here. Strössner is being buried up at the arcades, not far from the main gates. A posh 'un like him gets his own crypt, of course. A Vienna pyramid, so to speak."

Leo groaned and turned to Julia. "We should have known. A proper privileged funeral. After hours and right at the top by the arcades."

Rothmayer seemed intrigued. "Why are you attending the funeral? Is there news about the curse?"

"Know what, why don't you just come with us?" Leo suggested. "We're in a rush. I'm afraid the funeral's already started."

"And who's going to watch Anna while I'm away, huh? Only yesterday I had another letter from the welfare office. I'm not leaving her alone even for a moment!"

"We won't be long, promise," said Julia. "And no government official ever turns up after clocking out—they're all at home, eating their roast dinner." Anna peered out from behind Rothmayer. Julia waved her bundle, winking at the girl. "Why don't you try on what's in here in the meantime, Anna? There are two skirts, too, used but pretty. Take a look, see what you like, all right?"

Rothmayer hesitated, then nodded. "Very well, then. Before one of you walks into my new alarm system on the path—I came up with something special." He grinned. "Your swinging scythe wasn't far off the mark, Herr Inspector."

"You ought to quit this nonsense," warned Leo. "Before something really does happen."

Rothmayer said nothing. He slipped into his black coat and marched ahead. The entire way to the front gate, he muttered under his breath, "Want to take Anna away from me just to stick her in an orphanage! A fat lot of good that's going to do! She'll know no one, and most of the ones in there will end up as beggars or whores in the street. I won't let it happen! I have ideas, new ideas how I'm gonna show them exactly what I . . ." Rothmayer painted vivid pictures for Leo and Julia about his various plans.

But Leo wasn't really listening. He was much too tense, eager to find out whether Professor Walter Kerfeld would be among the funeral guests—and who else might show up. He hoped to find some sort of clue, something that would help him solve this mystery.

"By the way, I did a little more reading in my books, and in those Professor Hofmann kindly lent me," said Rothmayer as they walked along the rows of graves. "The eye of Horus is a well-known symbol among Egyptologists. It signifies immortality."

"Well, humans still haven't found a fountain of youth," said Julia with a shrug. "Not even Big Elli."

Dusk had fallen across the cemetery by now. The countless crosses and tombstones stood out darkly in the gray of evening. In the shadows beneath the bushes and few trees, it was already night. A deer grazed on an overgrown grave; a small owl hooted somewhere. Not a soul was about. Leo thought of all the ghost stories about cemeteries—about revenants, ghouls, and grave robbers . . . Oddly, though, he felt quite at ease. Maybe that was because of the perpetually babbling gravedigger at his side.

About two hundred yards north of the main entrance lay the so-called arcades, housed in a semicircular brick building in a

Renaissance Revival style. Inside, niches with statues marked entrances to crypts. Leo saw tacky marble angels and temple-like columns, sculptures that might be deities or sleeping beauties. There was even a grotto with dwarves. It seemed to Leo like a sad and senseless attempt to make death a part of the world of the living.

As if one could buy immortality, with enough money, he thought.

To his right, about a dozen people stood gathered in the dim light. The men were dressed in black with top hats, conversing quietly. Farther back toward the entrance, several elegant carriages stood parked. Several lanterns had been set up to illuminate one crypt in particular. Underneath the arch of the arcade was a pyramid as tall as a man bearing bronze lettering. At its top shone the Egyptian ankh, a symbol of immortality.

"As if we were in Alexandria instead of Vienna," grumbled Rothmayer, stopping with Leo and Julia in the darkness of a niche. "A few fat angels would have done the trick. And just a stone's throw away, they have to share shaft graves by the dozen! In ten years, they'll all have the same white bones, whether they're in a pauper's grave or an imperial crypt." The gravedigger grinned. "I haven't found no skull of gold yet!"

It seemed the coffin bearing Strössner's body had already been stowed in the crypt; the ceremony was over. Leo saw Professor Hofmann from the forensic institute and Dr. Dedekind from the Museum of Art History deep in conversation. Close to the pyramid, the Rapoldys were speaking with a gentleman with wavy black hair and a mustache, who, strangely, wore tall riding boots with his tailcoat and top hat. Professor Kerfeld was nowhere to be seen.

"I don't believe it," whispered Julia. "The man speaking with the Rapoldys—the one wearing the riding boots—is Friedrich Knauer, the director of the zoological garden! I met him on Monday."

"This society is a fairly illustrious group. Museum curators, directors, professors . . ." Leo removed his homburg hat. "I'm going to go over there and see what these gentlemen can tell me about the whereabouts of their esteemed colleague Kerfeld. Maybe I'll glean something useful."

"I better stay here with Herr Rothmayer," said Julia. "It was risky enough when I came along to interview the Rapoldys with you. And now the zoo director is here, too. He knows who I am."

Leo nodded. "You're probably right, it's too risky. Leinkirchner will have our heads." He thought it best to say nothing at all to Leinkirchner of this unplanned visit to Central Cemetery.

Hat under his arm, Leo strode toward the group on his own. Charlotte Rapoldy was the first to spot him. Her face was concealed behind a veil, but still Leo thought he caught a look of irritation behind it.

"Herr von Herzfeldt, as much as it gladdens me to see you much recovered, I'm surprised at your presence here. This is a private ceremony." Her voice sounded hoarse.

"I'm sorry to intrude, Frau Rapoldy," said Leo. "But I'm still looking for Professor Walter Kerfeld. I hoped to find him here."

"Well, he isn't here," butted in her husband. "You can see that." Clemens Rapoldy limped closer with his walking stick. The ivory jackal head gleamed dully in the light of the lanterns. "I already told you that Professor Kerfeld is highly unreliable."

"And you're not at all concerned that something might have happened to him?" asked Leo. "He failed to show for one of his lectures at the university. He isn't at home. Kerfeld would be the fourth from your group to die or vanish mysteriously."

"So now you believe in the curse, too," breathed Charlotte.

"I didn't say that, but—"

"Can I help?" Friedrich Knauer stepped up to them. The zoo's director eyeballed Leo distrustfully. "This is a private funeral. I don't believe I've seen you at our committee meetings, Herr . . . ?"

"Herr von Herzfeldt is a friend of the family," said Charlotte Rapoldy quickly, shooting a look of warning at Leo. "He merely wished to express his sympathy."

"Oh, well, in that case," muttered Knauer. "Apologies, I wasn't aware."

"Charlotte and I are acquaintances from long ago," said Leo. "Uh, once upon a time I considered studying Egyptology. She told me many exciting stories, including about her father's expeditions."

"Well, and now it seems one of those expeditions cost him his life," said Knauer regretfully. "Malaria is a nasty disease. Professor Strössner was a luminary, a titan of Egyptology! The archaeological society loses its greatest man with him."

"What is it exactly that your society does?" asked Leo.

"Well, we've dedicated ourselves to the preservation of ancient Egyptian history," replied Knauer. "We host seminars, conduct small research trips. Some of our members are among the most generous patrons of Egyptology in Europe." He nodded toward a group of older gentlemen behind them. "The gentlemen Seilkamp and Scherding have both dedicated their fortunes to Egyptology. Franz Ritter von Hauer is the director of the Museum of Natural History, and—"

"Thank you, um, I already know those gentlemen," said Leo, wanting to avoid the attention of Dr. Dedekind and Professor Hofmann. So far, no one except for the two of them and the Rapoldys knew his true identity.

"You're welcome to attend any of the society's events as a guest," said Knauer amiably. "With a sponsor, it would be no problem at all. I, for example, invited young Rebers. His presentation on the subject of ancient Egyptian ideals of beauty was well received. Carl Rebers is my assistant at the zoo and a biologist like me." He pointed out the only younger man among the group, currently in conversation with Clemens Rapoldy. The gangly youth with bright red hair and freckles was dressed in a black suit a couple of sizes too small. Like Knauer, he seemed ill at ease in mourning attire.

"You see, it's never too late to take up a new interest," he continued. Our members come from many different backgrounds. And we could do with some young blood. Look at us old men!" Knauer laughed, then stopped abruptly when he noticed Charlotte Rapoldy's stern look. "Forgive me, Charlotte, that was out of place . . ."

There was the crunching sound of wheels on gravel. Leo turned to see a carriage drawn by six black horses approaching from the main entrance.

"Are you expecting another guest?" he asked, intrigued.

"He . . . he said he'd come," said Knauer quietly. He squared his shoulders, almost like a soldier standing to attention. "But we didn't think he'd . . ."

The carriage door opened and out climbed an older man Leo recognized only from pictures. He wore a plain military uniform adorned with so many medals that it seemed to weigh him down. The bushy beard on his cheeks was white. His resemblance to his powerful relative uncanny; like the emperor, Archduke Rainer Ferdinand was an imposing figure.

"As an honorary member of the society, His Excellency wishes to express his sympathies to me and Clemens," said Charlotte Rapoldy quietly to Leo. "Incognito, of course. Please excuse me." Her head held high, her face still concealed behind the veil, she strode toward the archduke, who removed his hat and bowed to her. As Leo watched the scene, one thing became very clear to him.

If His Excellency the archduke Rainer Ferdinand was also a member of the archaeological society, this case was much more delicate than they'd thought.

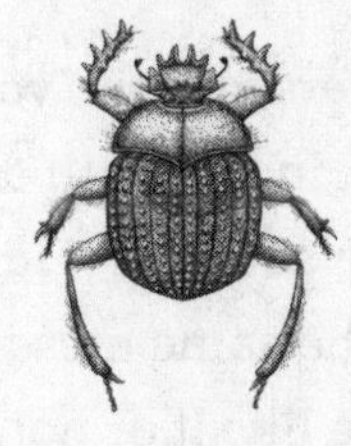

CHAPTER 11

When Leo arrived at the office the next day, he could barely feel the wound on his head—and still, it had taken all his powers of persuasion to prevent Frau Rinsinger from applying another bandage.

Erich Loibl was already at his desk. He looked up from his files and gave Leo a nod.

"Paul told me about your little accident. Something to do with a covert operation, was it?" He pointed at Leo's head. "I don't suppose you'd like to share?"

"As you just said, it was a covert operation," replied Leo, sitting down. He wanted to write up his report for Leinkirchner and make a few telephone calls, but first there was something he needed to take up with Loibl.

"It's rich, I have to say," complained Loibl, scratching his unshaved chin. "We sit here, day in, day out, working together as friends and colleagues, and suddenly everyone's keeping secrets. Would never have thought Paul to be like that. Oh, well . . ." He pushed some files over toward Leo. "He reckons you're to support me with those hustler murders, despite your oh-so-secret operation. There's been a second case, in the sixth district. Maybe you already heard from, well . . . other sources." He winked at Leo. "Fräulein Wolf took pictures. It was the same mess as in Meidling. We'll have to share the job, whether we like it or not."

"I hear it's actually the third case already," Leo said pointedly.

That gave Loibl pause. "Who told you that?" He peered at Leo suspiciously. "Fräulein Wolf again, was it?"

"It doesn't matter. Apparently you mentioned something—something about a case in Leopoldstadt, near the Prater. You might remember vaguely?"

Loibl frowned and thought for a while. "Oh, that!" he exclaimed eventually. "But that was more than a year ago. A fisherman found a sack in the Danube Canal. A sack with body parts—the arms and torso of a younger man. No head. And someone had done some chopping down below. There wasn't much left that would have helped in any way. The sack had been in the water for a few weeks."

"And you only mention this now?" asked Leo.

"Listen, that wasn't the first time someone discarded body parts in that way. Sometimes it's tiny newborns! You'd know if you'd grown up in Vienna, not in small-town Graz. We were never able to identify the victim, which isn't ideal, but—"

"Don't you see, Loibl? Three young men were found with their penises and testicles cut off—all three in different districts! That's not the work of a pimp with a grudge! They always stick to their own turf."

Loibl bit his lip. His eyes turned to the drawer, where, presumably, he kept his bottle of booze. "The . . . the victims might have been found in different districts, but they might all come from the same place originally," he said hesitantly. "That's still an option."

"Christ, use your brain!" Leo groaned. "Assume for a minute that the case is what you say and some pimp is trying to mark his territory. His message to the boys would be: 'watch out!' And he would leave his message out in the open. He would leave the body in *his* district, somewhere where it would be easily found. Unlike in our cases." He gestured at the photographs on the table in front of him. "I think these cases are about something else. The murderer hid the bodies and on top of that tried to mislead us by making them look like hustler murders. He's trying to divert from his real motive." Leo rose.

"What are you going to do?" asked Loibl.

"What do you think? I'm going to see chief inspector Leinkirchner and report to him. I believe we aren't looking for any murderous, vengeful pimp but some madman who targets young queer men. Someone who poses as a customer. Perhaps he's a homosexual himself."

"You stay where you are!" Loibl rose, shaking. Leo saw how pale he looked, noticed he was unshaved, dark rings under his eyes. "Paul put me in charge of this case. You . . . you're merely assisting! I've had enough of everyone telling me how to do my job. The Leopoldstadt case, you heard that from Wolf, too! I'm going to make a complaint. I won't stand for womenfolk taking over our investigations."

"Are you saying you're simply going to ignore the third case and its implications?" asked Leo menacingly.

"No . . . no, I'm not." Loibl held on tight to the desk like a man drowning. At last he sighed and threw up his hands. "Please understand, Herzfeldt. If you go over there now, how does that make me look? I . . . things aren't great at the moment. My wife . . . well, she no longer lives with me. Says I drink too much. But it . . . it'll work itself out. I'm aware that my work hasn't been the best as of late. Then the zoo case came along and I thought things were looking up . . ." He faltered, beads of sweat on his forehead. "I'm asking you as your colleague, Herzfeldt. Let me go to Leinkirchner and tell him about this. I know it was a mistake—I should have mentioned the third case. I . . . it simply slipped my mind!"

Leo sat back down. He felt sorry for Loibl. He knew nothing about his colleague, except that he liked to sneak the occasional drink at work and that he avoided hard work when possible. Leo had had no idea about marital problems, just like he hadn't known that Paul Leinkirchner was married and owned a dog.

We know so little about one another, he thought, wondering if the same held true for him and Julia.

"Fine." He nodded. "You tell Leinkirchner. I've got that other case, too, and I'm supposed to be writing a report. It's all a bit much at the minute, to be frank." Leo pointed at the bump on his forehead, smiling peaceably. "Who knows, maybe I'm a little forgetful these days."

"Thanks, Herzfeldt. I owe you one." Loibl swallowed visibly again. His hand moved toward the drawer but then jerked back. He pushed back his greasy hair, ran his fingers over his walrus moustache, then went on his way to Leinkirchner's office.

Leo drew a deep breath. Then he picked up his fountain pen and paper and started to write down all that had happened in the last two days. It wasn't an easy task, mostly because he hadn't made any progress whatsoever. He interrupted his work several times to make phone calls to the university as well as to Walter Kerfeld's home, but the professor still hadn't resurfaced. And his search for the doctor issuing Father Gregor's death certificate in Graz was still a dead end. It was infuriating!

Deep in thought, Leo gazed out the small window. Had he found out anything new at all during his visit to Central Cemetery? Well, at least he knew now that the archduke was very close with the Rapoldys—which didn't make things any easier.

After the funeral at the arcades, Leo and Julia had gone back to Augustin Rothmayer's. Anna had been immensely pleased about the visit and also with the clothes Julia had brought. For a while they'd been almost like a small family, as if Augustin Rothmayer was their grouchy grandfather. But then it was time for Julia to return to the Blue Dragoon. Rothmayer let them both out though a smaller gate in the cemetery wall and Leo had gone home to his rented room. He'd told Julia his head still ached, but in truth, it was also because the incident with the walking mummy was still on his mind. There had to be an explanation! He had a sense that he'd seen something in the Rapoldys' garden that might help him along, but he couldn't figure out what it was for the life of him.

Loibl was still over at Leinkirchner's; the conversation seemed to be taking a while. Or else the chief inspector had sent Loibl on an assignment—perhaps to interview more witnesses in the hustler murders? The photographs still lay in a disorderly pile on the desk.

Leo moved his unfinished report aside and studied the pictures Julia had taken at the most recent crime scene. Sometimes he regretted having landed Julia this job. So much blood, so much horror, each image telling a new story with a terrible ending. This time, the victim had been found in a barrel by the side of the road. The same gruesome details—stab wounds all over the body, one well-aimed thrust to the heart. The penis nowhere to be found. Again, the victim was young and exceptionally handsome. Could their murderer be a crazed punter who was on the hunt all across Vienna, castrating his victims and then disposing of them in remote corners? At least it was a rock-solid murder case. There were no walking mummies or curses from an Egyptian priest who had died millennia ago.

Leo was about to focus back on his report when the telephone rang. He picked up in the hope it might be the doctor from Graz.

"Inspector Herzfeldt speaking," he answered.

"Ah, the baron himself!" warbled a female voice. It was Margarethe from the phone exchange, a former colleague of Julia's. "Just the person I was after. I have someone on the line for you, inspector."

"From Graz, by any chance?"

"Um, no, not from Graz. From Vienna. A certain Professor Walter Kerfeld. Says it's urgent."

Leo breathed a sigh of relief. At last a little light on the horizon of their investigation. "Put him through."

There was a click. Next, Leo heard strange rattling breathing on the line. Was it a bad connection?

"Herr Professor . . . ?" he asked carefully.

"Inspector Herzfeldt, it's you, yes?" It definitely was Kerfeld's voice. But it sounded strange, slightly distorted. "Are you . . . are you alone?"

"Uh, yes I am. What is this about, Herr Professor? I've been trying to get ahold of you. You haven't been at the university, nor did you attend the funeral at Central Cemetery last night. I think we better—"

"My life is in danger! That's why I moved into a hotel. Listen, I have important information. Information about Strössner's mummy. The whole thing has been planned well in advance! He isn't who he claims to be!"

"What . . . rather, who do you mean?"

"I can't tell you on the telephone." There was a rustling sound as if the professor was holding his hand to the mouthpiece. His voice dropped to a whisper, barely intelligible. "I . . . I believe I'm being watched. Let's meet at a public place—that seems safest to me." Kerfeld was breathing heavily. "Say, St. Stephen's Cathedral in half an hour? And make sure you come alone!"

There was a crackle on the line and then it was cut. Leo hung the earpiece back on its holder. His heart beat wildly. He leaned back in his chair and breathed deeply.

At long last he'd find out what truly lay behind the mysterious mummies and the curse—or so he hoped.

His report would have to wait a little longer.

A short while later, Leo rushed out of police headquarters, his coat billowing behind him.

He was much too early, really. It wasn't even fifteen minutes from Schottenring to St. Stephen's Cathedral, and Professor Kerfeld was meeting him in half an hour. But Leo couldn't bear to be in the office a moment longer. What in God's name did the professor have to tell him? The man felt threatened. And, apparently, by someone in particular. That's what he had suggested on the phone.

He isn't who he claims to be. . . . Those had been Kerfeld's words.

Leo passed the stock exchange, which was already busy at midmorning, and entered the first district, the city's wealthy center. The doors of the shops and coffeehouses stood open with the summery weather. Their first patrons sat outdoors, sipping their coffee, enjoying the sun on their faces. Leo would have liked to join them. Instead, he was on the trail of a mummy. Two, in fact, if he counted the Egyptian princess, whose mummy was also missing.

He isn't who he claims to be. . . .

Who was Kerfeld talking about? Well, Leo would soon find out.

Just before Lugeck corner he turned right and headed toward the cathedral square, which was bustling with life. Women carrying parasols and shopping baskets strolled across the square; businessmen were looking for an early lunch. The wide, cobblestoned area was busy with numerous beggars and street musicians, and two uniformed constables looked bored doing their rounds.

Leo checked his watch. He still had fifteen minutes. He decided to wait a little. Maybe he'd be able to observe which direction Kerfeld came from and whether he was being followed.

When no one appeared ten minutes later, Leo approached the large open entrance to the cathedral. Inside, it was dark and unpleasantly cool, as if winter had sought refuge here. There weren't many visitors in the pews. Up above the main entrance, someone was playing Bach's "Toccata and Fugue" on the organ. Leo knew the piece from his childhood in Graz. The bass notes droned, and the high notes echoed through the nave like the voices of lost souls.

Leo looked around. He'd only met Kerfeld once, but the professor was a memorable figure, with his long gray hair and full walrus moustache. It shouldn't be difficult to make him out among the few churchgoers.

Leo's eye scanned the rows of pews as the music reached a crescendo. There, at the front, in the second row! A man in a black, slightly tattered coat was clearly Walter Kerfeld—his hair was easily recognizable. He was sitting hunched forward, as if he were praying.

Relieved, Leo hastened down the aisle toward the altar. The pews in front and behind Kerfeld were empty; he sat all alone. His body was slumped forward, and Leo thought he saw the professor was trembling . . . because of the cold?

Leo pushed along the narrow pew as swiftly as he could until at last he reached Walter Kerfeld. The professor still didn't look up. His squished and dusty top hat lay carelessly between his feet.

"Herr Professor," whispered Leo. "It's me, inspector von Herzfeldt. You wanted to . . ."

Then the professor looked up, and Leo flinched. Spittle ran from Kerfeld's lips, his eyes wide with fear, his pupils tiny pinholes. His face was frightfully pale, almost yellow.

"*Paternoster* . . . ," gasped Kerfeld. He was trembling all over. Something was wrong with his trousers, too. They bulged at his abdomen as if they contained something large.

"*Paternoster* . . . ," he stammered again, then grabbed Leo by the collar. "*Pater . . . noster!* You . . . you must . . ."

Just then, the church bells began to toll.

The din drowned out the professor's final words as well as Leo's desperate shouts for help.

"Careful, Sisi, the rocks are slippery!"

Julia was sitting on a sunny rock, watching her daughter cautiously navigating the streambed. It was only a small creek, the water no more than ankle deep, the bed made up of slippery gravel and some larger stones that Sisi had placed her feet on.

Julia knew how important it was for Sisi to gain confidence in her own abilities. And the worst that could happen was a wet dress. Still, her maternal instincts won out—her shout of warning had come from a place deep down inside.

Even though she can't hear me, thought Julia wistfully.

Her daughter was wholly absorbed in her own world. Her face set in an expression of concentration, Sisi placed one little foot in front of the other until she reached the other side.

"Well done!" exclaimed Julia and clapped her hands. "When you come back over here, I might just have a piece of cake for you."

Sisi turned to her, and Julia's heart skipped a beat. Had her daughter heard something? But then Sisi gave her a puzzled look. The sudden movement had been pure coincidence.

"Would you like some cake?" asked Julia again, enunciating clearly. She gestured as if she were eating and pointed at the picnic basket. Sisi nodded enthusiastically. She made her way back across the rocks, doing quite well for a three-year-old. When Julia watched her daughter in moments like these, she realized once more that though Sisi was deaf, she was a perfectly normal child—even if some people thought otherwise because she didn't speak and sometimes made strange sounds.

First thing that morning Julia had decided that the day would belong to her daughter. There was no work for her today at the police detention cells at Theobald Lane, where the police camera equipment was kept. And if an emergency should arise, the photography studios on Mariahilfer Street could always fill in for her. And so she had called the police station from the Dragoon and called in sick. No one could blame her, following recent events—even if her male colleagues would probably interpret her absence as another reason women weren't meant to work in the security bureau .

To be fair, the day before in Mariahilf had almost become too much for her. The dead youth in the barrel, butchered like a pig, blood spilled everywhere like wine, and, as always, all those men from the police station looking at her, watching her in case she made a mistake or fainted.

When the May sun sent her milky rays into her bedroom this morning, Sisi was already awake. Julia had packed a few pieces of cake from the evening before into a basket alongside a bottle of homemade lemonade and a little bread and cheese, and then she and Sisi had been on their way. They took the horsecar tram out to Neuwaldegg, a popular destination at the edge of the Vienna Woods. There was a small castle and a lovely, sprawling park. Since it was midweek, there weren't many others about, and they had strolled through the woodland alone until they came across this small babbling brook.

To Sisi, this was paradise.

In the meantime, she had made her way almost back to this side of the creek. Julia spread her arms. "Jump, darling! I'll catch you!"

Perhaps Sisi couldn't hear her, but still, she leaped into her mother's arms. Julia squeezed her tight, planted a kiss on her nose, and tickled her until Sisi giggled.

Julia felt a pang in her heart. She would have liked to go on such excursions together with her daughter and Leo, but Leo preferred to be alone with her. And he was far too tied up in his work; there never seemed to be time for anything more than brief Sunday trips or visits to the theater. Rarely if ever had the three of them spent a day together. Last night at Central Cemetery, they'd had a lovely evening with Augustin Rothmayer and Anna. But then Leo had gone back to his room without her. Julia chewed her lip. Leo wasn't comfortable around Sisi, that much was obvious. Maybe it had something to do with Sisi's disability? Sometimes Julia had the feeling that Leo was suspicious of anything that wasn't perfect.

But life isn't perfect, thought Julia. *Never.*

She led Sisi over to a rock that had warmed in the midday sun. She spread out the picnic blanket, placed two plates upon it, and divided the cake. Sisi devoured hers hungrily. Julia was filled with a deep sense of gratitude as she watched her daughter, the mossy rock, the gurgling water with the light reflecting off it, the green fir trees beyond . . . It was a perfect moment. She walked over to her camera case and set up the apparatus. She was well practiced at this now, and it only took her a few minutes. For once she wanted to capture something beautiful—not the dead, but the living. The police paid for the photo plates, but surely no one would notice if one or two were missing. Plates were fragile, after all.

The light was ideal. A butterfly appeared, dancing around Sisi's nose. Sisi looked up, and Julia pushed the release.

They both smiled.

Her daughter was so beautiful and so fragile at the same time. Sometimes, an overwhelming fear gripped Julia—what would happen to Sisi if one day she was no longer there to look after her? She understood Augustin Rothmayer's fears well. He was just as worried about Anna.

She took three or four more pictures before packing away her camera. When she stowed the dry plates, her eye was caught by some developed plates left in the bag. They were the ones from the day in chief Saidrovuni's cell at the courthouse. So far, she hadn't taken any of the images around to the porter or the warden. The thought alone repulsed her—as if by doing so, she would be delivering the chief to his tormentors all over again.

Carefully, Julia took out one of the plates and studied it closely. The chief's gaze was proud, his facial features chiseled, his eyes free of fear. During the last few months, Julia had taken the pictures of many suspects. She believed by now she could tell by their eyes if they were indeed guilty. She often found out later that her hunches had been correct.

The chief's eyes staring at her from the photograph showed no guilt.

Julia's gaze turned to Sisi, who was crumbling her cake into small bits before stuffing them into her little mouth, her lips and chin sticky with sugar. Saidrovuni had a child, too. When he was arrested, his baby's wailing carried on long after the prison wagon had left. The sound had almost broken Julia's heart.

The things Saidrovuni had told her were strange, as if out of a grim fairytale: a demon with teeth made of iron; a key vanishing mysteriously . . . And yet Julia didn't believe that he was making excuses.

Saidrovuni had seen something in that moonlit night. Or rather, someone.

Julia cast one last glance over his portrait. Then she packed it away decisively. This day was meant to belong entirely to Sisi. But she didn't want to fail Saidrovuni, either. Something needed to happen.

Only, what?

And then she had an idea how she might manage both at once.

Sisi and Saidrovuni.

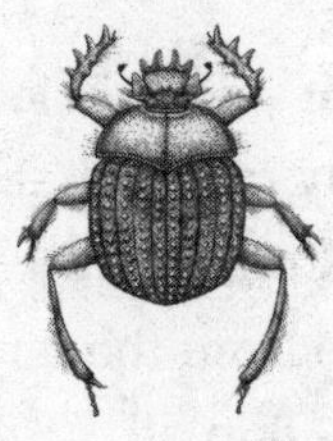

CHAPTER 12

From *Death Rites Around the World* by Augustin Rothmayer, written in Vienna, 1894

> **A particularly infamous form of funeral is cannibalism. In some remote parts of the world, people consume their dead relatives, for they believe that in doing so they imbibe their souls. In some cases, the ashes of the burned corpse are what is consumed; in other cases, the raw or roasted flesh. It is said that the flavor resembles that of pork.**

Morning mist hung in the streets. A few housewives and maidservants shook out feather beds from open windows, a lone horsecar tram jingled from the direction of the Ring, and the paper boys were beginning their first rounds. The air smelled of coal stoves and the horse dung that lay everywhere in the streets. Soon the dung gatherers would come and pick it up. Horse dung made for sought-after fertilizer, especially now, in May.

Leo buttoned up his coat and hurried through the empty lanes of Josefstadt. He was rarely out and about at this hour. Not even Frau Rinsinger was up yet. Consequently, all he'd had to drink was a cup of cold and bitter coffee from the day before. He hadn't shaved, which was highly unusual. All in all, he felt rather rumpled.

He hadn't slept much the night before, just like the previous nights. Yesterday's events had rattled him. Professor Walter Kerfeld had died right before his eyes in St. Stephen's Cathedral! A physician who happened to be in the church was able to do nothing more than to confirm his death. The doctor guessed it was a sudden hemorrhaging of the lungs, or a stroke.

However, neither theory explained a certain dubious symptom: the swelling in Kerfeld's pants that Leo had noticed while in the church. The professor had clearly had an erection right before his death.

Leo felt certain the man hadn't died a natural death. Walter Kerfeld had wanted to tell him something important. He'd mentioned that he was being watched, that he was hiding in a hotel . . . All of it suggested that someone wanted to silence him, and succeeded. Kerfeld had died before he could say anything else.

The previous afternoon had been hectic. Once Kerfeld had been pronounced dead, Leo had arranged for his transport to the forensic institute. Leo had finished his report and then proceeded to inform Leinkirchner and superintendent Stukart. Stukart had not been amused, mildly put.

"Vengeful mummies haunting the streets of Vienna, a professor and suspect dead at St. Stephen's Cathedral with an erection," Stukart had moaned. "What will you bring me next, Herzfeldt? Archduchess Maria Theresa risen from her tomb?"

The police president had personally inquired about the case. Nothing about the mummy case had leaked yet, not even to the papers. On Leinkirchner's orders, the cleaning woman from the Museum of Art History was still in custody. But that could change any day.

And Leo hadn't made the slightest progress.

On the contrary, everything was getting more complicated by the day. Leo almost envied Erich Loibl, who was throwing all his energy at the hustler murders. The angry sermon from Leinkirchner about the forgotten case in Leopoldstadt hadn't eventuated; instead, the chief inspector declared that he was putting together a bigger team to speed up the investigation.

This morning, Leo had risen from bed at six. He knew Professor Eduard Hofmann to be an early riser. It was a fact that the director of the forensic institute occasionally conducted an autopsy before breakfast, whistling a merry tune.

Leo passed by a public fountain where two laborers were washing sleep from their eyes. Then he turned onto Lazarett Lane. A nearby church bell struck half past six. There were no lights in the windows of the forensic institute. Leo cursed softly. What had given him the idea the professor would be at work at this hour? Now he'd have to stand around waiting! Should he go look for a coffeehouse that was open this early? In the nearby university quarter, perhaps?

He was still considering his options when a familiar figure approached the institute. Professor Hofmann was carrying a briefcase and a walking stick, swinging the latter back and forth cheerfully as if he were out on a Sunday excursion in the country.

"Herr Professor." Leo stepped forward and doffed his hat. "I bid you good morning. I'm aware of the early hour but—"

"Ah, inspector von Herzfeldt!" Hofmann stopped as if it were perfectly normal to bump into an unannounced police inspector first thing in the morning. He lifted his top hat. "A good morning to you too. I hear you attended Alfons Strössner's funeral? What a pity I missed you!"

"I thought it best if we weren't seen together. After everything that . . . that's happened," explained Leo.

"I understand." The professor nodded, then wagged a stern finger. "You sure are creating a lot of work for me at the moment."

"I'm afraid I don't follow . . ."

"Well, not you personally. But your department. First Alfons Strössner as a mummy, then those castrated young men. And now poor Walter!" He shook his head remorsefully. "I haven't even had a chance yet to say a proper farewell to him."

"You mean Walter Kerfeld? Uh, that's why I'm here. I don't suppose you've . . ."

"Conducted the autopsy?" Hofmann gave a laugh. "I might be able to work some magic, inspector, but miracles take a little longer. Do you think you're the only department bringing me dead bodies to examine? Yesterday alone we had four suicides: three gas and one fifth-floor balcony jumper. The economic situation isn't what you'd call rosy; in fact, it's a little like 1873, around the time of the world's fair. Even my investments—"

"Herr Professor, do you think you could prioritize the Kerfeld case nonetheless? It really is very, very important."

"Oh well, I suppose I was going to make a start on Walter today anyway. My assistant doesn't arrive until seven. Although . . ." Hofmann's face lit up. "You can give me a hand."

"Me? But . . ."

"Come! The early bird catches the cause of death, as we forensic pathologists like to say." The professor laughed at his own joke and unlocked the door to the institute. Leo followed him down the empty corridors, which smelled of bitter medicines. In hindsight, he was pleased that he hadn't yet breakfasted. Together with Hofmann he entered the familiar autopsy hall. The professor gestured at a table in passing. Underneath a sheet lay the outline of a body. A handwritten tag was attached to a toe.

"Korbinian Meurer," Leo read. *"17 years. Found in 6th district."*

"The lad from Mariahilf," Hofmann said. "Same pattern as the Meidling case. Here, too, it's safe to assume that the penis and scrotum were removed postmortem. Again, there was a well-placed thrust to the heart followed by random stabbing. My report will be sent off with the tube mail later. But you're here for Walter. One moment, please."

Hofmann walked over to the refrigerator and soon returned with a stretcher on wheels bearing a naked dead body.

With his full hair and his walrus moustache, Professor Kerfeld looked like a sleeping Kaiser Barbarossa. Only now did Leo notice how emaciated he was—the body of an old man who had lived a hard life. His face was a dull yellow, a little like rancid butter.

Hofmann studied his dead acquaintance with gentle regret.

"Good old Walter. He never had it easy, but he never made it easy for others, either. Blew his lid the moment someone didn't share his views. I guess it had something to do with his humble origins—quick to use the elbows."

"Did you know him well?" asked Leo.

Hofmann shrugged. "No more or less than I knew the other committee members from the archaeological society. We met occasionally for a glass of cognac, or to lead discussions, attend lectures . . ."

"How did Kerfeld get along with the other committee members?"

"Like I said, he was a difficult man. He clashed in particular with Alfons Strössner and the Rapoldys. He spread some nasty rumors . . ."

"About Strössner and the Rapoldys growing rich from antique treasures? I heard. What do you make of these accusations?"

Hofmann frowned. "I wouldn't have thought Alfons Strössner

needed it. He lived for his research and his reputation. He probably would have been pleased to learn that he ended up as a mummy." He gave a shrug. "Money was never an issue in that family. Properties, bond papers, good connections . . . the usual."

"What about the other committee members? Anyone else struggling with Kerfeld?"

Eduard Hofmann considered this. "Well, Franz Ritter von Hauer is the director of the museum of Natural History. Naturally, there were one or two scientific disputes, also involving Seilkamp and Scherding. Dr. Knauer from the zoo and young Rebers—his assistant, I believe—tended to keep out of it. Those debates could be quite out there. Arguments about embalming techniques across the various epochs; the journey of the dead and various interpretations, deities, and rituals; perceptions of immortality and eternal youth . . ." Eduard Hofmann regarded Kerfeld's body like an interesting exhibit at a museum. "Well, we all of us ought to forget about the idea of immortality. Rest in peace, Walter." He pointed at his scalpel case. "Let's get to work, then. *Small scalpel*, please."

Leo blanched.

"What is it, inspector? We all know this isn't your first dead body."

"But it's the first I'm cutting open!"

"You're only meant to assist. Pull yourself together! By the way, I thought your witness statement from yesterday was interesting. I read your report."

"You mean the saliva and pinhead pupils?" Leo handed Hofmann the scalpel, trying not to look as the professor made the first incision. The knife cut through the wrinkly skin as if through paper.

"Typical signs of poisoning, yes. As is the yellowed skin. And there was something else. An absurdly erect member."

"I noticed it right away. The physician in the cathedral was startled by it, too. I mean, inside a church . . ." Leo swallowed hard when Hofmann, having severed the muscle strands, proceeded to saw open the ribcage. The crunching sound made Leo's blood run cold.

"Yes, it is strange," said Hofmann pensively. He lifted out both lungs before turning his attention to the heart and stomach. He cut out the stomach pouch and held it up to Leo's nose as if it were a sack of candied almonds. The stench made Leo feel sick.

"We'll know more once I have examined the contents of the stomach," said Hofmann. "And his liver and kidneys. But I am prepared to voice a suspicion at this point."

"Which . . . is?" groaned Leo.

"Have you heard of the Spanish fly?"

"You mean the aphrodisiac?"

"*Lytta vesicatoria*." Hofmann nodded as he continued to work. "A green blister beetle that carries the chemical cantharidin. For centuries these beetles have been ground up and sold as an aphrodisiac, as you mentioned. If too much is ingested, the kidneys and liver suffer catastrophic damage, and death occurs about twelve hours later."

"And you believe the professor was poisoned with this?"

"Well, all the signs suggest it. I hope Walter was at least able to enjoy his . . . uh, swelling before he passed." The professor put aside the scalpel. "If you could now assist me in removing the skullcap, Herr Inspector. The bone saw is just over there."

WHEN LEO ARRIVED AT POLICE HEADQUARTERS LATER ON, HIS stomach still queasy, Leinkirchner met him in the hallway. The chief inspector shot a reproachful glance at his watch.

"Slept well, did we? Nice for some. I already got another phone call from the superintendent because of Kerfeld's death this morning, and he in turn got a call from the police president. They await results!"

"Results which I can deliver," said Leo flatly. He had managed to not vomit during the autopsy, but his appetite was truly spoiled. He wasn't sure whether he'd ever be able to enter another butcher's shop without thinking of Professor Hofmann's unnerving whistling. "I've just been to the forensic institute."

"Ah, that's why you look a little pale. Can't handle the sight of corpses anymore, it seems. Well, you better get used to it in Vienna." The chief inspector beckoned Leo toward his office. "We better find a little more privacy. There are some . . . well, changes I must inform you about."

Leo said nothing as he followed Leinkirchner. Not a single word of praise for doing his job this early in the morning, moreover as a corpse-dissecting assistant. Nothing but sneers. But he was used to it from his superior. In Leinkirchner's office, Leo didn't even take the time to sit down before cutting straight to Professor Hofmann's suspicions as to Kerfeld's cause of death.

"He's still awaiting the results from the stomach contents," he said in the end. "But the professor is quite certain: Kerfeld was poisoned with an overdose of Spanish fly."

"Hmm. But that doesn't answer the question of whether it was accidental or not," murmured Leinkirchner, sitting behind his desk and lighting a cigar.

"How do you mean?"

"Well, isn't it obvious?" Leinkirchner waved his match to extinguish it. "Our colleagues have found the hotel where Kerfeld was hiding out for the last few days. It's a small cheap place near Praterstern. Plenty of prostitutes coming and going. There's a good chance the professor met up with one of them—or several of them. According to the hotel staff, Kerfeld never left his room at all, even had his meals taken up to him." Leinkirchner grinned.

"Perhaps it wasn't working the way it was supposed to, and so a little Spanish fly was used . . . And in the end it was too much for his lusty old heart. I could think of worse ways to die."

"Do you really believe that?" asked Leo skeptically. "The professor was trying to tell me something. Something so secret and delicate that he feared for his life. And just before he tells me, he dies from poison. The obvious conclusion is that someone poisoned him to shut him up."

"Have you asked yourself why the man went to St. Stephen's Cathedral?" Leinkirchner snatched Leo's folder from the table and leafed through it. "Yesterday, you stated that Kerfeld muttered a few words before his death. Here! '*Paternoster*.'" The chief inspector pointed at the words in the file. "That makes it perfectly clear. The old sinner went there to pray! Look at it this way, Herzfeldt: Kerfeld amuses himself with a few whores who offer him some powder to help him perform better. He's overcome by a guilty conscience and he goes to church to pray—and then, *bam*. End of story." He flipped shut the folder and tossed it back on the table.

Leo shook his head. He could scarcely believe that Leinkirchner would come up with such an absurd theory. "Beg your pardon, chief inspector, but that's laughable. I still believe that—"

"Let me tell you what I believe," said Leinkirchner, cutting him off. "I believe this case is becoming too big for you. You're losing perspective, Herzfeldt. And then you lie in wait for the Rapoldys at Central Cemetery, asking rude questions!" Leinkirchner's voice grew louder. "Did you really think I wouldn't find out? Clemens Rapoldy himself wrote to the police president to inform him of your faux pas. It was a private ceremony, and one with high-ranking guests. With very high-ranking ones, damn it!"

Leo sighed softly. He hadn't mentioned his visit to Central Cemetery in his report. But he should have known that his little excursion wouldn't remain a secret. At least Leinkirchner didn't seem to know about Julia.

"You said yourself that we must make progress in this case," he tried again. "Where else would I have been able to speak with the committee members of the Vienna Archaeological Society on short notice? Once the cleaning woman is released—"

"Forget about the cleaning woman. She won't say a word. It's been taken care of."

"What . . . what do you mean?"

Leinkirchner leaned back and took a long drag. "She's no longer in Vienna. Don't worry, she's fine. And she has enough money to go looking for a better position elsewhere."

"You bribed her and then made her disappear?" Leo felt compelled to sit down after all. He was stumped. First Leinkirchner was cranking up the pressure to solve this mysterious mummy case as swiftly as possible. And now, suddenly, he seemed intent on concealing any evidence. "The imperial court's behind this, isn't it?" he guessed after a while. "It was an order from high up."

"What were you expecting, smarty-pants?" Leinkirchner gave a shrug. "Something like this was bound to happen, at least after your sniffing around at the cemetery when the archduke showed up. And now the indecent death of Professor Kerfeld . . . His Excellency must be shielded from becoming entangled in all this. It would be a catastrophe!"

Leinkirchner leaned his bulky body across the table and spoke in a calm, firm voice. "I'll tell you what we're going to do. We're closing the case Strössner. The venerable Professor Alfons Strössner died in Cairo from a tropical fever, rest his soul. I'm going to inform Dr. Dedekind and Professor Hofmann right away. No curse, no walking mummies out for revenge. I'm certain those two gentlemen are able to keep a secret. Just like yourself, inspector . . .", Leinkirchner added with a menacing undertone.

"But what about the incident in the Rapoldys' garden?" protested Leo. "Someone tried to—"

"Enough!" Leinkirchner brought his palm down hard on the table. "You had your chance, Herzfeldt. But enough is enough. I can assure you the Rapoldys share my view. We have more important things to do than chase after mummies. The case with the young hustlers is taking on unexpected proportions. If there is indeed a madman out there cutting up queers, I'll need every hand on deck! This very afternoon we're calling a special commission meeting. Stukart wants you there." He leaned back and sucked on his cigar. He eyed Leo inquisitively. "By the way, any idea where Fräulein Wolf might be?"

"Why do you ask?" said Leo tersely. He still couldn't believe they were taking this case away from him. It seemed like everyone was conspiring against him.

"We made a few arrests yesterday and could have done with photographs of the prisoners. Fräulein rang in sick yesterday. I'm guessing all the blood at the crime scenes is getting too much for her. Womenfolk are too sensitive and also a little hysterical, aren't they?" Leinkirchner grinned. "Well, and today we haven't been able to get ahold of her, either. There's this telephone number, but the lady that answers it is pretty harsh—to put it mildly. Not very helpful. The landlady, I guess, a tough old witch." His large body tilted forward again. "You know Fräulein Wolf . . . uh, more closely. Any idea where she might be? In your bed, perhaps, Herzfeldt? A wild mixed-race union . . ."

Leo didn't stoop to Leinkirchner's provocation. Like hell would he tell the man that he planned to take Julia to the theater that night. "I can't help you, chief inspector," he merely replied.

Leinkirchner leaned back, crossing his arms. "Pity. If you happen to see her, please tell her that she's very close to losing her job. She meddles in things she has no business meddling in, and clearly isn't suited to crime-scene photography. I don't think the superintendent will tolerate her behavior much longer. I'll see you at the meeting this afternoon, Herzfeldt. Meanwhile, give Loibl a hand."

Leo rose without replying. As he left the office, from the corner of his eye he saw Leinkirchner toss his report on Kerfeld's death into the trash can.

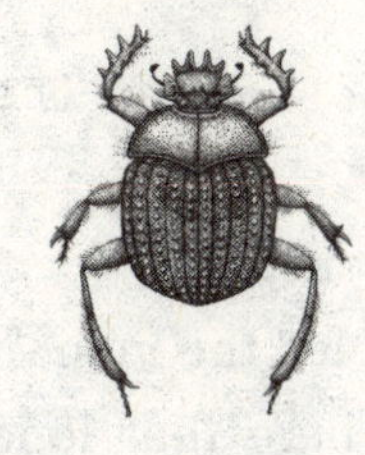

CHAPTER 13

The elephants' trumpeting echoed all the way over to the Praterstern.

Julia grasped Sisi by the arm and beamed a cheerful smile at her. It was a shame her daughter couldn't hear the animals. Well, at least she'd see them soon.

Julia waited for a cart and a single-horse fiacre to pass by before crossing the busy Laufberger Lane, heading toward the entrance of the zoological garden. The idea to visit the zoo with her daughter had occurred to her the day before. During her last visit Julia had noticed how lovely Vienna's latest attraction was—and much more centrally located than the menagerie at Schönbrunn, which was beginning to show its age. Sisi would enjoy the outing and Julia would be able to take a look around. She couldn't stop thinking about Saidrovuni's fate. Julia believed he was innocent. Maybe she'd learn something here at the zoo that would help.

The porter in the small pay booth looked up tiredly from his newspaper. It was early afternoon and quite warm, almost as hot and sticky as the middle of summer. The man had probably been about to nod off.

"One child, one adult," said Julia, opening her porte-monnaie.

"Fifteen kreuzer," grumbled the man. "Gates close at six."

"I don't think we'll be here that long. Thanks anyway." Julia counted out the coins. Not even the famous sharp tongue of Vienna was able to spoil her mood today.

It was the second day in a row Julia was spending with her daughter. Let the police headquarters think she's sick. In some ways, she was—her soul ailed. The last few weeks had been draining. Dead bodies with bullet and stab wounds; suicides; a brutal jealousy murder with an axe; and then a few accidents with those new automobiles that were growing in number. Not to mention those gruesome hustler murders . . . It was a miracle she hadn't collapsed sooner. She deserved this time off.

For tonight, Leo had asked her out to the popular and expensive Ronacher theater. They'd both had a hard week and Julia looked forward to the date—even if she was still a little miffed that Leo had spent the night a few days ago on the Rapoldys' chaise longue instead of her bed. She felt Leo distancing himself from her. Or was she distancing herself from him? Either way—what mattered was that she focused on her daughter.

All the better if she could combine it with a little private snooping. Because that was what she had in mind.

Sisi blossomed under her mother's attention. She laughed a lot and squeezed Julia's hand hard. Julia had had to suppress a grin when, earlier on at the Dragoon, she'd noticed that Bruno was almost a little jealous when she took Sisi with her. Side by side they strolled along the gravel paths past goldfish ponds and bubbling fountains. They stopped at the bear cage and watched the big brown mother bear playing with her two cubs. Sisi gurgled happily as she pointed at the little ones as they chased each other across the rocks. They looked just like teddy bears. An older couple looked over at them and started to whisper, pointing at Sisi. Julia felt a stab in her heart. She knew what people called it when the deaf communicated.

Monkey speak . . .

"Come, I'll show you the other animals," said Julia, pulling Sisi along by her little hand.

They walked on to the zebras, the giraffes, and the elephants, stopping in awe. But Julia also kept her eyes open, though she didn't really know what for.

The idea to investigate at the zoo had come to her during their trip to Neuwaldegg the day before. Saidrovuni had seen a demon in the lion's enclosure: someone or something that had bent over the young keeper. An animal or a person? Julia tried to think. To find out more, she'd probably have to visit the lion. She tapped Sisi's shoulder. Her daughter reluctantly pulled her gaze away from the gray giants, who were currently being fed.

"Would you like to see the dangerous big cats?" asked Julia, moving her lips clearly. She pretended to hiss and mimed a mane around her face. She didn't know the proper sign for it, but perhaps it looked similar to what she was doing. "Grrr! The lion? You know it from your picture book."

They walked in the direction of the lion and other large cats. There was a mangy panther, pacing the perimeter of his cage lonesomely, and even a tiger, but the pavilion with the lion's enclosure was closed off. Someone had nailed a few boards across the entrance. Through the barred windows Julia saw that the cage behind the rows of seats was empty.

She tried to imagine what Saidrovuni had seen. Maybe he'd stood right where she and Sisi were standing. He would have peered through one of the windows, and it had been dark. He couldn't have made much out.

Julia hesitated, then tugged on one of the boards. It wasn't coming off. She spotted a pitchfork, the kind the zoo staff used to muck out the cages. The pitchfork was leaning against the pavilion's side wall. Julia picked it up and winked at her daughter.

"Mama is going to do something naughty. You can't tell anyone, all right? It's our secret."

Intrigued, Sisi watched her mother as she loosened one of the boards, using the pitchfork as a lever. The resulting gap was large enough for them to slip through. Sisi visibly enjoyed their secret game.

Inside, Julia took a close look at the empty, cleaned-out cage. She checked the lock and the pulley used to open the sliding door at the back. Saidrovuni told her that the door had been locked, the lion safely in the rear partition. If it had been a person who had murdered the keeper, then he had come from the front. Either the door was still open, or . . .

Julia paused in her step.

Or because the keeper had known his murderer and let him in.

Someone had entered the cage, killed the young man, and then let the lion back in with the body to conceal his tracks. Once the animal had finished with the corpse, no one would have been able to tell what really happened.

Could that be what had happened?

Saidrovuni had spoken of a demon with long teeth made of iron. *Asan-Bosam*, that's what he called it.

Teeth made of iron . . .

Julia gave a start when her eye landed on the pitchfork she'd set down next to the cage. Its long prongs were the perfect murder weapon. The metal spikes really did look a little like teeth. So, what if someone snuck into the enclosure and—

"Hey, what are you doing here? The pavilion is closed."

Julia hadn't noticed the man stepping out from the rear feeding compartment. He was glowering at them. Fright shot through her when she recognized him as the old keeper, Lenz.

"You aren't supposed to be here, fräulein," said Lenz. Then he stopped, looking hard at Julia. "Hey, I know you. You're that photographer!"

"I'm sorry, we must have gotten lost. Come, Sisi."

Julia grabbed her daughter and slipped back through the boards.

"Hey, wait! What were you snooping around here for? Stop, damn it!"

As quickly as she could, Julia rushed along the graveled paths holding Sisi's hand, the angry voice of the old keeper behind them. Then there was the sound of metal clanging. Presumably, Lenz was leaving the enclosure to pursue them.

Without knowing where she was going, Julia grabbed her daughter and turned right, jogging past the bird cages and then past an enclosure holding buffalo and antelope. Sisi whined unhappily, unable to understand why her mother was rushing past these amazing new sights. A large building now appeared in front of them. Julia had noticed its dome-like turrets from the entrance. The building looked like a small, slightly derelict castle. Wide steps led to an open entrance. Was Lenz still following them? Julia didn't dare turn and look. Dragging Sisi along, she rushed into the dark interior of the building.

They were received by damp warmth, as if they'd arrived in the jungle. The air smelled of rot, soil, and dung. Outside noises became muffled. Weakly lit corridors led off in different directions. There were fish tanks shimmering in a blue light, algae and ferns softly waving, small colorful fish flitting about. More glass enclosures followed, containing green and black snakes dozing on rocks. In others there were frogs, lizards, and newts.

Another corridor branched off to the right, leading them past a handful of visitors to an enormous cage the size of a small cottage. The front of the cage was made of thick glass, allowing for an unobstructed view of the pond inside. At the pond's edge, a number of large crocodiles lay as motionlessly as if they were stuffed. Julia calmed down a little. She regained control over her breathing and listened, catching the muted voices of the visitors but no hasty footsteps, no shouting.

They'd shaken Lenz off.

Julia took a closer look at their surroundings. The crocodile enclosure was situated in one of the building's side wings, illuminated by kerosene lights on the wall. Not much daylight came in through the windows, making the visitor feel as though they were at the bottom of an ocean or concealed somewhere deep under the jungle's green canopy. The effect was soothing, almost hypnotic.

In the cage next to the crocodile enclosure, two giant snakes dangled from branches like fat vines. Just then, a young man wearing tall boots, an apron, and gloves stepped through the branches and leaves. In his hand he carried a sack, and now he pulled a rabbit out from it, almost like a magician with a hat. He held the rabbit out to one of the snakes, and Julia saw to her horror that the rabbit was alive and squirming. The man set down the animal, and it stayed where it was, trembling and apathetic, while the large snake slithered off its branch and moved toward its prey. Then it opened its huge jaws and struck, the rabbit disappearing down its throat. The outline of the twitching meal was still obvious through the leathery skin, slowly moving downwards.

Julia shook herself. This truly was no sight for a little girl. She was about to move on with Sisi when her eye fell on the keeper again. She recognized him now. He was the same young man who'd attended the funeral service at Central Cemetery together with Dr. Knauer. He had stood next to the zoo's director. That day, the lanky youth in his mid-twenties had worn an ill-fitting funeral suit. But his red hair made him quite recognizable. He was lifting a second rabbit from his sack. Julia reached out her arm for her daughter. Sisi really didn't need to see—

Her hand felt nothing but thin air.

"Sisi?" said Julia anxiously, looking around. "Sisi, where . . . where are you?"

Her daughter had gone.

"Sisi!" Julia called out, even though she knew her daughter wouldn't be able to hear. After deliberating for a moment or two, Julia ran down the dark passageway, past the snakes, lizards and frogs. No sign of Sisi. She couldn't have gotten very far! Julia ran past several visitors, then stopped breathlessly and addressed a young woman pushing a baby carriage.

"Have you seen a little girl? Three years old, she's wearing a red jacket and a blue skirt?"

The woman shook her head sympathetically. Julia thought. If Sisi hadn't come past here, she had to be in the reptile area still. Her heart pounding, Julia spun around and retraced her steps to the crocodile enclosure.

And that's when she saw Sisi.

Her daughter hadn't run far at all. She had somehow managed to squeeze though the bars in the cage's side walls. Sisi was standing at the edge of the pond, about to balance across the stones just like she'd done the previous day at the brook in the woods, alone, where there'd been no crocodiles lurking on the banks.

"Oh God, Sisi, get outta there!" screamed Julia, banging against the glass pane. "Get out!"

But her daughter neither heard nor looked up. She deftly placed one foot in front of the other, hopping across the stones. Several of the previously lifeless-looking reptiles glided into the water. One swam directly toward Sisi, its head almost entirely underwater, only the nostrils sticking out like some abhorrent prehistoric monster.

Julia screamed and kept slamming her palms against the pane as Sisi balanced along the stone with outstretched arms.

Suddenly, Julia was shoved aside. It was the red-haired keeper, still holding the second rabbit. He tossed it right over the glass front and the poor creature landed in the water with a splash. The alligator who had been speeding toward Sisi changed course and snatched at the rabbit. Sisi still didn't look up, entirely absorbed by her game.

The man took out a bunch of keys, opened a gate on the side and strode into the enclosure. The remaining crocodiles stayed where they were; perhaps because they knew the keeper. He reached Sisi in just a few steps and grabbed her by her collar. Sisi cried out in shock and surprise as she was lifted away from the stones and through the gate. The door shut with a clang and the thick-skinned reptiles returned to their state of inertia.

Crying, Sisi ran to her mother and clung onto her. Julia was still paralyzed with fear.

"Thank you . . . ," she managed eventually. "If you hadn't been here . . ."

"The beasts are quite placid so long as you don't go in the water," said the lanky young man, breathing heavily. "Most likely, nothing would have happened to your daughter on the rocks. But if she'd fallen in . . ." He broke off, then shook his head. "I told the board several times already that the bars on the sides are too far apart! It's a miracle that nothing happened before today. We should put glass around the whole enclosure, not just the front. But that's too expensive, apparently."

He held out his hand to her before realizing that he was still wearing dirty gloves. A little embarrassed, he withdrew his hand.

"Carl Rebers," he murmured, brushing red hair away from his forehead. With his freckles he looked a little like an oversized rascal. "I'm in charge of the vivarium. It was lucky it was feeding time—normally, I'd be out back in the laboratory."

"Then heaven must have sent you." Julia still held her daughter tightly. Carl Rebers didn't seem to recognize her. Thank goodness she'd stayed in the background at the cemetery, or else this encounter might be much more awkward. "I'm sorry I—"

Rebers brushed her off with a flick of his hand. "Don't worry. We all have reason to be thankful. I can't bear to imagine if something like this had happened again after—" He stopped himself. Julia guessed Rebers knew about the incident in the lion enclosure. But of course the public couldn't find out. She helped him out by changing the subject.

"Aside from this unplanned adventure, this building is really impressive. You really think you're by the sea or in a jungle. Except it's much safer here." She smiled. "Well, normally."

"You think so?" The young man beamed at her. "I'm glad to hear it. The vivarium is getting a bit run down. Originally it was just an aquarium, but then we added the reptiles." He motioned over his shoulder. "Over in the other wing, Hamburg businessman Carl Hagenbeck had an Arctic sea enclosure built. Our fat walrus, Oscar, tosses a whole table set into the water three times a day in front of an audience, crockery and all. That might be a bit nicer for your daughter."

"Yes. Well, at least we've experienced a proper jungle adventure," said Julia.

Rebers laughed. "You're right, of course. I'm not a big fan of those kinds of tricks. Animals aren't meant to be throwing around plates—they can be of real use to us, for scientific research. That's why I became a biologist—not to train animals."

"Some people even train other people like animals." Julia gestured out the window. "I recently saw your so-called ethnic show. Those poor indigenous people are kept like beasts. It's a disgrace, if you ask me!"

"It is a disgrace, yes." Rebers' face darkened. "I completely agree. But don't say that out loud to Friedrich Knauer, our director! I may be his assistant, but we disagree on that topic. As well as on several others . . . ," he added. He gave Julia a shy look, seemed to be weighing something up.

"Can I ask you something?" Rebers said eventually.

"Of course."

"Your daughter is deaf, isn't she? I thought so, earlier, when she didn't look up. And now the noises she's making . . ."

"She's just afraid," said Julia tightly. "And she's hungry." She picked up her whining daughter and held her close. "But aside from that . . . yes. You're right. My daughter is deaf. We really should be—"

"I didn't mean to offend you—I apologize." Rebers lifted both hands. "What I meant to do was to offer some hope. I believe that we may be able to cure deafness in just a few years. Once we know more about how hearing and articulation work in humans. That's what I mean when I talk about scientific research with animals. They can help us, with experiments, for example. That's so much more valuable than teaching them to balance balls on their nose or trot around in a circle."

"You . . . you're probably right," said Julia slowly, feeling bad for her gruff reaction. He had meant well with Sisi. "Thanks again. If there's anything I can do . . ."

"Not at all." Rebers waved, smiling a little sheepishly. "I only hope you'll visit our lovely zoo again, despite the fright. And . . . well, if you wouldn't mind not telling anyone what happened? Or else we may as well close our doors right away. I probably told you more than I should have." He looked at her intently. "My boss will be livid if he finds out."

Julia tried to imagine skinny freckled Carl Rebers next to belligerent Friedrich Knauer. Rebers's position probably wasn't an easy one; it sounded like Knauer steered the new zoological garden with a heavy hand. And he had mentioned differences in opinion. The first time she'd met Knauer, Julia had thought his jovial demeanor had been an act.

"We'll be as silent as the grave, won't we, Sisi?" Julia stroked her daughter's hair. "We want to visit the zoo again in the future. Maybe not the crocodiles, though."

"Thank you!" Rebers breathed a sigh of relief. "Now if you'll excuse me. I need to go feed the frogs and lizards. They're much less dangerous."

Julia gave Carl Rebers one last smile before turning toward the exit.

Once she and Sisi were back outside, she glanced around cautiously. With all of the excitement in the vivarium, she'd almost forgotten about Eugen Lenz and his pursuit of them. But there was no sign of Lenz.

Julia thought about the pitchfork and Saidrovuni's words about the demon with long teeth of steel. What had the grumpy old keeper been doing in the lion's enclosure earlier, anyway? It was empty and closed to the public. What was he up to? Covering up evidence?

"Come Sisi. It's getting late. We've had enough adventures for one day."

Julia took her daughter by the hand and strolled toward the exit, wrapped up in thoughts. Perhaps her encounter with Carl Rebers would come in handy. He might be able to help her find out more about Lenz.

And about Friedrich Knauer, too.

Because Julia couldn't shake the growing suspicion that the zoo's director hadn't told the whole truth in the case Saidrovuni.

That Friday, Leo waded through files until late.

Paul Leinkirchner had dumped a whole stack of potential witness statements from the two hustler murders on him, presumably so that Leo had no opportunity to investigate the Strössner case any further. There were plenty, especially for the second case—from beggars, peddlers, drunks, and harlots. But barely any of the statements proved useful or even made sense, which slowed Leo's work down even more. There was not a single clue about a possible perpetrator.

In the second murder, the body had been identified swiftly. Seventeen-year-old Korbinian Meurer came from Mariahilf, the same district where he was murdered. He was one of the more typical male prostitutes: neglected, no family, living in the street. Presumably, no one would have noticed his disappearance if he hadn't been murdered in such a spectacular manner. The fact that the killer hid the body in a barrel told Leo yet again that this wasn't an act of revenge by a pimp, who would have surely exposed the body as a warning to other hustlers.

And then there were the body parts found in the Danube Canal. Chief inspector Leinkirchner had sent Leo down to the archives, but there was nothing on the case. If a file was ever started on it, then it had long since disappeared into the void of bureaucracy. Just another unidentified victim of the city of Vienna . . .

Leo listened to the ticking of the clock on the wall, which told him it was past six in the evening. He and Julia had agreed to meet at half past seven at the Ronacher. They'd gotten into the habit of visiting the theater once a month. Tonight was also an opportunity to show Julia how much she meant to him. On the program this evening was a potpourri of chansons, artistry, jugglers, magicians, and a Chinese illusion show—just the right recipe for a little diversion.

Erich Loibl had taken his leave quite a while ago, ostensibly, to question more witnesses—but Leo suspected he was hiding in some tavern or other to quench his thirst.

In the meantime, Leo had been going through the files. But he struggled to focus. He still felt utterly outraged that Leinkirchner had taken the mummy case away from him. Since Walter Kerfeld's death, it was crystal clear to him that one person was behind all those strange events.

He isn't who he claims to be. . . .

Who was Kerfeld talking about?

Was the imperial court involved? Leo felt pretty certain that the order to shelve the case had come right from the top. So, if he didn't want to lose his job, there was nothing he could do.

At least not here in Vienna . . .

A thought struck Leo. A few days ago, Leinkirchner had suggested that he ask his father to help him in the case of Father Gregor in Graz.

You Jews are connected. . . .

Well, his father certainly wouldn't lift a finger for him. Not after all that had happened back in Graz before Leo had fled to Vienna. Nor would Leo consider asking his father for anything, ever; he was too proud. But there was someone else he could call.

Leo's hand moved to the telephone.

"Operator," he said. "Please connect me with Graz." He stated a number which was answered a short while later by a familiar voice.

"Leo, is that you?"

Leo smiled.

It felt good to hear her voice.

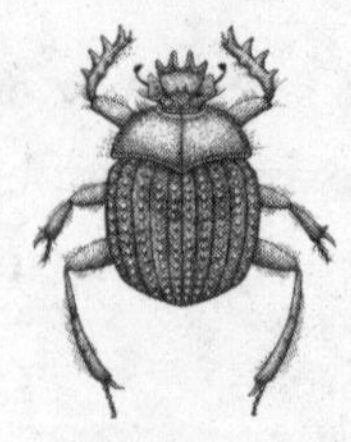

CHAPTER 14

From *Death Rites Around the World* by Augustin Rothmayer, written in Vienna, 1894

> In the fourth book of Moses, the Bible tells of a strange custom the Jewish people allegedly adopted from the Egyptians. If a wife is accused of adultery but denies it, she is brought to the temple and made to drink so-called bitter water. If she is guilty, she dies from the poisonous water—if she is innocent, she lives. It is unknown which toxin this drink contained. It is possible there are substances that are deadly for one person while another feels nothing at all.

The streets of the first district were so busy this Friday evening that one might think it was already Saturday. The warm month of May seemed to have put the whole of Vienna in the mood for outings and amusements. Carriages clattered along the narrow lanes, and men in tailcoats and top hats thronged the sidewalks with their spruced-up companions, trying in vain to avoid the foul-smelling garbage in the gutters.

Julia waited forlornly outside the Ronacher's entrance, holding her umbrella up high so that Leo would better be able to see her. It was the same as always. They had agreed on half past seven, and now the show was about to begin. Why couldn't this man be on time for once? Most theatergoers were making their way to their seats. A bell rang out.

Where on earth . . . ? There!

At last he was running toward her, one hand holding on to his homburg hat, the other swinging a walking stick. As always, Leo's appearance was impeccable. Julia liked to tease him that he spent more time on his wardrobe than he spent with her. And she was only half joking. With his cutaway suit, spats, and walking stick, he looked like a right British dandy. Several women turned to look him over.

"I'm sorry," said Leo breathlessly when he reached her. "The traffic is mad. First I was in a fiacre. When nothing moved, I carried on on foot. I was at the office beforehand, then quickly went home to get changed. You can't imagine—"

"I put a child to bed, cleaned my room, dressed up for you, and took a tram from Neulerchenfeld," she interrupted him. "Don't you tell me anything about office work and getting changed. And now move! Do you have the tickets?"

He looked flustered. "I thought you were buying . . . ?"

"Me? What makes you think I—" She broke off when she saw his grin as he drew out two tickets from the inside pocket of his suit. "Oh, you incorrigible oaf! And I fall for it every single time."

The Ronacher, formerly the Vienna City Theater, was situated between Himmelpfort Lane and Schelling Lane. Following a fire a few years ago, it had been completely overhauled, and now boasted a ballroom seating a thousand guests, boxes, a conservatory, and even a hotel. And it was the first theater with electric lighting. Anything the heart desired in a variety theater was offered here, from half-naked coupletists to magicians and fakirs. The shows weren't cheap, but they were more affordable than those at the Hofburg, and the tickets easier to get. Leo would pay for this evening like he had for others, including snacks and a glass of champagne—Julia would never be able to afford this kind of amusement.

She had decided on a tight-fitting dress with a feathered hat, knowing Leo liked this combination. Both stemmed from Elli's costume wardrobe but looked respectable enough. While Julia had waited, she'd studied tonight's program. She was particularly excited about the illusionist show at the end of the night. Julia loved being led on a journey to another world. In America, they had so-called kinetoscopes: boxes with a peephole through which the viewer was able to see moving pictures. Here in Europe, they still used older techniques like thaumatropes, *laterna magicas*, and phantoscopes. Nevertheless, Julia happily allowed such illusions to sweep her along.

"You wouldn't believe all that's happened," groaned Leo as they pushed their way through the packed foyer to the cloakroom. "They took the Strössner case away from me! The whole thing is simply being dropped—probably at the behest of the court."

"What?" Julia stopped, baffled. "Why would they . . . ?"

"Because things were getting too hot for them. Especially after what happened with Professor Kerfeld." Keeping his voice low, Leo told her of the professor's death in St. Stephen's Cathedral and the likelihood that he was poisoned.

"Murdered?" breathed Julia. "Are you sure?"

Leo nodded. "The suggestion that Kerfeld spent his time at the hotel with prostitutes and then, blinded by his lust, accidentally poisons himself is simply absurd!"

The cloakroom attendant, holding out her arms for Leo's hat and walking stick, looked at him with bewilderment.

"I beg your pardon?" she asked.

"Uh, a new play at the Deutsches Volkstheater," said Julia. "My friend doesn't like it very much." She considered telling Leo about her visit to the zoo today. She had hoped she might be able to get Leo to pick up the Saidrovuni case. But Leo was much too agitated.

"I'm so close to solving the riddle," he whispered as they walked over to the auditorium to look for their seats. "I can feel it. So very close! At least I now have someone in Graz to help me find Father Gregor's death certificate. A highly reliable person that I'm well-acquainted with."

"A colleague from the local police?" guessed Julia.

"Not quite. It's my sister, Lili." Leo grinned. "I should have thought of her sooner! As the wife of a wealthy but boring cloth manufacturer, Lili is grateful for any diversion. This will be more fun for her than embroidery or choosing the furniture for their new villa in Geidorf—Graz's posh quarter. She's going to ask around at the hospitals."

"So long as you don't employ your mother next," said Julia sarcastically.

They arrived at their seats. At the Ronacher, theatergoers sat at tables where they also ate and drank. They shared a table with an elderly couple, a matronly woman with an enormous hat and a gray little man who seemed to have nodded off already. The woman shot Julia a distasteful look and pushed her champagne flute forward as if marking her territory. No sooner had they sat down than the bell rang for the third time. The lights went out.

"I hope you like the show," said Leo. "Not what you'd call fine arts, but—"

"Ssshh!" hissed the older woman next to him. Her husband snored softly. "Intermission is for conversation. This is a theater, not a common tavern." Julia said nothing, merely passing the program to Leo as the curtain opened.

The show began with a man playing the hurdy-gurdy and a little monkey who continually pinched his owner's hat and adorably played around with it. When the monkey clambered into the auditorium and searched the audience for items of clothing worth stealing, the laughter was raucous.

"If that beast pisses on my suit there'll be murder," muttered Leo. The woman turned to him again, glowering angrily.

"Quiet already!"

"Or maybe two murders," Leo added softly.

The monkey reminded Julia of what happened at the zoo today, of the grave danger Sisi had been in. She struggled to concentrate on the act. There was but a small leap from trained animals to trained humans. Nor was she able to stop thinking about the demon with the metal teeth.

The hurdy-gurdy man and his little monkey were followed by colorfully clad artists riding unicycles and juggling bowling pins, throwing them to one another. They were accompanied by Spanish dance music of the kind that Julia loved, and she slowly relaxed. Maybe they'd have a drink or two at the restaurant next door later. They just needed to spend more time together, like they used to in the first few weeks of their relationship. During that time, they'd been very close, and not just when they were dancing or in bed. Julia recalled the animated conversation Leo had led with Charlotte Rapoldy. She had seen by his face that the woman fascinated him, and then, later on, he'd even stayed overnight.

"By the way, Leinkirchner is not happy about you taking sick leave," whispered Leo. "You've got to be careful, Julia! You're already not the most popular person at headquarters at the moment—they feel like you're meddling."

"Let them find someone else who'll stand to attention at any time for a pittance," said Julia quietly but firmly. "I called in sick through all the proper channels. For the first time ever! I was always available, all those months, even on Sundays!"

The woman at their table was about to snap at them again when the music swelled and, accompanied by smoke and thunder, a magician in an elegant coat and top hat appeared on stage. He danced with a ballerina, magically making her clothes disappear one by one, much to the amusement of the audience, particularly the male portion.

"Christ, am I spared nothing today?" complained Leo. "That's just cheap! The Ronacher used to have a good reputation. Is it going to be one knee-slapper after the next? Maybe next time we should try the Hofburg." He glanced at the program leaflet in his lap. Suddenly he made a strange sound, almost as if he were in pain. Julia gave him a startled look.

"What is it? Are you unwell?"

"I'm such an idiot," he said, slapping the paper against his forehead. "Such a goddamned idiot!"

"I've told you as much before. But . . ."

He laughed out loud. "I'll be damned! How could I have been fooled this easily? I know what happened. It's so simple!"

"Shut up already, you loudmouthed lout!" The older woman had reached the end of her tether. Several other guests also turned to look at Leo. People started to whisper, and even the magician on stage glanced into the audience.

"There's one thing I need to check," said Leo, lost in thought. He didn't seem to care that half the room was staring at him now. "But I'm almost completely certain."

"I don't need to put up with this!" spat the lady at their table. "If you can't shut up, leave the theater this instant!"

"That's precisely what I intend to do." Leo rose.

Julia grabbed his arm. "Have you lost your marbles?" she whispered urgently. "What are you doing? You can't just—"

"Julia, I will explain everything later. I see it clearly now! Once I've obtained absolute certainty, I'll send word to you. I love you!"

With that, Leo pushed through the rows of tables and chairs, accompanied by exclamations of protest from the audience members, and rushed toward one of the emergency exits.

"If that's your husband, I would file for divorce right away," said the old woman.

"Oh, why don't you shut your trap, you stupid old hellcat!" snapped Julia. She pointed at the sleeping husband at her side. "You better watch that *your* husband doesn't stop snoring and die of old age during the show."

"You . . . you insolent . . ." The woman looked as if she might have a heart attack. She gulped for air before evidently deciding to ignore the insult. She turned away demonstratively and positioned herself in a way that meant Julia could hardly see the stage over her large hairstyle.

Julia stiffly remained in her seat. The rest of the show rushed past her while she felt people's eyes like pinpricks in her back. To the audience, it must look as if her partner had ditched her ignominiously. And he had, in a sense. Not for the first time . . . Being with Leo was like climbing from a warm bath into a cold one and back again. Julia picked up her champagne flute and drained it in one gulp.

Once again she wondered whether Big Elli was perhaps right after all: maybe she and Leo simply weren't a good match.

Leo promised the driver two extra kronen if he drove faster. Most Viennese were by now enjoying their Friday nights inside taverns, coffeehouses, or theaters, or simply at home; the streets were quieter than an hour ago. Still, there was enough traffic to slow their progress. Leo impatiently shuffled in his seat.

"If you go via the Ring and take Mariahilf Road, you'll be quicker, I think," he suggested to the driver.

The man gave a bored glance over his shoulder. "Wanna drive yourself? No problem! I'll sit in the back and make clever comments."

"Forget it." Annoyed, Leo slumped back in his seat. There was never any point arguing with a fiacre driver. "I'm sure you know best."

"I'd damn well say so." The driver cracked his whip and turned down a side street. Leo was forced to admit that there was less traffic here. As the iron-ringed wheels clattered across the cobblestones, he went through everything in his mind once more. The solution had been right in front of him and yet he'd allowed himself to be fooled! Had he been blinded by the pomp and sophistication? Perhaps, because he'd been more taken with a certain person than he cared to admit?

Speeding through Wiental and along Hietzinger Main Road, the fiacre arrived at last at the new villa quarter. Leo handed the driver the agreed sum, climbed out, and hurried toward the dark house. Was he making a mistake, coming here this late and alone? He weighed his walking stick in his hands. Well, worst case, he'd be able to defend himself. He wouldn't allow himself to be taken by surprise again.

Like before, he pulled on the bell rope and the low, soft gong droned. This time, it took a long while before someone answered. He rang three more times before lights went on in the house. Then the door opened. The aging maid squinted into the darkness.

"Who's there?"

"Inspector Herzfeldt," said Leo. "I need to speak with your mistress. I apologize for the hour, but it's urgent."

"The mistress and the master have already gone to bed—"

"Then rouse them," countered Leo impatiently.

The maidservant went back inside, shaking her head. A few minutes later, the mistress of the house appeared, wearing a dressing gown that she must have quickly slipped into.

"Herr Inspector, do you have any idea how late it is? What are you doing here at this hour?"

"A police agent is always at work, Frau Rapoldy," said Leo. "I have some questions that can't wait."

She shook her head regretfully. "With all due respect, I was already in bed and—"

"Of course, I could come back tomorrow with a few of my colleagues. Or better still: why don't you visit us at headquarters? And please do bring your magic lantern. The Vienna police do so enjoy illusion tricks—so long as they aren't used against them."

Leo thought Charlotte Rapoldy was growing a little paler. She hesitated for a moment before speaking. "Please wait here. I . . . will call my husband and get dressed."

"Too kind. If it's not too much trouble, I'd like to speak in the conservatory. The view from there is just so lovely." Leo waited, his eye traveling across the garden. The statues, the pyramid . . . farther back, the sarcophagus and the tall wall behind it. Now that he knew, it was very simple.

The door opened once more. Charlotte Rapoldy had quickly changed into one of her shift dresses, her tousled hair swept back with the silver tiara.

"My husband and I will see you in the conservatory, inspector."

She strode ahead and Leo followed her down the dark hallway, past the library and into the conservatory, which was bathed in the dancing light of a kerosene lamp. The Rapoldys sat down beside each other. One of Clemens Rapoldy's hands rested on his walking stick, the other on his wife's leg in a gesture of support. His suit was creased. Without a hat his thinning hair lay bare, and in the dim lighting, the man suddenly looked much older.

"You have something to say, Herr von Herzfeldt?" Clemens

Rapoldy said sharply. He jutted out his chin. "Forgive us for not offering you anything to drink. Our maidservant Mathilda had a long day."

"So did I," said Leo, who, unlike the Rapoldys, hadn't taken a seat and was standing in the center of the conservatory. "It's probably better if this conversation stays between us for now." He gestured at the large window. "A lovely view, as I said. Could almost be a theater set, don't you think?"

"What are you getting at?" asked Clemens Rapoldy.

"Well, when I visited here the last time, your wife claimed that you had set the table in the conservatory especially for me. It was actually a rather chilly night, if you recall? And still it was very important to you that we eat out here. Your wife praised the lovely view of the garden from here. Of the Egyptian statues, the pyramid, and especially the sarcophagus . . ." Leo paused for a moment. "But actually, the view is blocked by something. Namely by the freshly whitewashed wall. And my guess is that the very same wall was of great importance to you that evening." He looked at Charlotte. "You own a *laterna magica*, don't you?"

Charlotte Rapoldy fidgeted nervously with her tiara. "It . . . it belonged to my father. But how—?"

"I saw the box during my first visit at your library, up on the shelf. I didn't think much of it at the time. Sometimes you only really notice something once it's missing, right? When, several days later, I was lying injured on your chaise longue, the magic lantern had gone. I'm guessing because it was needed elsewhere: out in the sarcophagus. Am I right?"

The Rapoldys said nothing, and Leo continued. "I've just been to an interesting show at the Ronacher—"

"What are you telling us these ridiculous stories for, inspector?" flared up Clemens Rapoldy. He thumped his stick onto the parquet floor. "Make your point already!"

"I'm trying to. Like I said, I've just been to the theater. A typical variety program: singers, dancers, magicians—and also a Chinese illusion show. The program booklet promised exotic images and landscapes, taking the audience on a faraway journey to China. And do you know how they take the audience on such a journey? That, too, was printed in the program. With a very old trick . . ."

"With . . . with a magic lantern," breathed Charlotte Rapoldy. She covered her face with her hands as if she might keep reality out.

Leo nodded. "Exactly. With a magic lantern, also known as *laterna magica*. A simple construction that's been around for several hundred years. All you need is a powerful source of light, a concave mirror, lenses, and some images painted on glass. Did your father own images of mummies, Frau Rapoldy? For his scientific lectures, perhaps? A magic lantern is often used for such purposes. I saw it often enough during my time as a student in Graz."

She nodded silently, and Leo went on, his tone beginning to sound as if he were giving an academic lecture himself. His hands clasped behind his back, he paced up and down in the conservatory.

"The projection screen is important. A white wall is just ideal! Distance also plays a role. The farther the lantern is moved away, the larger the image becomes, and also blurrier. But who would expect a ghost to have clear outlines? So long as he is big and frightens the living daylights out of the beholder." Leo stopped by the large window, gazing outside. "The only thing I don't yet fully understand is how you managed to make the image appear at just the right moment—just when the storm was setting in. The perfect staging! My guess is you had an electrical switch?" Leo eyed Clemens Rapoldy with curiosity. "I suspect that was your job. Just like the task to strike me down."

Clemens Rapoldy pressed his lips together defiantly. Both hands now clasped the pommel of his stick. "You have no proof," he said eventually. "Nothing at all!"

"But a whole lot of evidence," retorted Leo. "Enough to warrant an investigation, at least. One such piece of evidence is your stick." He nodded at Rapoldy's cane. "At your father-in-law's funeral two days ago, I noticed that the beautiful ivory jackal head is cracked. It would seem my skull was harder than the pommel of your stick."

"Clemens never intended to strike you down!" said Charlotte Rapoldy. "We . . . we never expected you to venture out in that ghastly weather. I swear to God we only wanted to give you a fright!"

"Charlotte, be silent!" Her husband stared at her in warning. "There is no proof."

A sob broke out of Charlotte Rapoldy. "I am so sick of this farce, Clemens! I haven't been able to sleep in days—no, weeks! It all would have come out sooner or later."

"Charlotte, I'm begging you—"

"Herr von Herzfeldt," said Charlotte, cutting off her husband. She wiped the tears from her face. "I have come to know you as a gentleman and a man of honor. As . . . as one of us. Will you promise me that what I'm about to tell you will never be made public?"

"I can promise you to try my best. But if the law was broken, if crimes were committed, I'll be forced to pursue it. I'm duty bound as a police agent."

"That's precisely it, inspector." Charlotte Rapoldy gave a wry laugh. "No crime was committed! It all was a terrible accident. And now this story is growing out of hand, growing into something monstrous. It really is like a curse that cannot be taken back. Please, inspector, you must believe us. It wasn't meant to happen like this . . ."

And then Charlotte Rapoldy told her story.

Leo listened with bated breath.

The case Strössner was so much more bizarre than he could ever have guessed.

Benedikt Warnbrunner stood at a corner in the fifth district, near the Wien canal, starving. What wouldn't he give for the butt of a cigar, or even just a few crumbs of tobacco? About an hour ago he had searched the gutter for any discarded bits that he might be able to wrap up in a bit of newspaper to smoke. But all he'd found was a blood-spattered handkerchief and an apple core, which he'd swiftly proceeded to devour. He hadn't eaten anything since breakfast, and that had merely been a few spoonfuls of porridge from the holey pot that he shared with his five siblings.

Since then, Benedikt had roamed the streets, waiting for night to fall—time to make a little money.

Benedikt was the eldest of his brothers, not quite seventeen, but with his tall frame; his black, matted hair; and stubbly chin he was often taken to be older. His mother sometimes said he took after their father. The only way to verify this was with a faded photograph his mother wore in a medallion around her neck. Father had died years ago from the accursed cholera; Benedikt barely remembered him. The other tenants in the large tenement block near Westbahnhof where they lived also said that he was just like his father. The same handsome good-for-nothing who had turned their mother's head way back when. No money, no future. Eyes like a gypsy. The same black, fiery eyes that Benedikt had. They had come in useful many times.

A while ago he'd found out that it wasn't just the girls who liked him, but also quite a few men. They were mostly older men stealing through the streets at night, heads low, searching for pretty lads like him. When the first one approached him, Benedikt had run away. But by now he knew what they wanted and how to handle them, and he was able to speak up when something was too filthy or too rough for him. Most of them were weak, sissified sort of fellows who turned to putty in his hands. Together they would go into some quiet corner; sometimes Benedikt would pay another boy a few kronen to stand guard, and a few minutes later, it would all be over—and Benedikt had enough money to enjoy himself at the taverns and cheap coffeehouses, acting the big shot.

The shame didn't come until the following morning, alongside the hangover.

Benedikt discreetly scanned the busy road. Margareten Square was busy with night owls at this hour, many of them drunk. Benedikt tried to steer clear of the drunks—they were often aggressive and couldn't be reasoned with. Then there were the young men who were after whores and who threatened him with beatings, as if they were better than him. Sometimes the girls flirted with him, but their pimps soon called them back. Benedikt really had to look out for pimps, who made short work of small-time hustlers like himself. They cut off their noses or scarred their faces with glass shards. That's why he worked a different district each weekend. Pimps were worse than the police! All the police did was give you a few whacks with their sticks and chase you away before resuming their rounds.

And then there was the phantom, of course.

The other hustlers Benedikt occasionally met spoke of it in whispers. A ghost has been haunting the city for a few months now, they said; it dragged boys down into Vienna's innards and ate them up alive. They whispered about bones sucked clean, bloodied scraps of clothing, and ripped-out hair; sometimes the remains of those poor devils were found in the sewers. But Benedikt didn't believe any of it. They were nothing but scary stories the pimps spread in the streets to freak out occasional hustlers like himself.

A garbage cart cluttered past Benedikt, followed by a pair of raucously singing drunks. They stopped at a streetlight so one of them could vomit, then staggered on. Music streamed from one of the nearby taverns, and Benedikt could smell smoked meats.

His stomach grumbled audibly. Not a single punter in sight! It was maddening. Where were they all? Probably at home with their good wives, who mustn't know of their little secret . . .

Benedikt thought about moving on to another district or perhaps at least to another spot when he noticed a man in a long black coat. He was standing directly beneath a streetlight, the same light where the drunk men had just been singing. Benedikt blinked a few times. Strange, he hadn't noticed the man arrive. The stranger wore a top hat, a black tuxedo, and held a walking stick like an elegant gentleman. From time to time, wealthy men braved the jungle of the outer districts to seek adventures with handsome boys. Such occasions invariably brought a lot of money.

A smile traversed Benedikt's hollow-cheeked face. Maybe this night would have a happy ending after all. He could already taste the goulash on his tongue, the cool beer.

The man with the top hat left the bright circle of the streetlight and was immediately swallowed up by the dark of night. Just like a . . .

Phantom, thought Benedikt, immediately swiping the thought aside.

There were crunching footsteps, the tapping of a walking stick on cobblestones. There he was! The man was walking straight toward Benedikt. Then he stopped abruptly, looking the boy up and down appraisingly as if he were a piglet or calf at the market. And then something odd happened: the man drew his hat, as if he weren't greeting an insignificant hustler but a gentleman.

"Lovely mild May night, isn't it?" said the stranger softly, his voice an icy breath. "Too nice to spend alone. Would you care to keep me company, young sir?"

"Depends . . . depends on the price," said Benedict reluctantly. He tried to appear more confident than he felt. The man was somehow . . . strange. As if he wasn't of this world, as if he'd hovered down on the tails of his coat from a cloud or from the pale moon. He placed five shining kronen in Benedikt's hand.

"I'll pay you the same again later. Come with me, my boy."

Benedikt's fingers closed over the coins. This was more than he could have hoped for, much more! Where was the man taking him? Normally, the punters followed Benedikt like puppies. This was exactly the other way around.

They turned down a side alley that lay dark and deserted save for the garbage cart from earlier. The old nag hitched to it stood patiently, not even lifting its head. It smelled of trash and . . . of something else.

"Here?" asked Benedict.

"Here," said the man.

The stranger lifted his walking stick, sliding a long narrow blade from its pommel. He used the blade to pierce Benedikt's heart right through his ribs, with a movement as casual as if he were putting a chicken on the spit. It happened so fast that Benedict didn't even have time to scream.

As blood rushed in his ears and his world turned black, Benedikt felt the phantom grab him by the collar and drag him away.

Away to a place that was even darker than the eternal night descending over him.

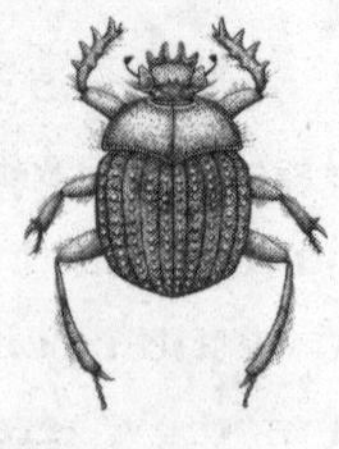

CHAPTER 15

"I loved my father dearly, inspector. Sometimes I feel like he's still here, somewhere in this house. As if he'd never left me. When I hear floorboards creak, I keep thinking it's him."

Leo was sitting at the table with the Rapoldys in the conservatory. The kerosene lamp flickered above Charlotte Rapoldy, casting her face in an unhealthy bluish light. A nightingale sang somewhere in the garden; other than that, all was eerily still.

Charlotte Rapoldy removed the silver tiara from her hair, her fingers absently sliding over the green scarab. She drew one more deep breath, then continued. "None of us are getting younger, are we? My father never let it show, but he'd been suffering from diabetes for a few years. His breathing was heavy and he struggled with the heat. But still he wouldn't let anyone take the lead of the Deir al-Bahari expedition from him. His biggest dream was to bring all those wonderful treasures back to Vienna! My husband and I originally intended to pay the dig site only a brief visit before setting off on our cruise on the Nile. It was our honeymoon, after all. . . ."

Charlotte smiled weakly, and Clemens Rapoldy held her hand. "We ended up staying longer. My husband is a doctor. That way, we were able to keep an eye on my father. Clemens prescribed diabezerin."

"Diabezerin?" Leo gave the Rapoldys a puzzled look. "What's that? A medication?"

"An extract from porcine pancreas," replied Clemens Rapoldy. "It's a very recently developed therapy. However, it is promising in the treatment of diabetes. The substance isn't cheap, but I thought it appropriate to treat my father-in-law with it."

"Father received an ampoule of it every morning. When we were back in Vienna, too," said Charlotte. "We have a refrigerator here at the house that we use to store other important substances, too. I injected him with the medicine myself. It was our daily morning ritual. Until that accursed February morning . . ." Her face darkened and she clearly found it difficult to find the words.

"You don't have to do this, Charlotte," said her husband, still holding her hand. "You don't need to go through this—"

"I . . . I still can't explain it to this day," said Charlotte, ignoring her husband. She spoke as if in a daze. "Like I said, the refrigerator also contained other substances that needed to be kept cold. Among others, samples of a poison my father had brought with him from Egypt and which he intended to study more closely in due course. It was toxin from the Strophanthus plant, which leads to nausea, vomiting, and a slowing of the heart rate, and in the worst case, to complete heart failure. Father suspected Strophanthus was used against grave robbers in the pyramids, and that it keeps for thousands of years."

"A trap for unwelcome visitors," said Leo, forced to think of Augustin Rothmayer's booby traps in Central Cemetery.

"A treacherous, invisible poison, yes." Charlotte Rapoldy nodded. "There is some suggestion of it in old writings. Father planned to test it on animals to see whether it was still effective after all this time. The Strophanthus ampoules looked similar to those Clemens used for diabezerin. I wasn't feeling well that day; I was in a rush. For some reason I . . . I mixed up the ampoules."

"You injected your father with deadly poison?" asked Leo, horrified.

"By accident! Good God, it was an accident. And the toxin . . . it was still effective. I would give my life to undo that day! My life!" Charlotte burst out in tears and her husband consoled her.

He continued to speak in her stead. "It took several hours for his heart to stop completely. There is no cure and no antidote. My father-in-law knew that, and he also knew that Charlotte wouldn't be believed." His voice was calm and factual, probably to spare Charlotte further distress.

"Why not?" asked Leo. "It was a tragic accident—"

"Look around you!" Clemens Rapoldy gestured at the luxurious furnishings. "My wife is his sole heir, as well as a well-known Egyptologist herself, who should have known her way around ancient toxins. And then she mixes up the ampoules! I never touched them. Damn, I should have taken greater care that they couldn't be confused!" Clemens Rapoldy sighed deeply. "Alfons loved his daughter above all else. And so he came up with a plan to avoid Charlotte falling under suspicion. The mummification was his idea."

"Professor Strössner *wanted* to be embalmed?" Leo forgot to close his mouth with amazement. He shook his head. "You can't be serious."

"Father occasionally talked about wishing to be buried that way," said Charlotte, dabbing at her tears with a handkerchief. "He thought of everything. He only had a few hours. And so he booked a passage in his name from Genoa to Cairo via telephone. Then he called up the museum and said that he'd be traveling for a while. He even wrote a few letters, which he sent to a trusted friend in Cairo, who then mailed the letters back to Vienna."

Leo groaned. "The riddle of the letters! So that's how he did it."

"Everything was planned through to the last detail," Clemens Rapoldy added. "That's how my father-in-law was. The perfect plan for everything, even for his own death. As far as the world knew, he vanished without a trace somewhere in the Egyptian desert. No suspicion would fall on Charlotte. He even found a solution for the removal of his body, albeit a rather . . . well, unusual solution. But it was his dying wish, after all."

"Did you . . . *mummify* your own father?" asked Leo, looking at Charlotte Rapoldy, who sat stiffly in front of him. He still couldn't believe it. And yet everything the Rapoldys were saying made sense. All the pieces of the puzzle suddenly came together.

Almost all, thought Leo.

"It was his dying wish," said Charlotte. "Father was very persuasive, even as he lay dying. Before he closed his eyes for the final time, he looked at me. He . . . he said I had to do it, with the help of Clemens. Not least for the sake of science! Very few researchers still know the ancient techniques. Once he passed, we prayed together. Then I focused on my work. It . . . it was my final act of love for him. He would have been proud of his daughter's work . . ."

Charlotte swallowed. "I gave Father his beloved pocket watch, the same way the ancient Egyptians gave their family members something for their journey to the realm of the dead. It seemed like the right thing to do. Clemens and I then transported him to the Museum of Art History in a carriage. It wasn't unusual for Father to study something at home and later have it taken to the museum. We stored Father at the back of the depot. There are so many mummies and old finds, no one would ever have noticed. He could have rested there for all eternity—"

"If it weren't for the thieving cleaning lady," concluded Leo. "That's how it all came to light." He shook his head. "It's quite incredible. So incredible, in fact, that I'm leaning toward believing it. But what about those other two mummies, the priest Ta-bek-en-chon and the princess? The curse?"

Charlotte Rapoldy smiled tiredly. "Sometimes stories are so powerful, so colorful, that they come to life. Wouldn't you agree, inspector? Come, we'll show you something."

TOGETHER THEY WALKED DOWN THE HALLWAY TO THE ROOMS at the rear of the villa. There, a steep staircase led downward in a curve, a red rug adorned with hieroglyphs guiding their way. Leo felt stunned. What the Rapoldys had just told him solved the mystery. Strössner's phone call at the museum, the letters from Cairo, the pocket watch in the bandages . . .

But still, some questions remained, and Leo couldn't shake a certain feeling he knew from previous cases.

Something was wrong.

Clemens Rapoldy led them down the cellar stairs, which ended in front of a door barred with a heavy padlock. He fished out a key.

"Our personal depot," he explained. "This is where we store our most significant and precious finds—as well as the deadliest poisons. This was also where we conducted the, uh . . . mummification."

He opened the door and Leo peered into a low-ceilinged, musty-smelling cellar that reminded him of an Egyptian burial chamber. A single lamp illuminated shelves stacked with gilded death masks and painted wooden tablets showing faces of the long deceased. There were small statuettes and mummies of animals like the ones Leo had seen at the museum. On a large, scuffed wooden table in the center lay two mummies wrapped in very old, brittle bandages, one of them a little smaller and daintier than the other. The bandages had been unwrapped in places, the dried-up faces lying bare.

"The priest Ta-bek-en-chon and the unknown princess," said Charlotte Rapoldy reverently. "Reunited at last, here at Villa Thebes."

"But Dr. Dedekind claimed the mummies were missing," said Leo.

Charlotte Rapoldy smirked. "They were never missing. Father had them brought here. He was always of the opinion that he should be examining Ta-bek-en-chon himself. He found him in the desert sands, after all." She bestowed the millennia-old corpses with a look of tenderness. "Father brought them back together after an eternity of separation."

"How can you possibly know they were a couple when they were alive?"

"Maybe it's nothing but a beautiful story." She gave a shrug. "But marriages between high priests and children of pharaohs were not uncommon. Just think of Imhotep, genius architect and advisor to the pharaoh Djoser and later revered as a god—he, too, married a princess, according to legend. And then there are the emerald eyes making these discoveries so very special."

"It is crucial those eyes are returned to the museum alongside the mummies," said Clemens Rapoldy. "They're of immeasurable value, not only to Egyptology." He shot Leo a questioning look. "You don't happen to know where they are currently . . . ?"

"They're in the police's evidence room," replied Leo. "A place almost as safe as the Great Pyramid of Giza—trust me."

"Good." Charlotte nodded. "I hope your colleagues will release the emeralds soon." Drawing a deep sigh, she looked again at the pair of mummies. "How did things come to this? We'll have to tell Alexander and also Professor Hofmann what really happened. Save them from believing in a curse. I'm sure those two can keep a secret."

"What are you going to do with us now, inspector?" asked Clemens Rapoldy. "Now that you know everything." He gave an abashed smile. "I'm terribly sorry for hitting you over the head. I was panicking, afraid you'd find the magic lantern. Like Charlotte said, all we wanted to do was give you a fright. We hoped you might leave us alone after."

"It was an exceptionally stupid idea," said Leo. "And it hasn't helped your situation at all. And I don't mean the blow with the stick—I'll get over it, I have a thick skull. I mean the other matter . . . I'll have to speak with my superior."

"You do that, inspector. And put in a good word for us." Charlotte Rapoldy looked at him from pleading eyes. In the dim light of the cellar, framed by all those Egyptian artefacts and the two mummies, she looked more than ever like Queen Cleopatra.

"Our fate, Herr von Herzfeldt, lies entirely in your hands."

The following morning, Leo and Paul Leinkirchner sat in the superintendent's office. It took the duration of two of Leinkirchner's cigars and four of Leo's Yenidzes to tell the whole story and answer all their questions. Stukart was so flabbergasted, he even forgot to tell them off for smoking in his office.

"This is the most outrageous confession I've ever heard! A professor who is accidentally poisoned and orders his own mummification . . ." The superintendent polished his glasses and peered through them as if they'd help him verify Leo's report. "And yet it all sounds plausible, somehow."

"I confiscated the ampoules in question and took them to Professor Hofmann first thing this morning," said Leo. "He'll give them a closer examination. I expect he'll reach the same result. Why should the Rapoldys lie about this? They would have known we would check the contents. One vial contains the Strophanthus, the other the diabezerin. Both glass vessels truly do look very similar."

Stukart returned the glasses to his nose and turned to Paul Leinkirchner. "What do you make of this?"

Leinkirchner shrugged his shoulders. "Hard to say. At least it answers all the questions."

"Not quite all," said Leo. "A few remain."

Last night, Leo had gone over everything again in his head. The feeling that had overcome him in the cellar remained—had intensified, even. He would have liked to discuss his thoughts with Julia, as well as explain his sudden departure. But when he'd tried to call her at the Dragoon before coming to Stukart's office, Elli had merely told him curtly that Julia was unavailable.

"What do you mean, Herzfeldt?" asked Moritz Stukart. "Which unanswered questions?"

"The case Kerfeld, for example." Leo cleared his throat. "His sudden death at St. Stephen's Cathedral isn't solved at all. On the contrary, it's quite the mystery. Clearly, Professor Walter Kerfeld was being followed. He knew something that he wanted to share with me at the cathedral. And then he dies! I still believe that he was poisoned. Only question is, why? Kerfeld doesn't feature in the Rapoldys' story. And then we have Father Gregor Mayr from Graz. I'm hoping to soon—"

"Jesus Christ in Heaven, we've already discussed this matter!" snarled Leinkirchner. "Professor Kerfeld died from an overdose of Spanish fly after visiting some prostitutes. He went to St. Stephen's Cathedral to confess his sins. If he was trying to tell you something, his last words would hardly have been the Lord's Prayer. *Paternoster*! You remember? That's what he said to you."

"I still believe something's not right. We don't know the whole story yet." Leo looked at Stukart. "Superintendent, sir, I urge you to wait before shelving this case! It's too soon."

Stukart said nothing for a long while. His silence told Leo that the decision had already been made.

"Well, dear colleague . . . ," began Stukart, dithering uncharacteristically. "You know I'm an experienced police agent, just like chief inspector Leinkirchner here. Together we've solved many a case. And the police agent in me agrees with you. This case is difficult . . ." He sighed. "But I'm no longer just a policeman but also the director of this institution. I have political obligations."

"Let's not beat around the bush," said Leo. "You've been given orders from the top to drop this case, am I right?"

"Just think, Herzfeldt," replied Stukart. "What's the alternative? Keep investigating? Then the whole affair will reach the public, sooner or later. We should consider ourselves lucky the press hasn't yet found out. Numerous powerful gentlemen are affected, and I'm not just talking about the Rapoldys. There's Friedrich Carl Knauer, renowned zoologist and director of the new zoological garden; Dr. Alexander Dedekind, curator at the Museum of Art History; there are other important patrons of science, and then there's the archduke himself! Just imagine the headlines, especially from the journals not favorably inclined toward the court. The Rapoldys' confession takes care of everything."

"How handy," muttered Leo. He'd half-expected this decision, especially after Charlotte Rapoldy asked him the night before to put in a good word for them. Had she known that he had no say here? Probably.

"And what about the Rapoldys?" he asked.

Pensively, Stukart arranged his sharpened pencils on his table. "Sure, we could open an investigation. But what's to gain? It clearly seems that Professor Strössner's death was an accident. You said so yourself. A trial would stir everything up again . . ."

"I see." Leo stood. "Then my presence here is longer required."

"Sit down, Herzfeldt," growled Leinkirchner. The scar in his face twitched menacingly. "Who do you think you are? You don't decide when you leave this room—the superintendent or myself does!" He pointed at Leo's chair.

"I would have phrased it differently, but my message would have been the same," said Stukart, gazing sternly at Leo.

Reluctantly, Leo sat back down.

"Good. There are other matters to discuss, too. More important matters." Stukart nodded at him. "Those hustler murders. We have a new case, the third already. Last night a certain Benedikt Warnbrunner was found dead in Margareten, fifth district." Stukart leaned forward. "But this time there's some good news: two drunk men saw the murderer. The description isn't terribly detailed, but it's a start. The witnesses spoke of a man in a black tailcoat, with a top hat and a walking stick."

"Black coat, top hat, walking stick—that describes every other passerby in Vienna," said Leo with a shrug.

"You're right. But it's better than nothing." The superintendent pushed the case file toward him. "Professor Hofmann has already taken a look at the body. Same modus operandi as with the last two victims. A single fatal thrust with a long, thin blade, perhaps something like a rapier. Then the penis and testicles were removed before the body was stabbed indiscriminately." Stukart sighed. "If we still had doubts, this removes them once and for all. We're dealing with an insane repeat offender. I want you to take the lead in this case together with Leinkirchner. The chief inspector has already put together a team of capable police agents."

"You want *me* to take the lead?" asked Leo, stunned. He wondered how Erich Loibl would feel about this, considering he'd led this investigation until now.

"Together with me," barked Leinkirchner. "Don't let it get to your head. I'm still your boss."

Stukart lifted his hands in an appeasing gesture. "I know you're a capable detective, Herzfeldt. If you weren't I'd have long sent you back to Graz on account of your impertinence. And Loibl is, well . . . a little out of his depth with this case. View it as a gesture of recognition, also with regard to your work on the Strössner case—provided you agree to stop investigating that one," he added. "I want you and Leinkirchner to work closely together. You can benefit from each other, believe me."

"If you say so," replied Leo tersely.

"Yes, I do say so." Stukart flipped the folder in front of him shut and gave Leo a close look. "Oh, by the way, have you seen Fräulein Wolf? We've been unable to reach her via the telephone. I know she called in sick. But we needed her to take photographs of the murdered lad in Margareten last night."

She was at the theater with me then, thought Leo. *Despite reporting sick . . .*

"I'm afraid I can't help you there," he said. "If I run into her, I'll tell her to get in touch with you."

The superintendent shrugged. "That probably won't be necessary. I've come to the conclusion that women are too sensitive for such tasks after all—and, it would seem, too unreliable."

"But she's sick," replied Leo.

"Women are constantly sick with something or other. And if they're not sick, they're indisposed, hysterical, or pregnant. No, no, my decision stands." Stukart shook his head. "Fräulein Wolf is to be relieved of her duties. The dismissal notice will be sent out today."

The superintendent rose and brushed some specks of dust off his waistcoat. "Gentlemen, I'm counting on you! Show the world that experience and scientific methods can work hand in hand to the benefit of all. I expect a report from you every morning."

Leo opened his mouth to say something, but Stukart's eyes told him any objection would be futile—with regard to both the mummy case and to Julia's fate. Leo hoped fervently that he'd get to speak with Julia before news of her dismissal reached her.

But she remained unavailable that Saturday, and also on the days that followed.

CHAPTER 16

From *Death Rites Around the World* by Augustin Rothmayer, written in Vienna, 1894

> Sarcophagus: from the Greek "sarkophagos," meaning flesh-eating. The Greeks and Romans frequently used limestone for their stone coffins, and it is said corpses decomposed within forty days inside such coffins. Lime can indeed be aggressive. It wasn't for no reason that during the Middle Ages, plague victims used to be covered with burnt lime.

"Herr Rothmayer, please calm yourself. And for God's sake, put down the spade! Or one might almost think you intend to strike me with it."

Julia halted, hid with Sisi behind a rusty cross, and tried to overhear the argument. They were at the far end of Central Cemetery, near the wall, in an area where few visitors strayed. Julia had heard the voice just as she was about to turn down the path to Augustin

Rothmayer's cottage. She signaled for Sisi to keep quiet and peered out from behind the cross.

What she saw didn't exactly reassure her.

When Julia decided that Sunday morning to take her daughter on an excursion to Central Cemetery, she'd looked forward to catching up with the peculiar gravedigger, maybe over a cup of coffee, maybe during a stroll. The disastrous evening with Leo had only been two days ago and she needed some distance, both from Leo and from her work, which was no longer her work. She'd received the dismissal notice yesterday, at her postbox at Westbahnhof Station, which she'd acquired to keep her address secret. In a few brief words the superintendent wrote that her services were no longer required. They wished her all the best for her future career.

She was out.

No reasons for her dismissal were given in the letter, nor did it acknowledge that she had called in sick. But she already knew why they'd fired her. Just because for once she wanted to spend some time with her daughter! Was that really too much to ask for?

The realization that she'd lost her income hadn't yet fully registered. To take her mind of things, she'd headed to Central Cemetery with Sisi, hoping to find a little normalcy. Instead she found Rothmayer looking ready to commit murder with his spade raised, facing off with a bald man. The man wore a pince-nez and a freshly ironed black suit. Rothmayer towered over him by almost two heads.

"There are graves need diggin'," grumbled Augustin Rothmayer. "We'd best each be on our way before something bad happens. Goodbye, sir."

"Herr Rothmayer, there's no point! You know full well that I won't go anywhere. I'm your employer, for God's sake! And now, take down that spade already!"

It was then that Julia remembered the short man—he was the cemetery director. She'd bumped into him once or twice in the past.

On those occasions, he'd struck her as a friendly, surprisingly affable man in view of his profession—quite the contrast to Augustin Rothmayer, who was still wielding his spade as if it were a bayonet. Julia decided it was time to step in. She emerged from behind the cross and swiftly strode toward the two men. The director turned to her with obvious relief.

"Fräulein Wolf, thank heavens! Please talk some sense into him. I'm here because of the girl—"

"No one takes Anna away from me!" cried Rothmayer.

"I don't want to take her away from you," said the director in a placating tone. "I understand how you feel. Listen, Herr Rothmayer, I have four daughters of my own. Perhaps Anna could play with them sometime? But you must see that the child needs to return to school at some point, and besides—"

"Damn it, I . . . I need Anna!" went on Rothmayer, his voice cracking. "She's learning a whole lot with me. And I can't keep up with all the work on my own anymore. The cemetery grows larger every year but you never hire more people. The sweeping up of the bones in the ten-year graves alone is . . . well, I'm literally being worked to the bone! The small, quick hands of the child make short work of it. And then there's the wreath-braiding—"

"May I make a suggestion?" Julia lifted both palms in a gesture of goodwill, turning to the director. "I would like to speak with Herr Rothmayer. Alone. I'm sure we can find a solution."

The cemetery director wiped the sweat off his bald head and nodded gratefully. "Talk to him, fräulein. He's as stubborn as an old mule. Three times already the welfare has been by. I won't be able to fob her off again."

"Let her come—she'll get the surprise of her life, huh," grumbled Rothmayer. "Just you wait and see." Julia had no trouble imagining the kind of surprise he was referring to, after what Leo had told her.

The director raised a finger in warning, though in view of his height, he wasn't particularly intimidating. His eyes blazed angrily behind his pince-nez. "You might come from a famous family, Herr Rothmayer—well, in our trade, at least—but I can't protect you forever. At some point enough is enough! I won't tolerate your escapades any longer, do you hear me?"

Julia knew what the director meant. Augustin Rothmayer's lineage traced back to the famous Vienna musician Marx Augustin. During the great Vienna plague, more than two hundred years ago, the singer had, drunk as a skunk, emerged alive from a pestilence grave into which he'd been tossed, presumed dead. The song of dear Augustin had traveled around the world. Since then, the Rothmayers had produced many gravediggers and buried a number of well-known personalities, unto this day.

Augustin Rothmayer sunk the spade into the ground with force and folded his arms petulantly. He looked like a medieval sentry, his feet firmly planted in the middle of the path.

"Over my dead body," he said, a turn of phrase which Julia considered a little odd.

The director turned to her and spoke in a low, imploring voice. "You know as well as I do that the welfare will never agree to an adoption. Anna may be an orphan, but this here is a cemetery and Herr Rothmayer . . . well, he isn't the easiest of people, is he?"

"You don't say," said Julia softly.

The gravedigger continued to stare daggers at them. Julia tried a smile. She pointed at Sisi, still cowering behind the cross, looking frightened. "Won't you look at my daughter, Herr Rothmayer? She's scared of you! When she was so excited to play with Anna. Why don't we go inside together? What do you say?"

Augustin Rothmayer scratched his head, spat on the ground, and plodded off.

"I believe that means yes," said Julia.

The director let out a deep sigh. "Persuade him, fräulein! Or else I won't be able to guarantee anything. Anything at all! I bid you a good Sunday." He strode off, shaking his head and casting scrutinizing glances at the graves as he passed. Julia took Sisi by the hand and together they walked to the gravedigger's home.

Augustin Rothmayer sat on the little bench outside his cottage, repairing something on his spade. When he saw Julia walk up he smiled and set aside his tool. This was something that never ceased to stump Julia—moments ago he'd wished the plague on the director, and now he had the mien of a kindly, slightly eccentric old man who wouldn't hurt a fly.

"It's nice of you to come visit with Sisi," he said with a tip of his hat. "Even if the timing isn't great. By the way, the clothes fit Anna perfectly."

"Where is Anna?" asked Julia, looking around. She enjoyed having a normal conversation with the strange old codger. It diverted her from her own worries.

Rothmayer rocked his head from side to side, considering, then he gave a shrug. "Well, I guess we can risk it now." He stuck two fingers in his mouth and whistled, and moments later Anna emerged from among the trees.

"The nasty man is gone, Anna," said Rothmayer in an affectionate voice that didn't at all go with his usual grumpiness. "Wanna go play with Sisi? Why don't you show her the shaft graves, yes? Don't fall in, will you?"

"I'm not a babysitter!" said Anna defiantly.

"I'll play you something on the fiddle later, all right?" suggested Rothmayer. "Some Schubert, your favorite."

Anna seemed persuaded. She took little Sisi by the hand and together they disappeared among the trees. Julia said nothing for a while, gazing across the rows of graves, which looked like narrow streets to nowhere in the slanting light of morning. The blooming rose garden around Rothmayer's cottage was the only speck of color around.

"The cemetery director is no nasty man," said Julia eventually. She sat down on the bench next to the gravedigger, enjoying the sun on her face. "He's only trying to help."

"Don't need no help." Rothmayer made a throwaway gesture. "Let's talk about something else. You look unhappy, fräulein. I can tell. Face like a funeral, like a corpse, even."

"Thanks for the compliment." Julia smiled wryly, then her expression darkened. "But you're right. I've been better."

"Well, then tell me what's bugging you." The gravedigger grinned. "I'll be as silent as the grave."

"Where to begin . . . ?" Haltingly at first, but with increasing ease Julia told him about her dismissal and her trouble with Leo. She had come to the conclusion that she needed a break, especially now that she had lost her job. And then there were those awful hustler murders . . . She just couldn't shake the images out of her head.

"Taking photographs of corpses isn't a job," said Augustin Rothmayer eventually. "Be thankful you don't have to do that any longer."

"Oh, but burying corpses is a job, is it?" Her eyes were challenging. "How am I supposed to afford the expensive medicines for Sisi now? I have some savings, but they won't last longer than a few weeks!"

"I'm sure a solution will be found. Perhaps your fancy baron could—"

"To hell with the fancy baron and all his important assignments! I haven't seen him since this disaster of a Friday night, and that's for the best."

"Hmm." Augustin picked at some dirt from under his fingernails. "He isn't that bad a fellow, your Leo. A little vain and full of himself, like many young men. But a clever copper, no doubt about it. I wouldn't mind hearing what he's found out about the mummies. For my new almanac alone . . ."

"Then why don't you ask him yourself," retorted Julia. "You two make for a much better couple. Besides, what do we care about those ancient mummies? There are other cases involving the fates of people alive here and now. Right this moment an African chief is sitting in prison—a man they kept like . . . like an ape at the new zoo! And now they're accusing him of a murder that he most likely didn't commit!"

"A proper chief, eh? From the Matabele tribe?"

Julia was dumbstruck. "You know of them?" Rothmayer's vast knowledge never ceased to amaze her; it didn't at all go with the picture of a grumpy old gravedigger.

"I've read about them. The Matabele are a proud people with some interesting death rites. I was planning to include some in my almanac. Is it possible to speak with this chief?"

Julia sighed. "Unless a miracle occurs, he'll soon be undergoing his own death rite." She summarized the events at the zoo for Rothmayer, who listened with interest.

"What did you say the name was of that young keeper? The one eaten by the lion?"

"Stefan Moser. Why?"

Rothmayer said nothing for a while, then answered with another question. "And you don't believe that Saidrovuni was the murderer but someone else? Hmm . . ." He frowned, then his face suddenly brightened. "I have a proposal for you, fräulein. You help me with Anna, help make sure she stays with me. In return, I'll look into this chief. Perhaps I'll be able to find something. Also about this strange demon."

"And how do you propose to do that?"

"Trust me, fräulein. It wouldn't be the first dead body whose secrets I unearth."

For the first time in days Julia felt hope sprout inside her. Even if she wasn't doing so well, at least she could help others. The mystery would also help take her mind off things. "You'd do that for me?"

"I would. You scratch my back, I scratch yours." Rothmayer gave her an awkward pat on the knee. "Now we better go see what those two girls are getting up to over by the shaft graves. They better not be bowling with bones and skulls. I've caught Anna doing that before." He gave a wolfish grin. "At least she has a good bowling arm."

BY MONDAY MORNING, LEO STILL HADN'T HEARD FROM JULIA.

He sat with Paul Leinkirchner in Leinkirchner's smoke-filled office, working in concentration and, mostly, silence. Leo had moved from his normal office into Leinkirchner's; it seemed the natural thing to do, since he and Leinkirchner were leading this case together—even though Leo never really felt at ease in the chief inspector's presence. Also, the air in this room was so thick with tobacco fumes, it gave Leo a headache.

The hustler murders had been keeping police headquarters on their toes. It wasn't entirely clear whether the three recent cases were the only ones. Ever since Erich Loibl mentioned the body in the Danube Canal in the second district, one theory suggested there were other earlier victims of the same murderer. But there were so many unsolved cases from the last few years that Leo soon lost track. To his horror he learned that only about half of all murders in Vienna ever got solved.

Sticking to his word, Stukart formed a special commission. A notice went out to all the Vienna newpapers with a vague description of the killer: black tailcoat, top hat, walking stick . . . Leo had spent the entire weekend in meetings with Leinkirchner, Loibl, and their other colleagues, which was so time-consuming that he had no chance to look further into the mummy case—fact aside that he'd been ordered not to.

And slowly but surely, it had dawned on him that Julia was more than a little annoyed with him. Leo hoped very much that she'd forgive him once he had a chance to explain what had been behind his sudden departure from the theater. If Stukart really had dismissed her, which was likely, then they really needed to talk. But Big Elli only fobbed him off on the phone. And so far, he hadn't found the time to travel out to Neulerchenfeld what with all this madness.

There was a knock on the door and Erich Loibl trudged in. He shot Leo a sullen look. Loibl apparently still hadn't gotten over the fact that Stukart had transferred the lead of this case to Leo and Leinkirchner. For the last two days, Loibl had only spoken to Leo when absolutely necessary.

"Any news, Erich?" asked Leinkirchner without looking up. "If so, make it snappy. I still have a whole pile of files of poorly written witness interview transcripts from the various constabularies around town. All of them unsolved cases from the last few years. A damned pigsty, I tell you!"

Loibl coughed. "Well, I went through the missing persons reports back to 1890." He scratched his head. "It's quite the stack. I don't think it'll get us anywhere. There are just too many of them. I mean, married couples argue, young men take off to find happiness elsewhere, young women fall pregnant and disappear . . . Anyway, it's just a few hustlers. Why don't we let this madman clean up a little? A few boy whores less. In other places, they call that hygiene." Loibl smirked at his own joke.

"Clean up, huh?" Leinkirchner looked up from his files for the first time. "Who do you want to clean up next in Vienna, Erich, huh? The Serbs, the Slavs, the whores, the Jews?" He shot Leo a brief glance. "The Itzigs aren't my favorite people, but that doesn't mean I'm going to kill them. So, if you don't have any better ideas, let us get on with our work here."

Loibl hesitated, still standing near the door.

"I might have something," he said after a while. He clearly felt uncomfortable. "I searched the files one more time for the case in Leopoldstadt. The case that temporarily slipped my mind . . ."

"What of it?" asked Leinkirchner. "Herzfeldt said there was no file for the case. Don't tell me you found one after all? Behind the cupboard, or as blotting paper?"

"I haven't. But I found something else." Loibl drew out a tattered piece of paper and read from it: "March '93—so over a year ago. Children found an arm in the sewers while they were playing. It was near the place where the torso was found in the canal, in the second district."

"The victim's arm?" asked Leo.

"That's what I thought at first. That's why I didn't think too much of this note at first." Loibl nodded, visibly relieved to be back in the game. "But then I remembered something. The body back then was only missing its legs and head. It still had the arms. So, the arm stemmed from yet another victim. Presumed a young man, around twenty. They weren't able to determine anything else—the arm was too far gone. And here . . ."

With quiet triumph, Loibl presented another page and read from it. "Constabulary report from September '93. In a canal in the sixth district, canal workers found the remains of a strongly decomposed human skull with some hair still attached." He looked up expectantly.

"Christ, Loibl!" Leo shook himself. "Are you saying the entire Vienna underworld is filled with . . . with human remains?"

"This is Vienna, a metropolis. Not small-town Graz, Herzfeldt." Leinkirchner gave a derisive snort. "People come, people go, people vanish. Erich is right. In the last ten years alone our population has grown by a quarter million. No wonder the odd one goes missing along the wayside, freezing, starving, diseases, accidents . . . Doesn't always mean murder."

He lit another cigar and puffed. "There are poorhouses and other places for the homeless to go, but those are usually full or crawling with lice. So, many opt to go underground. It's warmer in the sewers, especially in the winter—and they don't get bothered by the likes of us. Well, and then people vanish down there. In a way, the sewers are also a kind of cemetery."

"They vanish in the sewers? Hmm . . ." Leo leafed through the files in front of him, the files of the four cases in the order they occurred: Leopoldstadt, Meidling, Mariahilf, Margareten . . . A thought had taken root in his mind, an idea he needed to check. "Interesting," he said eventually. "Very interesting."

"I'd be ever so grateful if you cared to share your *interesting* insights," grumbled Leinkirchner. "What are you doing, leafing all nervously through the old cases? You were meant to look for older ones!"

Without answering, Leo rummaged in a drawer for some pins that he normally used to fasten handkerchiefs to his breast pocket. He stood and walked over to the large map of Vienna on the wall, where he placed several pins. Then he used a pencil to draw several lines. Loibl and Leinkirchner watched for a while.

"What's this all about, Herzfeldt?" asked Leinkirchner impatiently. "Some new game?"

"Leopoldstadt, Meilding, Mariahilf, Margareten," said Leo thoughtfully, ignoring his colleague's sneering remark. "That's where the victims were found."

Loibl shrugged. "But we know that already."

"Yes, but the exact locations are interesting." Leo tapped on the map with the pins and pencil lines. "They're all close to water, to the Danube Canal and the Wien Canal. Isn't there construction on the sewers of the Wien at the moment? And at the Danube Canal also?"

"There are," said Leinkirchner. "But—"

"What if the murderer intended to dispose of the bodies in the sewers and was disturbed?" went on Leo. "Perhaps by the construction works. What if our four victims are something like . . . mishaps, in the eyes of the killer? The other victims are deep down in the sewers . . ."

"There are weirs blocking all of the sewers," said Loibl. "If he didn't want the bodies to be noticed, he'd have to cut them into smaller pieces."

Leo turned to Loibl. "But you just said yourself that body parts have been found! And we only have the torso and arms of the first body. Maybe there are plenty more body parts down there! Our cases might be just the tip of the iceberg."

"Think, Herzfeldt." Leinkirchner puffed a cloud of tobacco smoke in Leo's direction. "The fellow murders all those pretty boys. And then he carefully cuts them up in the street to dispose of them in the sewers? How would he accomplish that? Someone would have seen him, especially considering how many times he's been at it. No way."

Leo thought for a while, staring at the points on the map. At last he sighed. "You're probably right." He returned to his chair. "I probably jumped to conclusions."

"There might be something to it yet." Leinkirchner sucked on his cigar, shaking his head. "Damn. Maybe I just don't like accepting the thought that we're not just dealing with a few murders but with years of butchering." He pushed the files away as if they carried a deadly disease. "Compared to *this*, Jack the Ripper wouldn't be more than a bloody joke."

FOR THE REST OF THE MORNING, LEO AND PAUL LEINKIRCHner trawled old cases, but Leo struggled to focus. This was partly because of Julia. He yearned to tell her that he was sorry, wished he could make it up to her. Three days without her had shown Leo how much she meant to him, that he needed her. But he just couldn't get hold of her. Should he up and leave for Neulerchenfeld, abandon his work? He could tell Leinkirchner that he planned to visit one of the constabularies out in the districts, but he didn't feel entirely comfortable at the thought.

When it was close to lunchtime, Leo suddenly had an idea. Margarethe! Julia used to work alongside her at the telephone exchange office at headquarters. Their friendship wasn't as close as it used to be, but Julia had mentioned her old friend only recently. Perhaps Margarethe would be able to speak with Julia, put in a good word for him. He stood.

"Are you taking lunch?" Leinkirchner looked up disapprovingly. "This early? Or have you simply run out of genius ideas?"

"There's something I need to do. I'll be back in time for our afternoon meeting."

"Well, saves me offering to get lunch," replied Leinkirchner.

"Thanks, too kind." Leo smiled a little. "Another time, perhaps." Their relationship remained cool, but at least Leinkirchner had refrained from provoking Leo with his anti-Semitic remarks. Earlier, during their conversation with Loibl, he'd practically defended him.

Leo picked up his hat and coat and went to the third floor where the telephone exchange was located. Police headquarters had recruited heavily in the last few months. Now there were two telephone rooms filled with wooden boxes and tin machines, with more than a dozen women sitting in front of them, speaking into mouthpieces and endlessly re-plugging connections. In the last year, telephone lines in Vienna had nearly doubled.

Margarethe sat in the second room at the back. She broke out in a surprised smile when she noticed Leo.

"Ah, the baron! Don't tell me you're taking me out for lunch?"

Leo returned the smile. He knew that in the beginning, Margarethe had been envious of Julia for landing herself an inspector, and one from a wealthy home to boot. Margarethe liked to tease him, but he knew she liked him—maybe even more than liked.

"How do you feel about a coffee over at Sluka?" suggested Leo. "My treat."

"I would hope so, Herr Baron. A simple switchboard operator such as myself can't afford coffee at Sluka. Why not? It's nearly break time, anyway." Margarethe rose with a sigh. "Why can't I shake the feeling that I owe this invitation not to my new hairstyle, but to something else?" She dropped her voice conspiratorially. "Or should I say, someone else? I'm right, aren't I?"

Leo merely passed her her coat by way of reply. Over at Sluka on Rathaus Square, he waited for the stuck-up waiter to bring them two cups of overpriced coffee before coming out with it.

"You're aware that Julia and I still . . . well . . ." He faltered.

Margarethe grinned. "There's a lovely Viennese word for that, Herr German. You should learn it sometime. But yes, I'm aware." She raised a hand. "And I swear I haven't blabbed this time. If anyone claims I—"

"It's not about that, Margarethe. Julia and I . . . we had . . . well, things aren't going great at the moment. And now it seems she doesn't want to see me anymore." He gave her his best puppy look. "Would you talk to her, maybe?"

"Hmm, maybe." Margarethe took a slow sip of her coffee. She was quite clearly enjoying torturing him a little. "Though maybe she just wants to spend a little more time with her daughter. Maybe she doesn't want to see a copper for a while, not even you. Now that she no longer works for the police," she added in an ominous tone.

Leo groaned. "So Stukart really did fire her."

"Yes, he did. Apparently, Julia was unreliable and, being a woman, too sensitive. Stukart's secretary typed the dismissal notice—she told me." Margarethe frowned. "The boss isn't all wrong. About the sensitive bit, I mean. Photographing murder victims! That really isn't for us women. I would faint at the first victim. What am I saying? At the first drop of blood!"

"Listen, Margarethe," said Leo. "I really need to speak with Julia. Now more than ever. I want to tell her that . . . that I love her."

"Oh, inspector!" Margarethe fluttered her lashes. "You're such a romantic. A proper baron."

"Please tell her that I want to make it up to her, tonight. That I . . ." Leo thought. "That I'll take her back to the Ronacher. And dancing and champagne after."

"Inspector, I'm swooning. Stop it, before I start to cry."

"Ask her to come to my room at seven o'clock, will you? Tell her I'm sorry."

Leo placed a few coins on the table, rose, and bowed. "Forgive me, dear fräulein. Duty calls."

"Life is unfair." Margarethe fidgeted with her hair, crossed her legs, and shot Leo a cheeky look. "Some of us visit the theater with barons, while others spend the evening in a tavern with their fat fiancés, eating goulash."

Leo tipped his hat and quickly walked out of the coffeehouse.

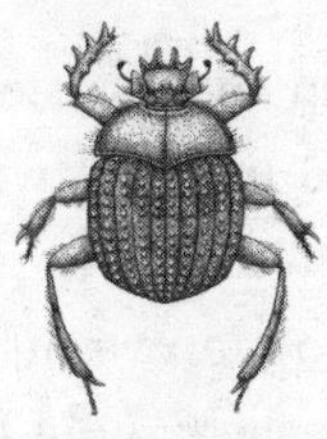

CHAPTER 17

A few hours later, Leo was on his way home. It was early evening, and the Ring was bustling. Most pedestrians were men on their way home from work, and many of them were clad in tailcoats and top hats. Unbidden, the thought popped into Leo's head how many of them were capable of murder, if the opportunity arose.

Nothing out of the ordinary had occurred during the afternoon hours at headquarters. Erich Loibl returned from another interrogation of the two drunk witnesses from Margareten with nothing new to report. The description of the killer remained vague. The witnesses had seen a man with a top hat and tailcoat drag the body into a side street. When they called out, he'd run away. One detail was interesting, however: the man had carried a walking stick, but he'd been very quick—no limp, no dragged foot.

Around five in the afternoon, Leo had taken his leave of Leinkirchner. He'd read in the *Neue Freie Presse* that a ladies' singing group from America who had performed at the world's fair at Chicago was performing at the Ronacher that evening. Five women on stage! Julia was bound to love it. Leo had sent an errand boy to the Ronacher and managed to snag two tickets. In a private box, even. That way, they wouldn't have to put up with any griping table neighbors. Leo began to plan what he would wear. He needed to be smart but not overdressed; Julia hated it when he acted the dandy. He himself didn't even notice. What was wrong with dressing nicely?

Deep in thought, Leo climbed the stairs to his lodgings and opened the door. His landlady, Frau Rinsinger, padded toward him curiously.

"An early finish tonight? I thought you'd be busy investigating the hustler murders. I read about them in the paper . . ."

"You know I can't tell you anything, Frau Rinsinger," said Leo. "Even if I wanted to. Classified," he added in a portentous tone. "Highly confidential."

"Of course. Classified. Highly confidential. I understand." Frau Rinsinger loved police jargon. Her eyes softened. "You work too much, Herr von Herzfeldt. Pardon me for saying, but you look tired and burnt out. Aged overnight! The bruise on your head probably hasn't fully healed. You'd do well to look after your health! My late husband, God keep his soul—"

"Well, if that is the case, you'll be pleased to know I'm headed to the theater tonight," cut in Leo to speed things up.

"Oh, with Fräulein Wolf? How delightful. That'll do you a world of good. A nice young lady, Fräulein Wolf. Although I still don't fully understand what it is she does at the police. Is she your secretary?"

"Uh, something like that. Now, if you'll excuse me, Frau Rinsinger. I need to change and freshen up."

Leo vanished into his room where he searched his wardrobe for the right outfit. More than half a dozen suits hung on the hangers, from casual dinner jackets to tuxedos. Most of his clothes were still from his Graz days, although some he'd purchased here in Vienna, where, in his own humble opinion, the best tailors resided, after London and Paris.

Leo's measly police wages would never cover those purchases. But he felt confident that his mother would approve of such expenses. Her check arrived regularly. His sister Lili, whom he'd asked for assistance only last Friday, had inquired after him with genuine concern. His mother and sister missed him—unlike his father. Even his older brother, Viktor, who had started at the Herzfeldt family bank as junior boss, hadn't been in touch in a long while. What would straightlaced Victor say to the tiny rented room at Frau Rinsinger's? Leo gave a wry smile. Well, at least he'd always been better dressed than his brother.

After dithering for a while Leo decided on the plain black chesterfield suit, adding a touch of color with a red handkerchief and a dark-blue tie. He washed his face and hands, shaved, dressed, and tidied his hair in the mirror.

The doorbell rang and Leo gave a jump. His pocket watch told him it was only half past six. His heart made a joyous leap. Julia! She actually came, and she even was a little early. That was a good sign! With one last glance into the mirror, he stepped out into the hallway with a smile on his face. Frau Rinsinger was just opening the door.

Standing in the stairwell was Paul Leinkirchner.

"What are you all spruced up for?" asked Leinkirchner gruffly instead of greeting Leo or the landlady or even tipping his old hat.

"I . . . uh . . . the theater," stammered Leo, too surprised to string a sentence. "Must have forgotten to mention . . ."

"Theater? You can forget about that. We have work to do."

"Now?"

"Yes, of course now! Are you slow or what? I couldn't get ahold of you over the telephone, so I came by in person. Fiacre's waiting outside. It's a matter of urgency!"

Frau Rinsinger wrung her hands. "Oh, how exciting! May I ask where you're off to? Another murder, yes? Is the fräulein going, too?"

"What fräulein?" asked Leinkirchner.

Leo swiftly pushed past his landlady and past the chief inspector into the stairwell. "Let's discuss this outside."

Leo rushed ahead, hearing Leinkirchner clatter down the steps after him. Indeed, a service vehicle waited for them in the street. They climbed in, the driver cracked his whip, and they raced down Lange Lane at breakneck speed. Everything had happened so fast, Leo hadn't even had time to clean the shaving foam off his neck.

"The theater, was it?" Leinkirchner grinned. "May I ask which *fräulein* your landlady was referring to?"

"No, you may not." Leo stared straight ahead. How was he supposed to explain this to Julia? He'd made this evening out to be his great apology, and now this . . . His only hope was that Frau Rinsinger would be able to explain everything. And who was to say Julia would even show up? Maybe she was well and truly through with him.

"Nice suit," said Leinkirchner, looking Leo up and down. "With handkerchief, even. Is that how one wears it these days? Unfortunately, it's about to get a little grubby."

"Where are we headed?" asked Leo.

"The Danube Canal, Alsergrund near Rossauer Landing. We're going down into the sewers."

"Into the sewers?" Leo shot Leinkirchner a look of disbelief. "Are you saying . . . ?"

"Yes, I am, smarty-pants." Leinkirchner gave a snort. "Our killer struck again. He's getting bolder—it's not even full dark yet. The victim, a young man, was able to cry for help before he died. Two street sweepers heard him and saw a man wearing a top hat and a black tailcoat dragging a lifeless body into the sewers. The murderer is probably still down there."

"What makes you think that?"

"We're guarding all access points. The underground sewers along the Danube Canal are quite new. There aren't that many entryways, and most of them are still sealed." Leinkirchner nodded grimly. "The fellow's trapped down there like a mouse. We've got him."

The chief inspector paused for a moment before continuing. "Your theory about the sewers might not be all that far-fetched, after all. We've had more reports from the constabularies come in. Body parts are found down there all the time. Bones, part of a bottom jaw, a finger . . . No one really looked into it because we all know who lives down there. The sewers are like underground cemeteries—no one really worries. But the sheer frequency of finds in the last year is disconcerting."

Why must things get really bad before we wake up? wondered Leo. But he said nothing. It was astonishing enough that Leinkirchner admitted that Leo might have been right.

The carriage clattered across the Ring and on toward the ninth district. It rolled to a halt next to the squat Rossauer barracks. In the glow of a gas streetlight, a group of uniformed constables awaited them as well as several civilians. A little off to the side stood a garbage cart, an old nag hitched to its front, eating from a bucket. Leinkirchner and Leo climbed out and approached the group.

"Who's in charge here?" asked Leinkirchner in his gruff tone.

"That would be me, inspector." An older man in uniform with a neatly twirled mustache stepped forward and stood to attention. He nodded toward two civilians in filthy clothing. "That's the two sweepers who witnessed the incident."

"Struck the lad like a pig, he did," said one of them, a hard-looking old man with few remaining teeth. He pointed at the ground. "See—full of blood. What a mess!" He was right; the cobblestones gleamed with blood in the light of the streetlamp. The constables struggled to keep curious onlookers away from the crime scene.

"We read about it in the paper, inspector," said the second street sweeper, a younger man. He kneaded his dirty old hat nervously in his hands. "A fancy gentleman with a fancy hat and a stick. That's how we knew straightaway that he—"

"Speaking of stick," said the chief constable with the moustache. "Take a look at what we found." He passed a stick that was missing its handle to Leo. The wooden stick was hollow inside.

"So, that's how he does it." Leo nodded. "A sword stick. And then he took the victim down below ground. Where did he go down, actually?"

"Through the tower, of course," replied the older sweeper.

"The tower?"

The old man gestured at a man-high pillar, which Leo had mistaken for an advertising column. "Those are the entrances to the sewers. They're quite new still. They're meant to be locked."

"The lock isn't difficult to crack," said the chief constable. "A picklock or a filed-down key would do it." He raised one hand to his temple in a salute. "Chief inspector, sir. All entries are under guard, as instructed."

"Well done," replied Leinkirchner approvingly. "Three of you, come with us. The rest—get rid of those gawkers, bleedin' parasites! Your men are armed, right?"

"Gasser revolvers," said the chief constable proudly. "Latest model. Not enough room down there for rifles, anyway. I've also taken the liberty of sourcing a few kerosene torches."

"Good man. Once we've got that bastard, you can expect a promotion."

The chief constable nearly burst with pride.

Leo turned to the older street sweeper. "Do you know what we can expect down there? Aside from rats and dirt."

"No self-respecting man goes down there, inspector. Only beggars and vagabonds live down there. And the kanalstrotters, of course. Sewer sifters. But you know all that."

That gave Leo pause. "The what?"

The old man gave the chief inspector a look of uncertainty. Leinkirchner made a sound of derision.

"The Herr Inspector isn't from Vienna," he said. "And he's likely never seen a canal before—save, perhaps, the Canal Grande in Venice!"

"Well, so . . . the kanalstrotters work down there," explained the old man with a shrug. "They pick up coins, spoons, bits of jewelry, buttons, anything of value. Poor bastards, the lot of them, but not as poor as the fat fishers. They sift the sewers for bones, meat scraps, fat. Then they sell it to the soap boilers for a few kronen."

"And then the inspector pays a few kronen for soap smelling of roses for his soft inspector skin," jeered Leinkirchner. "Or he uses it to launder his fancy suit. Even the handkerchief." Leo noticed that several of the constables were trying to stifle grins. He couldn't blame them. In view of their destination, he looked utterly out of place—like a snobby German on his way to the theater.

"Well, you've made your point," said Leo. "Now let's go do our job." He walked toward the pillar, where a tin door stood ajar. Narrow winding steps led downward. "A lamp," he demanded.

One of the men passed him a kerosene torch, and Leo led the way. If he didn't want his reputation ruined entirely, he needed to show initiative.

The steps led down a few yards before ending in a wide corridor with brick walls, high enough for Leo to just about stand upright. In its middle, a murky stream carried various bits and pieces, some unrecognizable. There were leaves, scraps of paper, and something that was probably a rat cadaver. It was cold, and it didn't stink quite as badly as Leo had expected. The metal stairs creaked and groaned as other men followed him.

Once they'd all reached the bottom, Leinkirchner raised his lamp and looked around.

"Is there only the one sewer?" he asked the chief constable, who'd decided to come along.

"This is the right-hand main sewer," the man replied. "It's not quite completed yet. Apparently, several side sewers drain into this one."

"There isn't a map, perchance?" asked Leo.

"We were unable to obtain one at such short notice. It's after hours, and no one answered the telephone at the department."

"Of course, no murders allowed after hours in Vienna," commented Leinkirchner dryly. "Orders from the top. Why oh why doesn't anyone follow them?" He searched the ground with his lamp. "If the killer dragged his victim down here, there should be blood."

"Not if he pulled the body along in the stream," said Leo. "It's quicker and saves him carrying his victim." He paused. "Question remains, why does he bother in the first place? We can assume the boy was dead, or else he would have put up a struggle. The murderer achieved what he set out to do. Why does he drag his prey off, almost like . . . like an animal?"

Leo couldn't help but think of the *Asan-Bosam*, the demon with metal teeth the chief from the zoo spoke of. A chill ran up his spine, and not just because of the cool temperature.

"To answer that, we'll have to find the murderer," replied Leinkirchner. "If your theory proves correct, he would have walked downstream. So, let's do the same. Follow me."

As Leinkirchner rushed ahead, Leo noticed his colleague's limp once more. Why was the chief inspector putting himself through this? He could have stayed up the top and left him, the younger man, to do the dirty work. Stukart had placed both of them in charge of this case, after all.

Simply because he grudges me any success, thought Leo.

Together with the other men he followed Leinkirchner, running down the right-hand side of the stream. The walls were filthy, and in some places slimy, covered in a gray film. Whenever a horsecar tram clattered down the streets above them, brick dust rained down from the ceiling. Leo's suit was covered in filth after a short time. He had loosened his tie to make breathing easier in the stuffy, tight space, and he'd long since lost his silk handkerchief. It was probably floating down the sewer somewhere ahead of him.

After a while, a narrower corridor branched off to the right, water spilling out from it into the main channel.

"Damn it all. If there was blood, it's long been washed away," groused Leinkirchner. "No idea where our man has gone to. We'll have to split up." He pointed at Leo. "Keep going along the main sewer with the chief constable. Me and the two others will go check up here."

With that, he vanished into the darkness, the two constables quickly following suit. Leo's eyes followed them. It really was amazing how nimble Leinkirchner was in spite of his handicap.

Together with the older chief constable, Leo continued down the wide corridor. Their steps echoed, but other than that there was only the trickling of water and the occasional distant rumbling, as if the city's intestines were churning. The constable walked ahead with his revolver drawn, shooting occasional glances at Leo.

"I was en route to the theater when the call came," explained Leo. "In case you're wondering about my suit."

"It's not that, inspector. I was merely wonderin' where your pistol is."

"My—" Leo reached for the inside pocket of his jacket. "Damn, I didn't think of it in the rush!" He could have slapped himself. How could anyone be this stupid? But everything had happened so fast earlier.

"Oh well, maybe you've brought your opera glasses," remarked the constable unhelpfully and kept walking.

Thanks, dear Leinkirchner, thought Leo. *Thanks a bunch for making a fool out of me in front of our subordinates.*

Suddenly, shouts rang out behind them, then a shot fired. The chief constable spun around. "They've got him!" He ran back up the corridor, followed closely by Leo. Another scream sounded. Moments later they reached the fork where they'd separated from their colleagues. Running up the side sewer, Leo found that another corridor branched off shortly thereafter. Another shot cracked through the tunnels, but it was impossible to tell where it came from. The sewers were a maze!

"Keep going straight!" ordered Leo. "I'll take the other way."

The chief constable gave a nod and vanished into the darkness of the sewer.

The pipe Leo followed now was much lower and narrower. He was forced to walk hunched over, his suit scraping against the damp ceiling, dust trickling into his eyes. One bend followed another, so Leo couldn't see very far with his torch. Other, even narrower drains led off to his left and right. Leo couldn't hear any more noises, no voice, no shot, nothing. He was clearly headed in the wrong direction.

He was about to turn back when something large and black swooped at him like a huge bird of prey from a nook.

Leo fell, upper body first, into the sewer's cold waters, his torch slipping from his grasp. For a moment he saw the glint of metal flash before his eyes, then a figure in a coat running past him.

Lying in the muck in front of him was a top hat.

He struggled to his feet, about to rush after the figure when he heard someone groan in the opposite direction. Leo listened.

"Chief inspector, is that you?" he asked quietly.

"Yes, damn it! Don't tell me you let him get away."

Leo felt for his lamp. When at last he found it, he raised it high and saw the tunnel empty, the footsteps gone. "Looks that way. But if the exits are still under guard, he shouldn't get away. Do you need help?"

A muttered curse came from the darkness, followed by another groan. Leo proceeded slowly until he found Paul Leinkirchner around a corner. The chief inspector was alone. He sat leaning against a wall, his right leg angled unnaturally. Leo saw blood shimmer on the ground in the light of the torch.

"You're hurt!" Leo ran the last few steps. Now he saw that Leinkirchner's right trouser leg was saturated with blood.

The chief inspector gritted his teeth, his face ashen. "The bastard took me by surprise. Came out of nowhere . . . got me with his rapier."

"Don't talk so much. Conserve your energy."

"You a Jewish physician now, too?" Leinkirchner gave a gasping laugh while Leo inspected the wound. The blade had stabbed through the right thigh but thankfully appeared to have missed the main artery. Still, the wound was bleeding profusely. Leo took off his jacket, tore it into strips and used them to apply a pressure bandage like he'd learned to do during his time as a reserve lieutenant.

"Your lovely suit," said Leinkirchner from between gritted teeth. "What's a rag like that cost?"

"Not as much as your life," said Leo. "Listen, I don't expect you to be grateful, but please bite back your stupid comments."

"Why didn't you shoot when the fellow ran past you?"

"I could ask you the same question."

Leinkirchner gave a laugh. "Damn, you're right." His eye turned to his revolver, uselessly lying on the ground. "He took me by surprise. I sent the two constables down another passage and carried on by myself. He . . . he must have hidden in a niche. But that's just an excuse. I'm getting old. In the war, this would never have happened to me."

"I understand." Leo nodded as he bandaged the wound.

"You understand jack shit!" snapped Leinkirchner. "What does the likes of you know of the war? Sixth infantry division, war of '78 in Bosnia! I was a sergeant during the battle of Sarajevo, and I was shot in the leg carrying two injured comrades behind our lines. Half our company had their heads ripped off by shrapnel. And our officer was one of yours . . ."

"One of ours?" Leo looked up. "What do you mean?"

"A Jew, of course! Came from a good house, knew how to order people around but had no idea of war. A goddamned coward, he was! Ditched me and the two injured comrades and took off. Our division was destroyed because of him. So many good men." Leinkirchner shook his head grimly. "Fate is a lousy whore. First I nearly lose my leg thanks to a filthy Jew. Now another Jew is trying to make sure I don't limp on the other, too."

Leo said nothing. That explained to some extent where Leinkirchner's hatred of all things Jewish stemmed from. But there was probably more to it. To former sergeant Paul Leinkirchner, Jews were people of money and influence who got away with things, who always swam on top. And who wore better suits . . . The fact that Leo didn't practice the Jewish faith—yes, that his father renounced his faith in order to evade the constant animosities—didn't seem to matter.

Once a Jew, always a Jew . . .

What a narrow-minded way to view the world! Would it ever change?

"I'd say we're even now," said Leo, continuing to work on the bandage. "Half a year ago, on Central Cemetery, you saved my life. Remember?"

"Oh yes, I remember," replied Leinkirchner. His jaw was clenched with pain. "That time you . . . you didn't shoot either."

And I'd rather eat my hat than tell you why, thought Leo. *For the same reason why I didn't shoot today . . .*

Yes, he'd left his service revolver at home. Maybe he did actually forget it. But Leo knew what the reason was, deep down: he didn't *want* to bring his weapon. Too much had happened in his past, too much ruined by a revolver back in Graz. A friendship, his future, a life . . . At Central Cemetery, when Leinkirchner saved his life, Leo had found it impossible to shoot. His hand had shaken too hard.

A policeman who doesn't shoot. Like a scorpion without a stinger, a tiger without teeth . . .

"You're right about one thing, Herzfeldt," said Leinkirchner into his thoughts. "It's strange that the murderer drags off his victims. What does he do with them, down here?"

"The castration," said Leo, glad his colleague changed the subject. "The cutting off of their manhood. That's what it must be about. Everything else is just for show. He can't seem to leave the victim alone until he's completed the ritual. That's what he brought the boy down here for."

"To cut off his willy in peace?" Leinkirchner winced, and Leo wasn't sure whether it was out of pain or disgust. "That is the sickest thing I've ever heard of. If I ever get my hands on that fellow . . ."

Shouts echoed through the tunnels.

"That's the chief constable and the others," said Leo. He shouted back, "We're here! Down here! We have a man down!"

"Christ, no need to blow it out of proportion," muttered Leinkirchner. "You bandaged the wound. I'm better already."

"Only moments ago you said a Jew was saving your leg. I insist on having my moment of glory." Leo continued to shout for help until the chief constable appeared at last with his torch.

"There you are!" said the man with relief. "We searched everywhere for you two."

"Finding the killer is much more important," replied Leinkirchner, straightening up with some difficulty. "Did you get him?"

"Well, uh . . . One of my men just came down to report to me . . ." The chief constable twirled his mustache, visibly abashed. "The fellow slipped through our fingers. Apparently, he came up one of the towers down by Augarten Bridge and sneaked past two of my men who . . . um . . . needed to relieve themselves . . . at the same time, unfortunately."

"Two pissing coppers." Leinkirchner groaned and sank back down. "I can't believe it! Your men could get a job in the puppet show in the Wurstelprater with that performance. This will have consequences, I hope you're aware of that!"

"Understood, chief, sir. Consequences." The chief constable clapped his heels together. It was clear from his stony face that at that moment, he saw his promotion wash away down the sewer. "Is there anything else I can do for you, inspectors?"

"Have a stretcher brought down here," said Leo. "And start looking for a doctor."

"I don't need no doctor," objected Leinkirchner. "Nor do I need a—"

"You're out of action, chief inspector. I'm taking charge of this assignment. And as the officer in charge I order you to undergo a medical examination." Then, dropping his voice so only Leinkirchner could hear: "Don't forget—your leg was bandaged by a Jew. We wouldn't want your lovely Germanic blood to become tainted now, would we?"

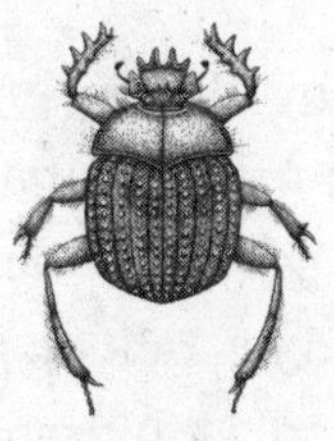

CHAPTER 18

From *Death Rites Around the World* by Augustin Rothmayer, written in Vienna 1894

> **In some areas of Europe, women who die in childbirth are still buried with shoes of the finest leather. There is a reason for this apparent waste: according to old belief, the dead mothers search for their newborn child for six more weeks. Sad, haunted figures, unable to die because of love . . . The expensive shoes make it so their shuffling footsteps aren't heard.**

The next morning, they shifted the meeting to the large conference room on the fourth floor. Superintendent Stukart had added to the investigative team, comprised nearly two dozen men. This was at least partly due to the sensational reports in the morning newspapers, about the sewer murderer and his spectacular escape. His victim had been found a short while later in a side sewer—a young man, bled to death by all appearances. Leo hoped the poor lad wasn't alive when his murderer cut away his manhood.

Moritz Stukart sat with Leo at the head of a long oval table. Leo thought about how he'd held his talk on new methods of criminalistics here just over a week ago. Leinkirchner had made a fool of him in front of everybody then. Well, at least that wouldn't happen this time. The chief inspector was on sick leave. The wound on his leg wasn't as bad as they'd feared, but the doctor had prescribed strict bed rest, and Stukart had made it abundantly clear that he didn't want to see Leinkirchner here for the next few days.

Meanwhile, he'd entrusted Leo with the lead of the team.

Leo's eye scanned the men sitting crowded in the smoky room. They returned his gaze with a mixture of distrust and curiosity. He was still the new guy, the snobby Prussian from Graz who kept turning up with newfangled investigation methods and who was generally considered an oddity and loner. Leo knew they whispered and gossiped about him behind his back. Among the things they gossiped about was the opinion that he was Stukart's pet—which was why no one would dare challenge his role as the lead officer. At least not until he made his first grave mistake.

Leo still hadn't heard from Julia. Apparently she hadn't turned up last night, and she never telephoned Frau Rinsinger, either. Well, their reconciliation would have to wait. The men in this room would only too gladly pounce on the juicy bit of news that he'd maintained a romantic liaison in house.

"Gentlemen," said superintendent Stukart, opening the meeting by tapping his pencil against the table several times with a clacking, unnerving noise. "I believe you're all aware of what happened last night. Perhaps you've read the papers. Let me begin by saying that the writers are quite wrong on one point but right about another. Point one: our worthy colleague Leinkirchner is neither fighting for his life nor was his . . . well, you-know-what cut off. He's doing well, given the circumstances. The second point, however, is entirely true: the Vienna police did not reap glory last night. In other words: we've made complete fools of ourselves. The killer got away because two constables followed the call of nature." The superintendent struck his pencil so hard against the table that the lead broke. "Four dead! We have four dead in just ten days, although the number might be much higher."

"What does that mean?" asked a wheat-blond young man at the front. Leo remembered him from his talk. "More victims . . . ?"

Stukart gave Leo an expectant look, and the latter pointed at Erich Loibl, sitting close by.

"Thanks to inspector Loibl here we've connected another unsolved case with our hustler murderer," said Leo. "The case lies more than a year back. Body parts were found in the Danube Canal, a torso with arms and parts of a skull. In that case, too, the victim's penis and scrotum were removed."

Loibl nodded, visibly glad that Leo had praised him instead of showing him up.

"Add to that further body parts that have been found in the sewers in the last few months," added Leo. "Bits of scalp, an arm, human bones . . . We're still sifting through the files of the district constabularies. We can't prove it yet, but it's possible that our killer is behind those deaths—at least some of them."

"Nought but riffraff living down there," uttered an older colleague from the back. "They're probably cutting each other's throats . . ."

"Possible," conceded Leo. "And yet there is one interesting point, one parallel that all the cases share. Recurring events suggest the same motive, the same perpetrator. Hans Gross writes in his *Handbook for Investigating Judges . . .*"

Several of the men rolled their eyes and Leo realized that he was going at this the wrong way. He rose and walked over to the large city map he'd mounted on the wall before the meeting. On it, he'd marked several points and numbers and connected them with lines—lines following the city's underground sewers. Red pins marked the four known crime scenes while green pins indicated locations where body parts had been found. The whole thing looked like a huge web spanning across Vienna.

"Our killer invariably strikes near the large inner-city canals," explained Leo, pointing at the markers. "The sewers along the Wien Canal, as well as the new one by the Danube Canal, as well as a few older sewers that were built decades ago. Our theory is that the murderer selects his victims randomly from among young hustlers, stabs them to death in a dark place, removes the penis and testicles, and then cuts up their bodies to dispose of them like garbage in the sewers. Individual body parts are harder to assign to an individual, and they disappear more quickly—that's why he's been able to go unnoticed for so long."

"How is that supposed to work? Cutting up the bodies and getting rid of the parts?" It was the blond, arrogant young man. "A butcher getting around with his butchery tools?" The young police agent looked around the room, smirking. "Are there mobile butcher shops? I've never heard of one."

"We're still figuring out how exactly he does it," said Stukart, backing Leo up. "But I think we ought to give consideration to this theory before ridiculing it."

"Is there at least a better description of the murderer now?" asked one of the men from farther back. "I mean more than tailcoat, top hat, and walking stick? After all you, Herr Inspector, and Leinkirchner saw him."

"Unfortunately it was too dark and it happened too quickly for an accurate description," replied Leo with a shrug. "But we know one thing now: his hair is black. The murderer lost his top hat at the crime scene, and I've been able to identify black hairs on it. Judging by the size of the hat, we're looking for a man of average height."

"Uh-huh, a man of average height with black hair, wearing a tailcoat and top hat," muttered an older colleague loudly enough for Leo to hear. "If this is the oh-so-great modern police work, even my grandmother could do it. Do we at least know more about the last victim?"

"We're still in the dark," admitted Leo. "A young man, handsome, boyish. Could be a hustler. He fits the typical prey of our killer, in any case."

"Goddamned faggots," a voice from the back of the room called out. "Serves them right."

Several men grumbled their assent.

"It would be useful to find out more about the sewers, about the people living in them," said Leo, choosing to ignore the comment. "There could be more witnesses." He was still standing in front of the map. Thinking, he traced the lines of the channels with his fingers once more. "Do any of you have ideas or suggestions? As you know, I haven't been here for very long."

He was met with thick silence. Nervously, he fidgeted with his tie. Could it be? It seemed as if the men in this room were sabotaging him on purpose. Had he been acting too pompously again?

Superintendent Stukart harrumphed. "Well, if there are no further suggestions, we better—"

"I might have an idea." It was Erich Loibl, raising his hand cautiously. "There's this place. The Zwingburg."

Leo gave Loibl a relieved look. He hadn't expected this. "The Zwingburg?" he asked encouragingly. "What's that?"

"May I?" Loibl stood and moved toward the map. He pointed at a spot near the Ring. "Here, at Schwarzenberg Square. I don't know any details, but apparently, there's some sort of secret camp down there. A base for beggars, kanalstrotters, and other scoundrels. They call it the Zwingburg because apparently it would be as difficult to take as a fortress."

Stukart pensively polished his pince-nez. Without the glasses, he looked like a wide-eyed owl. "You're right. I believe the constables from the city watch went there once, chasing a pickpocket. They were forced to abort their operation. The sewer over there is wide, and the fellows down there had virtually entrenched themselves. Just like a fortress."

"I, uh, I know one or two of the fellows down there," said Loibl. "They act as *agents provocateurs* for us. That mustn't come out, of course—but they'd be able to show us around. I'd gladly offer myself for the operation."

"Thank you, inspector." Leo gave him a warm nod, touched that Loibl of all people decided to help him out. "That's good news for once. I suggest you and I follow this up." He looked around the room. "Is there anyone else who'd like to accompany us?"

Another wall of silence. Leo tried to ignore it and focused on his next tasks. He put together investigation groups, issued orders, and sternly assigned tasks even if it meant working overtime. He dished out reprimands, and, once or twice, he even slapped a ruler onto the table, almost like superintendent Stukart.

Leo smiled grimly. He was no Paul Leinkirchner, but if this was how his colleagues wanted to play it, he was perfectly capable of being just as great an asshole as the chief inspector.

A deafening trumpeting rang out and Julia jumped. She had slept poorly and felt accordingly nervy. Still, she couldn't help but grin a little. How far had things come? Was she now afraid of elephants? She might as well forget about applying for a job at the zoo. She'd have to think of something else.

She was standing in front of the monkey enclosure, in the same place she'd stood with Sisi last Friday. It was already her third visit to the zoological garden.

Deep in thought, Julia watched the chimpanzees swinging from branch to branch, fishing for bananas. Others merely sat in a corner, resting. One of them, a chimpanzee graying with age, seemed to watch her carefully from his spot in a corner. As if it wasn't she regarding him but the other way around. She wondered what he thought, the old ape, when visitors stopped outside his enclosure every day, pulling faces and pointing their fingers. Just then a fat man holding his equally fat son by the hand laughed out loud, right next to her. Both of them wiggled their heads and poked out their tongues. Julia turned away with disgust. Charles Darwin had a point. Men were probably the biggest apes of all.

It was strange to stroll through the zoo on a Tuesday afternoon. Normally, Julia would have been at Theobald Lane by now, photographing the new inmates, or she'd be out on some assignment. She still found it difficult to grasp that all that was over now. Yesterday afternoon she'd met up with Margarethe at a coffeehouse. Margarethe told her about Leo's invitation and was appalled when Julia said she wasn't going to accept it. In Margarethe's eyes, Leo was the big ticket in Julia's life. Her friend simply couldn't comprehend how anyone could decline an invitation to the Ronacher with champagne and caviar canapés. And Julia wasn't entirely certain why herself. She only knew one thing: she needed distance from Leo. She had to go her own way, without his money, his grand gestures, his dreams and hopes for their future together.

This time, Julia had left her daughter with Bruno and Big Elli. She'd told them that she needed to be alone for a while. But she had another motive: the murder case at the zoo still preoccupied her thoughts. Deep down Julia knew that Saidrovuni was innocent. For days now the chief had been vegetating in a prison cell at the courthouse, awaiting trial and probably the death penalty.

Augustin Rothmayer's promise to find out more about the deceased keeper Stefan Moser had encouraged Julia to make some more inquiries of her own. Especially now that she had plenty of time. Perhaps Carl Rebers would be able to help. As assistant to the director, Rebers was bound to know a thing or two about internal processes, and also about director Friedrich Knauer, whom Julia found a little suspicious. And Rebers knew keeper Eugen Lenz, whose accusation of Saidrovuni had kicked the whole affair off.

Feeling indecisive, she meandered along the graveled paths until she came to the large aviary that formed the entrance to the show arena. A sign advised that the next show would start in half an hour. Already there was a small queue of visitors, even though it wasn't even Sunday or a holiday. The Matabele ethnic show was the zoo's great attraction and presumably brought in a ton of money. Among those waiting were the chubby father and son duo, the boy sucking on some kind of huge colorful candy. Chances were father and son would stare at the Matabele just as stupidly and pull faces as they'd done with the apes. Julia felt sick. But at least she now had an idea of what she could do. If anyone knew more about the case, surely it was the Matabele themselves. Maybe she'd be able to speak with them. Julia decided to join the queue.

After waiting patiently for a while, all of the visitors were admitted. The crowd streamed through the entrance and followed the wire tunnel into the inside of the aviary. Julia was once again gripped by the sensation of having entered the jungle. Screeching parrots fluttered among the branches above her; monkeys swung on vines. The aviary's net was barely visible, rendering the illusion near perfect. The path led to the large circular arena, where they sat down, chatting and laughing, on the wooden benches. The Matabele women had assumed their positions outside their huts, wearing skirts and furs and chanting a foreign-sounding harmony accompanied by monotonous drumming. The music rose to a drumroll before stopping abruptly. The audience watched in captivated silence.

Zoo director Friedrich Knauer himself entered the arena. Wearing a pressed three-piece suit, blackened leather boots, and a kind of safari helmet on his head, he looked the part of a European explorer somewhere in Africa. He gave a small bow.

"Ladies and gentlemen!" he droned. "It is my great honor to present to you the hunting dance of the Matabele! We are very proud to host this wild and primeval troupe here in Vienna. In just a few short weeks they'll be off to the next European metropolis. You will enjoy an exotic show, a glimpse into a kind of paradisiacal primal state that we civilized nations have long since left behind—a fact which some in today's audience might find regretful." With a wink he pointed at the bare-breasted Matabele women. Stifled laughter came from the men, while wives elbowed their husbands in the ribs.

Knauer raised a hand. "Allow yourself to be enchanted by the magic of Africa! Embark on a journey into the dark heart of this still unexplored continent!" With another bow he walked off and the drumming started back up. The women moved to the rhythm, singing and clapping their hands.

Julia studied the Matabele women more closely. She thought she recognized the younger woman from Saidrovuni's hut that day. Julia might have been imagining it, but she thought the woman's face was rigid with grief, her gaze empty.

With another drumroll, the men emerged from the huts, clad in nothing but loincloths and wigs made of horsehair. They wielded clubs and spears in a wild dance, ejecting loud cries from time to time and tossing the clubs back and forth like the jugglers at the Ronacher. The pantomime that followed appeared to tell the story of a thief being caught red-handed. He got away and the men pursued him, still dancing. In the end, the scoundrel was symbolically clubbed to death in the center of the stage.

To Julia, the show was a mix of carnival and cheap theater. There wasn't anything genuine about it, though the audience followed the spectacle with cries of amazement and laughter. The father and son duo seemed highly entertained. Julia watched the boy toss a piece of candy at the Matabele warriors as if he were feeding bread to ducks at a pond.

After half an hour, the show ended and the audience scattered. Julia moved to one side and hid behind a bush next to the rows of benches. When all the other visitors had left the arena, she walked over to the huts. The Matabele men had vanished back inside them, presumably to prepare for the next performance. Some of the women and children sat around the fire outside the huts, conversing in low voices. When they caught sight of Julia, they fell silent and gestured as if to shoo Julia away. Julia raised her hands and approached slowly.

"I won't bother you for long," she said, not knowing whether anyone understood her. "I'm here because of your chief. Because of Herr Saidrovuni. Does anyone understand me? I want to help him."

When the women heard the name of their chief, they began to whisper, and Julia called herself a fool. What had caused her to assume that the women would understand German? How would she react if she were in the middle of a foreign land and someone started talking to her in their strange language?

One of the women watched Julia closely. Julia recognized the young woman from the chief's hut. She'd been cradling a baby that time—was she perhaps something like his wife?

"Do you remember me?" asked Julia, looking at the woman. When there was no reaction, she formed a circle with her thumb and forefinger, holding it up to her eyes like a lens and making a clicking noise. "The photographer. I'm here to help you."

Recognition dawned on the Matabele woman's face.

"Your husband is in prison, but I believe he's innocent," Julia went on. "Do you know who might have hidden the key in his hut?"

When the woman again showed no reaction, Julia produced her own key ring and jingled it. "The key to the lion enclosure." She pointed at the hut. "How did the key get into the hut? Do you know anything about that? It's very important!"

Suddenly, the woman seemed to understand. She started to talk hastily in her tongue, making frequent clicking sounds. Tears streamed down her cheeks. Other women began to speak imploringly to her. They appeared to want to silence her, and an angry exchange ensued. Saidrovuni's young wife sobbed, her entire body quaking. Again and again she pointed at the keys. Julia thought she could hear two words over and over. They sounded like *umlilo* and *ikhanda*. But as much as Julia focused on the woman's gestures, she couldn't figure out the words' meanings.

She was about to speak to the wailing woman again when a deep, commanding voice boomed from one of the huts. A man emerged, no longer dressed in his loin cloth and horsehair wig but in linen pants and vest. Julia briefly wondered which was the costume: the linen pants or the loin cloth. Saidrovuni, too, had kept European clothing in his chest.

The man glowered at Julia. "Go away!" he barked with a hard accent. "Go away, woman! Leave us."

Hoisting his spear menacingly, he moved toward Julia. She decided it was time to retreat. She nodded at the women in farewell and hastily strode toward the entrance to the tunnel.

Once inside the tunnel, Julia suddenly heard familiar voices. It was Friedrich Knauer and the old keeper, Eugen Lenz.

"There was nothing!" Lenz was saying in his grating voice. "I swear, it's just those savages taking revenge. They were lying through their teeth. I'll make sure no one blabs. You know you can count on me, director."

"True or made up, it mustn't ever get out, you hear me?" Knauer replied angrily. "Never! It would mean the end of the zoo. . . ."

Julia looked around desperately. Lenz couldn't find her here! He'd already caught her sniffing around once. As quietly as she could she ran back to the rows of benches. She hid behind one of the tall backrests while Knauer and Lenz walked past some way away. The director still seemed quite agitated, but they were too far away for Julia to make out any more of what they were saying.

When she could no longer see them, Julia darted into the tunnel once more and ran as fast as she could toward the light at the other end. No voices yelled after her; no one seemed to have spotted her. Relieved, she stepped out of the tunnel and walked past the queue forming for the next show. She turned over Knauer's words in her head.

It mustn't ever get out. . . .

What did the director mean?

"That's a surprise! I didn't expect to see you back here so soon."

Julia jumped when someone addressed her from behind. Had they caught her after all?

She turned and found herself looking at the friendly face of Carl Rebers. She almost didn't recognize him, as he wasn't dressed in his apron and boots like in the vivarium. Instead, he wore a plain black suit that was a little too small for him. His red hair stuck out from under a scuffed bowler.

Rebers cast a searching glance about him. "Is your daughter not with you today, or has she run off again? Do I need to rescue her from some beast or other?"

"Don't worry." Julia smiled with relief. "I'm alone today. It's nice for a change."

"I see." Rebers nodded, then pointed at the entrance to the show arena. "Are you coming from the ethnic show? I thought you disliked our main attraction."

"I . . ." Julia hesitated. "I wanted to see it for myself. Well, my attitude hasn't changed—on the contrary, I'm more convinced than ever."

Carl Rebers gave her an inquisitive look. "I don't suppose you're from the paper?"

"What makes you think that?"

"I don't know. You sound like someone from the paper." He shrugged. "And I just remembered that old Lenz said something about a mother with a child snooping around the closed-off lion area. I believe it was the very same day I met you at the vivarium. And not long before that, a photographer visited, said Lenz . . ."

Julia blushed. She was completely busted. What a great detective she was! She decided to tell at least some of the truth.

"You're right," she said slowly. "I . . . I work for the Wiener Anzeiger. It's about the death in the lion enclosure. I was here as a photographer the day after it happened, and now my boss wants more information. A big scoop. But the zoo won't give me anything, and so I'm taking a look around myself."

Carl Rebers frowned. "It's understandable that the zoo won't comment on the incident. Just imagine what our visitors would think: a lion eating a keeper! And then your daughter nearly falls into the pond of Nile crocodiles . . . They would say the zoo isn't safe." Rebers sighed and shook his head sadly. "Well, looks like you got your story after all . . ."

Julia searched for the right words. She was sorry that Rebers was disappointed in her. He saved Sisi's life, or at least rescued her from grave danger. "The incident with the crocodiles stays between us, promise," she said. "But the dead keeper—there is information that suggests there might be more to it than . . . than just an accident."

"More than an accident?" Rebers pushed back his bowler, red curls tumbling across his forehead. He looked stumped. "Who told you that?"

"I . . . I have my sources." Julia considered briefly, then decided to confide in Carl Rebers. She had nothing left to lose. If Rebers told director Knauer about her, her clandestine investigation was finished. Worse, she might even face charges of willful misrepresentation. She cleared her throat. "Listen, I know the police have arrested the chief of the Matabele. The story goes that he opened the gate in revenge to let the lion attack keeper Lenz. Unfortunately it got young Moser instead."

"How did you . . . ?" Rebers paused, then gave a resigned shrug. "Oh well, sounds like you know everything. Congratulations. Your newspaper will love the story." He shook his head with disappointment. "You do realize what it will mean to the zoo if this article gets published, don't you?"

"But why would the chief have hidden the key in his own hut?" asked Julia by way of reply. "It makes no sense! I believe something else happened. I believe someone set a trap for him. And my guess is the Matabele women know something."

"A trap?" Rebers gave a laugh. "Your imagination is running wild, Fräulein Journalist. Who do you propose would have done such a thing?"

"Lenz of course! The two of them argued, apparently about the Matabele's food." Julia began to explain her theory. "The two of them fell out, maybe there were other factors involved, too. Lenz hates the chief. And maybe Lenz wanted to get rid of young Moser too. Then he'd have killed two birds with one stone . . ." She sighed. "Granted, it all sounds rather far-fetched. But something's off here, that much I'm sure of."

As they talked, they'd walked slowly along and had now come to the giraffe enclosure. The animals gazed down at them with bored expressions, chewing on some leaves.

"Hmm . . ." said Rebers. He seemed to think it over. Maybe he wasn't so sure anymore that Julia was spouting nonsense.

"Maybe your theory isn't all wrong," he said eventually, his eyes gazing into the distance. "Young Moser was about to be named head keeper. Lenz would have been out the door—he drinks too much and is getting forgetful." He gave a shrug. "Well, now everything stays as it was. Strange. But it doesn't necessarily mean anything."

"Earlier, I overheard Lenz and director Knauer arguing," replied Julia. "The director talked about something that must never get out. What did he mean? Do you think he . . . he knows something? Something to do with Stefan Moser's death?"

Rebers looked around. He waited until some visitors had moved past them, then he said in a lowered voice: "Put it this way—Dr. Knauer would do anything to avoid scandal, especially since the zoo has only just opened its gates, and finances are still shaky. He'll do anything to sweep certain things under the rug. And he sometimes has . . . well, rather queer views."

"Do you know the director privately?"

Rebers gave a thin smile. "Who really knows director Friedrich Carl Knauer? Probably not even his own wife. Scientists tend to be strange creatures . . ." He trailed off, and his face suddenly brightened. "Tell me, you didn't make up your daughter's deafness, did you?"

"No, no!" Julia shook her head. "Sisi was born deaf. It's not always easy . . ." She swallowed. "For either of us. Maybe that's why I got so worked up over the ethnic show. Because . . . well, because people sometimes look at Sisi just like that when she tries to speak. As if she were a . . . a savage. Or an ape."

"Well, I hope science will soon find a remedy. There are hopeful signs, fräulein—" Rebers paused and laughed. "We've been talking all this time and I still haven't asked for your name."

"Uh, Margarethe. Margarethe Löffler." Her friend's name was the first thing that popped into her mind.

"Well, Fräulein Löffler. I scratch your back, you scratch mine. You don't mention the incident at the vivarium, and in return you can do what you will with the information I've just given you. I might even find out more for your article." Carl Rebers raised a finger in warning. "But you have to promise me one thing: leave my name out of it. Or else I can kiss my position of assistant to the director goodbye. Agreed?"

Julia nodded and shook Rebers's hand. "You can count on me. You've really helped me, thank you."

"It's a pity we didn't meet under different circumstances." Carl Rebers gave her a wink. "If you'd ever like a guided tour of the zoo, call on me. That said, my specialty is frogs and other amphibians. I'm not sure how interesting that would be for you."

Julia feigned disappointment. "I'd prefer zebras and ponies." She laughed. "But thanks! Sisi likes tadpoles. Maybe we'll visit again soon, completely separate from journalism research or other ulterior motives. Promise."

"I'd like that." Rebers doffed his hat a little awkwardly. "I bid you a good day, Fräulein Löffler. It was a pleasure."

As he plodded off in his ill-fitting black suit, Julia felt the pangs of a guilty conscience for having lied to Carl Rebers. Oddly, she was reminded of Augustin Rothmayer just then, whose raven-black suits were always a little short, just like Rebers's. She grinned.

An amphibian expert and a gravedigger . . .

Those two would make an excellent pair.

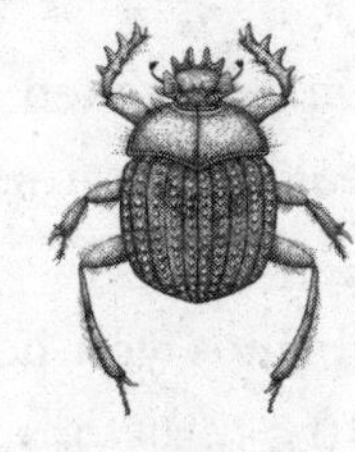

CHAPTER 19

In the light of the late afternoon, Augustin Rothmayer stood hunched in front of the cemetery administration building and scraped the dirt off his boots. Now that it was May, the ground was moist from spring rainfalls and soil clung to shoe soles like glue. Augustin sometimes emerged from a grave to find he'd grown by two inches, as if he wore high-heeled shoes. Once he was reasonably satisfied with his cleaning job, he pushed the electric doorbell.

There was a jarring sound inside, and the gravedigger grimaced. Parts of the cemetery administration were completely electrified, much to Rothmayer's dismay. He'd never get used to these blaring ringing sounds. There was nothing like the melodious chiming of a death knell announcing someone's final hour. Yes, that was a sound to warm the heart! Much better than these newfangled doorbells, which sounded as if someone's foot was being stepped on.

The door opened and the cemetery director gave him a look of surprise. He wore a large napkin tucked into his shirt; apparently, he was in the middle of a meal. Children's voices were audible in the background.

"Herr Rothmayer, what brings you here? You've finished work for today, as have I," added the director meaningfully. "I don't suppose you came to apologize for your demeanor last Sunday? That would be a novelty indeed."

Augustin removed his hat and played sheepishly with its brim. It wasn't easy for him, visiting his superior's private abode. Like himself, the director lived on the cemetery grounds, but right at the front, close to the main entrance and in much grander conditions. It was a nice ground-floor apartment with high stucco ceilings, and there was even a small garden. A swing creaked, and Augustin heard a girl's bright laughter.

"Uh . . . , good evening to you, too," he began awkwardly. "Um, yes, I s'pose I also wanted to apologize—"

"Was Fräulein Wolf able to change your mind with regard to Anna?"

"Um, I'm sure we'll figure something out," replied Augustin. "But I've actually come because of something else."

The director raised an eyebrow. "Uh-huh, and what would that be?"

"Well, I'm afraid something rather harebrained happened. There's been a mix-up of corpses."

"A . . . mix-up of corpses?" The director pulled off his napkin and gave Rothmayer a befuddled look. "What on earth do you mean, a mix-up of corpses?"

"Well, gravedigger Stockinger and myself, we've both been swamped with burials lately. Consumption, spotted fever, you know, the usual things for May." Rothmayer stared hard at a clump of soil on his boot that he'd missed. "And in all the rush, we must have mixed up two coffins in the morgue. They don't write no names on the coffins, do they. Anyhow, Stockinger buried a certain Lisbeth Bachmüller and I a Stefan Moser. Only, the wrong body was in the wrong coffin, you see, the other way round. Moser in Bachmüller and Bachmüller in Moser. Like I said, bloody stupid."

"Hmm, bloody stupid, you got it . . ." The director nervously dabbed his lips with a corner of his napkin. "Well, as long as no one knows . . . I mean, now they're both six feet under. Before God we're all the same, aren't we?"

"Yes, of course you're right, herr." Augustin Rothmayer scratched behind his ear, thinking. "But do you know councilor Bachmüller? Regular visitor at court. Brother-in-law of Major Kranicek, apparently, who met the kaiserin a few times at Schönbrunn while walking the dog. Anyway, councilor Bachmüller loved his wife Lisbeth very dearly and is going to visit her grave often . . ." He let his voice trail off.

"Christ, stop it," breathed the director. "If this gets out . . ." He used the napkin to wipe across his sweaty bald head. "You're quite right, Rothmayer. We need to put this in order. What do you suggest?"

"I can excavate both bodies at night, when no one's around. And swap them over. Then all's back in order."

"Order. Very sensible, Rothmayer. Order is good. You do that."

Augustin moved his head from side to side as if he were contemplating something. "Hmm, there's just one small problem. I don't know where Moser was put—the wrong Bachmüller, I mean. It was Stockinger buried—"

"I understand. That's easily fixed. Follow me."

A woman's voice called out from inside the apartment, "*Schatz*, are you coming? The beef bouillon is getting cold!"

The director shouted back, "Just a moment, dear. There's some paperwork I need to finish." He waved Rothmayer inside. Together they went up to the director's office above the apartment, where the short man headed straight for the boxes of files piling up on shelves along the wall. Rothmayer cast an admiring look down the long rows of boxes. Every burial was recorded here. Presumably, there were hundreds or thousands more of these filing boxes in the basements of the administration buildings. Order really did reign at Central Cemetery—at least when it came to its archives.

"Remind me of the dead man's name?" asked the director, searing through the files.

"Moser. Stefan Moser. Young, apparently. Zookeeper by trade. Unsure of his year of birth, sorry."

"Moser, zookeeper, hmm. Ah, here he is!" The director drew out a card. "Wasn't very long ago, thank goodness." He held out the index card to Augustin. "Sector 3, field IV, grave 39. Will you find it?"

"Will I find it?" Augustin smirked. "I know each and every grave here, sir. As if it were my own." He memorized the number, muttering to himself. "A shaft grave and Moser's right at the bottom. Blast it! That'll take a while. Much obliged, director, and pardon the trouble."

Augustin Rothmayer returned his floppy hat to his head and trudged toward the front door, his boots leaving wet, black crumbs of dirt behind like the slimy trail of a snail. Sighing softly, the director followed him downstairs to his cold soup.

The gravedigger smiled. He'd found what he'd come for.

Now all he had to do was dig deep.

The doorkeeper outside the cellar bar looked Leo up and down. He wasn't quite as big as Bruno from the Blue Dragoon, but he was tall enough to make Leo feel smaller than he already was.

"Ah, Herr von Herzfeldt, what an honor," said the hairy mountain, who knew Leo from previous visits. “A little late, aren’t ya? The lassie is halfway through her act.”

“I’ll just be happy if I get the lassie at a table alone later on,” replied Leo.

“A private performance, so to speak.” The doorkeeper grinned. “You’ve got good taste, baron. Well, in you go.”

With a nod at Leo he opened the door to the bar. Word had spread that goings-on at the cellar bar were on occasion debauched, so they’d become more selective in who was allowed through the door. Only Big Elli and a few others knew that Leo worked for the police, and that was good. The giant out front probably thought he was a real baron.

The vaulted cellar was so full of smoke that Leo’s eyes watered as soon as he stepped inside. He blinked repeatedly, and when he saw Julia up on the stage, his heart skipped a beat.

It was Tuesday night, one of the two nights a week that Julia sang and performed the tango here. Her exotic performance, so different from the traditional waltz, had become popular here in Neulerchenfeld. The audience consisted mostly of young men who gawked at her as she moved to the rhythm of the music in the close embrace of her dance partner, Pierre. She let her head fall back and closed her eyes dreamily as maestro Alfredo played the slightly out-of-tune piano. Leo hated seeing Julia like this, even though he knew Pierre and Alfredo posed no threat. Alfredo was ancient and Pierre preferred men.

Leo took a seat in a dark corner and signaled to the waiter. The first glass of absinthe enveloped his strained nerves like smooth honey. He lit a cigarette and stretched out his legs.

All day—during the morning meeting, while he made plans for tomorrow with Loibl—Leo’s thoughts kept returning to Julia. He missed her! His fear of losing her was growing by the day. And so he’d decided to take the initiative. Since Julia hadn’t returned his calls or responded to Margarethe, the cellar bar seemed his only option to see her, to talk to her and hopefully to make up.

From the corner of his eye Leo watched Pierre maneuvering Julia across the stage, body pressed against body, their eyes connected as if with wires. Leo remembered the times he and Julia had danced here in a similar fashion. Jealousy welled up in him. Had she spotted him yet? It didn't look like it, but perhaps she was making a point of demonstrating that his presence meant nothing to her.

A few songs later, the couple bowed and vanished backstage, accompanied by the audience's applause. Leo checked his watch. It was nine o'clock at night. He knew Julia had a half-hour break now. He quickly extinguished his cigarette, stood, and walked over to the stage. Next to it, a small door led to the dressing room. Old Alfredo sat in front of it, smoking a fat cigar. When he recognized Leo, his bushy eyebrows shot up.

"Perdon, señor, I don't believe the señora has time for you at the moment—"

"The señora can tell me herself," grumbled Leo and pushed past Alfredo, entering the small dressing room. Julia was sitting in front of a mirror, Pierre helping her get her hair back in shape. She was wearing the tight blue dress from Elli's collection that Leo loved—only, not when she wore it for everyone on stage.

A grin spread on Pierre's face when he spotted Leo in the mirror.

"Oh là là, an important visitor." Pierre blew him a kiss and chuckled. "You look dashing, inspector. A new suit?"

"Why don't you go treat yourself to a glass of champagne?" said Leo, placing a few notes in Pierre's hand. "The waiter's suit isn't too shabby, either, and he's got a nice arse."

Pierre shot Julia a look, but her expression remined neutral. The young dancer shrugged. "Why not? I could do with some fresh air, anyhow." He brushed his hand across Leo's jacket as he sidled past. "I like your perfume, inspector."

"Yours, on the other hand, is far too sickly," said Leo grimly. "And now out with you!"

When he and Julia were alone at last, an uncomfortable silence stretched. They could hear the patrons' laughter outside the door, the clinking of glasses. Alfredo was playing a popular hit and a few men were singing along.

Leo shook his head. "I'll never understand why you do this. Those people out there, they're scum. I mean—"

"Is that why you came?" asked Julia sharply. "To insult my audience and my dance partner and to tell me once again what I should be doing?"

Leo raised his hands defensively. "I'm sorry. That was probably not the best start to an apology."

"No. I'm afraid it wasn't," said Julia, continuing to powder her face.

Leo stepped behind her so that she might see his shamefaced expression. "Julia, I'm sorry I left you at the Ronacher on Friday. Would you give me the opportunity to explain?"

"You have fifteen minutes before I go back onstage."

Leo pulled up a chair and sat next to her in front of the mirror. He studied his own reflection. He looked drawn and tired. Hardly a surprise, considering all that had happened in the last few days.

"I solved the mummy case," he said.

"You solved it?" Julia turned to face him for the first time. "Just like that?"

"Well, not entirely, but mostly, yes." At least he now had Julia's undivided attention. He told her of his conversation with the Rapoldys Friday night and what he'd found out.

"So, the mummy's curse is nothing but a cover-up—the cover-up of an accident," she said at last, shaking her head. "No murder, no curse, no great mystery . . . just a plain juggler's trick. Who'd have thought?"

"Something's not quite right, though. Don't forget Walter Kerfeld's death!" Leo lowered his voice. "The imperial court flexed their muscles, that much is clear. Maybe some high-ranking gentlemen are involved personally, or even the archduke himself. And I'm still waiting to hear from my sister Lili in Graz about Father Gregor Mayr's cause of death."

He drew a deep sigh. "But I have so much going on at work that I don't really have the time to follow up on that. You might have seen in the papers that there's been another hustler murder. Another castration. Me and Leinkirchner were—"

"Listen, Leo," she butted in. "I'm out, as you know. Stukart fired me. And I'm actually not too unhappy about it."

"I could talk to Stukart," said Leo quickly. "I mean, crime-scene photography might not be the best job in the long run for a woman, but you could go back to the switchboard—"

"Stop it, Leo!" Julia's voice was cutting and determined now. "Stop constantly interfering in my life. It has to end."

"What do you mean?"

She set aside her powder puff and looked at him earnestly. "Listen. I've been thinking a lot in the last few days and nights. Thinking about us. Maybe we should take a break for a while. We . . ." She paused. "We just aren't a good fit, Leo. I mean, look at you." Julia gestured at his pressed black suit. His small silk handkerchief probably cost as much as Pierre's shoes. "This here isn't your world and it never will be. You've said so yourself many times."

"You can't be serious! You can't . . . I mean, why . . ." Leo found himself lost for words. His throat was suddenly parched.

Her eyes softened. "Leo, things can't always go your way. When have you ever done anything that helps *me*?"

"I . . . the camera equipment . . ."

"That's what I mean. You bought me the camera equipment because you enjoy photography and wanted me to enjoy it also. You go to the theater with me because you like going to the theater. You take me to plush restaurants because you like dining expensively. And you like parading me through Vienna in an open fiacre when I wear my blue dress. But that's not me, Leo! That's just the Julia you like to see." She gave him a sad look. "The real Julia lives in a brothel, she likes to dance and sing in smoky cellar bars, and she has a fatherless daughter who can't hear or speak. But I'm afraid that's not the Julia you want. Someone like Charlotte Rapoldy would be a much better match for you."

Leo said nothing. He had come here expecting her to be mad at him. He'd expected a lecture, but not a final reckoning. Her words struck him deep down inside, not least because he sensed that there was some truth to them. Outside the door, the punters clapped their hands and called Julia's name.

"If everything you say is true, then why did you even bother with me at all the last few months?" he asked bitterly.

"Why?" A desperate laugh escaped her. "Because I love you, Leo! I love my dorky baron with all his quirks, his brilliant mind, his wit, and yes, even his arrogance. That's what makes this all so difficult!"

She made to rise but Leo stopped her. "How can I prove to you that I don't just think of myself? That you're worth it, that I'd walk through fire for you? That I love you for . . . for yourself!"

She hesitated, seemed to consider.

Then she uttered one word. "Saidrovuni."

He looked puzzled. "The chief? What about him?"

"I went back to the zoo. I am certain now that he didn't murder the young keeper. But no court in the world would believe me or him. Help me get him out."

"Out from the Vienna courthouse?" Leo's jaw dropped. "Are you . . . are you joking? How is that supposed to work? And even if I could . . ."

"You asked me for a way to prove your love. That's it." She tore herself free. "And now excuse me. The rabble demands its floozy."

She strode out the door and the crowd cheered. Alfredo struck a tune Leo knew well. Julia sang it often, a song from *Carmen*, an opera making the headlines in Vienna at the moment. Tonight, the words shook Leo to his core.

L'amour est un oiseau rebelle, que nul ne peut apprivoiser . . .

Love is a wild bird that no one can tame.

Leo looked in the mirror. Suddenly, his new suit, silk handkerchief, and the brilliantine in his hair seemed awfully corny to him. And for the first time, he asked himself if there was a real Leo behind the image in the mirror.

"Easy, girl. A coffin ain't no toy."

There was a rattling, creaking, and squeaking as the winch slowly turned. A dark shape rose from the blackness of the grave, eventually taking on the contours of a coffin. It was the last of four. Clumps of dirt skittered across the bright spruce boards and clattered into the depths. The coffin swung from side to side in the ropes as Anna continued to turn the crank.

"Slowly, I said!" grumbled Augustin. "Even a corpse'll feel sick with all that swinging."

Anna grinned as if it were all just a game.

And I suppose it is, for her, thought Augustin. *A forbidden game.*

He could operate the pulley himself, of course. He had built it a few years ago and was mighty proud of it. Normally, lowering a coffin required two gravediggers. Ropes were placed under the coffin at the top and bottom. That way, even the heaviest box could be lowered into a hole with relative ease. But Augustin preferred to work alone, and so he had built this pulley winch.

He had, however, never before used it to bring a coffin back to the surface.

Augustin had already thought about patenting his coffin crane. The construction resembled a wooden spider squatting atop the open grave. The gravedigger frowned. "Coffin spider" might not be such a bad name—easy to remember. With a hand crank and system of pulleys, even the heavier coffins could be moved by a single person. But tonight, Anna had pleaded with him until he'd caved and taken her along.

It was long past midnight. A kerosene lamp that was perched on the neighboring grave mound shed a warm glow on the gravedigger, the girl, and the crane. When the pulleys didn't squeak and Augustin didn't grumble, it was very silent, aside from the occasional fluting of a nightingale. Three coffins sat beside the hole. Stefan Moser's indeed proved to be at the very bottom of the nine-foot hole. Apparently, there'd been several more funerals that day that Augustin hadn't known about.

The story about the supposed mix-up had occurred to him on Sunday, right after Fräulein Wolf's visit. But it had taken until tonight for Augustin to gather up enough courage to pay the cemetery director a visit and ask about the grave. The director hadn't suspected anything. Why should he? He was just glad he didn't have to get his hands dirty.

Augustin trusted Fräulein Wolf. If she said that she would help him and Anna, then she meant it. And so he helped her, too. He knew that he wouldn't be able to keep up the cat and mouse forever. At some point the welfare would find Anna and take her away from him. What would happen then, he didn't know.

So much pain . . . so many memories . . .

As the coffin slowly swung to a halt above the grave, Augustin watched Anna from the corner of his eye.

She truly did remind him of his daughter, who had died of

cholera. She'd been their last child to live, and she'd been his favorite. Before his eyes, she had withered like a leaf in fall. The day after her death, Augustin found his wife Marthe hanging from a willow, close to the Sankt Marx Cemetery wall. Her empty gaze had been directed at the gray Vienna sky, a sky entirely void of fat, singing angels; violins; and God.

So much pain . . .

When Augustin had committed both coffins to the ground with his own hands back then at Sankt Marx Cemetery, a part of him had died too—crawled into a coffin, closed the lid, and curled up like a hedgehog in an eternal winter. Only this dear girl, also named Anna, had woken him from his hibernation. They mustn't take her away from him!

"Now, make sure the wheel locks and then come over here. Gimme a hand and pull the box over to the ground."

Anna carefully followed his instructions. Using another spool, they easily pulled the heavy coffin next to the hole and set it down. After one last clatter, silence set in.

"All done," said Augustin, wiping sweat off his forehead. "Right, lassie, you've had your fun. Now off to bed with you. I'm sure you can find your way home."

"But what about you, Herr Rothmayer?" asked Anna. "Are you staying?"

"I've still got work to do here."

She crossed her arms defiantly. "Then I'm staying, too."

"Like hell you are! That's not what we agreed on. I'll show you what I do with little girls who—" Augustin broke off. There was no point threatening Anna. It led nowhere. She resembled his daughter in her stubbornness, too. "Fine," he said instead. "I've got a suggestion for you. If you go home now, you may play on my fiddle for a little bit. But no bow, or else Lucie will take off and never return! You can only pluck it."

Anna's eyes grew wide. "Really? I can play on it?"

"Plucking, only plucking! And let me warn you." He raised a finger that was covered in grave soil. "If I find just one scratch on it later, you'll be sorry! I'll smack your bottom until you wish I'd buried you alive first."

"Whatever you say, Herr Rothmayer!" Anna brought her hand to her temple and grinned. "No bow, no scratches. Plucking only." Then she was gone, vanishing behind the nearest grave mound.

Augustin sighed. It had always been Anna's wish to hold the violin. So far, he'd only played for her. Maybe he'd buy her her own fiddle someday. But this one violin was sacred to him. Anna didn't know who it had once belonged to, and even if she knew, she probably wouldn't care. Augustin cared. The violin had been handed down in his family for generations. Allowing Anna to play with it tonight was a small acknowledgment that she was part of the family.

He was the last of the line, anyway. There was no other Rothmayer after him. Who would he leave the valuable instrument to if not her? Certainly not some idiots from some museum. They'd only put it in a glass case where it would gather dust.

The gravedigger waited a few moments longer, then produced a chisel and set it under the coffin lid. The nails hadn't been in the timber for long and were easy to pry loose. When he lifted the lid, the smell of decomposition, until then but a faint trace, wafted up like an invisible cloud. Normally, Augustin could tell by the smell how old a corpse was. He knew from the file that this one was only a week old. But the smell was much stronger.

Why?

He fetched the kerosene lamp and put it down next to him to see better.

They'd patched together the lad, or what was left of him, in a fairly rushed job. Augustin hoped the boy's family hadn't had to see him like this. In some really bad cases, when nothing could be done, the undertakers only left the head uncovered while the rest of the body was concealed.

But in this case, the head wasn't a pretty picture, either.

Augustin knew from Julia that Stefan Moser had been attacked by a lion. He knew what to expect. He studied the corpse, felt it, tried to discern any hints that might help him along. As far as he knew, this body hadn't been taken to Professor Hofmann, which seemed odd. Why hadn't it? After the accident the boy had been brought straight here and stored in the morgue for two days as the law dictated. Stefan Moser may not have been the victim of a crime, but Augustin would have thought the forensic institute would be interested in this case.

Augustin's fingers traveled across the body, plucking here and there. The gravedigger felt, sensed—smelled—a master of death. There was the story of a stranger, of some kind of demon bending over Moser's body. His murderer?

Augustin examined the body almost tenderly. He knew—corpses had much to tell him. Unfortunately, the wounds on this one were so plentiful that any stab or bullet wounds would be impossible to make out. At least not in the middle of the night at Central Cemetery by the light of a kerosene lamp with no medical instruments. The right arm was missing entirely, as well as the left leg. The throat was shredded. In addition, a week of warm May weather meant the body was decomposing quickly. The gravedigger's eye wandered down the torso. His first strange discovery was on the pants.

And then he saw something else.

Strange . . .

He bent down lower, examining the wound. There was no doubt.

But why . . . ?

Pensive, he hummed a melody, as he always did when he focused. It was Chopin's funeral march—a beautiful piece. Augustin dressed the body and replaced the coffin lid. To the rhythm of the music, he hammered the nails back into the wood. He didn't know what exactly his discovery meant, but he knew one thing.

He would telephone Fräulein Wolf first thing in the morning.

But first he had to get four coffins back in the ground.

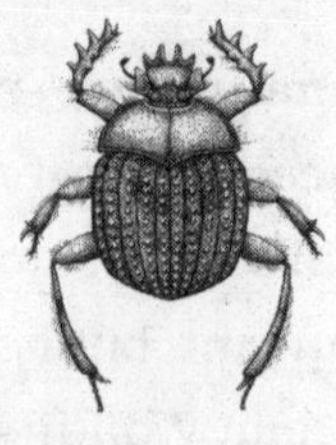

CHAPTER 20

From *Death Rites Around the World* by Augustin Rothmayer, written in Vienna, 1894

> People need funeral rites to grieve, and there's mighty little the high and mighty can do about it. Kaiser Joseph II tried to introduce the so-called economy coffin toward the end of the eighteenth century. The coffin was meant to be reused as many times as desired due to a trapdoor in the bottom which opened over the grave. But the Viennese didn't like the idea. Nor did they like the flat coffin lids made of cheap softwood, called "nose squeezers" by the people.

When Leo arrived at Schwarzenberg Square early the next morning, Erich Loibl was already waiting for him near a tobacconist's shop. Loibl looked reasonably well rested and didn't reek of schnapps. Apparently, Leo's praise in front of the entire team and the prospect of helping solve the case had lent him some motivation. With a happy smirk he sank his teeth into a bratwurst; fat trickled into his walrus bread.

"Want one?" Loibl nodded in the direction of a bratwurst stall, not much more than a crooked box nailed together with a few planks. "The wurst at Schwarzenberg Square is the best in all of Vienna. Try it!"

"No, thank you." Leo grimaced. "I didn't know they were selling bratwursts this early in the morning."

"Well, they're not the freshest," Loibl said with a full mouth. "They'll be from last night. But well seasoned and nice and greasy." Mustard dripped onto his collar, but he didn't seem to notice. "My man won't get here till seven. We've got a little time."

Loibl had spent the previous afternoon reaching out to his contacts in the underworld. And he'd struck gold. There was someone willing to show them the way to the Zwingburg and who would help—for the right price, of course—find people who would talk down there.

A horsecar tram clattered past. A little farther on, it rolled to a halt and spat out a few passengers. Schwarzenberg Square was still quite empty. Across the square towered the palais of Archduke Ludwig Viktor, one of the many new palaces built on the former glacis. The palace was also connected to a former case. The Wien Canal ran nearby, as Leo's nose testified. In a way Leo was glad he was at work this early in the morning—at least it allowed him to forget for a while that Julia had sent him packing last night. He'd stayed in the dressing room like a pillar of stone for a long time before sneaking out the back door like a thief in the night, Julia's question still echoing in his mind.

When have you ever done anything to help me?

He'd never thought about it this way. The bitter truth in her words pained him almost as much as the distance she had firmly planted between them.

"Who is this fellow we're meeting?" asked Leo abruptly, trying to divert his thoughts. His eyes grazed the newspapers displayed at the tobacconist's, fat headlines blaring the latest murder in the hustler scene. Even with no bratwurst Leo felt sickened by the sensationalist images the artist had created to accompany the articles.

"Oh, just a small fish. Wangler-Paul. You'll know him by his beret." Loibl wiped his mouth and fed the rest of his bun to the pigeons fluttering across the square. "A small-time black marketeer and pickpocket. Whenever the fuzz is onto him, he likes to hide in the sewers. Knows some of the lads down there and told 'em that we're after a madman murderer underground. 'Parently there's a fair few stories going 'round about the fellow already . . ."

"What kind of stories?" asked Leo.

"Paul didn't want to say. But in any case, the kanalstrotters and fat fishers are willing to talk to us. Ah, look at that, the good sir's on time." Loibl indicated toward a short bowlegged man wearing a beret waddling toward them. Wangler-Paul kept his eyes down, his head drawn between his shoulders like a turtle.

"Move, move," he muttered in their direction as he walked past without slowing down. "You don't know me, I don't know you, got it? Now behind."

Without a word they followed the man until they came to a tower just like the one Leo had seen down by the Danube Canal. Wangler-Paul produced a picklock and moments later a small door opened into the tower. The short man gave a mock bow.

"Welcome, gentlemen. In you go."

"Huh. We certainly wouldn't have needed any help to get in here," commented Leo.

Wangler-Paul stared at him through small, bloodshot eyes. His face was disfigured by boils. "A clever one, are we? Well then, good luck down there on your own. So long." He turned and made to walk off.

"The inspector didn't mean it," said Loibl quickly. Then, whispering to Leo, he added, "Believe me, we need a guide down there. And besides, no one will talk to us without him."

"So, what'll it be?" growled Paul. "You growing roots? Hand over the dough, will you."

Loibl counted several bills into the man's hand, and Paul made them disappear as swiftly as a magician at the Ronacher. "Wasn't that hard, was it now," he muttered. He picked up a kerosene lamp that had been placed strategically inside the tower's entrance and began to descend the winding steps. A few yards down, a hole opened up to the right, and Paul crawled inside.

Lanky Loibl raised an eyebrow. "Just as well that our chief inspector is still bedbound. Leinkirchner's paunch would never have fit through there."

Loibl crawled after Wangler-Paul and Leo followed behind. The hole was small, and the tunnel beyond was no larger. A foul-smelling stream flowed down the center. At least Leo wasn't wearing his best suit this time, but a sturdy woolen coat and equally sturdy pants. His beloved homburg hat had stayed home.

"This is one of the cholera sewers from the Wien Canal," explained Loibl as they made their way along the narrow passage. "They've been around for decades. The various city streams drain into these. The whole mess used to spill into the streets regularly, turning the whole place into a cesspit. They've finally begun works to regulate the Wien and put parts of it underground. Hopefully, that problem's now fixed."

Leo moved in silence. He thought about entire rivers that flowed underground, like the river Styx in the Greek Hades, inhabited by a myriad of underworld creatures. In a way, this place suited his current state of mind very well. Leo felt like Orpheus, only he'd already lost his Eurydice.

Wangler-Paul guided them onward, up and down steps, past catch basins, and through holes that had been smashed in brick walls. Leo was increasingly under the impression that Paul was leading them in circles, presumably to confuse them. If so, then he was succeeding. They crawled though several more holes before arriving at last in a larger sewer. The stream of wastewater was much wider and deeper than in the smaller tunnels. A few slimy, moldering planks led across the stream, almost like a drawbridge. On the other side, they saw a heavy door.

"The Zwingburg," murmured Leo. "Now I understand."

"Our fort. Like the stories from America's Wild West, only underground." Wangler-Paul grinned, displaying a few black teeth. With surprising nimbleness he stepped across the planks. Once on the other side, he knocked on the door in a rhythm. The heavy door opened and a pockmarked fellow with a broken-looking nose studied first Paul and then Leo and Loibl with scrutinizing looks.

"Those are the two coppers?" asked the man.

Wangler-Paul nodded. "Yurek knows." He waved to the two inspectors. "What are you waiting for? D'you need a special invite?"

Leo cautiously navigated across the slippery timbers and Loibl followed. Below them, the foul water swirled. A large lump of fur drifted past—the cadaver of a cat or a dog, perhaps—and vanished down an eddy.

The door led to a long room that was surprisingly warm and dry. Men were lying on the floor, wrapped up in sacks and holey blankets. It reeked of unwashed people, smoke, and old beer. A handful of kerosene lamps offered hazy light. In the room's center, a man stood with his arms folded. He was short, wide, and tousled like a bear. His hair and beard were one rampant mass, and his eyes glowed like pieces of burning coal, alert. With his build, he seemed made to live in such low, tight corridors. Leo couldn't help but think of dwarves from fairytales.

The man took a drag from a stump of tobacco that looked like it'd only just been fished out of the sewer. With a grim expression he addressed Wangler-Paul.

"You took them 'round like I told you to?" He spoke with an Eastern European accent. His voice was much higher than Leo expected for such a squat man.

"Course, Yurek." Paul grinned. "They don't know which way's up."

"Still. Bind their eyes on the way back. Just to be sure." Suddenly, the man's face broke into a smile. Clearly, he was something like a leader down here. His grim expression wiped away; he opened his arms in a welcoming gesture. "Welcome to the Zwingburg, inspectors. May I offer you a drink? Wine, schnapps? We even have a bottle of Scottish whiskey. You'd be amazed at the things that wash up in the sewers." The man, evidently called Yurek, drew a bottle of amber-colored liquid from his coat pocket. Leo saw Loibl run a hand across dry lips.

"Thanks, we're working," Leo said quickly.

"Suit yourself." Yurek shrugged and slipped the bottle back in his pocket. "You're looking for the phantom. I wondered what took you so long. But the fuzz have never been the brightest."

"The phantom?" Leo frowned. He hadn't heard the term in this context before. "What do you mean?"

"Well, what do you think? The madman you're after! That's what we call him."

"Do you actually know anything about him?" asked Loibl dubiously. "Or is it nothing but ghost stories you sell us for cash?"

"Do we know anything? Ha!" Yurek rolled his eyes and turned to Leo. "Look, inspector. To you coppers we may be nothing but riff-raff, but we're honorable kanalstrotters, hair and hide." He pointed at the men around them, eyeballing Leo and Loibl with interest from their places on the ground. "We're treasure hunters, really.

You wouldn't believe the things posh ladies and gentlemen throw into the gutter—or what ends up in the sewers through other ways. Follow me, I'll show you something."

Yurek led Leo and Loibl to an alcove where a wobbly trestle had been set up. Upon it lay the strangest collection of objects Leo had ever seen—bent tin soldiers; a scuffed pocket watch; a twisted, rusty nail; a brittle leather briefcase; glass marbles gleaming in the light; even one of those new lightbulbs, like the ones illuminating Volksgarten park, though this one was broken.

"My underground cabinet of curiosities." Yurek chuckled. "Perhaps not as grand as the Museum of Art History, but just as interesting. Every one of these objects tells a story, don't you think?" Tenderly, he picked up one of the tin soldiers. "Who might this little man have belonged to? Was it a boy's lost Christmas present? Were many tears cried over it? Or this watch . . ." Yurek picked up the pocket watch and flipped it open. "See the initials? 'With love from O. R.' Was it a gift from a wife to her husband? Or from his business partner, a long time ago? Or even a mistress? As for the briefcase—"

"Listen," said Leo, interrupting him. "Those are lovely stories, but we're here for a particular reason."

"Mm, no patience." Yurek shook his head with disappointment. "No one ever has patience. In the country I was born in, you let people tell their stories. It's called being polite. But I can tell by your language, inspector: you're Prussian. Everything must go fast, fast, one two three four, am I right?" He pretended to march like a soldier. "So, please. You see, I could build a different sort of curiosity show here." He cocked his head. "Well, more like a kind of a chamber of horrors. Because we also find things that are not so pretty. Rusty pistols, knives, cudgels, blackjacks, and from time to time, human bones or body parts. Not a pretty sight, but it's part of life down here. It all gets washed up, the beautiful and the ugly, life and death. But more recently, since a year ago or so . . ." Yurek paused, then turned to one of the men in the background. "Josef, wanna come closer?"

An old man approached them, dragging his feet. He was so skinny, he could probably fit through any hole in the sewers. His coat, his cap, his pants—everything was too baggy for him.

"Josef is our oldest fat fisherman," explained Yurek. "He's past sixty. It's a miracle he's still alive. Fat fishermen don't usually grow old. They sift the cold water for bones and bits of fat to sell to the soap factories. Always catching a fever. When we kanalstrotters find something that's of no use to us, we often leave it out for the fat fishermen, poor bastards. Josef, tell us what your colleagues are whispering about."

Josef scratched his louse-ridden scalp. When he spoke, his voice was heavy, sounding somewhat . . . wet and swampy, Leo thought, as if the old man had been crawling through the sewers of Vienna for far too long.

"Well, we always used to find bits and pieces every now and again," mumbled Josef into his beard. "Bits and pieces of a person, I mean. Happens. But lately, there've been more . . . pieces. Arms, legs, smashed skulls, bits of scalps, hands, fingers . . . Always cut up so they get washed away. Clearly, they know that a whole body would get caught in the weirs. And once or twice the phantom was seen."

"And who's that supposed to be?" asked Leo. "The phantom?"

"The phantom brings the body parts down here. In a sack. He's dressed in a top hat and a black suit."

"That's our man!" said Loibl.

Leo frowned. "I don't know, sounds like a fairytale . . . Do you know anything about him?"

Old Josef shook his head. "No one's ever got a good look of him. The lads down here are frightened of him, think he's a ghost.

Someone who brings misfortune. He appeared for the first time a year ago, and since then, he's appeared regularly. Empties out his sack of bones and vanishes, no one knows where to. One time, a few brave men followed him up top but he was gone! Like the devil!" The old man crossed himself and withdrew even deeper into his loose coat. "Just like the devil himself, I swear on my dead mother."

"Here. Fished it out last night." From the endless depths of his coat pocket, Yurek produced an issue of the Neues Wiener Journal. The cover page, wavy because it was wet, showed a cloaked, faceless man bent over a young, handsome lad. "The papers write that the phantom goes after pretty young hustlers. Is that right?"

Leo nodded slowly. "That's what we assume. And he castrates them."

"Dirty bastard!" snarled Yurek. He gave Leo a serious look before lifting his finger. "Listen, inspector. We've never allowed the fuzz in the Zwingburg before. We've done so today for one reason alone: we want you to catch that dog! I don't believe in no phantoms or ghosts. That's the work of a madman. We may not be the prettiest lads down here, but who knows when he'll start picking us off? We don't feel safe in the sewers anymore. And the sewers are our protection from all the filth upstairs."

"We're going to need your help if we're to catch him," said Leo, pensive. He looked around the low-ceilinged room. "How many of you live down here?"

"In the sewers? Hard to say—no one's counting." Yurek gave a shrug. "A few hundred, in any case."

"That's more than we have at our disposal at the police. Search for the man, split into groups, no fewer than four men. Safer that way. He's armed and dangerous, but he's human, and he can be hunted. So far, all we know is that he's of average height and has black hair. He lost his top hat during his last kill. But it's possible he's got a new hat. The hat and suit allow him to meld into crowds quickly."

"And we still don't know how and where he cuts up his victims after he kills them, before he brings them down here," added Loibl. "And how he manages to do so without getting noticed."

"We'll figure it out," said Leo. "I have a sense that we're getting close. Last time we almost caught him."

"All right. I'll put my men in groups of four." Yurek nodded slowly, then he gave another chuckle. "Who'd have thought we kanalstrotters would one day work together with the fuzz. By God, these are modern times indeed!"

When they reemerged from the tower some time later, Leo and Loibl looked like a pair of vagabonds. Their clothes were wet and filthy, even torn in places. Leo noticed an elegantly dressed woman eying them with disgust. On her head she wore a beast of a hat that seemed to have flowers growing out of it. He couldn't help but grin. He wondered how the woman's dress and hat would stand up to a tour through the sewers.

Fine feathers make fine birds . . .

On their way back, Wangler-Paul tied their eyes with fabric scraps, leading them along stinking streams, up slippery steps and ladders, and down slimy corridors back to the surface. Leo honestly couldn't say where the Zwingburg was located following their odyssey—maybe it was right below their feet.

"I'm afraid no fiacre will take us," said Loibl, gesturing at their dirty clothes. "They'll probably even boot us off the tram."

"Then we walk," said Leo. "It's not that far."

It was a strange experience for him, strolling along the Ring like a vagabond. He almost hoped a constable might stop them.

"So, what do you make of it?" asked Erich Loibl. "A phantom of the underworld!" He shook his head. "It does sound rather fantastical."

"And yet it supports my theory," replied Leo. "That's how our murderer disposes of his victims. It's been going on for a year, maybe longer. But more recently, he's been getting interrupted, forced to find different solutions. He's growing more careless, more hectic."

"But—just imagine," said Loibl. "If what Yurek told us is true, then we're not talking four of five bodies but dozens!"

"A scary thought, granted. But what's even scarier is that it took so long for those bodies to be noticed. So many people go missing and no one asks questions."

Loibl nodded. "Vienna is a leviathan. Each year, thousands of migrants flock to the city just to get swallowed up. And then the sewers spew out their remains." He shuddered visibly. "I still wonder how he does it. Cutting them up, I mean."

Leo said nothing. He, too, grappled with this question. He lacked a picture of how the killer proceeded—let alone a picture of the killer himself, aside from black hair and his clothing.

They were nearing Volksgarten park; it was close to noon. After the hours spent underground, the bustling promenade was unbearably loud and bright.

Erich Loibl headed for a flower stall. Fishing a few coins from his pocket, he purchased a bouquet of carnations. Catching Leo's questioning look, he shrugged and smiled.

"For my wife. We want to give it another go. Under the condition that I stay off the booze. Down there, I was sorely tempted. That bottle of whiskey . . ."

"Well, well, the temptations of the underworld." Leo grinned. "You resisted."

Loibl fingered the flowers, a little embarrassed. "I meant to thank you, Herzfeldt. For not reporting my mistake with the first victim to Stukart. And for saying nice things at the meeting. I think your methods aren't as bad as Paul makes them out. The map with the pins and lines—that made a lot of sense. We've never worked like this before."

"Now now, don't get ahead of yourself," jested Leo. "What will your mate Paul Leinkirchner say when he returns form his sickbed? That we've become blood brothers?"

"Paul isn't a bad fellow, trust me. He's just had some bad experiences . . . with . . . with people like . . ." Loibl faltered.

"With Jews—is that what you're trying to say?"

The friendly conversation dried up. Also, the carnations made Leo think of Julia. Loibl's bouquet was small and simple, but what if that was precisely what made it a better gesture—a better show of love than Leo's grandiose invitations to the theater or to French restaurants? Still, the proof that Julia had demanded of him seemed impossible.

Loibl cleared his throat. "Listen, I didn't mean to step on your toes just now," he said. "I don't believe—"

"Let's leave it," said Leo curtly. "We're here, anyway."

They'd reached police headquarters. The bored-looking guard at the large entrance made to shoo the filthy pair off when he recognized Erich Loibl.

"Inspector!" he said, bewildered. "Did you fall into a sewer? The flowers look fresh enough . . ."

"Covert assignment," grumbled Loibl. "If you don't mind, we'd like to change."

"Of course, inspector." The guard stepped aside, his eye catching Leo. "Oh, it's you, Herr von Herzfeldt. What are the chances! Someone just came for you, wanting to speak with you. I sent word upstairs but you weren't in."

"Who was it?" asked Leo, suspicious. "A skinny fellow with dirty boots and a floppy hat?"

"No, no. Fräulein Wolf. You know, our lovely photographer. She said she'd wait for you in a tavern nearby. A tavern you both know well. She'd wait until—" The guard checked his pocket watch. "Until noon. Well, that's now."

"Fr . . . Fräulein Wolf?" Leo's heart beat faster. "Thank you for the message." Hesitating, he looked at Loibl. "I know the meeting is about to start—"

"Off you go," said Loibl. "I can tell that it's important. I'll say you had to follow a few . . . well, private leads. Wouldn't be the first time."

"Thanks," said Leo. He turned on his heels.

"But don't you want to get changed first?" asked Loibl, bemused.

"I'm afraid there's no time." Leo was about to dash off but Loibl grabbed his sleeve. The inspector handed him the bunch of carnations. "Take them. I have a feeling you need them. I can get new ones later. Besides, they smell better than your clothes." He winked at Leo. "We all have our secrets, don't we?"

"You could be right." Leo gave a strained smile. "I owe you, my friend. See you later!" Then he took off.

He knew exactly which tavern.

"Another small wine, miss? Or can I interest you in a salad or a pancake soup?"

"What?" Absorbed in thought, Julia looked up. The waiter stood in front of her, holding a tray. "No, thanks. I think you can bring me the check."

"As you wish." The waiter marched off, but not without shooting Julia one more disapproving look. She'd been sitting here for over an hour, consuming nothing but a small glass of wine. Not the best way to make friends in Melker Cellar.

It was still too early to be very busy in the dark cellar tavern. Some regulars sat at the tables, but none of them were women. It smelled of tobacco smoke, sauerkraut, and smoked meat; the food was simple, cheap, and tasty. Julia used to come here often after work for a pork knuckle or a schnitzel with potato salad. She used to like coming here with Leo, too. It was here that they'd had their first longer conversation. They'd taken a liking to each other right away. Their conversations had been animated and cheerful, and they'd laughed a lot.

Leo . . .

Julia glanced at the old upright clock in the corner, quietly ticking away. It was past noon. Should she wait any longer? Augustin Rothmayer had telephoned her that morning from Central Cemetery. The administration building there housed a telephone that the gravedigger was loath to using. But what he'd had to tell Julia was too urgent to wait.

It changed everything.

Julia ought to have reported to the police right away. But that would have resulted in uncomfortable questions, questions she wished to spare Rothmayer. Opening the coffin of young keeper Stefan Moser had been a favor to her, after all. Also, Julia realized that the unexpected news gave her some bargaining power that might persuade Leo to help her with Saidrovuni after all. If she was being entirely honest with herself, though, she was here for another reason, too.

She wanted to see Leo.

When he had joined her in the dressing room last night, she'd been so angry. In that moment she'd been utterly certain: they simply weren't a good match. But then when he'd sat in front of her like a whipped puppy she'd almost felt sorry for him again. What was it that she was accusing him of? That he was the way he was? Wasn't that the very reason she loved him? Because of his quirks, his snobbishness, his sharp mind, his sense of humor—because he was different from any other man she knew?

Since she felt incapable of reaching a decision, she would let fate decide. She went to the police headquarters to find Leo. And when he wasn't in, she'd set an ultimatum for herself.

Noon. If he didn't turn up by noon, she'd leave.

The clock in the corner struck a quarter past twelve.

Julia was about to leave the money for the wine on the table when a commotion broke out by the stairs leading down to the tavern.

"Listen, ya dirty beggar, you're not coming in here," the waiter was saying. "Not in that getup. You stink! You don't have no money."

"How dare you?" spoke the other man. "One more word and I'll have you arrested! You . . . you plebeian! Do you have any idea who you're speaking with?"

Julia flinched, then smiled. That was definitely Leo. What on earth was going on?

There was a crash on the steps and then Leo tumbled into the cellar with the waiter in tow, who was beathing heavily and hanging onto Leo's arm. But was it really Leo? The man, who just then gave the waiter a decent push, looked like Leo. But he wore a dirty jacket and pants, which were ripped in places. His face was filthy, his hair matted with something slimy, his boots sodden. He clutched a bunch of crumpled carnations.

"Fräulein, this . . . this person is here for you!" exclaimed the waiter, still tugging at Leo's sleeve. "Claims he's with the police."

"Damn it man, didn't you see my badge?" snapped Leo angrily. "Would you like to see my pistol as well?"

The few patrons in the taverns tensed visibly. Chairs scraped across the floor; a murmur rose. Two men dashed into a neighboring room—whether they did so because of the threat of a gun or because he was police wasn't clear.

"It's . . . it's all right," said Julia, still staring at Leo with astonishment. "The gentleman really is with the police."

"Blimey, the fuzz isn't what they used to be," complained the waiter. He brushed some dirt off his shirt and walked out the room, shaking his head. "Tramp!"

Leo stood sheepishly for a few moments, then handed Julia the battered bouquet. "For you," he murmured. "They looked better just before."

"As have you," quipped Julia. She took the flowers and put them on the table in front of her. "Thanks. This is . . . well, different." She failed to stifle a grin. "Let me guess. Covert assignment, or your mother's stopped sending money?"

"The first," replied Leo, sitting. "Anway, I can afford my own suits these days. The carnations, though, are from Loibl."

"Uh-huh? And when are you two moving in together?"

"Julia, stop it. I apologized last night, and I'm ready to change."

"I named my condition," she said, more coolly than intended.

"And I told you what you're asking is impossible." The other guests had settled again, only occasionally still glancing at Leo. Nevertheless, Leo lowered his voice. "We can't free your chief from the courthouse prison—no way!"

"Well, you might change your mind once I tell you what Augustin Rothmayer told me on the phone this morning."

"Rothmayer again!" Leo groaned. "Rothmayer here, Rothmayer there . . . I can't get away from the old codger."

"I asked him to take a look at the body of young Moser, you know, the keeper mauled by the lion," Julia continued, unfazed. "And guess what he found?"

"What?" asked Leo, not particularly interested. "Julia, I have bigger problems at the moments. These hustler murders—"

"Moser was castrated. Like your hustlers."

"What?" Leo's mouth gaped. "He was castrated?"

Julia nodded. "No doubt about it. Rothmayer said the wound looks just like the one on the other victim. He saw one of the others at Professor Hofmann's. And Moser's other wounds also suggest he was killed by a person before being castrated. A stab wound to the heart. The lion was later. The animal was probably let in to cover the crime. Rothmayer also found rotting meat on Moser's clothing. As if someone rubbed it intentionally on his jacket and pants. As if they wanted to encourage the lion to eat the body." She leaned across the table and whispered, "Your hustler murderer and the murderer from the zoo are one and the same, Leo! Do you understand what that means?"

"But . . . but why should our phantom go to the trouble of breaking into the zoo to commit murder there?" Leo asked, befuddled. "That doesn't at all fit with his usual modus operandi."

"I don't know. But I know one thing." Julia narrowed her eyes. "The murderer covered up his deed. And not just that. He diverted suspicion onto someone else by planting the keys in Saidrovuni's hut."

"Planting them there?" Leo still wasn't convinced. "How could he be sure someone would go looking for them there?"

"Easy." Julia Looked at Leo intently. She spoke the next words slowly and deliberately. "By denouncing Saidrovuni to the police. And it was Eugen Lenz who did that."

"The old keeper? You . . . you're saying he is our hustler murderer?"

Julia shrugged. "He's not that old and he's quite agile. As the keeper of big predators, he knows how to cut up cadavers—he does it every day at feeding time. He has the right tools. What if Lenz was attracted to Moser and the younger man didn't requite his love? What if Eugen Lenz lives a second life haunting the streets of Vienna and cutting down pretty lads? I overheard a conversation between him and director Knauer. The two of them are hiding something. What if it's Lenz's relationship with

Moser? Or with other young keepers? Don't forget: it was Lenz who led me and Loibl to Saidrovuni. That's how we found the keys!"

Leo didn't immediately reply, thinking. "It's nothing but a theory so far," he said eventually. "And a pretty wild one. But I must admit it's more than strange that our phantom murdered at the zoo."

"Didn't you say the phantom has black hair?" asked Julia. "Lenz has black hair!"

"Many people have black hair, Julia," replied Leo with a shrug. "That doesn't mean anything. How can you prove that it really was Lenz?"

"When I went back to the zoo on Saturday, I spoke briefly with the Matabele women, with Saidrovuni's young wife. I'm certain she knows something! She kept using the same two words . . ." Julia thought. "*Umlilo* and *ikhanda*. Yes, that's it. Or something very similar. But I have no idea what they mean!"

Leo sighed. "I'm afraid it'll be difficult to find someone in Vienna who can translate Matabele."

"Yes, there is someone." Julia smiled darkly. "You know who I mean."

"Saidrovuni." Leo rolled his eyes. "So that's what you're getting at. We free the chief and he gives us Lenz."

"I'm certain Saidrovuni knows more than he's told us so far. And he's the only one who can tell us what his wife meant with those words. I believe she saw something. Something that helps us catch the murderer!" She gave him a pleading look. "Leo, I went to the courthouse this morning. I asked to see Saidrovuni, made up a story about the pictures not turning out. But they wouldn't let me see him. He's unwell, I just know it! They beat him up before—they'll do it again. To the prison wardens he's nothing but an animal."

"Julia, that doesn't change anything." Leo shook his head. "It's impossible to break into the courthouse and escape with a prisoner. You'd need an army for that!"

"Or a good plan," countered Julia. "And I think I have an idea at least." She waved to the waiter, who'd kept sourly to his corner. "Let's order two more wines. And then you hear me out. It always begins with an idea."

Leo listened.

By the time they'd finished their wine, Julia's plan was taking shape.

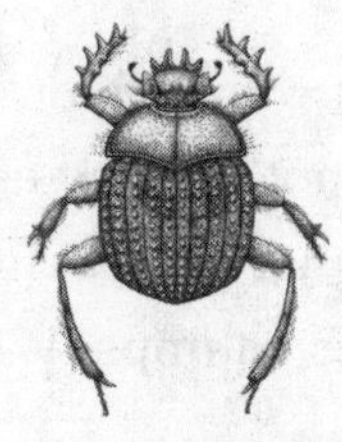

CHAPTER 21

The same day, at precisely five before six in the evening, Leo entered the courthouse. An aging porter stared sleepily at his newspaper. At the sight of the unexpected visitor, the man peered at the large wall clock hanging in the entrance hall. His face spoke volumes. Five minutes until knock-off time, and some idiot turned up wanting something?

"What can I do for you?" said the man automatically.

Leo flashed his badge. "Schneider, Security Bureau," he said by way of introduction. "I'm here for a brief interrogation of a prisoner. A certain . . ." He raised an eyebrow. "Saidrovuni. Not sure if that's the first or family name. It's a strange one, that's for sure."

"The savage? No clue if that one's got a family name. Hmm . . ." The porter pushed back his cap and scratched his head. He studied the badge then looked back at Leo. "Schneider, you say?"

"*Inspector* Schneider, if you please," retorted Leo harshly. "New generation, fresh from law school. Superintendent Stukart only reminded us just last week how important it is to respect titles!"

"All right, all right, Herr Inspector." The porter gave a wave. "With all due respect, it's not as easy as you imagine. Requesting a prisoner for questioning just before closing time. It takes a whole lotta paperwork, signatures, stamps. Why don't you come back in the morning—"

"It's urgent. And besides, there's no need to transport the prisoner. A quick interrogation in the cell will suffice."

"Well, in that case." The porter was visibly relieved. The end of his workday moved back within reach. He rang a large handbell, and not long after, a round, pimple-faced guard appeared. "Schorsch is in charge of the upstairs floor," explained the porter. "He'll show you the way. How long will you be, do you think?"

"Don't worry, not long. We all want to get home, don't we?" Leo tipped his head, all conscientious policeman. "And apologies for the trouble."

"Always a pleasure to help the young 'uns," said the porter, eyes already back on his newspaper.

As Leo and the warden followed the corridors to the prison tract, Leo's hand kept touching his glued-on pencil mustache and Vandyke. It was lucky that he hadn't been to the courthouse much, unlike Julia, who used to come on a weekly basis as crime-scene photographer. The porter obviously hadn't recognized him, even if he'd shot him a suspicious look.

It had been a good idea to turn up just before closing time. They wouldn't have managed much sooner, anyway. After the tavern cellar meeting with Julia, Leo returned to police headquarters. His and Loibl's report of the events underground had caused a stir. Stukart ordered additional investigations of the various canals, sewers, and weirs. Leo decided against mentioning the kanalstrotters' offer to help with the investigation—no need for Stukart to know absolutely everything. Since Leinkirchner was still out sick, Leo was the sole lead detective in the case—a circumstance which didn't bother him at all.

Unlike the current situation.

Rarely had Leo felt this naked and exposed. If his mission failed, he would lose his employment as police agent, and that was probably the least of it.

To add to his disguise, he'd left his homburg and suit at home and replaced them with a bowler hat, huge coat with a stand-up collar, and thick glasses that turned the world blurry. Julia had borrowed the fake beard and glasses from the cellar bar's stash of costumes. Leo gave a grim smile. He looked like a ham actor from a Wurstelprater theater.

But it seemed to be working.

When Julia first told him her idea at lunchtime, he'd been dismissive at first. There were too many counterarguments—the risk was too great. But it was clear by the look in Julia's eyes that that was precisely what she expected from him: that he take a risk for her. They tossed each idea back and forth until a plan emerged—a rather daring plan, but a plan nonetheless.

Leo was sweating under the coat and glued-on beard. He'd been terrified down at reception that the scratchy mess would fall off, revealing his true identity to the porter.

So far, so good. The largest obstacles, however, still lay ahead of him.

He followed the guard up many stairs, down corridors, and across courtyards. At last they reached the upper prison tract. The chubby guard, breathing hard, stopped outside a red door with a little hatch. He opened the hatch and cast a probing look inside before unlocking the door and stepping aside.

"Sir," bellowed the warden, standing to attention. "Prisoner Saidrovuni."

Even from this distance it was clear to Leo that Saidrovuni wasn't merely sleeping but that he was unwell and injured. He cowered on the hard cot, his head slumped forward. His right eye was swollen shut, and there was dried blood on the floor in front of him. Next to the blood, food had spilled from a battered bowl.

Leo bit his lip. Julia was right. They were treating Saidrovuni like a dog. He corrected himself: *You wouldn't even treat a dog like this. Beaten and chained up in a stuffy hole. And yet his condition is our luck . . .*

In order for their plan to work, it was important that Saidrovuni looked unwell. The prison guards had more than obliged.

"Christ, what did you do to the man?" snarled Leo. "He's in no fit state to be questioned!"

"Uh, the prisoner showed himself uncooperative," mumbled Schorsch, who, as the guard responsible for this tract, would be held accountable. He stared at the ground. "Didn't want to eat . . ."

"And so you thrashed our good old Viennese cuisine right into him, alongside the bowl? Christ in heaven, how am I meant to get answers to my questions? He's beyond talking!"

The guard said nothing, studying the tiled floor by his feet and fidgeting with the buttons of his uniform.

"Very well." Leo drew a deep breath and pretended to be thinking hard. "I'll tell you what we'll do. We're going to take the prisoner over to General Hospital. You still have the old connecting passageway, don't you?"

"Sure, the passage is there . . ." The guard nodded reluctantly. "But we'd require reinforcements. And there are forms to fill out—"

"So, you'd like more people to learn what has occurred here?" blustered Leo. "You want the whole shebang, do you? Would you like me to notify the press, too, that prisoners get beat up in here? How about the imperial court, huh?"

"But . . . but he's just a savage . . ."

"And a crucial witness in a murder investigation!" thundered Leo. "God Almighty, do you want to be held accountable for the sabotage of important police work? Do you?"

"Of course not—"

"Then stop staring at the ground and twisting your buttons, and go fetch the goddamn stretcher! That's an order!"

"Yessir, as you wish, sir! A stretcher." The guard hurried off and Leo breathed a sigh of relief. If there was anything one could count on in Viennese administration, it was absolute obedience, no matter how harebrained the order was. The key was to shout loudly enough.

With soft steps he approached Saidrovuni and bent closer. They'd done thorough work on the man. Saidrovuni seemed sick and unaware of what was going on around him. Fury rose up in Leo. He still wasn't entirely convinced that this man was innocent, but this was a step too far.

"I'm getting you out of here," whispered Leo. "Hang in there."

Behind him, the guard's heavy steps returned. Schorsch, out of breath, set a stretcher down in the cell. Using one of his many keys, he undid Saidrovuni's chains, and together they dragged the prisoner onto the stretcher. Schorsch awkwardly tried to shackle Saidrovuni to the frame.

"What in God's name are you doing?" demanded Leo.

"Um, I think we ought to chain the prisoner up."

"And where do you think he's going to go, in his state? To Café Central for a coffee? Come on, we don't have all the time in the world!"

Leo grabbed the handles on one side and, after a moment of hesitation, the guard followed suit. Together they lifted their human cargo and stepped into the corridor.

In all his agitation, Leo didn't feel his mustache beginning to peel.

SCHORSCH CLASPED THE STRETCHER'S HANDLES ANGRILY AND tried to ignore who it was he was carrying.

A Black!

That's how far they'd come—a proud Austrian carting a savage around in a litter. The fellow had his eyes closed, probably enjoying the ride. He was probably faking it! Sure, Schorsch had given him a few slaps to wipe that bleeding arrogant look off his face. As if he were the kaiser himself and not a prisoner and murderer, a cannibal, even, if his colleagues were to be believed! The savage hadn't wanted to eat their food—probably because it wasn't human flesh—and had even spat it out right in front of him. That had been the final straw.

The young fräulein who'd taken the photographs a few days ago had looked just as arrogant as the inspector now. And Schorsch never received the promised picture—apparently because they hadn't turned out. And now this patronizing fop dared to tell him off in front of the savage! They'd probably serve him coffee over at the hospital, and porridge with honey, and they'd fluff his pillows for him!

Schorsch, sweating and sullen, kept his eyes fixed to a spot on the inspector's back. They walked past a few of Schorsch's colleagues who watched them with bemusement. Some of them grinned. Great—his reputation was finished!

This inspector was an oddball. He kept touching his beard, and he was dressed as if they were still in the middle of winter. For a moment the man had seemed familiar to Schorsch, but he figured he would have remembered a strange one like this. He gave a strange impression, he did.

If we were to meet in the street at night, I'd flatten you, you midget!

But life was unfair. Instead of going home as he should have by now, or telling this bleeding idiot exactly what he thought of him, he was forced to cart a savage around.

Just you wait—when you get back from hospital!

They carried the stretcher down several flights of stairs and arrived at the basement. The inspector seemed hesitant, unfamiliar with the way, and Schorsch considered leading him in circles on purpose. But then he realized that he'd get home even later that way.

It was surprising that the inspector knew of the passage. Not many police did—it was rarely used. The passageway had been built decades ago as a fast and easy way to move prisoners from the courthouse to Vienna General Hospital. It was meant to make an escape in the street impossible. Apparently, there'd once been a spectacular attempted escape, and afterward they'd grown more cautious.

"One moment, inspector. The door." With a groan Schorsch set down the stretcher, intentionally dropping it the last few inches. The savage moaned. Well, at least that was the end of his beauty sleep. Schorsch had led them to a door with a large, cross-shaped metal handle and an additional padlock.

"The connecting passageway," he declared, not without pride. "You're lucky I've got the key for it. As the guard responsible for the entire upstairs tract, I—"

"If you want to get home tonight, quit telling stories and open the door."

"As you wish, inspector."

And kiss my ass, you imp!

The inspector was playing with his beard again. Was he a faggot, maybe? Or what was this ridiculous behavior about? Earlier, Schorsch even thought that the beard was missing briefly. But he must have been mistaken.

Seething on the inside, Schorsch opened the lock and turned the handle. There was a lot of creaking—presumably, this entrance hadn't been used for months. The door opened into the dark corridor beyond. Schorsch felt for the light switch, and moments later, lights flickered to life on the ceiling. Parts of the hospital had been electrified the previous year. Schorsch couldn't fathom why they'd bothered with this seldom-used passage, but at least it meant they didn't have to trudge through the dark now.

The corridor in front of them seemed to stretch into eternity. The air was damp and musty.

"It's a fair way over to the hospital," said Schorsch. "A few hundred yards at least."

"Then let's get it over and done with. And, up!"

The inspector lifted his end of the stretcher and the warden followed suit. Together they lugged the prisoner down the dimly lit corridor.

They'd gone maybe halfway when suddenly the lights went out.

"Damn!" cursed Schorsch. "You've gotta be kidding! That's what you get with that new electricity stuff. Why—"

"Moaning won't help," said the inspector impatiently. "Do something! The switch at the door must be defective. Go on—go back and sort it."

"You want me to . . ." Schorsch looked around nervously. It was pitch black. He couldn't see the walls, let alone the door that lay somewhere behind them.

"Or I can report to your superior that you shat your pants because the lights went out. Would you like me to go ahead and—?"

"No, no. I'm going." Schorsch set down the stretcher and started down the way back. He held his arm stretched out before him to avoid bumping into walls or the door. His steps echoed in the darkness. How long was this damned passage? Shouldn't he be back at the door already? Behind him, there were scraping and scratching sounds. Schorsch started, then relaxed. What was he afraid of? Ghosts? Buried Turkish tunnelers from the days of the siege of Vienna? The sound was probably just that queer inspector, or maybe the savage showing signs of life. To think anything else was ridiculous.

At last! His hands felt the door's cool metal. Schorsch fumbled for the light switch. It was one of those new porcelain ones. He didn't know much about these modern electrical things, but maybe he should turn the switch from side to side a few times.

He turned the switch to the right and the lights came abruptly back on.

"There we go," said Schorsch with relief. "Wasn't that hard."

When he looked back, the corridor was empty. Only the stretcher sat on the ground, like a poorly chosen farewell gift.

What the hell . . . ?

In that moment, Schorsch realized that his evening was ruined once and for all.

LEO HASTENED THROUGH THE DARKNESS, GUIDED BY A TINY light in front of him bouncing up and down like a will-o'-the-wisp. How long until the guards turned up? Five minutes? More? Schorsch hadn't seemed very bright, but he'd still report the missing prisoner right away. Just as well that he hadn't seen that Leo's thin mustache had fallen off completely.

The light in front of him held still for a moment, and then Julia's face appeared in its glow, holding up a kerosene lantern. She looked around.

"Here are the steps to the ground floor," she said, her breath coming fast. "From there we can get to one of the hospital's courtyards. It's the quickest way out. Can you lift Saidrovuni?"

"I'm sure I can cope for this short bit." Leo grabbed the wheelchair carrying the unconscious chief and yanked it backward up the steps. Its wheels were freshly greased.

The trick had been so simple that Leo still couldn't believe it had worked. Julia had waited with the wheelchair at the other end of the passage. When Leo, Schorsch, and Saidrovuni were about halfway along the corridor, she had switched the light off from her end. Under the cover of darkness, she'd rushed toward Leo and his human freight.

They'd wrapped the chief in a gray dressing gown and plunked a large sun hat on his head, making him look like a slightly neglected patient. She'd found a nurse's gown with a bonnet in Elli's costume rack. The disguise was good enough to mislead an unsuspecting onlooker for a short time, but it wouldn't last for long.

Julia was right—the stairs led to a cluttered backyard. Vienna General Hospital was a maze of yards, buildings, and additions that had grown gradually over the last two hundred years. Part of the complex were the morgue, the forensic institute, and the *Narrenturm*—the former madhouse. Leo hoped fervently that they wouldn't bump into Professor Hofmann. A stone archway led them to a larger courtyard. There, they ran into their first hospital staff—two doctors in white coats. Thankfully, they merely bestowed the strange trio with passing glances.

Leo was amazed how well Julia knew her way around this place. She'd visited a few times with her daughter but hadn't received much help. But she had an excellent sense of direction. A few months ago, a young orderly who probably had a crush on her had shown her the passageway to the prison. And right at this moment, a high-ranking doctor who owned the necessary keys was amusing himself—sans keys—with one of Elli's girls. He probably wouldn't even notice until the morning.

"We can't forget to thank Elli," whispered Julia as they pushed Saidrovuni across another courtyard. "Without her, my idea would have stayed just that—an idea. The good doctor was rather surprised when he received Elli's invitation to a special liaison in the middle of the afternoon."

It had been Big Elli who'd reminded Julia that among their regulars were doctors from the hospital, even some quite influential ones. Elli had sent word to the doctor and the man hadn't hesitated.

"I fear a simple 'thank you' won't cut it with Elli," replied Leo as they walked. He ripped off the remaining beard, having deposited the glasses into the garbage a few moments ago. "You'll owe her a favor."

"You're right. And I already know which."

Without further explanation, Julia pushed against the large courtyard doors. Both sides swung outward, and they spilled out onto busy Alser Street. Dusk painted the street in a warm, orange glow. Not far away, a one-horse carriage stood ready. The driver looked like Cerberus turned human.

"Bruno," sighed Leo. "Elli doesn't leave anything to chance, does she. I shudder to think what the favor will be."

Elli's doorkeeper shot Leo a dark look and climbed down from his seat. The hulking man bent down to the wheelchair, curiously studying its load.

"That the savage?" he wanted to know. "Looks normal to me. Only an African."

"He's no savage but a sick and injured man," said Julia. "The guards mistreated him. You be gentle, you hear me?"

"Course. As if he was a porcelain jug." Bruno picked up the wheelchair with his huge hands as if it were a small parcel and deposited it into the carriage. Leo and Julia also climbed in and they took off. Outside the carriage the first gas streetlights sputtered to life here and there as they drove.

"So? What now?" asked Leo after a while. Both of them were exhausted. Saidrovuni moaned softly, still unconscious.

"He gets a room at Elli's," said Julia. "We can't question him in this state, anyway. He'll have to get better first." She hesitated. "I'm afraid his real illness is incurable, though."

"What do you mean?"

"He's lost everything." Julia's face darkened. "His wife and child are in the zoo. What is he supposed to do now? Even if the cops don't find him, he can hardly return to his family."

"Well, at least he's safe, for now," replied Leo. "We probably saved him from the gallows."

"Thank you, Leo," said Julia. She moved suddenly closer to him and kissed him long and hard. "I'll never forget this."

Leo smiled. For himself, at least, this stunt appeared to have been worth it. But he felt better for another reason, too. Something had become clear to him during the last couple of hours: they'd rescued a man. Not a savage, not a cannibal, not a zoo exhibit.

Just a man who was probably innocent.

An hour later they were sitting together at their patient's bedside. Sisi was with them, snuggled against her mother, eyes clasped on Saidrovuni from a safe distance. The man's breathing had steadied. Julia had cleaned his wounds and dressed him in fresh clothes. There was a bandage around his forehead now. Big Elli had given Saidrovuni a small attic room; next door, girls moaned in routine fashion and beds creaked. For many of the girls, dusk was the start of their workday.

"His outward injuries aren't as bad as I thought," said Julia, sipping a cup of hot tea Elli had brought up. A steaming teapot and two more cups sat on a side table. "The guards gave him a black eye, a bump on the back of his head, knocked a few of his teeth out. But that's it. If only his fever wasn't so bad . . ." She sighed. "It's probably from being chained up with almost no clothes in that cold, damp cell."

"I'm sure that's thanks to Schorsch, that fat chief guard," said Leo, nodding grimly. "I should have punched him in farewell."

"I think his punishment will be bad enough. He let a prisoner escape." Julia gave Leo a serious look. "Do you think anyone recognized you?"

"I don't think so. Although the porter did give me a suspicious look." Leo smirked despite himself. "Can't wait to hear what they'll say at headquarters tomorrow. A ghost inspector vanishing into thin air together with a prisoner. The latest supernatural mystery after the spooky mummy."

Leo had peeled off the big coat by now and put on a fresh shirt. The remnants of costume glue on his face itched like crazy. Sisi slid off her mother's lap and cautiously approached the sleeping patient. Reaching out one hand, she touched the tight curls of his black hair.

"She's never seen an African before," said Julia, studying her daughter pensively. "How would she have?" She shuddered. "Awful to think that until a couple of decades ago keeping slaves was acceptable in America."

"Things aren't that much better here," said Leo. "The only places you'll see people like Saidrovuni are at ethnic shows or on advertisements for cigarettes. I guess it'll be a long time yet before they'll be treated as equals. Perhaps they never will be." He paused. "Strange," he said then. "I've never really thought about that before. I suppose because it isn't every day one breaks a black-skinned man out of prison."

He stuck his hand in his pocket and drew out a packet of bonbons. Sisi couldn't hear, but, like most children, she seemed to practically sense candy. She turned toward him and made a happy sound. Giggling, she climbed onto Leo's knees and opened the little bag.

"Hey, that's bribery!" exclaimed Julia.

"I meant to give them to her this afternoon before we headed to the courthouse," said Leo apologetically. "But I forgot all about them in all the excitement."

Julia grinned. "Without the candy she'd never have sat on your lap." She gazed at him with a mixture of love, sadness, and helplessness. "Maybe you should have brought some candy sooner."

"Julia, I made so many mistakes," replied Leo as Sisi stuffed her mouth, beaming. He looked at her with pleading eyes. "I can see that now. Give me one more chance? I'm more than just a man for cozy hours."

She sighed. "What am I supposed to do when you look at me with those puppy eyes? But first we need to focus on Saidrovuni. And those terrible murders. If there's a connection to the zoo, he's the only one who can help us find out more. And perhaps young Carl Rebers, the director's assistant. But I probably put him off with my lies."

Leo nodded. Julia had told him about her encounter with Rebers and about his hints with regard to director Knauer. Leo still couldn't quite imagine how these cases might be connected. What on earth was the phantom doing at the zoo? Or was it naught but an unfortunate coincidence?

"If it's true what the kanalstrotters are saying, this case is so much bigger than we'd thought," he murmured. "I could almost believe in something like an Asan what's-its-name—the African demon the chief spoke about. I think I preferred the mummy." He rubbed his eyes. "Maybe we'll know more tomorrow. I can't think straight anymore. All that excitement—I'm done for! I could fall asleep right here with Sisi."

"Then why don't you? You only need to go down one floor." Julia smiled. "If you like, you can stay in our room for the night. I'm sure Elli will turn a blind eye. But no funny business!" She held up a stern finger. "Sisi may not be able to hear, but she has eyes like a cat at night." Her look turned speculative. "Or would you prefer to spend the night on Charlotte Rapoldy's chaise longue?"

"So someone can knock me out again in that place? No, thank you!" Leo laughed. "Trust me, Julia, I've learned my lesson. I don't like shift dresses, I don't like endless discussions about mummification, and I don't like Egyptian trinkets. What I do like is you."

"Well, in that case, I think there might be some room in my bed," said Julia, watching Leo give a long yawn. "But don't expect me to carry you downstairs. Sisi's quite enough for me."

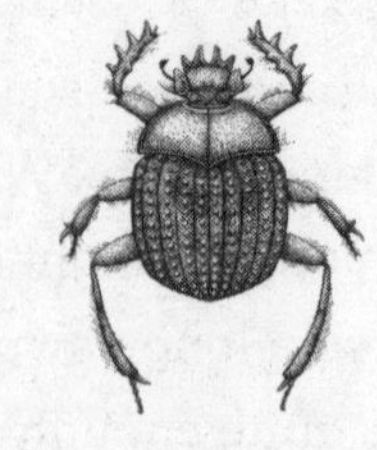

CHAPTER 22

From *Death Rites Around the World* by Augustin Rothmayer, written in Vienna, 1894

> While in many cultures cremations are the typical way to bid farewell to the dead, Christian nations still struggle with this concept. Why is that? Anyone who has ever seen or smelled a decomposing corpse would consider the pure ashes of a cremated family member a gift from heaven. I can imagine keeping such urns on the mantelpiece or on a bookshelf so that we can remember our dead on a daily basis, but I doubt such a custom will ever be possible in Austria.

Superintendent Moritz Stukart played with one of his many sharpened pencils as he gazed out the window. The usual noises of Schottenring reached them through the sooty pane—the rattle and jingle of horsecar trams, their horses whinnying; the shouts of street vendors; the cussing of fiacre drivers; bells tolling in the distance; the wistful melody of a hurdy-gurdy.

"Do you sometimes feel as if Vienna were a large beast?" asked Stukart, still staring out into the busy May morning.

"Uh, beg your pardon, superintendent?" Leo rubbed his eyes, still feeling a little sleepy. He and Erich Loibl were sitting on the other side of Stukart's desk. It was eight in the morning. Stukart had asked them to see him before the morning meeting, and Leo desperately needed another strong cup of coffee.

The night at Julia's had been lovely, even if they hadn't done more than kiss. Sisi had slept between them, and they'd been like a small family. Leo had soon nodded off, sleeping without nightmares for the first time in a long time. He'd felt oddly at home—even if that home was a dingy brothel in Neulerchenfeld.

"A huge, untamed beast. Monstrous and evil, don't you think?" Only then did Stukart turn to face his visitors. "The streets are the bones; Hofburg, Parliament, and city hall, the most important organs. We humans race along the thin lines of nerves, day in, day out. And the sewers are this monster's gut." The superintendent used the pencil to scratch his balding forehead. "That makes us criminal detectives poor animal tamers. We'll never get this beast under control. It quiets down for short periods of time just to strike even more cruelly . . . But let's leave that." His eyes focused. "Do we have any idea yet how many more victims we are dealing with?"

"The kanalstrotters weren't explicit about that." Leo shrugged. He found it difficult to sort his thoughts. Too much had happened in the last twenty-four hours. Only one day had passed since he and Loibl had been in the Zwingburg. They now knew that this case was even bigger than they'd assumed until then. But aside from that, they were still in the dark. Yesterday's meeting hadn't changed that. Nor had they heard back from the kanalstrotters.

"According to our witnesses, the body parts started to increase a year ago," Leo continued. "There could be a handful of victims, or there could be dozens. Most pieces of evidence are likely either completely decomposed or turned into soap. Or—"

"Damn it, man, do you understand what you're saying?" The pencil in Stukart's hand broke with a crack. Livid, the superintendent sent both halves flying into the waste basket. "If that's true, then we're dealing with a series of murders the likes of which Vienna has never seen before. And we have nothing but guesswork!"

"We lack the proof to draw definite conclusions," said Loibl defensively. Erich Loibl was in a much better state than usual. Leo suspected it had something to do with meeting up with his wife yesterday.

"There are plenty of missing persons reports from the last few months, but the reasons could all be entirely different," Loibl went on. "And countless new people move to the city all the time. Maybe it's nothing but scary stories and we'll only have the cases we can already prove. But the description of the killer the kanalstrotters gave us matches our own—top hat, cane, black suit, black hair."

"But we have nothing else!" groaned Stukart. "I send out my best men—we set up a special unit the size of half of Vienna's police force—and all we get is a hat, a walking stick, and a few black hairs!" He turned back to Leo. "Damn it, Herzfeldt, this might be your chance to prove yourself—to prove what the new techniques can do! Instead, you and Loibl wade through filth in the sewers as if we're stuck in the time of Archduchess Maria Theresa!"

"At least we've now doubled the number of constables at the points of interest," offered Leo, "where we suspect he might dispose of possible murder victims. The kanalstrotters are keeping their eyes peeled. And warnings are being sent to all pimps and hustlers across all districts."

"How lovely, the police, your friends and helpers, are now in the hustler business!" jeered Stukart. "Maybe you even plan to offer yourself as bait, dear Herzfeldt?"

"That's not the worst idea," murmured Leo. But then it dawned on him just how big Vienna was, how many hustlers there were. What were the odds of the phantom picking him? They were miniscule—too small to waste his time on and risk his life for. "You're probably right," he conceded. "There's little point in focusing solely on all the possible locations and victims. There are just too many. But there's only one killer. We must focus on him, using the means of psychology."

"Psychology, I see. Is that what your Graz mentor, crown prosecutor Gross, advises? You're starting to sound like that insane Viennese doctor."

"What is the murderer's motive?" said Leo, ignoring Stukart's comment. "Why does he do what he does? Cuts off his victims' holiest of holies, discards them like trash. Why doesn't he just kill them and leave it at that? If we can figure out his motive, we'll be a good deal closer."

"He hates faggots," said Loibl. "Perhaps he's queer himself. I still think that's the most plausible theory. He cuts them off because they're dirty. Because . . . because it makes him think dirty thoughts. Thoughts he doesn't want to think."

Leo sighed. "That doesn't really narrow down the pool of suspects. There must be hundreds—thousands of men in Vienna who like men. Always have been." He considered. "His dress and method suggest he may be from a well-to-do family."

"We have some lists of men who've been brought in for sodomy before or who've been caught in brothels," said Loibl. "There's a few high-ranking names among them. I took a look at those lists last night." He gave a shrug. "Problem is, several names have been erased or never even made it into the files. Those who have money use it, or Herr Papa makes a phone call to the authorities. Sodomy is punishable up to twenty years in the slammer in Austria, not to mention the ruined reputation. But most of the time, only the poor ones get convicted."

"I see." Stukart nodded. "I'll ask around higher up. Maybe there still are some other copies of those lists. Copies where the names weren't erased." He brushed lead dust off his hands. "That's a start, at least. We need some positive results, gentlemen! Especially after what happened at the courthouse last night."

Leo straightened up. "What, uh, happened?"

"That savage from the zoo escaped," grumbled Loibl. "The one that I arrested! I just heard about it out in the hall." He shook his head. "A scandal, that is. Apparently he feigned illness so that he'd be taken to the hospital. And that's when he escaped."

"He had a helper posing as an inspector," added Stukart. "The whole thing is a mystery. We're at the very beginning with our investigation."

"Posing as an inspector?" Leo raised his eyebrows, trying to don a mien of innocence. "Bizarre. What do we know about this . . . uh, fake inspector?"

"Nothing. But soon we'll know more. And then God have mercy on him!" Loibl nodded. "He's made a fool of all of us! If I get my hands on the bastard, I'll hang him from a streetlight with my own hands!"

BACK IN LEINKIRCHNER'S OFFICE, LEO TRIED TO FOCUS ON work. Loibl sat opposite him in the chief inspector's chair. Apparently Leinkirchner would have to stay home a few more days, which Leo didn't mind at all, unlike their boss. Loibl had given Leo the list of those convicted of sodomy over the last few years together with the corresponding photographs, as far as they existed. Maybe two pairs of eyes would be more effective than one.

Leo scanned the various bertillonage portraits, which showed the men from the front and in profile. There were old men and young ones, and they all looked into the camera like wounded deer. Leo felt sorry for them. How could they help loving men instead of women? It was a whim of nature. He noticed the worn clothing of almost all the men in the pictures. He felt certain that didn't represent reality. In Graz alone, he knew of several men who preferred men. But they had money and influence, unlike the poor bastards in these photos.

Leo's fingers moved down the lists of names, ages, and addresses. But his thoughts drifted. What if they found out that *he* was the impostor who'd entered the courthouse under a false name and helped a prisoner escape? By comparison, a few years in prison for sodomy was a walk in the park. Leo swallowed. He'd taken a great risk for Julia, maybe too great a risk. But he regretted nothing.

There was a knock and an errand boy entered. Erich Loibl, also absorbed in the files, looked up. "What is it, lad? We're busy."

"Telegram from Graz for inspector Herzfeldt," the boy said dutifully.

"From Graz?" Loibl gave Leo a look of surprise. "Were you expecting word from your family?"

"Not exactly. I think it may have something to do with an old case," said Leo evasively. Leinkirchner's order still stood: no one outside the case must know about the mummy. "I had made inquiries regarding a death."

Leo took the folded piece of paper. As expected, it was a telegram from his sister, Lili. Until recently, he'd have been grateful for any news from her. But the mummy case was closed and he had enough to worry about without it.

Leo opened the note and skimmed over the contents. Confused, he read it a second time.

When he read the lines a third time, he felt as if an electric current were running through him.

What the devil . . . ?

"Everything all right?" asked Loibl, looking at him with concern. "You're getting these red blotches on your forehead. Is it bad news from your family after all? A death?"

"Thanks, everything's all right. But I think . . . I think I'll take my break early today," said Leo, rushing to his feet. He folded the telegram back up and slipped it in his pocket. "I need to get a bit of fresh air, that's all."

"I hope you didn't catch a cold down in the sewers. Maybe we shoulda said yes to the whiskey." Loibl grinned. "I'm knocking off a little early tonight, by the way. Dinner with my dear wife in a fancy restaurant. There is life outside work, isn't there? Bad enough what with that phantom making us work overtime."

"You're telling me!" replied Leo. "I'll see you at the meeting this afternoon." He grabbed his hat and coat and slipped out the door.

A short while later, he emerged onto the Ring and breathed deeply. The telegram had reawakened the old mummy case, the same case he'd had to abandon at the behest of Stukart and Leinkirchner—even with several loose ends.

And another's just been added.

Well, what am I saying? More than a loose end—this is dynamite!

Leo laughed. His sister Lili had done solid work. Not only had she located the doctor responsible for the death certificate, but she'd also uncovered some highly interesting details surrounding the father's death. Lili would make for an excellent detective! Leo didn't yet know what to do. But one thing was very clear following this telegram: the mummy case was anything but closed, oh no.

He needed some space to think. He spontaneously decided to go over to Sluka. He'd be able to focus better with a strong coffee in tasteful surroundings than in the stuffy little office he shared with Loibl. There were so many unanswered questions—and not only in the mummy case. The murder at the zoo didn't seem to match the other hustler murders, and yet it suggested the same methods had been used. Leo wasn't entirely convinced by the theory about a wealthy man hunting poor queers. But he was forced to admit: it was their only attempt at an explanation. Why else should someone target handsome hustlers and castrate them?

Why?

What in God's name is his motive?

After ordering his coffee, Leo leaned back in a comfortable fauteuil and lit a cigarette. He watched the smoke as it rose to the ceiling and felt himself grow calm. The last few days had been like a constant merry-go-round ride. Julia, the odyssey through the sewers, the mad prison break, and now his sister's unexpected news from Graz. He hadn't had a moment of peace to think.

The cigarette smoke mingled with the coffeehouse's fragrant and smoky aroma. The voices around him, the clinking of cups and silverware, the shouted orders by waiters toward the kitchen—all of it melded together into a hum. It was this acoustic backdrop that allowed Leo to think the most clearly.

He reached for one of the newspapers lying available for patrons. It was the *Neues Wiener Tagblatt*. There were no reports yet of the spectacular escape from the courthouse, but the evening edition was bound to report on it in mocking tones. No way would they miss this one.

Leo leafed through the pages, enjoying his coffee. There were notices of balls at the opera next to reports of arson and murder. There were suicides and glamorous weddings, broken engagements and localized outbreaks of cholera. There were children run over by carriages and the latest gossip from city hall. Superintendent Stukart was right: this city was like one huge untamed beast.

On page twelve, under cultural notices, Leo spotted a piece that gave him pause. He set down his cup and thought.

And so we meet again . . .

Suddenly he knew what his next move would be. He couldn't tell whether it would lead him into the woods or to his goal.

But anything was better than sitting around waiting for the phantom to strike again.

"The book on the *Habsburg funerals*, the *Handbook of Medical Police,* and . . . uh, Sir Lionel Hardy's report on the burning of widows in India. That will be all, sir. Thank you kindly."

With an expression of indignation, the imperial court librarian pushed the three books across the counter, trying to keep as much distance as possible from Augustin Rothmayer. Augustin was accustomed to this treatment, even if he didn't understand what this fop's problem was. Augustin had donned his best suit—well, his only suit, to be fair—and brushed it clean, shaken it out repeatedly, and even rubbed off the soil stains on the knees. What fault of his was it if it was a funeral suit? The pompous sausage of a court librarian ought to be grateful that Augustin Rothmayer, in his position of officially appointed gravedigger, hadn't brought his spade!

Augustin muttered another thank you and wrote the titles and his name in the leather-bound folder. Then he picked up his stack and found himself a spot in the magnificent hall of the library.

The imperial court library, situated inside the Hofburg palace, was one of the largest libraries in the world, and a much admired hoard of knowledge. Centuries worth of books were housed here, more than a hundred thousand. Among them were Italian, English, and French volumes. For a few decades now, the library had been open to the public—a service which seemed to displease the chief librarian. The fellow probably would have preferred it if the imperial family alone visited, and only on certain holidays and with prior notice. Instead, professors, scholars, students, and yes, even plain Vienna citizens could all borrow its books. The librarian was unaware that one of these citizens was a gravedigger, and that was for the best.

Augustin soon found a quiet corner. There were smaller reading rooms outside of the great hall, but Augustin liked the big room.

As always, Augustin didn't immediately open his books, but instead soaked in the atmosphere of this holy place. The magnificent hall was almost twenty yards high with a dome and galleries—indeed reminiscent of a church, a cathedral, even. Rows of bookshelves made of gleaming nut wood stretched to the ceiling. Balancing on wooden stairs on wheels were librarians in shirts with stand-up collars and sleeve protectors. Reverent, focused silence filled the air. Those who came here sought quiet, not gossip, and Augustin valued this.

These days he visited almost weekly, whenever he managed to snatch a few free hours. Augustin had already consulted dozens of books for his latest work, *Death Rites Around the World*. Some—stored deep in the library's innards, in chests and trunks that groaned and puffed clouds of dust when opened—he had to order days in advance. In the beginning, the court librarian had been reluctant to help, but when Augustin turned up one day accompanied by Professor Hofmann, the decorated and knighted scientist, this had quickly changed. Augustin still wasn't treated warmly, but no worse than the other visitors.

After basking in the quiet for a few minutes, Augustin opened his writing book, took out his sharpened pencil, and turned to the first book. The heavy volume on the Habsburg funeral system was a hefty one; he had read about half. He worked through the pages with concentration, made a few notes, compared his previous notes with the sources listed.

He'd sat there for about an hour when he looked up for the first time. His back ached—a consequence of daily grave digging. Augustin stretched, cast his eye about, and spotted someone sitting at the neighboring table.

It was someone he knew.

Augustin blinked. In the dim light of the library, he took a few moments to place the person. But then he felt certain: he'd met this man not long ago. Augustin couldn't say whether the man had already been sitting there when he'd arrived. He seemed deeply focused, bent closely over some pages, taking notes, pausing, staring into the distance, then scribbling some more. There was something feverish about his demeanor, his lips quivering, occasionally drawing into a smile that made him look slightly mad. Then he would nod fervently or mutter soundless words.

Strange, Augustin thought. *Is that what they call the fever of scholars?*

He reached for Hardy's work on the burning of widows, but his focus was broken. His eye kept returning to the man hastily leafing through his books. Half an hour later, the man rose abruptly and hurried off, leaving the books on the table. He was probably going to ask for another book from the front desk.

Augustin only hesitated a second before standing. His curiosity was too great. He strolled over to the table, trying to look disinterested. He managed to catch a glimpse of the books. The titles were none he knew, but his interest was kindled—for the books were all on a particular subject.

A very particular niche subject.

Almost more niche than the subjects a gravedigger dealt with in his daily work.

Augustin noticed just in time that the man was returning. Indeed, he carried a few more heavy leather-bound tomes, sweat glistening on his forehead. He didn't seem to notice Augustin. The gravedigger took a silent step backward and disappeared into the shadows between the shelves. That was the upside of wearing a black funeral suit—one was practically invisible, as if people tried to avoid thinking of death.

Augustin returned to his seat and focused once more on his work. Thus the hours passed. In the late afternoon, when the slanting light through the windows turned first golden then dull, the man prepared to leave. He picked up his stack of books and carried it to the front desk. Augustin waited a few moments before following the man and queuing up behind him at the wide counter where books were issued, signed off, and returned.

"Reserve these under my name, will you?" said the man in a tone accustomed to issuing orders. "I'll be back Monday."

"As you wish, sir." The chief court librarian gave a small bow, evidently familiar with this customer. "I'll put them with the other books, as always. I bid you a good evening, sir."

Without a word of farewell the man headed outside.

Augustin stepped forward, his eyes on the books the librarian was about to put away. "Blimey, what are the odds," said Augustin. "Those are the ones I'm looking for. Lucky for you—you won't have to go find these ones for me!" He pulled the stack toward him.

"The gentleman has reserved these for Monday," replied the librarian with raised eyebrows. "I don't think he—"

"Well I'm sure he won't mind me borrowing them for just a moment. I don't plan to stay for the weekend, as lovely as it is in here. Excuse me." Augustin drew the folder toward him and, before the librarian could object, he set his name below the titles. "Thank you—too kind." He flashed his wolfish grin and carried the stack back to his spot. He set to work, fine dust tickling his nose.

After the first few pages, his hair stood on end.

He kept reading, his heart thudding.

Jesus, Mary, and Joseph! What in God's name . . .

As the gravedigger turned the next page, a piece of paper fluttered out. Augustin picked it up and read it.

The handwritten notes left no room for doubt.

So that's why . . .

Augustin Rothmayer clutched the note and hurried toward the exit.

"Hey, your books!" called out the librarian, indignant, behind him. "Sir, you . . . you must return your books in person! You can't just leave them lying on the table. Imagine if everyone did that. Hey, wait—"

But Augustin no longer heard him.

What he'd just learned was bound to interest the posh Prussian inspector, and Fräulein Wolf, too. Augustin had a deal with her, after all.

I scratch your back, you scratch mine.

Humming the commander's tune from Mozart's opera *Don Giovanni*, Augustin emerged onto Helden Square. The song seemed highly appropriate to him.

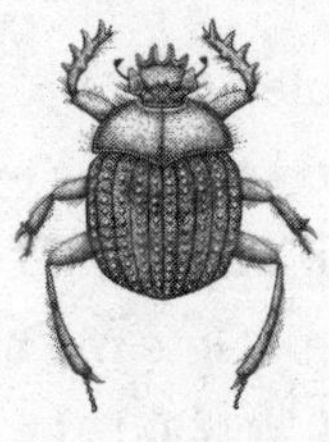

CHAPTER 23

As Leo crossed Maria Theresien Square that evening, the first gas streetlights came on. They flickered briefly before spreading their warm light, painting a mild glow over the couples in love, fiacre drivers waiting on their seats, and all those out for an evening stroll. The windows of the Museum of Natural History across the square were dark; the last few visitors exited the main hall, followed closely by a hunchbacked old porter who locked up behind them. Visitor hours were over at the Museum of Art History also, but the lights were still on in the right wing. The door stood open, and a foldout display board next to the door announced an evening event. The marble-gray board was cut in the shape of a sphinx. Leo walked over to it, reading the text which was rendered in stiff letters: "Presentation tonight hosted by the Vienna Archaeological Society: Perceptions of eternal life in ancient Egypt. Speaker: Dr. Friedrich Carl Knauer, director of the Vienna Zoological Garden. 7 o'clock start. Members only event!"

Leo stepped up to the ticket booth and asked for a ticket.

"You a member?" grumbled the porter, who probably thought he had better things to do than spend his evening in his little shack.

"This is my membership pass," said Leo, holding out his police badge with the double eagle. "Gets me into most places."

"Still costs ten kronen," replied the porter, apparently unconcerned about a police agent's presence at a talk on Egyptology. "And you're late. The gentlemen have already started."

"Well, then let's hope I won't be struck down by the pharaoh's curse," replied Leo, pushing a few coins across the counter.

The porter's face remained unmoved. "Up the right-hand stairs, hall V. And don't you get lost, or else my colleague will lock you in here over night. He don't give a damn if you're the fuzz or even Ramses himself." The porter counted the coins and then slammed down the shutter on his booth.

Leo hurried across the large foyer with its high dome and followed the signs to the presentation. When he'd seen the notice in the paper that morning, he'd decided to attend. After all, at Professor Strössner's memorial service Dr. Knauer himself had personally invited Leo to look up the society.

The day at police headquarters had brought no news. Superintendent Stukart had been in an accordingly foul mood for their big briefing, bemoaning Paul Leinkirchner's absence repeatedly while shooting reproachful looks in Leo's direction. All the while, Stukart himself hadn't achieved anything, either. His demand for a complete list of influential homosexuals had fallen on deaf ears. Probably because there were homosexuals at the imperial court, maybe even among the imperial family, Leo suspected. Their only lead led nowhere. So, what did he have to lose by pursuing his own suspicion? No matter how flimsy it was.

Leo passed through a large room with Egyptian columns. Its ceiling depicted a starry sky with vultures. He could hear the murmur of a voice from the next room, growing more distinct as he approached. Among the columns, about two dozen chairs had been set up; candles and lamps burned atop sarcophagi and glass display cases, bathing the room in dim lights. At the front, next to display cases with golden masks and other precious items, Dr. Friedrich Knauer stood speaking behind a lectern. His top hat sat next to his notes, which rustled as he leafed through them.

Most of the people in the sparse audience were gray-faced old men wearing black tailcoats and stand-up collars. Some of the men, Leo thought, looked like they were already mummified themselves, or at least asleep. Charlotte Rapoldy and her husband sat in the first row. Carl Rebers, Knauer's young assistant, was also present—the only person in the audience who appeared under thirty. Sitting next to him was Dr. Alexander Dedekind, curator of the Egypto-Oriental Collection, listening with closed eyes and a focused expression. Leo was relieved to see that Professor Eduard Hofmann wasn't here; this spared him unpleasant questions.

". . . eternal life wasn't the privilege of pharaohs alone, no, everyone was entitled to it!" Knauer was reading from his notes. His low, imploring voice echoed through the large room. "It was important to have a well-preserved and, especially, young body, made possible by embalming and subsequent masking. A veritable fountain of youth! The journey to the next world was fraught with danger. The so-called book of the dead served as a kind of guidebook. Yes, you may imagine this book like a Baedeker for the voyage through the realm of the dead." Knauer paused to let his little joke sink in. As he looked up, he noticed Leo for the first time, leaning against a column. The zoo director frowned, visibly thrown by this late attendee.

"Uh . . . where was I? Yes, the voyage to the realm of the dead . . ."

Knauer's hesitation drew the attention of the other guests. They glanced around, clearly annoyed by the disruption of the presentation. Leo lifted his hands apologetically and squeezed past several elderly guests to an empty seat. A white-haired gentleman with a walrus mustache bestowed him with a look of distaste.

"However, the dead person does not begin their journey in old age," Knauer went on eventually, seemingly forgetting momentarily that most of his audience were of old age. "No other society of antiquity was as obsessed with the ideals of beauty and eternal youth as the Egyptians. Not a single report from the old dynasties mentions age or illness! Neither in life nor in death. Youth, fertility, and beauty outshine everything else in ancient Egypt."

As if on cue, Charlotte Rapoldy turned to Leo then. She looked at him with a puzzled, bemused expression. Leo gave a shrug and, smiling, pointed at one of the sarcophagi by the wall, as if that explained his unexpected presence. Then he leaned back and continued to listen to the talk, which went into complex descriptions of the Egyptian soul. Apparently, an Egyptian had three of them, bearing strange names like *akh*, *ba,* and *ka*. Leo's thoughts trailed off.

Julia's suspicion that keeper Eugen Lenz was the phantom might have been far-fetched but not entirely implausible. The phantom had evidently struck at the zoo, and Knauer and Lenz had spoken about some sort of secret that mustn't come out. A secret to do with the phantom? And there was something else . . . Gazing at the lectern, Leo noticed something. Eugen Lenz wasn't the only one with black hair—director Knauer's was, too.

And he wore a top hat.

". . . and next time we will take a closer look at the highly interesting parallels between the ancient Egyptian religion and Christianity. I thank you for listening."

Leo gave a start. Absorbed in thought, he'd missed that Dr. Knauer was reaching the end of his talk. The guests applauded and the director gave a small bow, then walked over to Charlotte Rapoldy to pay his respects. Knauer smiled; evidently, they exchanged niceties. The remaining guests also rose from their seats.

Some food was served on one of the sarcophagi, so-called sandwiches, a popular food in England. A waiter in uniform passed around champagne in delicate blue glass flutes. Everyone seemed to know one another, standing together in small groups, debating. Leo tried to look at ease. He picked up a champagne glass from a waiter's tray and strolled past the glass display cases.

Friedrich Knauer was speaking with a gray-haired, hunched man, apparently discussing the finer differences between *ka* and *ba*.

Leo used a brief pause in the conversation to jump in. "Congratulations on your presentation," he said, raising his glass. "Quite refreshing. May this champagne be as reviving as an ancient Egyptian ritual!"

Knauer seemed confounded for a moment; then he smirked. "Well, some do believe champagne is a magical substance—life-giving, even?" The older man Leo had interrupted turned away, looking offended. Friedrich Knauer squinted at Leo. "Don't I know you, Herr . . . ?"

"Herzfeldt," said Leo. "Leopold von Herzfeldt. We met at Professor Strössner's funeral. I'm an old friend of Charlotte Rapoldy's. You invited me along to one of your meetings, remember?"

"And now you've come." Knauer smiled. "How kind of you. Do you plan to join the society? We could do with some young blood."

"I'm contemplating it," replied Leo. "I am very interested in Egyptology indeed. What you said earlier about eternal life and beauty—"

"Well, our dear Leopold isn't yet at an age where one thinks too much about death and what comes after. Or are you, *Leo*?"

Leo turned toward the sharp voice. It was Charlotte Rapoldy, moving toward him with her husband. She wore a blue velvet gown with gold hieroglyphs embroidered upon it. Her hair was adorned with the same silver tiara holding the green scarab she'd worn on their last encounters. She smiled stiffly. "Clemens just asked me where the two of us met. Wasn't it during our student travels through Palestine?"

"Uh, yes, I think you might be right . . . ," said Leo.

"You were already just as inquisitive back then," went on Charlotte Rapoldy. "Unstoppable in your quest for knowledge." She turned to Dr. Knauer. "I hope Leo isn't taking up too much of your precious time? He can be quite a persistent little pest."

"Oh, not at all." Knauer laughed. "But I see you two have old memories to revisit." He gave a bow. "You'll excuse me." He then made his way to the other guests.

When Charlotte and her husband were alone with Leo, Charlotte's smile vanished as abruptly as if a switch had been flipped. "Herr Inspector, may I ask the reason for this unexpected visit?" She raised a hand, a green diamond sparkling on one of her fingers, perfectly matching the tiara in her hair. "And don't tell me you've developed a sudden interest for Egyptology. I'd never buy it."

"Well, why not?" Leo raised his glass toward her. "As an inspector investigating a series of murders, the prospect of eternal life seems highly appealing."

"A series of murders?" Charlotte Rapoldy frowned. "What are you saying? And what does that have to do with our . . . well, case, inspector? I thought that was all closed."

"And so it is. Upon a request by the police president himself." Leo looked around. "May I ask where His Excellency the archduke is tonight? No interest in this talk?"

"The archduke can't simply attend a public talk," replied Charlotte coolly. "It would cause a stir. Don't you know that?"

"Just as great a stir as if the public learned that the archduke had taken part in the desecration of an Egyptian mummy."

"Inspector, where are you going with this?" asked Clemens Rapoldy, who'd so far merely listened. "Are you suggesting our case isn't being investigated just because it casts the court in a poor light? I thought we'd discussed this. My father-in-law's death was an accident, a terrible mistake! My wife has paid for it a hundred times over; she dreams of it every night. She mixed up the vials, and everything that happened thereafter happened because my father-in-law wished it! And now please excuse us. Other guests also wish to speak with us. Are you coming, Charlotte?"

Clemens Rapoldy furiously limped off with his stick.

Charlotte lingered for a moment. "You don't believe us, do you?" she said. "You think we're keeping something from you."

"Indeed. There are simply too many loose ends—not only in your case." Leo sighed. "I'd hoped to get a little closer to the truth. In an amicable conversation," he added. "This is no interrogation."

Charlotte hesitated. "I still can't believe how this could have happened to me. With the vials. Mixing them up seems so improbable. It . . . really is like a curse."

Leo set his glass down on a sarcophagus. "May I ask you something else? How long has Dr. Friedrich Carl Knauer been a member of your society?"

"Fritz?" Charlotte frowned. "One or two years, perhaps. He's a very active member. He's fascinated by the thought of eternal life in the ancient Egyptian worldview. He's convinced we Christians adopted much from the Egyptians." She smiled. "And he's a great recruiter for our aging club. First he turns up with young Rebers, and now you. The two of you lower our mean age by at least a decade. Why do you ask?"

"No reason. Nothing in particular, anyway. Just a hunch."

"Hunches can spoil any relationship, trust me." She turned serious. "There is something else I've been meaning to tell you. It's—"

"Charlotte, are you coming? Franz Ritter von Hauer is sharing news about his latest acquisitions for the Museum of Natural History."

Clemens Rapoldy was standing with a gentleman sporting an

enormously bushy beard—the same gentleman who'd shot Leo a disgruntled look during the presentation. Clemens stared expectantly at his wife.

"Shame we had to meet in these circumstances, inspector," said Charlotte Rapoldy. "Perhaps in another life . . . *Au revoir*." She allowed him to kiss her hand, then hovered away like a ghost. Leo's eyes followed her, feeling somewhat at a loss. He'd never understand this woman.

He took a few more unenthusiastic turns about the room, stopping here and there to gaze at an artwork, sipping his champagne. He could tell he was being avoided. Presumably, the Rapoldys had shared his true identity with the others, ruining the possibility of another unguarded conversation.

Leo decided to at least take a good look around the exhibits so that his visit wasn't entirely wasted. A statue of polished black basalt in a hidden corner drew his attention. He suspected it had been placed in this spot because some visitors might find it indecent. The statue was of a small man who bore a disproportionally large penis. The huge penis protruded horizontally from his body, almost like a sword. A plaque informed the beholder that the figurine was of the Egyptian fertility god Min.

Leo couldn't help but grin. He read the text, which spoke of a feast dedicated to Min during which a bull would be sacrificed. The animal's testicles would be burned as an offering for a fertile harvest.

The testicles would be burned . . .

That gave Leo pause. The text and the statue set some gears into motion in his brain. So far, the results of his thinking were very vague, like fog that molded into a shape, just to dissolve a moment later.

Testicles . . . a fertile harvest . . .

Leo cursed under his breath. He needed peace and a cigarette to focus and order his thoughts. He glanced one last time at the gray-haired members of the society, now gathered around Dr. Knauer, apparently congratulating him once more on his presentation. Words from Knauer's speech flashed through Leo's mind.

Youth, virility, beauty . . . age and illness . . .

Musing, he left the hall and followed the dimly lit corridor back to the foyer where the porter waited impatiently.

"Hey, you, how much longer are they going to be?" the man asked Leo. "It's long past knock-off time!"

But Leo didn't answer. He stepped outside, lit a cigarette, and took a long drag. Nicotine streamed into his arteries and his thoughts slotted into the right places, one after the other.

"That could be it," he murmured to himself, deeply absorbed by his thoughts. "Why didn't I think of this sooner? His motive—"

That's when Leo saw the cart.

It was parked a little off to the side, toward the end of the right museum wing. The only reason Leo had noticed it was because a lone streetlight shone upon it.

And because a garbage cart seemed a little out of place in the clean museum forecourt.

The filthy double-axle wagon was about the size and shape of a circus trailer. Trash would be shoveled onto the cart through a dented tin door at the back. An old horse was hitched to the front, munching oats from a pail. Leo suddenly remembered where he'd seen a similar cart before. By the column that led down into the sewers, near the Rossauer barracks, right where the murderer dragged his victim into the depths of the city. And now Leo also remembered that a garbage cart like this one had been mentioned in several witness statements. Always as an aside—no one had paid it much attention.

Who takes note of a garbage cart?

Leo tossed aside his cigarette and approached the wagon, his heart hammering. The door at the back opened easily, swinging outward with a soft squeak. Leo peered inside.

The sight froze his blood.

My God, what on earth—

A blow struck him on his temple. Leo gasped, staggered, reached out a hand toward the shadow that had suddenly appeared behind him. But his hand only grabbed thin air. The shadow wielded a heavy object for the second time.

Just before the blow landed, catapulting Leo into the blackness of unconsciousness, he registered that the object was a small Egyptian stone figurine. It was black, in the shape of a man with the head of a jackal.

"Give my regards to Anubis, inspector," said the phantom. "Unfortunately, you'll be traveling without the book of the dead."

Then the man dragged his prey inside the stinking cart.

Julia sat on Saidrovuni's bed, wiping his sweaty forehead with a cold cloth. She'd visited him regularly throughout the last few hours, listening to the man mutter in his sleep. On the second day following his arrival at the Blue Dragoon, Saidrovuni was still a little feverish, but he appeared to be over the worst. He had gained consciousness a few times since yesterday, and Julia managed to spoon-feed him a little soup and tea. It was evening now and soon she'd have to put Sisi to bed, but she wanted to check on her patient one more time.

She winced when there was a knock on the door.

Have they found us . . . ?

But it was only Big Elli, entering with a cup of tea in her hand.

"Still sleeping, the savage?" asked Elli with a note of impatience in her voice. "Our African Snow White . . ." She handed Julia the cup of tea. Then she cocked her head and studied their guest. "Hmm, he looks fine all right. I know several women and men who—"

"Don't you dare!" hissed Julia. "This man has a family. He's no plaything for you to do with as you please."

"Oy, watch your mouth, lassie!" Elli wagged a fat finger. "I'm no Hottentot hotel, just you remember that. The girls aren't talking about anything else. I could make a fortune selling admission tickets for him!" She rolled her eyes. "I've always been too soft for this world. You remember our deal, don't you?"

"Course I do. Saidrovuni stays until he's well, and then you get what you want."

Elli grinned. "That's better, girl." She fondled Julia's hair and bent down to her. "The German inspector was here again last night, wasn't he? Bruno told me. So, the fellow's playing family man now. I thought you sent him packing!"

"It's not that easy," replied Julia without much energy.

"He's not the right one for you, I've been telling you this for a long time. And trust me—I know men. He'll bring you nothing but trouble. An arrogant baron and a German to boot, bah—"

"And a good man," said Julia. "At least most of the time. Like it or not, I've fallen for him. You can grouse as much as you like."

"Oh, kiss my arse. By the way, if you're looking for Sisi, she's downstairs, plucking Bruno's hairs one by one. Everyone in this house just does as they please."

Elli pulled the door shut with gusto. In the hallway, Julia heard her thumping footsteps walking away. She sighed and rubbed her tired eyes. Elli was right—Leo was so different from herself. But didn't some say that opposites attracted? He'd taken a huge risk for her. And he really was trying: last night he'd played with Sisi and brought her sweets, and he said he'd come back tonight. Maybe they'd go for a drink somewhere close by . . . Leo telephoned earlier to say that he'd be attending a talk by zoo director Knauer after work, at the Museum of Art History. He hoped to find out more about the zoo murder and the hustler murders there. Maybe he'd already learned something new?

"*Amanzi* . . . water . . ."

Julia gave a start. Looking over at Saidrovuni, she saw that he was stirring, looking around with confusion. It seemed he was at last fully conscious.

"Where . . . where am I?" he asked.

"Don't be afraid. You're safe." Julia leaned down and wiped his forehead once more. "A friend and I, we freed you from prison. You had a fever and you've been sleeping for a long time. Since yesterday."

"I . . . I remember. The cell . . . the men swore at me and beat me." Saidrovuni gave Julia a puzzled look. "You're the photographer, right? Why are you helping me?"

"Because I don't believe that you're a murderer. I believe you were set up and—"

"My wife and child." Saidrovuni sat up abruptly. "I must go to them—"

Julia gently pushed him back down. "They're fine. No one arrested them." She didn't really know this for certain, but she didn't want to worry Saidrovuni any more.

"What place is this?" asked Saidrovuni. "A hotel?"

"Uh, something like that. You can stay here until you're better. No one knows you're here. No one except for me and my friend."

No need to mention that my friend is with the police, thought Julia.

"Here, drink." She guided the cup to Saidrovuni's mouth and he drank thirstily. Soon she set the empty cup back down. "I'll bring more water and broth. And something more solid, too. You must be hungry . . ."

Julia hesitated. Saidrovuni seemed much better, but he was still weak. Still, it was crucial they learned more about the events at the zoo as soon as possible.

"Listen," she began. "There's something I need to speak to you about. I spoke with your wife about the young keeper that was killed, and about Lenz's accusations. Unfortunately, your wife speaks no German. But there were two words that she kept repeating." Julia frowned, digging in her memory. "They were *umlilo* and *ikhanda*, or something like that. Do you know what they mean?"

"*Umlilo* and *ikhanda*?" Saidrovuni shook his head. "You must be mistaken. Those make no sense."

"What do they mean?"

Saidrovuni straightened up. His face looked ashen and tired. "Well, one of the words means—"

In that moment, there was another knock on the door and again it was Big Elli. She entered the room, breathing heavily and clearly in a foul mood.

"If you think I'm your errand boy you can think again!" she complained. "This was the last time! But I just can't get rid of the fellow. He's outside the door and insists on speaking with you. Says he won't budge until you come down."

"Leo?" asked Julia, hopeful. She'd expected Leo a while ago. She hadn't worried until now, but something about Elli's demeanor made her listen up.

"Trust me, lassie, if your German made a fuss like that, Bruno would have turned him to pulp long ago." Elli snorted. "No, it's someone else. A strange bird, this one. Bruno was going to smack him one, but Sisi grabbed the man's arms and whined and fussed. Looks like she knows him. Looks as if he's come straight from his own funeral, what with his floppy hat and muddy black coat. Brrr! He's creepy, I tell you."

"Oh, I think I know who it is," said Julia. "And he said it's important?"

Elli nodded. "Reckons he knows who you're looking for. And why the fellow cuts off the willies of all those pretty lads." She shook herself, her rings and necklaces jingling. "I told you the fellow's creepy. By God, it's as if the devil himself was outside our door. Go on already and find out what he has to say."

There was a clattering, groaning, and creaking as if from a giant grinder. A huge pyramid filled with rollers, gears, and millstones. Leo rattled along on a leather belt made of the skin of thousands of slaves, moving him toward a funnel as big as a whale's mouth. A monstrous bone mill that would grind him into white dust to fertilize the fields of the Nile valley . . .

Clattering . . .

Leo groaned. Tried to open his eyes. He couldn't. Was he blind?

Groaning . . .

Damn it, where was he? He squinted, blinked, tried again to open his eyes. But his eyes were glued shut by something warm and sticky. He also felt the warm stickiness on his face, which felt strangely numb. Was he still dreaming?

Creaking . . .

The dreams receded and memories returned. The gathering of the Vienna Archaeological Society at the Museum of Art History . . . Knauer's presentation . . . the conversation with the Rapoldys . . . he'd learned something—only, what? The garbage cart outside the museum. He had opened the door and looked inside. Something terrible had been inside.

Creaking . . .

The cart! Leo's heart rate shot up. This was no bone mill and no pyramid. This was the garbage cart! Someone had knocked him out and dragged him inside it. What he was hearing were the rhythmic noises of the moving cart.

He tried to sit up but couldn't. Something seemed to be . . . pinning him down. Damn, what was wrong with him? The feeling was familiar. As a boy, Leo had sometimes experienced it in his dreams. Physicians called it paralysis; the people called it *Hexendrücken*, as if a witch were holding one down. He remembered being awake and yet asleep, unable to move a muscle, as if he were buried alive. And he used to see ghosts in this state of semiconsciousness.

Back then, Leo would force himself to open his eyes or at least move his pinkie—a difficult process that seemed to take half an eternity. When at last he succeeded, he would wake up drenched in sweat.

What was that damned stickiness in his face? Warm and sticky . . .

Only then did it dawn on Leo that it was probably blood.

His own blood, chances were.

The garbage cart clattered down the streets at a leisurely pace. The horse whinnied; somewhere, a tram jingled. The song of a drunk man rose, then faded away. The wagon smelled odd, not like garbage but like something . . . *else*.

At last Leo managed to open one of his eyes a tiny bit. At first there was only darkness, but then he began making out shapes. The sparse light of gas streetlights seeped in through gaps in the poorly installed timbers of the wagon's walls. He was lying on a low steel tabletop that took up most of the wagon's center. His numb fingers felt a groove running down the edge of the table. With almost superhuman effort he managed to turn his head the slightest bit.

Hanging on the walls were tools that jangled merrily to the rhythm of the ride.

Saws, pincers, knives, scalpels . . .

Next to them, hung neatly in a row on hooks, were a top hat, a black suit, and a black wig. There were also a number of bloody rags.

Now Leo knew what the smell was. It wasn't really what you'd expect in a garbage cart but at a slaughterhouse.

It reeked of rot, decay, and blood.

Leo moaned; a shudder ran up his body. He didn't know how much time had passed since he was struck down. Minutes, hours, days? At least he now knew where the phantom cut up his victims before discarding them in the sewers. They'd always wondered how the murderer managed to do the dissecting in the streets without being noticed. Well, turns out, he really was doing it in the streets—in a way.

He cut up the bodies inside a garbage cart.

A perfect hiding place. There were garbage carts all over Vienna and no one paid them any attention. And no one came close to them, as they stank and were dirty. Leo remembered what one of the young colleagues had jeeringly said in a meeting a few days ago.

Are there mobile butcher shops?

That's exactly what it was. The killer was getting around in his own butchery on wheels, and no one had noticed a thing.

Now Leo recalled what he'd seen at the museum. The figurine with the absurdly large penis. And the train of thoughts this statue had triggered in him . . .

Suddenly, the wagon stopped. There was another creaking sound as someone climbed off the driver's seat. Footsteps approached the back door, which opened with a squeak. The beam from a kerosene lamp flooded the inside of the cart. Someone climbed in, reached for the large saw on the wall, and bent over Leo.

With his blood-encrusted eye, Leo looked the phantom straight in the face. He gasped.

Good God, who would have guessed . . . ?

Then he watched as the rusty saw blade moved toward his right upper arm.

And still he couldn't move.

"Before you tell me what you came here to say, answer me one question, Herr Rothmayer. How in God's name do you know where I live?"

Julia was sitting in Elli's office with Augustin Rothmayer. Her landlady had grudgingly allowed them to use the office, though not without considerable cursing. It was a small room decorated with erotic paintings, which the gravedigger studied with interest. It reeked of rose perfume. Before Julia left the attic, Saidrovuni had explained to her what the two words meant in Matabele, but to her disappointment, she wasn't able to make sense of them.

With one last glance at two large-bosomed nymphs and a poorly dressed Pan with a huge erection, Rothmayer turned to Julia. "I did a little bit of digging. Well, not me, but Anna. A few weeks ago, she was bored, so I asked her to follow you from Central Cemetery. Anna is quite good at things like that."

"That's quite rude, Herr Rothmayer. You know that."

"I beg you, fräulein, it was for a good cause!" Augustin Rothmayer clearly felt sheepish. "You helped Anna so much, brought her clothes and whatnot. I . . . I wanted to show my appreciation. Was going to send you a bunch of chrysanthemums, with a note."

"Aren't chrysanthemums what you give at a funeral?"

"Maybe." Rothmayer looked sulky. "But they're beautiful flowers, and they represent loyalty." He turned back to the paintings. "Is this house what I think it is?"

"Yes. But I'm not what you think I am and—" Julia drew a deep breath. "You know what? I don't care what you think. I have enough to worry about at the moment. So, what is it you came to tell me? Elli said it was about the castrated murdered boys?"

Rothmayer nodded eagerly. "I believe I know who's behind it! I watched the fellow at the court library today. And so I came to find you."

"Why didn't you tell inspector Herzfeldt or another policeman about your discovery?"

"Fräulein Wolf!" Rothmayer looked appalled. "You and me had

a deal. Remember? You help me with Anna and I help you with this strange case. And that's why I came to Neulerchenfeld today. I just had to tidy up some old bones first, and there was the crooked window at the morgue—"

"Herr Rothmayer, you're impossible! Tell me what you know already! Who did you see at the library and what makes you think he's our murderer?"

Augustin Rothmayer noisily wiped his nose with the back of his hand.

Then he told Julia the name.

"Are you sure?" She frowned. "I thought that . . ."

And suddenly Julia knew how the words *umlilo* and *ikhanda* fitted in.

A sound of sheer desperation escaped Leo's throat. It was no more than a hiss, but it was enough to make the phantom pause. The man lowered the rusty saw and bent down, looking intrigued. His face was all shadow.

"You're still alive? Interesting." The phantom reached for the kerosene lamp he'd set down on the table and held it over Leo. The man carefully wiped away dried blood before pulling Leo's eyelids up one after the other, closely studying his twitching pupils. "Highly interesting! You see, I injected you with a venom I developed myself. It's based on curare, an outstanding jungle poison. The natives of South America brush it onto their arrowheads. Paralysis ought to have spread to the lungs, but my recipe is very new and unfinished. I'm working on it. It's just so much better to perform a dissection when the subjects don't squirm."

"Grrrch . . . .," was all Leo managed. "Grrrch . . . grrrch . . ." He strained desperately, trying to lift his hand, but he couldn't. The phantom raised the saw once more.

"I wonder if you'll feel pain. What do you think?"

Sweat trickled down Leo's forehead. His jaw felt as if it were tied shut. His heart raced so madly, Leo thought it might give in at any moment.

"I can see in your eyes that you're afraid," said the phantom mildly. "Well, I guess that's to be expected given your current situation. Listen, that's the reason why I developed this poison. So that no one has to suffer unnecessarily. It's never about inflicting pain. Not with rabbits, not with frogs, newts, mice, or humans. It's only ever about the cause. Isn't it?"

"Grrrch . . . ," said Leo again. Spittle bubbled from the corners of his mouth.

"What are you saying?" The phantom frowned, studying him. "Oh, it's all so vexing! You don't fit my experiment criteria. You're too old. On the other hand, you're handsome, your skin has preserved its youthful complexion, and you have hardly any facial hair. Hmm . . ." The man bent down low over him, still holding the saw. Leo smelled aftershave cream and champagne.

"Still, I don't think it would work," the man carried on, straightening back up. "Puberty lies too far back with you. So far, none of my donors were past twenty. Except for Stefan Moser from the zoo, he was a touch older. Also very good-looking! And he had me figured out, too, just like you. Who would have thought?" The phantom shook his head, clearly agitated.

"I took this little figurine and followed you out of the museum," he went on after a moment. "When I saw you open the cart, I knew I had to act. I'm so close to my breakthrough, you see. I can't afford any glitches. Well, and here you are, still alive. What now?" The phantom hesitated. Then he put aside the saw.

"You know, mankind just isn't ready for something this big. I'm certain that, a few decades down, my research will be celebrated! One of humanity's greatest dreams turned reality: age and ailing will soon be matters of the past. A shame you won't be there to witness it. But the risk of you betraying me and destroying my life's work is too great. You understand, don't you? Do you understand that?"

The phantom grabbed Leo's arms and pulled him off the table. He landed on the ground with a thud but felt barely anything. Then the man dragged him outside. Leo heard the trumpeting sound of an animal nearby, the screeching of birds, the hungry growl of a large cat . . . From the corner of his eye, Leo saw a building with domes, towers, and wide steps, like a gloomy castle. The air was filled with the pungent stench of animal feces, soil, and jungle.

In the light of the kerosene lantern, the man's hair glowed fiery red.

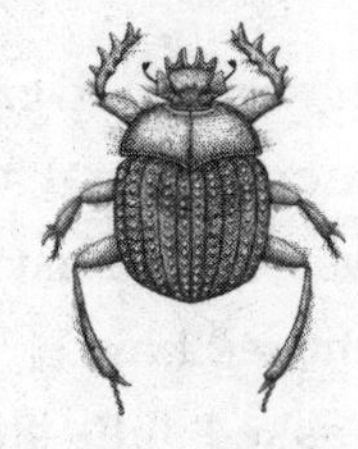

CHAPTER 24

From *Death Rites Around the World* by Augustin Rothmayer, written in Vienna, 1894

> A strange custom is said to be practiced in the West Indies. Occasionally, a person is given a poison that makes them appear dead. They are then buried in a well-aerated manner, just to be exhumed alive a short while later. A second poison takes away their wits, forcing them into a vegetative existence, much like the undead. They are then forced to serve their supposed saviors as slaves. The locals call these unfortunate creatures zombies.

"And it really was Carl Rebers you saw at the library?" asked Julia.

They were now sitting in a fiacre taking them toward the inner city. Under the watchful, suspicious eye of Bruno, Augustin had told her everything in Elli's office. Julia was still gobsmacked, barely able to grasp it all.

Rothmayer nodded. "I have a good memory for faces. The fellow was at Professor Strössner's funeral, that's where I remembered him from. And his name was on the list at the library. It's hard to overlook him, with his bright red hair."

"And those books . . . ?" asked Julia slowly.

"Strange scientific stuff. Took me a while to understand anything at all. But the little that I did glean was enough. Does the name Brown-Séquard mean anything to you?"

"I don't think so."

"Me neither, at first. But I read up on him. He was a doctor who, years ago, injected himself with an extract from animal testes. Reckoned it turned him thirty years younger. He wrote a book about it titled *The Elixir of Life.* Didn't help him, by the way. He died not long ago." Rothmayer gave a chuckle, then turned serious. "Carl Rebers had borrowed this book and several other works on so-called modern fountains of youth. Mostly they're about the consumption of animal parts that are supposed to rejuvenate us. The testicles of monkeys, tails of tigers, some kind of horns from Africa. Something to do with so-called glands." The gravedigger shook his head. "And these are supposed to be modern times! Soon we'll push those glands like buttons on an automaton and our body will drive like an automobile."

Julia tried to follow her companion's slightly convoluted deliberations. "And you really believe that—"

"Oh yes, I do!" exclaimed Rothmayer. "Rebers noted down some of his crazy thoughts on a piece of paper which he left behind in one of the books." He waved a crumpled piece of paper that he'd pulled out of his coat. "Here it is in black and white. Rebers follows this Brown-Séquard's theories, only instead of using dogs, monkeys, and guinea pigs, he uses humans. Young, handsome men! He chops off their willy and balls and uses them for experiments. Makes me want to spew!"

Julia swallowed. Augustin Rothmayer had already given her the brief version at the Dragoon, but the atrociousness was still sinking in. If everything Rothmayer was saying was true, then all those men had to die for a megalomaniac scientific nightmare. She'd gotten to know Carl Rebers a little at the zoo. Could this lovely, educated man who always seemed a little awkward really be the phantom? Was he the link between the death at the zoo and the many hustler murders? It was the Matabele words that persuaded her in the end. The two words Saidrovuni translated for her.

Umlilo and *ikhanda*.

That's what Saidrovuni's wife had said over and over. *Umlilo* and *ikhanda* were the Matabele words for "fire" and "head." Until just before, they'd meant nothing to Julia. But that had changed.

Fire head.

The Matabele women had been speaking about ginger-haired Rebers—and they'd clearly been afraid of him. Presumably, it had been Carl Rebers who'd hidden the key to the lion's enclosure in the chief's hut. And he set the lion on Stefan Moser, the young keeper.

Fire head.

When Rothmayer told her the name Carl Rebers earlier on, Julia remembered with a shock that Knauer's assistant was also a member of the archaeological society—the same society whose event Leo had attended at the Museum of Art History earlier that evening. He should have long since been back. Had something happened to him? She'd asked Rothmayer to head to the museum with her. Most likely she worried for nothing, but it wouldn't hurt to make sure. Elli had sensed her fear, too, and slipped Julia something that weighed heavily in her handbag now.

It was a small, loaded revolver.

"I'm not letting you go alone with that weirdo without the gun," Elli had whispered to her, shooting a sidelong glance at

Rothmayer. "I need you back in once piece. Not least so you can keep your end of our bargain. And now run along before I set Bruno on you."

Then she'd picked up Sisi tenderly, as if she were a baby chick, and carried her to bed.

The evening was nearing midnight. Here, around Neulerchenfeld, the streets of Vienna were still busy with punters seeking pleasure in various establishments. The carriage followed Lerchenfelder Street before turning onto the Ring and then Maria Theresien Square. Gas lanterns illuminated the large monument of the archduchess in the square's center, and a few pigeons scattered as they drove up. Julia asked the driver to stop, paid him, and walked with Rothmayer over to the museum.

The building was as black as the night; not a single light shone in any of the windows. The large entrance was locked.

"As expected," sighed Julia. "The talk is long over. Where might Leo be? He said he would come straight to the Dragoon afterward."

"Maybe he went somewhere else first," said Rothmayer with a shrug. "Herr German Inspector likes to do as he pleases."

"True. But somehow I don't believe it, not this time. More recently Leo has been . . . well, reliable."

"Then let's go see if there's another way in." Rothmayer turned left along the long, dark building. Then he stopped abruptly. When Julia caught up, she saw why.

On the ground near the museum on the Ring side were traces of blood. Close to the blood lay a dented homburg hat that looked familiar.

It was Leo's hat.

"Good God," breathed Julia. "Leo . . ." Her heart raced. She had to stop herself from screaming out loud. "What . . . what did that monster do to him?"

Only now, in the moment she saw the blood, did Julia realize just how much Leo meant to her. He had become an important part of her life, and now it looked as though Carl Rebers might have murdered him in cold blood, discarding him like he had all those other young men before. Her knees trembled and she leaned against the wall of the museum, battling tears.

In contrast, Augustin Rothmayer remained remarkably calm. Getting down on his knees, he searched the ground around them, crawling along like a huge black insect.

"There are fresh wheel marks," he said eventually. He rose, brushed off his hands, and pointed at a spot on the ground. "Close to the blood. My guess is he put the inspector into a cart and drove him somewhere. If that's true then maybe he's still alive."

"We have to call the police! I must tell Loibl . . ." Julia was turning to leave but Rothmayer held her back.

"And tell them what? Herr von Herzfeldt was out on his own. Remember? Carl Rebers has a few powerful friends."

Julia hesitated. Rothmayer was right. Leo had received clear instructions to leave the archaeological society alone. She couldn't just call them now with the hair-raising accusation that one of its members was the insane hustler murderer. Even if she managed to convince Loibl or superintendent Stukart, it would take far too long.

And they didn't even know if Leo was still alive.

"You're right." Julia nodded. "We have to find another way. Where would Rebers have gone?" She thought hard, and then something clicked. "The vivarium at the zoo! Rebers told me he's set up a laboratory there. He told me when we first met."

Carl Rebers carried Leo across his shoulder as if he were a stuffed puppet, lugging him up the wide steps to the vivarium's entrance.

Rebers was surprisingly strong—stronger, in any case, than one would have expected of the pale young man at first glance. He set down his human freight outside the door and fished for the keys inside his coat pocket, all the while talking to Leo as if he were a regular conversation partner instead of a pile of limp muscle.

"You don't know how privileged you are, getting to see the laboratory, inspector! I only set it up last year. Dr. Knauer leaves me to my own devices—he doesn't know what exactly I do in there. He isn't overly interested in laboratory work—he just isn't a scientist like myself. I have a vision of a center for biological experiments—the first one of its kind. You'll be amazed!"

Rebers opened the doors, switched on the emergency lighting, and dragged Leo's limp form into the high-ceilinged entrance hall, then past aquariums and glass cages holding snakes and frogs that stared at them with large black eyes. Farther along, larger enclosures followed. Outside, monkeys cackled as if to mock Leo's desperate situation.

"At least our chance encounter at the museum gave me a fantastic idea," Rebers prattled on as he dragged Leo along by his collar. "So far, I disposed of my donors in the sewers, in small portions. That draws the least attention. But recently I've had . . . well, some difficulties. I was forced to leave bodies behind. I was noticed. Rather annoying. And then it occurred to me, it's so much easier to dispose of the bodies here! For example at the crocodiles next door. Lions are less ideal, I've learned. I tried with young Moser, but lions aren't keen on human carrion. Too much remains uneaten."

Rebers breathed heavily as he pulled Leo around another corner. At that moment, Leo noticed a change in his body. He could feel more—the effect of the poison was wearing off. But he was still unable to move his head, arms, or legs.

"Stefan Moser caught onto me one day when he went to clean

my laboratory," continued Rebers, wholly absorbed in his own world. He paused to wipe sweat off his forehead, a dreamy smile on his lips. "A terribly handsome lad. He saw an amputated human scrotum on the table—stupidly, I'd left it there briefly. It was a real shame, having to dispose of him. And the other handsome young men. It was never easy for me, oh no!"

With a sigh, Rebers shook his head and dragged Leo farther down the dark corridor, continuing his monologue. "But the risk of Moser stopping me so close to the conclusion of my research was simply too great! And so I snuck the key into the hut and planted the idea in Lenz's head that that savage was out to kill him." Rebers laughed softly. "Maybe they'll let me have his testicles after his execution, do you think? They'd make an excellent addition to my scientific investigations."

Carl Rebers opened a small door that was concealed in a wall behind some fish tanks. He fidgeted with a light switch. Gas lights flamed to life and he dragged Leo inside. Leo's head lay tilted to one side so that he was only able to see part of the room. There were long tables holding cages with mice racing about wildly and squeaking; there were test tubes, a Bunsen burner, a centrifuge, a tray with gleaming scalpels. There were terrariums with small frogs; and two gray-haired capuchin monkeys screeched fearfully in their cages, rattling the metals bars. The images seemed to glide past Leo like pictures in a stereoscope.

His eye snagged on a framed yellowed photograph hanging off-kilter on the wall—the portrait of an older man with long, bushy sideburns; a stiff collar; and a stern expression. It looked somewhat out of place next to the test tubes.

"My father," explained Rebers as if he'd noticed Leo's glance. His tone was calm once more, as if he were chatting with Leo over a cup of tea. "Dr. Kurt Leonhard Rebers. You might have heard of him? He was a leading Viennese surgeon, a true philanthropist! Tough but fair, with his only son, too. I hung his picture here to remind myself why I'm doing all this work. Sometimes it feels as if he's watching over my shoulder as I work."

"Chrrr . . . ," went Leo. His tongue felt like a fat slug.

"What did you say?" Rebers lifted an eyebrow and turned to his victim on the floor. "You can see the resemblance? I don't know . . . I think I lack the masculine determination that defined him. Father always said I was mollycoddled. He was always trying to set me up with some young woman or other from a good family. But me, I . . . well, my interests lay elsewhere."

Carl Rebers straightened the picture and studied it for a long moment. When he spoke next, his voice sounded distant. "Lunacy took him practically overnight. It's a disease that's not uncommon in our family. He seemed to age all of a sudden, far too soon. Father was only fifty when his wit and his memory seeped away like water on dry soil. Toward the end, he'd swear at me, call me a stranger and an intruder. When it was me who cared for him all by myself, all this time! Me alone!"

Leo stared with a rigid gaze at the young assistant with the red hair, calling himself a fool. He had played with fire, marched naively into the presentation at the Museum of Art History and straight into the lion's den—and lost everything. Of all the men at the museum, he'd suspected Carl Rebers the least, in part because of his red hair. He had focused on Friedrich Knauer, simply forgetting his assistant. He had fallen for a black wig and a top hat, for cheap theater tricks.

And now the curtain falls, he thought.

Carl Rebers wiped a tear from the corner of his eye. "It's all been a little . . . much lately. Do you understand? You understand that, don't you? All that stabbing, violence, and cutting up. But someone had to take it upon themselves, in the name of science!"

"Chrrr," said Leo again, and Rebers nodded.

"You see! I knew you'd understand. You're an educated gentleman."

Leo's face remained impassive, but he could feel his strength return ever so slowly. He thought about how he would fight sleep paralysis growing up, focusing all his energy on one tiny movement. Lying on the floor now, Leo channeled all his strength into his left little finger. It felt as if he were moving a mountain. His forehead started to sweat.

Christ, you can do it! It's just a damned little finger . . .

The finger twitched.

Carl Rebers didn't notice. He was turning to the double-walled ice cupboard next to the test tubes. "My experiments haven't shown any positive results so far. I've been injecting only monkeys, rats, and rabbits. But I can tell that I'm this close to my big break!" He opened the cupboard door and a cool breeze brushed Leo's face. Rebers lifted out a metal box with a lid, about the size of a bread container. "My stores are nearly depleted. I only have four testicles on ice left. Hmm . . ." His expression turned thoughtful, and he eyed Leo with scientific interest.

"Oh, well. I think I'll take your testicles after all, if you don't mind. In the meantime, you can watch me puree and filter the others. It truly is highly interesting."

The noise of the Prater grew louder and louder as the fiacre neared the zoological garden. The nosy driver had tried his best to find out what connected the young woman with the strange older fellow dressed in black. But Augustin Rothmayer had put him off with a few snarled remarks, and refused to give him a tip as they disembarked.

The zoo was surrounded by a ten-foot wall. Even out here in the street Julia could smell the stench of animal urine. The tall gate between the two towers with stone lions was locked with a heavy chain. A few passersby walked past them toward the Prater, mostly couples and tipsy night owls. Julia slowed to a halt. She realized now that she hadn't thought about how to get into the zoo, let alone into the vivarium. Her fear for Leo blocked her logical thinking. Rothmayer seemed to notice her hesitation.

"Let's go see if the wall isn't a little lower over there," suggested the gravedigger, already walking off. Julia rushed to keep up. They turned off Laufenberger Lane down a smaller side street. In this section, the wall was topped with smooth bricks and built in curved sections, which was probably meant to look exotic. Barred holes like arrow slits allowed glimpses inside.

"There we go! It's not so bad here." Augustin Rothmayer stopped at a spot where the wall curved downward. He braced himself against the wall and knitted the fingers of both hands together. "Up you go, fräulein! I won't look up your skirt. This is how we young gravedigging apprentices used to go a-boozing across the cemetery wall."

"You used to get drunk among the dead?"

"Well, I liked to think the dead were glad that something was happening. And now go! What are you waiting for?"

Julia removed her shoes, placed them in her handbag with the revolver, and climbed up on Rothmayer. A musty smell emanated from him. She managed to heave herself onto the wall. From up here, she could see the many lights of the Wurstelprater in the distance. The zoo, on the other hand, was a black vastness, the handful of buildings as dark as the night—expect for one toward the back.

"The vivarium," whispered Julia. "There really is a light on there. You'd think the night watchman would notice."

"Not if young Rebers often works late at night," said Rothmayer. "And now pull me up before a copper comes by and arrests me!"

Julia reached down, and after a considerable amount of groaning and straining, Augustin Rothmayer too reached the top of the wall. Sharp glass shards protruded from the bricks in regular intervals.

"I wonder if they're there to keep people from getting in or to keep beasts from getting out?" pondered Rothmayer. "Hmm." He peered down. "I wonder what lives in the water down there?"

"Oh God . . ." Only now did Julia see that directly beneath them lay a small artificial lake. "That's why the wall is lower here."

"Well, then we'll have to swim, won't we," said Rothmayer and made to jump, clasping his floppy hat in both hands.

"You don't mean to—" But Rothmayer had already jumped, feet first. There was a splash, and after a while, the gravedigger's head emerged in the dark water.

"It's not that cold. Just a lot of weeds. And something just brushed past me. Bah, I'm sure it won't be no crocodile." He waved at her. "Are you coming? Or would you like me to organize a pleasure boat for our night-time outing?"

Julia knew the crocodiles were housed in the vivarium. But what about nasty hippos? Slimy monster snakes? And weren't there things like piranhas . . . ?

She closed her eyes, squeezed her nose shut, and jumped, holding her handbag above her head. The water was indeed not as cold as expected, probably because the lake was quite shallow. Julia's naked feet struck algae and mud. There was a splash nearby and she thought she could see a shape in the water.

A shape that swiftly moved toward her.

Julia screamed, paddled, and kicked wildly. She desperately clutched some reeds and pulled herself up the muddy bank. When she looked back, she saw a swan swimming in slow circles.

"Oh well, almost a lake monster," said Rothmayer, sitting on a bench by the side of the lake. With a grin he donned his dripping hat. "Only, white and with wings."

"Hilarious." Julia wrung her wet hair. She was shivering with cold, fury, and embarrassment. "Whose incredibly stupid idea was it to break into the zoo across the wall?" But then she remembered the lights at the vivarium and Leo, probably in grave danger inside it, if he was even still alive. "Let's agree to avoid lakes, lion's cages, and bear enclosures from now on, all right?" She slipped back into her shoes, shouldered her handbag, and marched ahead.

They moved silently across the zoological garden, sticking to smaller paths, watchful of possible night watchmen as they passed different cages, enclosures, and kennels. Julia felt as if all the animals were watching her distrustfully. There were sounds of rustling, hissing, and squeaking, and, from the nearby elephant house, deafening trumpeting. Julia felt as if she were navigating her way through a vast, clamoring jungle. She wondered how the Matabele ever got any sleep, what with all the noise.

The vivarium shone like a candle in the dark, making it easy for them to locate. Julia remembered her visit less than a week ago. That day, Carl Rebers had probably saved her daughter's life—and now she was chasing him as a serial killer.

Maybe as Leo's killer, too . . .

"Look," said Augustin Rothmayer quietly, pointing straight ahead. "The door to the vivarium is open a crack. Ha, and there's the wagon! I was right." He pointed at a filthy cart that was parked among bushes; a horse grazed peacefully beside it.

"Looks like a normal Viennese garbage cart," whispered Julia. "What is it doing at the zoo?" She walked over to it and looked inside. She flinched, nauseous, and had to hang on to the side of the wagon.

So, that's how he did it! Good God . . .

"What's inside?" asked Rothmayer.

"I'll tell you later. Quickly now, we must find Leo!"

Julia had already rushed to the vivarium's door and was pushing it open. What she had seen inside the wagon mobilized new strength inside her. Fear gave way to boundless fury. Julia knew: the only way to keep her fear at bay was to act. Now! Or else her imagination would overwhelm her.

Saws, pincers, knives, scalpels . . . Leo, where are you? What has he done to you?

Trembling, she pulled the small revolver out of the handbag and held it out in front of her, arms straight. A handful of gas lamps glowed dully down the corridors and in rooms.

"Do you even know how to operate one of those?" whispered Rothmayer.

"Well, I assume you squeeze the trigger. Can't be that hard. I—"

There was a scream and Julia nearly dropped the gun. It took her a moment to realize it was the screech of a monkey.

"That came from the hall down to the right," she said. "Where the crocodiles are." She remembered a door by the crocodile enclosure—Rebers had emerged from that door the first time she saw him. Hadn't he spoken about a laboratory? "Quick!" she called out.

She was running down the corridor, revolver raised in front of her, when another scream rang out.

Carl Rebers picked up a slender dagger from a table and walked over to Leo, who was still lying rigidly on the floor.

"I'm ready now," said Rebers. "First, I'll cut you out of your clothing, keep things tidy. Lovely suit, by the way. Wholly unsuitable for laboratory work, of course."

Leo gave a small twitch. The past hour he'd watched Rebers at work. The last two murder victims' testicles had been chopped up finely and then ground up in a kind of mill. Then Rebers mixed the whiteish pulp with a liquid. Other ingredients went in, too, but Leo hadn't been able to make them out. Lastly, Rebers had filled several ampules and placed them on a silver tray as if they were precious jewels. The pair of capuchin monkeys nervously rattled their cage bars and cackled throughout. Leo couldn't tell whether they cackled with fear or mockery.

"Once I've processed your testicles, I'll start one last series of experiments with the monkeys, rats, and rabbits." Rebers tested the dagger's edge with his fingertip. "And humans, too, at the end, of course. I'm sure many of the elderly gentlemen from the archaeological society will be only too glad to volunteer. What did you think of Knauer's talk on the subject of eternal youth in ancient Egypt tonight? I've always found his research inspiring. He has no idea, of course, about the research I'm conducting here in the laboratory. This here is my realm! A realm of science, based on research and experiments. No dumb dressage or ethnic shows for the masses."

Rebers placed the scalpel and, with one swift move, cut open Leo's shirt right down to his pants. Another cut undid his belt and pant buttons.

"We were this close once before, inspector," said Rebers tenderly. "Remember? It was down in the sewers. A shame that our second meeting must come to such an abrupt ending. He brushed the dagger gently across Leo's naked chest. "I recognized you right away at the museum tonight. I knew you were on to me. I had to act, you see? Even if it was hard for me . . ." The stiletto moved toward Leo's groin. "I will take your testicles while you're alive. Fresher that way. I think you won't feel much, thanks to the poison. It'll only hurt a little. So, take a deep breath in and—"

Leo's hand shot forward and clasped Rebers's fist holding the scalpel. The poison's effect had abated sufficiently in the past hour for him to make simple movements. Practice from his childhood and youth had helped.

First just a knuckle, then a finger, then the whole hand . . .

Rebers was too surprised to defend himself at first. He knelt above Leo, frozen just like his victim, like an evil mirror image, their hands knotted, the scalpel just an inch or two away from Leo's crotch.

"This . . . this is astonishing," gasped Rebers eventually. "Your body appears to be younger and more resilient than I'd thought. Outstanding research material." His left hand clutched Leo's throat and started to squeeze, while his right hand still pushed down on the scalpel. Leo felt himself run low on air. He still couldn't move his torso. The scalpel's point bored through the fabric of his pants.

"You don't have to fight it," urged Rebers, loosening his grip on Leo's throat. "Just let it happen! What is the death of a single person if it serves the entirety of humanity? Eternal youth . . ."

A long, low scream rose from Leo's throat as if his vocal cords had only just been released. Rebers broke off. Leo used the moment of surprise to command all his muscles to throw himself to the left.

Come on . . . If you let me down now, I'll never need you again!

And finally he was able to move again—not much, but enough to unbalance Rebers, forcing him to let go, flail his arms, and grab the edge of the table where the syringes sat on the tray. With a loud crash, the tray of syringes landed on the ground. Rebers turned away from Leo and groaned with dismay, collecting the syringes like a morphine addict hunting for his next injection.

"What are you doing?" he cried. "What a waste!"

Leo crawled away from Rebers on all fours, as slow as a tortoise. Once Rebers had gathered up all his syringes, he picked up the scalpel once more. He threw himself at Leo and sank the blade into his back. Despite the poison, Leo felt pain and roared with fear and rage. He kept crawling until he collapsed.

So this is how it ends, thought Leo.

"I will feed you to the crocodiles," gasped Rebers. "You don't deserve anything else." He pulled the scalpel out of Leo's back, preparing to strike again. "I was mistaken about you. You foolish, self-indulgent—"

In that moment, a shot split the air. Test tubes and syringes shattered. Rebers cried out and let go of Leo.

When Leo lifted his head with some difficulty, he saw Julia standing in the laboratory, her hair wet, a revolver in her hands. And behind her, the gravedigger, holding his ears.

A hallucination, thought Leo. *I must be hallucinating . . .*

Shooting a gun, so Julia had just learned, wasn't so difficult. It was hitting the target that was the hard part. Her shot had blown some test tubes and syringes off the table, and the kickback had been so hard she nearly dropped the gun.

Within a split second, she took in details of the room: cackling monkeys in cages, Leo's oddly frozen expression, scientific tools, squeaking rats, blood on the floor, and syringes, some of them broken. Then there were the eyes of Carl Rebers, wide with madness, in his hand a scalpel.

"Drop the knife!" yelled Julia. "Right now, or else I shoot!" She didn't know where the strength for this command came from. Her eyes darted between Rebers and Leo. Now she noticed a dark stain spreading on Leo's shoulder.

Carl Rebers brought the scalpel down again.

"Stop!" Julia squeezed the trigger again. This time she hit the freezer next to Rebers, decorating it with a black-rimmed hole. Carl Rebers left Leo's side and instead ran at Julia, scalpel in hand. Just then something flew past Julia. It was a glass balloon that shattered against Rebers' head. Its liquid contents streamed down his face. Rebers roared with pain and dropped the scalpel. He rolled on the ground, rubbing his eyes.

"Water!" he cried. "I—I'm burning!" He struggled to his feet and staggered down the side of the room, hanging onto the edge of the table as he neared the door.

"Go after the madman!" shouted Julia in Rothmayer's direction. She still aimed the revolver at Rebers. "I'll check on Leo!"

"I know what to do with blood and wounds better than you," replied the gravedigger with astonishing calmness. "If you dress wounds as well as you shoot, the inspector's done for." He nodded at the door. "I doubt he's going to get far. If I read correctly, that flagon contained nitric acid."

"Water, water!" cried Rebers again. He had staggered out the door and into the reptiles hall. "Oh God, what—" Suddenly, they heard something shatter loudly, followed by a splash.

Then there was silence.

"Well, seems he's found his water in the end," said Rothmayer into the silence.

The screaming that started up moments later was almost not human. It crescendoed to an utterly tormented roaring and screeching.

"Jesus, Mary, and Josef, what . . . what is going on?" asked Julia, only to answer her own question. "The crocodiles! He fell into the crocodile pond."

She remembered how Carl Rebers saved her precious daughter from the very same crocodiles just a few days ago. After a moment's hesitation she ran outside with her weapon. The heavy glass pane to the crocodile enclosure lay shattered. The pond beyond was blood red and alive with bubbling and gurgling. Occasionally Julia caught glimpses of wide-open jaws, a mangled hand, scraps of clothing, a shoe with a bloodied foot inside, and dark-green, leathery skin . . .

The screaming stopped. The troubled water gradually calmed. The longish dark shadows were down low in the water now, the ancient predators dragging away their prey.

Standing on the stones in the middle of the enclosure was a man.

In the dim light of the emergency lighting, Julia couldn't make him out at first. For a brief moment she thought Rebers had returned as a spirit, but this man was much taller and more muscular. He seemed like a stone monument, standing perfectly still. Then he raised a hand in a silent greeting.

"Saidrovuni," breathed Julia. She lowered her revolver. "What are you doing here?" she called out.

Saidrovuni was dressed in a shirt and pants that were too small for him. Julia recognized them as Leo's clothes, the ones he kept in her room at the Dragoon. The chief was barefoot, his shirt wet and only halfway buttoned up; he was trembling, possibly still from a fever.

"The *Asanbosam* took the fire head," said Saidrovuni in a low voice. "His just punishment. His soul may never return to his people."

"Christ, did you walk the whole way here from Neulerchenfeld?" asked Julia. "That's madness! You're ill—"

"My family," said Saidrovuni tiredly. "I had to check on my family. But then I heard screaming from the vivarium. I came here. The fire head saw me, or maybe he didn't. Maybe he saw the demon. He ran away from me, jumped through the glass . . . He was crazed with fear."

The water was perfectly calm now. The huge Nile crocodiles, more than three yards in length, had returned to their resting spots on the large rocks at the outer edge on the pond. A few scraps of fabric floated on the surface.

"It was the firehead who killed the young keeper. Umlilo ikhanda."

Saidrovuni nodded. "I know now. My wife saw him in our hut. He hid the keys there. Evil man."

"Now he's dead," replied Julia with one last glance at the crocodiles and the scraps of clothing. She shivered. "Chopped to bits just like his victims." She winced. "Leo! I must get back." She raced back to the laboratory, Saidrovuni following.

Augustin Rothmayer had removed Leo's shirt by now and examined his wounds. Using strips from Leo's cut-up pants, he had bandaged his back.

"So?" asked Julia anxiously.

"I've seen many stab wounds lately, but—" began Rothmayer.

"Oh my God." Julia clung to one of the tables. "Leo!" She couldn't hold back the tears.

"Christ, let me finish first! On the victims, the stab wounds were much deeper. Here the scalpel only went in an inch or so. Still, the herr inspector is losing a lot of blood. And Rebers seems to have poisoned him with something devilish, though the effect seems to be waning. We should get a doctor as soon as—" Rothmayer broke off when he noticed Saidrovuni. The tall chief had just entered the laboratory.

"Jeepers, what's the savage doing here?" growled Rothmayer. "Did he eat Rebers in the end?"

"The crocodiles took care of that," said Julia. "Herr Saidrovuni is a friend. I already told you about him. But the police mustn't find out about him. The whole business is a little . . . well, complicated." She considered. "May I ask a favor of you, Herr Rothmayer? One last one?"

The gravedigger studied Saidrovuni in silence for a few moments. "You haven't forgotten about our deal, have you, Fräulein Wolf?" he said at last.

"I haven't, Herr Rothmayer. I know how much you've helped me already. Please?"

"Who could deny you anything, with that doe-eyed look?" Rothmayer sighed and spread his long, spidery arms. "Well, out with it."

"Please escort Herr Saidrovuni back to the Dragoon. With his wife and children. You'll find them at the Matabele village here at the zoo. I'm sure a man like you knows ways of making sure the driver keeps word about his unusual passengers to himself. And send my regards to Elli. Tell her I . . . I will honor my promise in the next few days. In return she's to take Saidrovuni's family in, just for a short while."

"Hmm." Rothmayer frowned, but then his pale face broke into a grin. "Oh, what the heck? A bunch of savages and me through the Vienna night . . . Anna is going to love this story tomorrow." He turned to Saidrovuni. "Well, why don't you go ahead and show me where you live in here. Perhaps we can find some decent clothes for you, too, Herr Saidruthingy. No need to frighten our poor fiacre driver more than absolutely necessary. He's probably never even seen Africans before."

Saidrovuni shot Julia a questioning look.

"You can trust him," said Julia. "He's a gravedigger, but he cares for the living. No matter their skin color."

"I'll take that as a compliment," said Rothmayer. He tipped his hat. "Take care, fräulein. And give my regards to our herr inspector when he comes to. German weeds are hard to kill."

Together with Saidrovuni, the gravedigger left the laboratory. Their footsteps crunched on broken glass. Augustin Rothmayer stamped another full syringe on his way out.

Julia bent down to Leo and stroked his cheek. He opened his eyes and gave a lopsided smile, the numbness not entirely worn off.

"Youff godda learn to shoof," he slurred. "No free yards away ann missed . . ."

Julia gave an involuntary smirk. "Look who's talking! Which of us is meant to be the cop?" She rose. "There must be a telephone here somewhere. I'll call a doctor and inspector Loibl. He needs to come here with a few men and see all this. I guess we've solved the case."

"Nof quite yet," said Leo. "Nof . . . quite . . . yet . . ."

Julia gave him a puzzled look, but Leo's eyes had closed once more.

She couldn't tell if he was sleeping or merely thinking very hard.

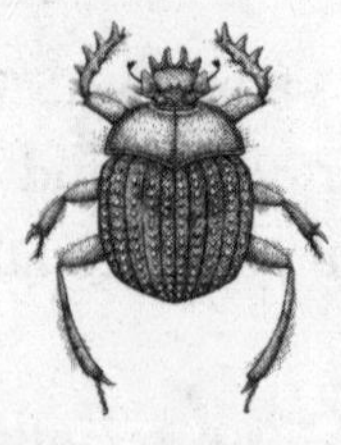

CHAPTER 25

Four days later

Leo lay in his bed, staring at the ceiling, where the nicotine-yellow stucco formed an unholy alliance with the flowery wallpaper. He sat up with some difficulty, groaning as he fumbled for the cigarettes on his nightstand. His back hurt as if he was being poked with glowing needles. Smoking helped him forget about the pain a little bit. He lit one of his beloved Yenidzes, the fourth that morning, and listened to Frau Rinsinger's footsteps. She was dusting the paintings in the hallway while belting out an aria from some operetta.

Leo had been on bedrest for days now. At least he'd been allowed to leave the general hospital the day before, Sunday. Julia had accompanied him home to Lange Lane and supplied him with all the necessities: cigarettes, cured sausage, schnapps, and candy. They both knew that Frau Rinsinger would put him on a strict and meager diet. The stash she'd brought him was well hidden under his bed.

Thankfully, the stab wounds Carl Rebers had inflicted with the scalpel weren't deep. They just hurt like hell. Worse were the aftereffects of the poison, which still hadn't entirely worn off—his feet were numb and his hands tingled—but with each day they got a little better. During a visit to the hospital, Professor Hofmann had said that it was probably a rare and little studied form of the curare poison, and that Leo ought to consider himself lucky that he was alive at all. "You're a joy to science," Hofmann had said. "You'll probably make it into some textbook or other. Congratulations!"

Since then, Leo had been lying here, thinking. He'd asked Erich Loibl to make a few phone calls, and Professor Hofmann, too, had done him a couple of favors. Leo hated to be this helpless. But at least all his mulling had reached a result. The small notebook lying next to the cigarettes on his nightstand was completely full of scribbled notes. Its contents were as astonishing as they were obvious.

Leo smiled. Sometimes it helped being forced to lie in bed, having the time to sort one's thoughts.

Maybe we should make a habit of it at the Vienna police station, he mused.

The doorbell rang. Frau Rinsinger paused her aria to open the door. Leo listened. Judging by the deep murmuring, it wasn't Julia coming to visit. She said she'd come by this afternoon. So, who could it be?

When there was a knock on his door, he quickly extinguished his cigarette and hid the ashtray under his bed next to the cured sausage. "Yes?" he called out.

"Herr von Herzfeldt, you have visitors," said Frau Rinsinger. "Uh, two gentlemen from the police."

Leo flinched. Could they have found out that he was behind Saidrovuni's escape from prison? He drew a deep breath.

"Send them in," he said.

The door opened and in came Erich Loibl and Paul Leinkirchner. Leinkirchner was clutching a bottle of brandy with a red bow, while Loibl awkwardly carried a box of candy.

Leo's jaw dropped with amazement.

"I told the gentlemen repeatedly that you cannot drink alcohol at the moment. I consider sweets inappropriate also, and—" Frau Rinsinger lifted an eyebrow, sniffing. "Herr von Herzfeldt, you smoked again!" She strode to the window, yanked open the curtains, and opened up the window. "Do you even want to get better, huh?"

"Would you mind leaving us alone with our colleague, please?" said Paul Leinkirchner in his usual blunt manner. "We have things to discuss."

Frau Rinsinger obeyed, leaving the room in obstinate silence. When the door closed, Leinkirchner gave a wide grin.

"An even greater dragon than my wife. Congratulations, Herzfeldt." He looked around the small, smoky room. "Well, well, so this is how our herr baron lives. The grandeur, practically imperial . . ."

"I would offer you two chairs," said Leo, still unable to gauge what this visit was for. "But I only own one."

Erich Loibl gave a wave. "We sit too much at work anyway. Today alone, we spent the whole morning sitting in superintendent Stukart's office for the closing briefing." He gestured at the bottle of cognac in Leinkirchner's hands. "That was Stukart's idea. However, someone else thought of it first . . ." With a grin, Loibl pulled another bottle out from under his coat. It was whiskey, the bottle scratched and dirty. "You remember this one? Greetings from Yurek, the leader of the kanalstrotters. He wishes to thank you for catching the phantom. Oh, and the sweets are for Fräulein Wolf. Handpicked by Stukart. He asked for her to get in touch with him. He'd like to discuss her possible return to the police."

"Indeed?" Leo tried not to let them see how pleased he felt. It would seem Julia's heroic action at the zoological garden had impressed the superintendent, too. "And why are you coming to me with this?"

"Well, you and Fräulein Wolf . . . ," Loibl stammered sheepishly. "We thought perhaps you see her from time to time. You know, after everything that happened at the vivarium."

"Possible," replied Leo curtly. He looked at Paul Leinkirchner. "How's the leg?"

"Probably better than your back." Leinkirchner grunted. "I'm back at work as of this morning. And for my first task, Stukart sent me here to thank you in the name of the entire Vienna police force. As if I were some kind of errand boy." He plunked the bottle on the nightstand. "Well, enjoy!"

"I'll drink to your health and wish you a mazel tov." Leo failed to stifle a grin. "Are you saying the case is closed?"

"It is." Loibl nodded. "We found notes in Carl Rebers's apartment that prove his crimes. Then we have the list of books from the court library, those horrendous remains at the laboratory, not to mention the garbage cart turned butchery at the zoological garden. Rebers is our man. Congratulations, Herzfeldt! Now, we're keen to hear how you figured it out. The superintendent awaits your report."

Leo hesitated. After Julia had telephoned the doctor and the police, the constables had secured the evidence from Rebers's labarotory in the vivarium: syringes with their macabre contents, his few remains, and the terrible contents of the garbage cart. He and Julia agreed to tell the detectives a slightly adjusted version of events. According to their version, Leo had visited the vivarium at night to question Rebers. The latter took him by surprise and injected him with the poison. Julia had worried about Leo and followed him to the vivarium, where the final confrontation had taken place. The police would learn nothing of Rothmayer's presence, nor of Saidrovuni's.

"You can count your lucky stars that you're alive," said Loibl, shaking his head. "Why didn't you take me or another colleague along to the vivarium?"

"I was only going ask Rebers some questions," replied Leo. "I'd received an anonymous tip-off from the court library and wanted to get to the bottom of it. When I got there, I caught Rebers red-handed."

"Red-handed, uh-huh." Leinkirchner seemed unconvinced. He studied Leo closely. "And what about that gravedigger? Professor Hofmann told us the old codger called him up because he noticed something about the young keeper's body."

"Um, yes, that's true," admitted Leo. "That was my second lead. I know Herr Rothmayer a little. When he told me that young Stefan Moser was castrated before his death in the lion's cage, my suspicion grew firmer. Although I must admit that at first I suspected director Friedrich Carl Knauer," he added with a shrug. "Tailcoat, top hat, black hair—everything seemed to fit. And then his talk about eternal life . . ."

"All evidence leads to the zoological garden, I understand." Loibl nodded grimly. "So that chief is innocent, after all. But then why did he escape from prison? We still don't know who helped him. And apparently, now his entire family has vanished from the zoo! The whole story is growing more mysterious by the day."

Leo said nothing, gazing out the window where a few clouds drifted across the otherwise blue May sky.

"Well, at least the hustler murders are solved," said Leinkirchner after a while. "I can't stand drafts of wind. I'll catch my death with all that air." He stamped over to the window and shut it. Then he opened the bottle of whiskey from the kanalstrotters and looked around for glasses. He found some on a dusty shelf and poured for himself, Loibl, and Leo. He raised his glass in a toast. "To keeping your balls!"

The men drank and sat in silence. Leo noticed that Loibl set his glass aside almost immediately. Apparently the effect from his reconciliation with his wife was lasting, at least for now.

"We still don't know how many victims Rebers is accountable for," said Leinkirchner after a while, studying the amber liquid in his glass. "And since the crocodiles ate him, we'll probably never know. But at least now we know how he did it." He took a long sip then shuddered. "A mobile butcher's shop, God, how sick! And all of it just to find the secret of eternal youth. By the way, Professor Hofmann reckoned that there might actually be something to Rebers's research. Something to do with glands—I didn't really get it. Never mind." He drank again before turning to Leo. "Even if I don't believe everything you've told us—still, you've solved the case, Herzfeldt. And for that you deserve our gratitude."

Leo sipped the potent liquid. It wasn't all that bad for whiskey from the sewers. Then he said: "Well, I believe the case isn't solved entirely yet."

"Not solved yet?" Leinkirchner almost choked. "Bloody hell, what do you mean?"

"The hustler murders are solved," replied Leo. "But there's still a fat knot of unanswered questions. And I spent the last few days unraveling this tangle."

"Do those telephone calls I made for you have anything to do with it?" asked Loibl.

"Yes, that's right." Leo nodded. "I suggest we top up our glasses and then I'll tell you what I've come up with. And then it's up to you to decide what we'll do next."

"Herzfeldt, Herzfeldt." Leinkirchner pulled out one of his fat cigars and lit it. "You sure can be annoying as hell. But at least you're always good for a surprise."

Smoke filled the small room and the three men disappeared inside its fumes.

Blue lampions flickered in the dark of night when Leo stepped out of a fiacre in Hietzing almost two weeks later. On account of the occasion, he wore a top hat instead of his usual homburg. The elegant hat went perfectly with his velvety black tailcoat and starched white shirt. Leo tipped the driver generously and rang the bell on the garden gate of Villa Thebes.

A string quartet was playing a soft waltz inside the house; small groups of people stood gathered in the garden among the pyramid and Egyptian statues, sipping from flutes of champagne and conversing in low voices. It was Charlotte Rapoldy herself who opened the sphinx-guarded gate, inviting Leo into the garden.

“Herr Inspector, what a pleasure to see you!” Smiling, she held out her hand for a kiss. “And congratulations again on solving that ghastly case. The papers have been singing your praises. You’re famous!” She dropped her voice. “Speaking of, if I may pass on His Excellency the archduke’s regards, too. He is impressed with your work and eager to meet you in person one day. Unfortunately that can’t be here, in public, as I’m sure you’ll understand.”

“Well, tonight I’m neither famous nor an inspector,” replied Leo, breathing a kiss on Charlotte’s hand. “Just a friend of Egyptology.”

His hostess smelled strongly of some exotic, probably very expensive perfume. She wore the silver tiara with the scarab and a flowing, tan costume with so many layers of fabric that it rustled with each movement. Her unconventional beauty shone like one of the lampions.

"Well put, Herr von Herzfeldt," she said. "We are all looking forward to your presentation. Come, I'll introduce you to our guests."

"Too kind, madam." Leo followed Charlotte through the garden, stopping here and there to chat with guests. Leo could feel approval in the looks of the guests, who now knew his real profession. Leo's dangerous, almost deadly mission at the zoological garden's vivarium was still a popular topic of conversation in Vienna, just like his spectacular rescue by a young woman. The papers had come up with a few heart-rending illustrations of him and Julia, and the police president personally praised them, offering Julia her job as crime-scene photographer back. Carl Rebers's macabre research served as a grim reminder of where madness could take a scientist—even if some Vienna doctors were unwilling to discount his theories.

Leo sipped his champagne. Clemens Rapoldy was in conversation with Alexander Dedekind, the curator of the Egypto-Oriental Collection at the Museum of Art History, and several older gentlemen in top hats and tailcoats, whom Leo recognized from Knauer's talk at the museum. They all stood near the sarcophagus; daffodils bloomed inside it. Knauer himself was just heading toward Leo and Charlotte from across the terrace.

The director of the zoological garden shook Leo's hand with a serious expression. "Herr Inspector, I owe you a debt of gratitude. Who could have guessed—Rebers, behind my back . . ." Knauer trailed off and sighed. "What lunacy! And it was I who introduced him to this venerable society. Eternal life!"

"I suspect it was Fritz's talk last year that gave Rebers the idea," said Charlotte Rapoldy thoughtfully. "The Egyptian god Thot is said to have had an elixir of life, and many ancient priests searched for its formula. Among them was Ta-bek-en-chon, the priest my father was so fascinated by."

"In any case." Knauer shook his head. "Carl Rebers thoroughly misunderstood the spirit of ancient Egypt. If only I'd realized sooner—"

"It's not your fault," said Leo. "It seems Rebers revered his father, and he was deeply affected by his loss from dementia. None of us noticed Rebers's madness—you can't see inside a person's head."

Leo thought about how Julia had first suspected keeper Eugen Lenz because of some secret he shared with Knauer. That, too, had been cleared up.

"I hear Eugen Lenz no longer works at the zoo," said Leo casually. "What the newspapers wrote, about the rape of a Matabele woman . . . ?"

"Is utter nonsense, of course," said Knauer, finishing Leo's sentence. "But I deemed it better to . . . uh, take old Lenz out of the line of fire, so to speak."

"I understand." Leo nodded, smirking inwardly. The papers had received an anonymous tip-off, claiming Eugen Lenz had raped one of the Matabele women. Saidrovuni must have known of it—perhaps the tip-off even came from him. So, that had been the secret that mustn't get out, for the good of the zoo . . .

"Let's not speak of such things," said Charlotte Rapoldy. "I don't want to hear any more horror stories today." She winked at Leo. "Stop torturing us already. What's the subject of your talk?"

Leo smiled enigmatically. "Allow yourself to be surprised, madam. I believe I've chosen a subject that is as instructive as it is entertaining."

Leo had telephoned the Rapoldys just two days prior, asking to become a member of the archaeological society. Tonight's "ball of pharaohs" was an excellent opportunity. The legendary event—the highlight of the society's annual program—always took place in mid-June at Villa Thebes. For the first time, the host wasn't Alfons Strössner, but his daughter Charlotte. Customarily the event included a presentation on a topic of Egyptology by one of the society's members, and Leo had volunteered. He hadn't yet specified what he would discuss, though.

Clemens Rapoldy, the only person dressed in white linen, approached the small group, leaning on his cane. He greeted Leo with a warm nod. "Herr von Herzfeldt, are you ready? I'll ask everyone to the library."

"Thank you. I'll keep it brief," said Leo. "I hear your wife is going to sing later?"

Charlotte chuckled nervously and adjusted her tiara. "Don't expect too much, inspector. Clemens will accompany me on the piano. The guests only tolerate it because we're the hosts."

Together they all entered the villa from the terrace and walked to the library, where chairs had been set up among the shelves. Those who didn't get a seat downstairs spilled into the gallery. Both rooms were illuminated brightly by many gas lamps. A lectern adorned with old Egyptian carvings and two dog heads had been set up for Leo, who sorted his notes and waited for everyone to find a spot.

He let his gaze travel from face to face one more time. There were about two dozen guests, most of them older men. Like in the museum, the Rapoldys and Dr. Dedekind were seated in the front row. Next to them sat director Friedrich Knauer, and even Professor Hofmann had come at the last minute. He shot Leo a brief look. Hofmann was the only one among the guests who knew what was about to happen. They had planned everything carefully.

The grand finale, thought Leo. *The staging is just perfect.*

He cleared his throat.

"Dear gentlemen, most venerable hostess." He nodded at Charlotte Rapoldy. "It is a great privilege to speak here before this illustrious circle. I thought hard about what I might speak about.

In the end, I decided on a subject that ties in nicely with my profession. The topic is justice in ancient Egypt."

Approving murmurs bubbled up. This topic had never been discussed before. Leo had specially referenced some books from the court library.

"Even ancient Egypt had police officers," he began. "They were called *medjay*. Originally, they were apparently nomads from the Sahara Desert, hired as mercenaries. It is possible that they spoke a different dialect, and therefore the general public may have been prejudiced against them." He winked. "You see, there are similarities to myself—the *medjay* were the Prussians of ancient Egypt."

There were a few laughs, and Leo went on: "Punishments in the Egyptian justice system were more brutal by far compared with those of today, ranging from lashings to burning and staking. Murder and grave robbery were considered the worst crimes. Fraud was also severely punished. Let's try to imagine the punishment for a grave robber and murderer who is a fraud at the same time! Perhaps they would have boiled such a person in oil. I haven't been able to find any such cases from ancient Egypt. But I do know of a contemporary case, and that's what I'd like to tell you about tonight."

The guests stared blankly at Leo. They probably expected him to make his way back to his original topic. But he didn't. Leo pushed aside his notes and looked at those in the front row one by one: beautiful Charlotte Rapoldy with her tiara; her husband, Clemens Rapoldy, frail with his cane; Professor Eduard Hofmann, and, next to him, thin Dr. Dedekind and tall Friedrich Knauer.

"There is one person in this room who has committed all these crimes," said Leo. "They concealed their dastardly deeds well, for many years. But today is the day of reckoning—the day of the *medjay*." He paused, looking sharply at a certain person in the room. The person gave the smallest twitch of the lashes, but otherwise remained perfectly calm, as if none of this concerned them.

No wonder you managed to get away with it for so long, thought Leo. *You even managed to fool your loved ones. . . .*

"You've been told that Professor Strössner died of a tropical disease," went on Leo. "But that's not true. He was poisoned."

"What are you doing?" interjected Charlotte Rapoldy. She looked angry and worried. "We agreed to keep this matter—"

"Poisoned," pressed on Leo. "Even though the killer tried to pin the blame on someone else. They hoped to get rid of two people all at once—two people who stood in the way of a golden future. Money, treasures of immeasurable value, and, in the end, this villa, too." He paused for a moment, his eye on a certain person in the front row. "It would all have been yours, doctor Clemens Rapoldy. Or should I say: Clemens *Carpati*?"

For a moment, icy silence filled the room. Then Clemens Rapoldy leaped up from his chair, angrily and surprisingly swiftly considering his handicap. "How dare you?" he snarled at Leo. "The cheek of it! And under our very own roof!"

"Clemens, calm yourself," said Charlotte. She pulled her husband back into his seat. "It's nothing but a poor joke." She turned to Leo. "Am I right, Herr Inspector? A silly joke as part of your presentation?"

"Unfortunately not, Frau Rapoldy," replied Leo. "It's the gruesome truth. Your husband is a wanted con artist. I've been making inquiries in the last few days and weeks. Clemens is his real first name, but he's had many last names. He has operated as a marriage fraudster in numerous countries—we've traced him across Europe. His true name is Carpati, and he's a murderer."

The guests began to mutter and cough nervously.

"What an incredible load of bollocks!" jeered Clemens Rapoldy.

"What are you on about? You're making an absolute fool of yourself! Where is your proof?"

"All in good time. Let me first tell you how I figured it all out, Herr *Doctor*." Leo's eyes flashed. "I first became suspicious of you following our very first meeting here at the villa. As a so-called doctor you spoke of your father-in-law's diabetes. What you couldn't have known was that my mother also suffers from diabetes. And so I know my way around the medical terminology a little bit. What you were spouting back then was complete rubbish. Diabetes melater . . . pancreatic disease . . . nothing but nonsensical jargon! I thought I might have misheard. But then you boasted about a miracle medicine, diabezerin. I asked around, and no such medicine exists. That's probably how you sold yourself to Charlotte, as a doctor and kind friend who would care for her father and inject him with some kind of expensive placebo. You met Charlotte in Cairo and immediately smelled wealth. You played your role perfectly, not just then but also later on, as the grieving son-in-law coming to identify the body at the forensic institute. I almost bought your performance—but only almost."

"Clemens, what . . . what is the inspector talking about?" Charlotte looked with horror at her husband, who was sitting with his arms folded and lips pressed into a thin line.

"It made sense, then, that it was you who thought up the trick with the *laterna magica*," said Leo. "I'm guessing you've used this trick before. To Charlotte, you sold it as a kind of self-defense. When I figured it out, though, you were forced to give away more of yourself than you'd planned. You told me about the unfortunate switch of the ampules. In a moment of absentmindedness your wife supposedly mixed up the two, the medicine and the Strophanthus toxin that your father-in-law was working on. But that's not true! Charlotte couldn't understand how the mix-up could have happened to her. What she didn't know: you swapped the two ampules beforehand. Because you intended for Charlotte to inject her father with the deadly poison! She probably would have gone to prison for manslaughter, and you would have inherited everything. You would have been a rich man . . ."

Leo paused, shooting a straight look at Clemens Rapoldy—now revealed as Clemens Carpati. The man's facade held.

"The old professor messed up your plan, though," went on Leo. "He didn't die promptly of the poison, but instead asked for his body to vanish as a mummy. That's when your troubles started—everything turned much more complicated. How were you to ignore the wishes of the man your wife loved more than anything?"

"Are you drunk, man?" Clemens Rapoldy shook his head, laughing. "Where do you get your stories from?" He turned to his guests, who were listening as if turned to stone. "The man's drunk! Please forgive him."

"I won't mind raising a glass after your arrest," countered Leo. "Let me finish my story first. We don't want to keep the honorable guests waiting for too long." He tapped his pencil against one of the dog heads on the lectern. In the front row, Charlotte Rapoldy, Dr. Dedekind, and director Knauer watched with obvious confusion. Professor Hofmann alone smiled knowingly.

"You had it all planned out meticulously," said Leo. "Even during your honeymoon you sold tomb treasures to dealers in Egypt without the knowledge of your father-in-law. But someone else caught onto you: Father Gregor Mayr, who was part of the expedition. Maybe Professor Walter Kerfeld did too, or at least he had a hunch. I haven't yet determined whether the fourth member of the expedition, Dr. Adolf Landinger, died of natural causes or whether he was another one of your victims. Not so with Mayr and Kerfeld, however. A while ago, I received a telegram from Graz. It wasn't easy to locate the doctor who'd issued Father

Mayr's death certificate. But a, uh, close friend of mine made inquiries and found him in the end. That doctor had a certain suspicion with regard to Mayr's cause of death. It would seem Father Gregor died of a poisoned rosary."

"A poisoned rosary?" Rapoldy sneered. "Your talk grows more bizarre by the minute."

"So-called paternoster peas contain a deadly toxin," Leo went on. "The red-and-black peas really do look like the pearls of a rosary. When they are pierced and threaded onto string, they can transfer their poison onto the hand and from there into the mouth. Mayr, who already had a weak heart, was known to kiss his rosary as he prayed, as a symbol of humility. The rosary was a gift from an unknown friend of the church, and it reached Mayr together with a letter. The letter has been forwarded to me, and it is in your hand, Clemens Carpati."

"How do you claim to know this?" asked Clemens defiantly.

"Because I am in possession of a writing sample of yours." Leo smiled. "Remember? You wrote to the police president to complain about my investigation. The hand is clearly the same."

For the first time, Clemens Rapoldy looked a little rattled. He nervously reached for his stiff collar and loosened it. "That doesn't prove anything," he declared. "Writing samples—that's modern humbug."

"The letters alone may not be sufficient. But that changes when there is a description of the culprit. And we have one for the murder of Professor Kerfeld."

Rapoldy laughed. "You want to pin that one on me, too?"

"Kerfeld had found you out," Leo went on, unfazed. "He hinted as much. First when I visited him at the university, and later on the telephone. He told me he feared for his life. 'He isn't who he claims to be.' Those were his words on the telephone. He was talking about you, con man and tomb raider!"

Leo scrutinized Clemens Rapoldy closely. "We found lists at Kerfeld's home that clearly prove which treasures you sold to Egyptian dealers! Professor Kerfeld must have found out what happened to Father Gregor, and he feared he would be next. At St. Stephen's Cathedral, close to death, he whispered one word: *paternoster*. Our father . . . but it was no last prayer. He was referring to the rosary peas you used to murder the father. He found you out!"

"But Kerfeld had no rosary peas on him!" objected Rapoldy stubbornly. "So I hardly could have poisoned him with any."

"No, you're right." Leo shook his head. "That would have been too obvious. You killed Kerfeld with a different poison, the Spanish fly, because you thought it might pass as an aphrodisiac. You located the hotel Kerfeld was hiding in and poisoned his food. Scared as he was, Kerfeld had his food brought up to his room. My guess is you simply acted as room service. But first you made your next mistake." Leo paused for effect. The members of the archaeological society listened, spellbound. Charlotte Rapoldy was weeping quietly.

"Because you were in a rush, you bought the poison yourself at a pharmacy," Leo said to Clemens Rapoldy. "My colleague visited every pharmacy in Vienna that sells Spanish fly as an aphrodisiac. There aren't many. And during the time period we're interested in, there was only one single buyer. And his description matches yours exactly!" Leo pointed at Clemens. "You are a grave robber, a con artist, and a repeat murderer. You are herewith under arrest, Clemens Carpati!"

There was silence. Then Charlotte Rapoldy sprang to her feet, screaming, "Clemens, please tell me this isn't true!" Tears streaked down her face.

"Darling, it's nothing but a nasty conspiracy against me," her husband said, trying to reassure her. "Some kind of grudge this fop wants to vent on me. Maybe he's jealous. He flirted with you the first time he laid eyes on you. He has no proof! He's got some handwriting and some sales list, a vague description from a random apothecary. So-called facts about my former life. Bah! Nothing but a cheap charade." He turned to Leo, his expression confident. "No court in the world will accept this."

"I saved my most important piece of evidence for last," said Leo. His voice was low but fervent. "It concerns the two ampules. You told me your wife was the only one who injected her father. You never touched the ampules in Vienna—correct?"

"That's the first time you're making sense," replied Clemens Rapoldy. "That's right! I never touched those damned bottles once, by the devil!"

"Then how come we found fingerprints on both ampules? And not only from one person, but from several? Probably yours, too."

"Finger . . . what? What kind of modern nonsense is that now?"

"I've had the two ampules which you kindly lent me examined by Professor Hofmann. There is a new technique which allows us to show fingerprints on objects. Herr Professor?" Leo looked at the professor. This was his cue.

Hofmann rose, cleared his throat and turned to the other guests. "Young Herzfeldt is right," he began in a loud voice, accustomed to lecturing. "This new technique is called dactyloscopy. Each unique fingerprint corresponds with only one individual. It's a very new technique, but it will soon replace bertillonage. A double murder was recently solved in Argentina using this method. I myself am currently working on a groundbreaking essay on—" The professor caught Leo's look. "Uh, I am digressing. Well." He pulled out an ink pad from his pocket and turned to Clemens Rapoldy.

"Like I said, I found several sets of fingerprints on the two ampules. I would like to ask you now to press your fingers onto this pad and provide me with a print. That way, we will know beyond any doubt—"

"You goddamned smart aleck of a peacock!" The man calling himself Clemens Rapoldy jumped to his feet. He rushed to the lectern and hurled it to the ground. There was no trace of a limp. "I'm going to kill you!"

"Just like you killed the others?" asked Leo, his fists raised defensively. "You probably would have killed your wife in the end, wouldn't you have? Just like her father . . ."

Clemens grabbed his cane and drew a long blade out from it. He stabbed it at Leo, who managed to dodge by stepping swiftly to the side.

A sword stick! thought Leo. *Like Carl Rebers's . . .*

He moved on the spot like a boxer, adopting a stance he remembered from his fencing lessons as a student. Some of the men in the room cried out with fright, but no one intervened. Even Professor Hofmann stood as if rooted to the spot, ink pad still in hand.

"The old bastard was incurably ill!" snarled Clemens, wielding his sword again. "I did him a favor. And then he goes and doesn't die straightaway—asks to be mummified instead. What a crazy old geezer!"

"You're not a doctor, or else you would have known that the Strophanthus toxin is slow acting." Leo ducked. The blade swooshed closely past him. "All the more surprising that you managed to conduct the embalming."

"That was Charlotte. I was merely holding the scalpels. I was under the impression she was enjoying herself. That woman is just as sick in the head as her father!" Carpati laughed sarcastically. "Obsessed with death, the pair of them! She would have only gotten what she longs for, deep down inside—her death!"

"Clemens, what—what are you saying?" cried Charlotte. "What

about our honeymoon, all your promises? The romantic cruise on the Nile . . . ?"

"A stinking, mosquito-ridden river and another ruin every few miles. I was bored out of my mind!" As he talked himself into a rage, Clemens kept trying to hit Leo with his sword. "The only thing that kept me going was the prospect that all those treasures would soon be mine! I was going to make money from all that trash, instead of letting it collect dust in a museum—there are plenty of fools willing to pay good money for such things."

"Stop it, you cretin!" Friedrich Knauer had risen to his feet, but Clemens kept him at bay with his sword.

"You're just another one of those drooling madmen!" gasped Clemens. "I should have done you in like Kerfeld and the others. Pity your assistant didn't chop your nuts off. You never had any to begin with—none of you here did!" He lifted his weapon and turned to Leo once more. "Well, now I shall—"

The sound of a shot fired rang out and Rapoldy froze. Out of nowhere, Paul Leinkirchner appeared up on the gallery, his gun still raised. He must have emerged from one of the other rooms on the second floor.

"Put down your silly toy and give up, Carpati!" called out Leinkirchner. "Your game is up."

Clemens Carpati hesitated just for a moment. "You'll never catch me, you bastards!" he screamed. "Never!" Cursing and swearing, he made for the door, running past Friedrich Knauer.

"Stop him!" cried Knauer.

Professor Hofmann seemed to wake from his trance, stepped forward and tripped up the fleeing man. Carpati stumbled and fell. "You senile old fools!" he ranted. "I will—"

In that moment, the downstairs library door opened and Erich Loibl stormed into the room with half a dozen constables. They threw themselves onto Carpati, who was struggling viciously, and pushed him to the ground. Someone took his sword off him. The con man fought and raged as handcuffs closed around his wrists.

Leo moved close to him and leaned down. "Now I'm going to have that drink," he said. "And a second one when they lead you to the gallows, Herr Carpati. I'm certain Anubis will deem your heart too heavy. The great devouress awaits you. Go to hell!"

Leo turned one last time to look at Charlotte Rapoldy, who was being held up by Friedrich Knauer and Professor Hofmann. She looked like she was about to faint.

Hofmann addressed him. "A good presentation, inspector. Even if the ending was unexpected." Leo noticed only then how pale the professor looked. "I must admit," Hofmann added, "I don't think I'm cut out for police work. I prefer criminals who are already dead."

"Well, you did help stop this criminal in the end." Leo smiled. "You can relay the story of your heroic intervention in your next lecture. Although—the greatest criminals usually stumble on the most trivial detail."

With that, he left to join Leinkirchner, Loibl, and the other constables in their arrest of Carpati.

ABOUT FIFTEEN MINUTES LATER, AFTER LEO, PAUL LEINKIRCHner, and Erich Loibl were back in the library. Leinkirchner settled onto the chaise longue with a cigar while Loibl examined the phonograph and *laterna magica* on the shelves. Many of the chairs still lay toppled, as did the lectern; one of the dog heads had broken off. One of the gas lights flickered occasionally, making it seem as if a lightning storm raged on the ceiling.

"What a palace!" commented Leinkirchner from the sofa. He stretched out his legs and gazed up at the glass dome and the stars sparkling above. "If Carpati's plan had worked out, all of this would have been his."

Leo nodded pensively. "As far as we can glean, Carpati was planning another trip to the Nile to sell more stolen goods. Maybe he would have pushed his wife overboard and made it look like an accident. He would have been the sole heir. He must have worked toward this goal for a long time. Since his engagement, I suppose."

"And in the end, a scrawny Jewish German ruins it all for him." Leinkirchner grinned. "Congratulations, Herzfeldt. We ought to threaten to cut off your balls more often—it seems to stimulate your thinking."

"It would have never been solved without everyone's help, including Professor Hofmann's," said Leo with a shrug. "It wasn't easy, exposing Carpati. I had nothing more than a hunch in the beginning, a feeling. But after the incident with the *laterna magica* and the walking mummy, I didn't trust the fellow any longer." He frowned. "No doctor comes up with tricks like that—only someone with experience in the field would. But we had no solid proof until right at the end. The list of sales we supposedly found at Kerfeld's were a straight-up lie—just like the claim that we were able to trace Carpati's trail as a con man over the years. There were suggestions, but not much more. I had to provoke him. So I thought, if I expose him in front of the assembled society, he might just lose his composure in the end. Luckily I was able to convince Professor Hofmann to play a part in my little performance. I think it was crucial that a recognized expert like him spoke up. It was at that point that Carpati realized that he wasn't getting out of this one."

"And still he nearly got away," said Loibl, replacing the *laterna magica* on the shelf. "The man was beside himself. Was still roaring in the *Green Henry*, fighting us with his hands and feet shackled! His final curse on the scaffold will probably be for you, Herzfeldt."

"All the more puzzling why you didn't step in sooner." Leo turned to Paul Leinkirchner with some annoyance. "You must have heard

Carpati's rantings and threats from the next room. He nearly got me with his sword!"

"I beg you! Surely you can fend off a weak man waving a flyswatter, Herzfeldt." Leinkirchner blew a cloud of smoke at the blue wallpaper. "As a former Jewish reserve lieutenant."

Leo studied the man closely. *Did you embrace the possibility that I might die?* he wondered. He shrugged. He'd never be able to read Leinkirchner. "Let's forget about it. At least this way his wife could see for herself what kind of a monster her beloved Clemens really is."

Charlotte Rapoldy was over on the sofa in the conservatory with her friends Dr. Dedekind and Friedrich Knauer, who were tending to her. One of them had fetched her smelling salts, and a doctor—a real medical doctor—wasn't far away.

The rest of the guests had departed, including Professor Hofmann. The scandal of Villa Thebes would soon begin to spread all across Vienna.

"Well, what about her?" asked Loibl. "Charlotte Rapoldy. Her reputation is ruined, in any case. I doubt the archduke will be in touch again."

"At least we can cross her off the list of suspects, after everything her husband confessed to tonight," replied Leo. "She truly didn't know of any of his plans. Seems a touch naïve to me." He sighed. "Our madam lives in another realm—the irritating present only rarely reaches her."

"Oh well, with all her money and Egyptian treasures, she'll soon find another prince," said Leinkirchner. "I mean, think of the emerald eyes alone, the ones in our evidence room. Carpati was probably after those as well. But they're nice and safe in our evidence room . . ." He cast a questioning look at Leo. "That's where they still are, aren't they? You took them there."

"Of course," replied Leo a little too swiftly. "And that's where they'll stay for the foreseeable future. If anything, those eyes are the property of the Museum of Art History, not that of Charlotte Rapoldy or any other individual."

Leinkirchner yawned. He was still stretched out on the chaise longue. "The woman's a looker, in any case. Admit it, Herzfeldt. You'd been eyeing her up, too. If you ask me, a lady from a house like this suits you much better than, well . . . certain other ladies." He gave Leo a wink.

"I'll decide for myself who suits me and who doesn't, thank you very much," retorted Leo sharply.

There was silence between the three very different men.

Then Erich Loibl cleared his throat. "You have to explain one thing to me, Herzfeldt. The thing with the fingerprints. It all sounds rather wild, what Professor Hofmann told us. That each fingerprint belongs to one person alone. Would you really have been able to see Carpati's prints on the ampules?"

Leo smiled. "To be honest, I don't know."

"You . . . you don't know?" Loibl gaped. "There is no such technique? The professor was telling a brazen-faced lie?"

"So far, there are only trial models." Leo shrugged. "But I do believe this method will soon break through and replace bertillonage. The double murder in Argentina really was solved that way. I read about it and thought this could make for a good final piece of evidence if the professor assisted me. And Carpati really did fall for it. It was the straw that broke the camel's back." He grinned. "Let's wait for Professor Hofmann's essay. Maybe we'll all have to learn the new technique at the police soon. The field of criminalistics is advancing relentlessly."

Paul Leinkirchner laughed heartily. "Damn it, Herzfeldt! You're an even greater con man than Carpati. If the police doesn't work out for you, you'll make it as a fraudster."

"A criminologist must always think like a criminal," said Leo.

“That’s what Hans Gross says in his *Handbook for Investigative Judges*. You should give it a read some time. A tiny criminal lives in each of us, even you, chief inspector. And now if you’ll excuse me.” He turned to leave. “I have a rendezvous with a certain lady.”

He lifted his top hat and walked down the fluffy rugs, past ancient vases and red silk wallpaper, out into the garden where the air was full of summer, woodruff, and new beginnings.

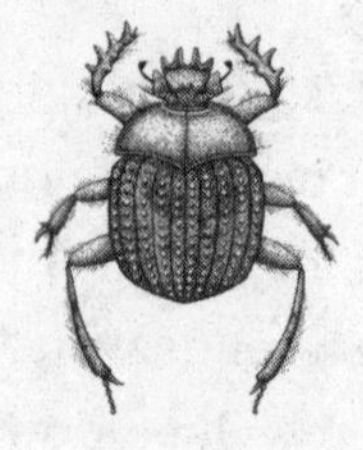

EPILOGUE

From *Death Rites Around the World* by Augustin Rothmayer, written in Vienna, 1894

> While necromancy—the conjuring of the dead—was once viewed as black magic and punished by death during the Middle Ages, nowadays spiritualists sprout like primroses all over Vienna. Everywhere you turn there are pendulums, shifting glasses, and letters that can make supposed contact with the dead. It's become a fashion much like noisy telephones or the driving of stinking automobiles. I believe it may be worth dedicating a whole book on its own to this cult.

Midnight had long passed when Leo at last rang the doorbell at the Dragoon. Inside he could hear laughter, the low voices of men, shrill cackling, and the occasional moan—a perfectly ordinary Saturday night. For Elli's girls, the night had only just begun.

The hatch at eye level opened and Bruno's ruffian visage appeared behind it.

"The lady awaits you," the giant grumbled. "Been getting impatient."

"And Sisi?" asked Leo.

"I put her to bed hours ago. Had to bounce her on my knees till I was ready to drop dead. The girl is more demanding than my boss."

Leo grinned. "I've come to believe Sisi is the true boss here, anyway."

"That's for sure. But don't let Elli hear you say that—if you don't want to lose your willy after all." Bruno opened the heavy door.

Leo hurried up the carpeted, well-worn stairs until he reached Julia's door. He knocked softly and entered.

He gasped with surprise, pausing on the threshold. The table, the shelves, the windowsill—every surface was covered in flowers in vases. There were red and white roses, carnations, daffodils, dahlias, chrysanthemums, and even a few exotic orchids. There was even a bouquet on the bed, right next to the sleeping child. The smell of flowers was so intense that Leo almost felt nauseous. Julia was sitting on her bed next to her daughter, dressed in her finest dress.

"Do you have a new admirer I should know about?" asked Leo suspiciously.

"You already know him." Julia smiled. "He likes to wear black, is in the excavating business, and smells a little."

"These— all these flowers are from Augustin Rothmayer?" Leo laughed in disbelief. "Did he rob a funeral parlor?"

"Don't ask me where he got them from. He came by this evening, together with Anna and an overwhelmed driver. Gave me the bouquets with a bow and a kiss on my hand."

"To thank you for keeping your end of the bargain, I take it?"

Julia nodded. "The welfare office gave their agreement today. In the end it went quicker than expected. Presumably because the orphanage on Alser Street is bursting at the seams. They're grateful for any foster family."

For multiple days Julia had trudged back and forth to the welfare office, speaking to the authorities. Based on their response, she had then spent a long evening pleading with the director of Central Cemetery and his wife, appealing to their better nature. Her idea had been simple: if a gravedigger couldn't adopt an orphaned girl, then how about a respected cemetery director—an upright, dry-as-bone official and husband and father of four?

In the end the director had agreed, especially because he didn't wish to lose such a capable gravedigger as Augustin Rothmayer, who was famous among his guild. On paper, the upstanding municipal employee and happily married father of four was now Anna's foster father. The authorities hadn't looked too closely. It might have had something to do with the fact that the director of the welfare office was a regular customer at Big Elli's. There would be one or two inspection visits and a little paperwork over the years, but the main thing was this: Anna would live with Augustin Rothmayer, perfectly officially as his apprentice.

"I still don't know what to think of a twelve-year-old girl spending all day every day at a cemetery, collecting bones and digging graves," said Leo.

"Other girls her age sell flowers or matches in the streets, or even their bodies," said Julia. "A cemetery can be paradise to a child. And the dead can't hurt you."

"You're right." Leo tiredly dropped next to Julia on the bed. "Unlike some of the living, even those from the best of houses. Do you want to know how my talk at the Rapoldys went?"

"Smug as you look, you're bound to have nailed the fellow in the end."

He laughed. "Yes, I have indeed. Though it was a close shave."

In brief words he filled Julia in on the evening's events at Villa Thebes. She knew most of his plan already since Leo had kept her in the loop during his investigations.

"The filthy pig," said Julia after he had finished. "I might almost feel a little sorry for Charlotte Rapoldy. But only a little. How could anyone fall for such a fraudster?" She considered. "Although sometimes, I don't know about you—maybe you're a con man, too. At least now you see how that woman might have been able to cloud a man's brain, but not another woman's. I thought her naïve and strange right from the start."

"She didn't cloud my brain!" protested Leo. "But I will admit, she inspires certain, well . . . fantasies."

"And I don't?" Her eyes blazed and she jutted out her chin, and Leo noticed once more how beautiful Julia was. More beautiful than Cleopatra and Charlotte Rapoldy put together—and not just because she was wearing an expensive evening gown.

He grinned. "Right now I have a whole lotta fantasies. But we'd need to be alone for those."

"Later. Elli is letting us have the room under the roof." She rose. "But first we go dancing. You promised me this night belongs to me. No fancy theater, no expensive restaurant. I want to dance and have fun."

"At the risk that I'll be too tired for anything else later." Leo yawned. "I had a big day. A murderer and con man doesn't catch himself . . ." He hesitated. "The fact that Elli is letting us have the room on a Saturday night is a little dubious. Such generosity isn't like her. Does it have anything to do with that mysterious deal of yours?"

Julia still hadn't told Leo what it was that Elli wanted in exchange for her help with Saidrovuni's escape. Julia had avoided Leo's questions, and he was beginning to fear that Julia was to sell her body at the Dragoon. He'd never allow it.

"Oh, why not?" Julia sighed. "You'll find out sooner or later regardless." She bent down and pulled a large, flat wooden box from under the bed. "This is what's it's about."

"That's your camera equipment. . . . Hang on!" Leo gave Julia an appalled look. "Don't tell me you're giving her your camera and your laboratory? Now that Stukart wants you back as—"

"Won't you listen? I'm not giving her anything—Elli doesn't even know how to use any of this. No, she wants me to take photographs from time to time. Photographs of clients."

"Secret pictures of clients . . ." Leo began to understand what Elli was planning.

"Elli wants to compile a small archive," explained Julia. "There are very powerful men among the customers here. She wants some security, and I'll help her get it. If any of her clients ever turn on her or if she needs a favor, she wants some leverage. Those men have jealous wives and a good reputation. They don't want to lose both."

"Photographs as a dirty currency. Hmm . . ." Leo smirked. He was relieved that Elli's demand wasn't what he had feared. "That might indeed be a lucrative business."

"It's disgusting. But it's the price Elli named. And I think it was worth it. By the way, I recevied a letter today. Look." Julia opened the drawer of her nightstand. "Postmarked from Genoa. That's where they're waiting for their ship. They're doing well."

Leo skimmed over the scribbled lines in poor German. The last few words appeared to be in the tongue of the Matabele.

"I'm guessing it's something like a blessing," said Julia. She moved beside him and hugged him tightly. "Leo, you did something much more important than arrest a murderer and fraud. You saved lives—or at least one."

"You wanted me to show you what really matters to me. You matter to me, Julia! Also because you . . . you . . ." He paused, trying to find the right words. "When I saw Charlotte Rapoldy one last time in all her luxury today, I realized something: this woman is forever preoccupied with the dead, with mummies, sarcophagi, lifeless treasures, and, in the end, with herself. You, on the other hand, you think of the living. You help the poor and the weak, and I love you for it."

He winked at her. "Well, and I did enjoy it a tiny little bit, breaking into the evidence room at headquarters. I left two glass marbles in place of the emeralds. Let's see how long it takes them to notice. I reckon it'll be years. Things get forgotten down there. This way, the jewels are a much better investment. Even if one of those eyes would have made a stunning pendant for you."

A deafening trumpeting rang out and for a brief moment Saidrovuni thought he was back at the Vienna zoological garden, back in the show arena, trapped between a cheap backdrop and wooden benches sticky with candy, caught under netting, the gray clouds pressing down on him. But then he felt the vibrating of the machines under his feet, heard the screeching of seagulls. He looked out at the wide horizon, a light blue line that melted into the darker blue of the sea. He squeezed the gunwale hard with both hands, deeply inhaling the salty, fishy breeze.

Just two more days . . .

He saw several other passengers gathered on the foredeck from the corner of his eye. They kept their distance from him, as if he suffered from a contagious disease. He was accustomed to such behavior, and it no longer hurt him. His skin had grown thick over the years. How strange it was that skin color should decide who was a civilized person and who wasn't. White men could be so stupid! He was wearing the same clothes as them, if not more elegant ones. The top hat suited him, and yet he felt dressed up, as if he were in disguise. He longed for the moment when he'd pull off all the nonsense. Soon.

Until this day he didn't know if the woman who had helped him in Vienna and slipped him the fat envelope of money was in reality an angel. That's what the Christians called those sent by God. It was as if she had washed away all the injustice, all the filth, all those bitter years he had spent in the traveling circus. During his darkest hour, back at the vivarium, he had looked evil in the eye—the *Asanbosam* in human form. He had vanquished evil and was richly rewarded.

It was like a miracle.

When they had recruited him on the coast of his home country years ago, he'd been young and impressionable. They'd promised him great things, spoken of a fun voyage during which he'd learn a lot and from where he'd return wealthy. None of it had held true. Well, at least he'd met a woman he loved and with whom he had a baby. There had been some lovely moments, though not many. They had seen many cities in Europe, but they'd all been the same: dirt, much stone, little green. The people there locked trees in so-called parks and animals in cages. They called people like him apes and gaped lustfully at the bare-breasted women of his people. Some of them did more than that.

The moment they had set foot on the steamship, his family had gone belowdecks, where they'd booked a small separate niche with hammocks. There was a lot of whispering and stares, but at least they were left in peace. The steward had checked their tickets doubly and triply, and even spoken with one of the deck officers. But all was in order.

Just two more days . . .

It would take the steamboat Alexandria two days and one night to make the passage from Genoa to Cairo. The tickets hadn't been cheap, and their clothing had cost a good deal also, just like the papers bearing false names, which the woman had helped get for them back in Vienna.

The photographer.

When he'd asked, she had gifted him the pictures she'd taken of him at the prison. He didn't want any part of him to stay behind in Vienna.

The horn blared again; the machines stamped like a thousand wild horses. A shudder went through the ship and the anchor chain rattled into place on its winch: they were setting off. The people around him cheered and waved their handkerchiefs.

Saidrovuni didn't look back.

Instead, he drew the crumpled photographs from his breast pocket, studied them one last time, and then ripped them into small scraps for the wind to pick up and carry out to sea.

Now his soul was free.

AFTERWORD

Readers Beware: Spoilers

I've always wanted to write a novel about mummies!

As a child I liked to read a comic book series called *Gespenster Geschichten, or* "ghost stories," which would invariably end with the legendary sentence: "It's strange, but that's how it was written." I remember the collapsing tombs, stalking monsters in bandages, and fearful grimaces of archaeologists beneath safari helmets. Later, I devoured short stories by Arthur Conan Doyle like "*The Ring of Thoth*" and "*Lot № 249.*" I loved the classic film *The Mummy* from 1932, as well as its rather sillier remake from around the turn of the millennium. And then of course I was enraptured when I heard of the legendary curse of the pharaohs, which was supposed to have struck all those who worked with Egyptologist Howard Carter in 1923 upon the opening of Tutankhamen's tomb. My book is filled with quotes and references to all of the above. You, my dear reader, must know: good writers don't steal, they merely stand on the shoulders of giants, who in turn stand on the shoulders of giants. . . .

MUCH OF THIS NOVEL RESTS ON HISTORICAL BACKGROUND—for example, the legendary finds of Deir al-Bahari. In 1871, the brothers Abd el-Rassul discovered a so-called hidden cache holding approximately forty sarcophagi, among them the mummy of the legendary pharaoh Ramses, in the mountains of Thebes. The brothers started a lucrative trade, selling their finds until they were caught ten years later. In 1891, a second cache was found in Deir el-Bahari, this one holding the mummies of a hundred and fifty(!) priests. The find was so enormous that the Egyptian government decided to gift large parts to select museums around the world. Among them, alongside the Louvre in Paris and the British Museum in London, was the Vienna Museum of Art History (Kunsthistorisches Museum Wien), which was first opening its doors right around that time. The treasures were assigned by the luck of the draw. And that's how the sarcophagus of a certain Ta-bek-en-chon landed in Vienna—alas, without its mummy. And that is where my imagination comes in. Sadly, I know of no Egyptian princess in Vienna.

Mummy parties really did exist, held mostly by the British aristocracy in the nineteenth century. Together the guests would unwrap a mummy, searching for precious amulets. In the German Empire, Friedrich Karl of Prussia, nephew of the Prussian king, held one such mummy party at his lodge in Dreilinden. The mummy was casually unwrapped atop a billiards table. I don't know of any such blasphemous acts performed by the archduke Rainer Ferdinand of Austria. The archduke really was a friend of archaeology, though. He gifted a valuable papyrus collection to the Vienna court library, entering the history books as "Papyrus Rainer."

Everything Augustin Rothmayer writes in his almanac on mummia, the use of mummies as fuel for fire, and on mummification techniques in ancient Egypt is the truth. And yes, there was a British lord who wanted to be mummified following his death: Alexander, Duke of Hamilton, known as a dandy and a fan of Egyptology. They do say the British have a penchant for the macabre.

Another topic based in historical truth is the beginnings of hormone research at the end of the nineteenth century (though they weren't called hormones yet). Since antiquity some have assigned healing powers to the consumption of animal organs. Animal testicles were considered potency enhancing. Driven by the longing for eternal youth, scientists later sought to use them as a remedy of rejuvenation. The British-French doctor Charles-Eduard Brown-Séquard (1817–1894) developed a hormone cocktail which he praised as an "elixir of life"—a miracle cure against aging—in his book. Even at the age of seventy-two he injected himself with an extract of puppy and guinea-pig testicles, convinced the remedy rejuvenated him by thirty years. Unfortunately, he died just five years later.

Later on, a certain Eugen Steinach reached such renown with his hormone therapy that, during the 1920s, even outside of Vienna the word "Steinachen" was used to refer to rejuvenation treatment. Steinach's competitor, French surgeon Serge Voronoff, was rumored to transplant the testicles of executed criminals onto elderly millionaires. Similarly, one Viennese newspaper reported that young men had been attacked in the street for their holiest parts (you can read more in *Sonderlinge, Außenseiter, Femme Fatales: Das "andere" Wien um 1900* by Michaela Lindinger, published by Amalthea Verlag). As always, my motto holds—history writes the best stories.

I invented the medication "diabezerine," but there were indeed attempts to treat diabetes with an extract from pig pancreas in 1869. It would be another fifty years before patients were successfully treated with insulin.

It was the same Eugen Steinach who, from 1912, led the physiological division of the Biological Experiment Center in Vienna. At the time, it was a unique institution where experiments were conducted on live animals. This center was indeed located inside a vivarium.

You see, even Carl Rebers's laboratory and his horrible experiments are rooted in truth.

AT THE TIME OF THE NOVEL'S SETTING, THE VIVARIUM AND THE zoo merged at the Schüttel. The first zoo opened in 1863 but was forced to shut only three years later because of bankruptcy. After its reopening in 1894, so-called "ethnic shows" were presented there, a term that downplays what was really happening: those shows were human zoos.

In Vienna alone, more than fifty of those disgraceful shows took place between 1870 and 1910. Entire families were lured away from their homes with empty promises and forced to playact a stereotype of foreign people to Europeans. Europeans may have spoken of enlightenment, but in truth, a racist view of the world was manifested in the conviction that the "white man" was superior to people from other parts of the world. Many of those put into such shows died during their travels, often from diseases new to them. Others broke down mentally. I recommend the tasteful documentary by Arte, the public European television channel, on the subject, available on YouTube. Contemporary witness Peter Altenberg writes in the book *Ashantee: Afrika und Wiem um 1900* about his impressions of the "African village" at the Vienna Prater in 1896.

A few years later, the zoo at Prater park closed again, and this time for good. The Vivarium remained until it burned down in the final days of World War II. All the scientific equipment was destroyed and all animals perished, among them a crocodile and an eighty-year-old tortoise. Today, all that remains as a reminder is a street name, Vivarium Street.

I came across an article in the *Wiener Zeitung* from 1895 that reports of a Matabele caravan at the Vienna zoo. The kingdom of the Matabele existed until 1893 and was put to a bloody end by the British. Its area roughly matched today's Zimbabwe, where, among other languages, Northern Ndebele is spoken. It was from this language that I borrowed my few words of Matabele in the book.

According to the newspaper article, the caravan was led by twenty-five-year-old chief Saidrovuni. Saidrovuni's appearance and the Matabele's ceremonial dance are also described. The character of Saidrovuni gave me the opportunity to give a face to those who suffered in those ethnic shows.

Some of the dialogue in this book uses racially charged language. Thankfully, the German word has been removed from the official vocabulary, and with good reason. It is derogatory and connected with a dark history. And even if some in the older generation insist that it's not meant in such a way, it still comes across that way to Black people. And that's the point. Language changes, and it creates reality—I know that only too well, as a writer.

And still I decided to use language in some places that illustrates the thinking from back then—the racism, the sense of superiority, the ignorance. I believe that if we present history in novels (and movies), we mustn't hide anything, or else we run the danger of some later generation claiming "it wasn't all that bad"—because they forgot how bad things actually were.

IN ALL MY BOOKS I TRY TO STAY AS FAITHFUL AS POSSIBLE TO THE PEriod in which they take place. Of course, sometimes I'm forced to make compromises. For example, I took some liberties with the layout of the Museum of Art History, and also with the zoo and the vivarium. And I also cheated a little bit with my description of the feast dedicated to Min, the god of fertility (an important clue for solving the mystery). I also took liberties with parts of the Vienna sewer system, which, at the time I was doing my research for this book, unfortunately wasn't open to the public. The right-hand main sewer at the south bank of the Danube Canal wasn't completed until later, and the Wien Canal was regulated and partially covered in 1895. So, please don't try to follow the same route as Leo and Loibl—you could get very badly lost! The so-called Zwingburg really did exist, though, just like the kanalstrotters and fat fishers. Underground channels have existed in Vienna for a long time. Many of the city streams were closed in during the cholera epidemic of 1830–31, but the main left and right sewers of the Wien Canal have existed for the same amount of time.

I gleaned many an exciting and interesting fact about Vienna's underground life from the book *Unter Wien* by Alexander Glück, Marcello La Speranza, and Peter Ryborz, published by Ch. Links Verlag. For example, that's where I read about the passageway linking the courthouse to the general hospital, possibly for moving prisoners. I couldn't locate the passageway however, and nor were experts able to confirm its existence.

That the *laterna magica* was used for entertainment much earlier, you can read in my novel *The Master's Apprentice*, in which the hero Johann Faustus uses it to seduce his Gretchen.

For an excellent travel guide of Vienna at the turn of the century I once again recommend *Ganz Wien in 7 Tagen* by Anton Holzer, published by Primus Verlag. For illuminating insight into the topic of mummies I suggest the heavily illustrated book *Mumien—Zeugen der Vergangenheit*, published by White Star, and as a good scene setter I recommend the audiobook episodes "*The Ring of Thot*" and "*The Mummy*" from the *Gruselkabinett* series, published byTitania Medien).

A note on the serial killer from this book: he too is based on a real-life case, this time from Germany. Fritz Haarmann, known as the "Butcher of Hanover," murdered twenty-four boys and young men at the beginning of the 1920s. He cut up their bodies and disposed of them partly in the toilet, partly in the nearby river Leine, where playing children found five human skulls. When they lowered the level of the river during the investigation, they found around three hundred human bone parts.

Like I say—history writes the best stories.

AS ALWAYS, MANY PEOPLE HELPED ME TURN A FEW VAGUE ideas into a book. But any mistakes that remain are my own.

First I'd like to thank Werner Sabitzer who with his vast knowledge of the Vienna police proved once again to be of immense help for this second installment of the series. Regina Hölzl from the Museum of Art History told me all about the findings of Deir al-Bahari, and took me to see the real mummy vault of the museum—an unforgettable experience!

At a typical Vienna coffeehouse, Werner Michael Schwarz from the Wien Museum told me much about the so-called "ethnic shows." Thanks also to Peter Ryborz, even if the tour through the sewers wasn't to be. His *The Third Man* Tour came highly recommended. Professor Magister Ewald Königstein from Bezirksmuseum Hietzing and Professor Vladimira Bousska helped me immensely. The Vienna district museums are each a pearl of their own and well worth a visit, not only for research!

Thank you also to Ullstein Publishing, who believed in the success of this series right from the beginning and has supported me in many areas. Thank you to my unmatched editor Uta Rupprecht and to Gerd, Martina, and Sophie from the Gerd F. Rumler Agency (and thank you for the many delicious brainstorming sessions at the Italian place). Thanks also to my father who once again provided the necessary medical knowledge, and, of course, to my wife Katrin, my patient first reader. We've been together for over twenty years now, and every year with you, dear Katrin, life is getting more beautiful!

UNTIL MY NEXT NOVEL, WHETHER IN THIS OR ANY OTHER TIME!

—Oliver Pötzsch

Here ends Oliver Pötzsch's
The Girl and the Gravedigger.

The first edition of this book was printed
and bound at LSC Communications
in Harrisonburg, Virginia, January 2026.

A NOTE ON THE TYPE

The text of this novel was set in Henriette, a Viennese-inspired font designed in 2012 by Michael Hochleitner. In the 1920s, seeking to standardize its street signs, the city of Vienna commissioned a typeface expressly for its signage, over time producing sixteen different variations. Hochleitner's Henriette is an homage to these resulting letterforms, adopting their clarity and sophistication in a versatile font ideal for headlines and text.

HARPERVIA

An imprint dedicated to publishing international voices,
offering readers a chance to encounter other lives and other
points of view via the language of the imagination.